"I applaud Sandy for capturing the lives of the ... character in this most humane story of Iskandar/Alexander, the young immigrant to America. He beautifully shares his heritage and history...so reminiscent of many immigrants to America from the shores of Syria and Lebanon. Remarkable!"

Helen Corey, Author

"This is a beautiful book. It brought back good memories of my parents' coming to America, Danny Thomas and the friends we made starting St., Jude's Children's Research Hospital."

Anthony Abraham

"I loved Sandy's description of the ambience of the Lebanese people and the description of the difficulties encountered by our parents in their quest for a new life. This beautiful love story should be read by all who love Lebanon, especially by those who are now in the United States."

Ruth Ann Skaff, Director of Planning and Future Development,
The Self-Ruled Antiochian Orthodox Christian Archdiocese

"Sandy Simon has captured the essence of the culture, history, character of the Lebanese people and their migration to escape poverty and tyranny to find freedom and opportunity in America which he has beautifully captured within a poignant love story."

Dr. Edward Eissey, President Emeritus
Palm Beach Community College

"I loved your book. Your description of Lebanon...the food, the ambience, and the people is wonderful...a great graphic description of the difficulties encountered by our parents in their quest for a new life. This is a beautiful love story that should be read by all who love Lebanon, and especially by those whose parents emigrated to the USA."

Richard C. Shadyac

"This beautiful love story wonderfully embraces a by-gone era. *Beyond The Cedars* is a tale about a man with a humble and impoverished beginning who lives an exceptional life never forgetting his first love. Woven into the story is an enlightening thread of world history that propels the reader into each decade. Everyone will enjoy this refreshing and impassioned novel from Sandy Simon."

LaRonda Denkler

BEYOND THE CEDARS

BEYOND THE CEDARS

SANDY SIMON

The Cedars Group
Delray Beach, Florida
2006

Library of Congress Contol Number 2006910692

ISBN 0 966 9625-5-9
Printed in the United States of America

Published by
The Cedars Group
220 MacFarlane Drive, Suite PH-6
Delray Beach, Florida 33483

This book is dedicated...

*to my father, Alexander Eassa Simon Chalhoub and my mother, Linda Helen
Zaine Thomé Simon on whose lives this book was based.*

*to all those tenacious, resilient, and dedicated immigrants from Lebanon and Syria
who, since 1850, have sought freedom and opportunity in America, and have
contributed their heritage, culture, and wealth to the fabric of their adopted country.*

*and, finally, to St. Jude Children's Research Hospital in Memphis, Tennessee,
which will receive a portion of the proceeds from sales of this book.*

Acknowledgements

I am most grateful...

To my mother and father whose life stories inspired this book.

To my family in Douma, Lebanon for their hospitality and insights.

To Papatya Bucak, Professor of Creative Writing at Florida Atlantic University, for her guidance and support.

To Consul General du Liban, Abdel Sattar Issa in Marseille, who graciously enlightened me to the historical presence of the Lebanese-Syrian community of Marseille, the *Panier*, and Marseille's role over the centuries.

To Richard Shadyac, my brother and mentor, for his incisive counsel.

To Anthony Abraham, John Moses, and Sally Benson for their suggestions and counsel.

To my graduate school roommate, W.H. "Bill" Stuart of Bartow, and to the Kissimmee Historical Society.

To my dear friend, Bill Finley, WWII B-17 pilot, Eighth Air Force for his detailed advice and encouragement.

Especially, I wish to acknowledge that this book could not have been written without the support, patience, and nurturing of Christiane Collins.

Thank you all.

Arabic Glossary of Terms

abayeh – *kaftan*-like, loose-fitting robe
afwan – you are welcome
aguilas/arguila – water pipe
ahlen wa sahlen – you are welcome
Allah – God
Allah y' rahamo (he) – may he rest in peace
Allah y' rahamha (she) – may she rest in peace
Allah ma'ak – be with God
allia hummah – may they rest in peace
arak – an alcoholic beverage made of anisette similar to the Greek drink ouzo
areeshi – grapes

baba – father nickname
baba ghanoush – paté made of eggplant, tahini, garlic, and olive oil
beit – home of...
Bekaa Valley – Lebanon's fertile valley that runs north to south between two mountain ranges
biyee – father
bulgar – cracked wheat
Butrus – Peter

darbuka – tambourine
debkeh – folk dance by groups
def – hand-held drum
dishdasheh – a loose-fitting ankle length gown

fistok – pistachios

ℋ

habibi – dear one
hafli – a party gathering with dancing

Hanna – John
hashweh – rice with pine seeds and diced meat
hummus – pâté made of garbanzo beans, olive oil, and tahini

I

ibn – son of …
Ibrahim – Abraham
imei – mother
insha Allah/inshallah – God be willing
imjadara ma' roz – lentils with rice
Ishmee – My name is
Iskandar – Alexander

J

jibneh – cheese
jiddy, jiddou – maternal, paternal grandfather

K

kafta – grilled meat, beef or lamb (no cracked wheat), mixed with parsley, and mild onion
khali – uncle
khai-yi – brother
khoury – priest
khudda – manure
khobaz – bread
kibbee – baked meatloaf of finely ground lamb or beef mixed with *bulgar*/cracked wheat
koosa/koosa mahshi – squash stuffed with rice and diced meat

L

la'a – no
laban – yogurt
lubiyye u roz – beans and rice

M

mahrharbahr – welcome
Markab el Bar – "Ship of the Land"
mezza – cluster of appetizers
mushthamah Libnani – Lebanese neighborhood

N

na'am – yes

O

oud – Arabic for lyre, a bowl-shaped guitar with bent neck, built of veneer wood

R

remáhni – pomegranate
remáhnet – pomegranate tree

S

sahbi – friend
Salim – Sam
Sayedna – My Lord, Your Grace
shaish-baish – 6-5
Shimal – the North
Shooishme – What is your name
shookrun – thank you
sitty – grandmother
souk – marketplace

T

tabouleh – salad of chopped parsley, *bulgar,* lemon juice, olive oil, and diced tomatoes
tahini – sesame seed paste
t'Fuduloo – let us dine
ta ha la hawn – come here
tanoos – uncle
towleh – backgammon game

W

wadi – dry river bed
wada-arreesh – grape leaves
Wadi Kadeesha – the steep and deep Valley of Passion, bisects northern Lebanon

Y

yabrah – rolled grape leaves stuffed with rice, ground beef or ground lamb
y'hara deen bladuk – may your country burn in hell
ya' haram – poor thing
yallah – hurry
y'eini – term of endearment, literally, "my eyes"
y'slemley – sweetheart

Z

zeytoon – olives

PROLOGUE

$\mathcal{T}$ he eighteen-year-old reached the lookout point on the grooved wagon path near the top of the mountain. He stepped to the ledge and watched as the morning sun gently rose over the barren mountains to the east, casting a brightening orange glow over the stone-filled soil and rock outcroppings of the steep, rugged mountains.

Iskandar, an imposing young man, nearly six feet tall and one hundred and seventy-five pounds, was ruggedly handsome. With a determined look on his face and an easy, friendly smile, he had a light olive complexion. His thick, wavy dark brown hair fell over his ears. He had broad, muscular shoulders and arms. His straight nose was smaller than most Middle Easterners.' Iskandar's eyes were his special characteristic. They were dark brown, sensitive looking, more sensual than those of others, and deeply set above his high cheekbones and strong chin. The women of Douma always told him he had the most beautiful man's eyes in all of Lebanon. His eyes would focus on someone else's so long that they seemed to pierce any protection the other person might try to employ. They especially affected women who found him instantly attractive and disarming with his gentleness and naiveté.

He was comfortable with himself, modest yet confident, slow to anger. His youth was spent climbing the rugged mountains, so he was strong and lean. He was a "son" of Mount Lebanon, as the Bible called the ancient region where he was born. And he carried in his veins all the genes of this historical land and his ancestors.

He stood at the path's grassy edge, put his makeshift wool valise on the ground beside the large, elongated stone and looked back down the slope at his village, perhaps for the last time. He could feel the sun's warmth touching his face now as he gazed longingly at the familiar small houses with their orange terra cotta roof tiles and flat dirt roofs that identified this mountain village called Douma, shaped like a scorpion. This was his family's home for more than twenty-three centuries. He was born here, and his heart was in the village. His eyes grew moist as he gazed down at two of the villagers working in the vineyards, tending their livelihood. *Life goes on*, he thought. *And so must mine.*

Iskandar was saying goodbye to his home, his extended family, his cousins, aunts, uncles and childhood playmates, and his way of life, all that was familiar. He slowly turned his eyes upward to the higher mountain ridge above him and looked on his beloved cedar trees, those ancient trees so unique to his Lebanon.

He was leaving his heritage, his land, his roots. He felt his heart constrict as he turned back toward the worn path and stopped to glance back over his shoulder one more time, squinting his eyes and raising a hand to shield them from the bright morning sun's rays. His heart was heavy, and his heightened emotions were a mixture of sadness, excitement and hopefulness. His father and sister were in America, his mother was no longer living, and his older brother had decided to remain in Lebanon. Here, for the first time, he stood alone feeling the tug-of-war between going back home to Douma and the new path he knew he must take...to America.

As he stood motionless absorbing his last views of the ancient, predominantly treeless mountains of his beloved Mount Lebanon, his eyes swept across the barren rocky protrusions, the ancient stone walls, the vineyards, the hilltops, and the path back down to his village. He saw a small stone by his shoe, reached down and picked it up. He brushed the grey sand from the stone, rolled it in his hand and, holding it in his outstretched hand, spoke aloud, "I will take you with me, my good friend. You will go with me to America." He put the stone in his pocket and, with a determined, self-assured expression on his face, turned his eyes from the east, to the ancient mountains, his past...then looked to the west, to the Mediterranean Sea, his future.

After a thoughtful moment, Iskandar took a deep breath and gazed on the inviting celestial blue waters of the Mediterranean. Focusing now on his new adventure, he stood tall, stiffened his muscular shoulders, lifted his tousled head, and smiled with a sense of optimism, perhaps a bit of bravado, as he picked up his valise and took his first steps down the mountain to the port in Beirut where he would board the ship. He was following his mother's dying wish to find his destiny in America...beyond the cedars.

PART ONE

CHAPTER ONE

The Bekaa Valley, Lebanon
1913

$\mathcal{T}$hey spoke in whispers, using arm signals to encourage each other and remaining constantly on the lookout for the feared Turkish soldiers.

The small group of mountain men in their ragged clothing, joined by young Iskandar, clustered on their knees in the forbidden wheat field gleaning the deep red soil of the rich farmland with their bare, callused hands, seeking the meager uncollected cut wheat. The 400-year occupation of Lebanon by the Ottoman Empire had been especially harsh for decades, but this year was the most severe. The people were desperate. Their village was impoverished. Their clothes were worn through. And they had to risk their lives just to find enough wheat to survive through the coming winter months. Survival was the best the villagers could hope for.

Iskandar, a small boy of ten, was crouched on all fours deep in the wheat fields of the Bekaa Valley, searching the soil for as many uncollected wheat kernels as he could find. His mother would make these morsels into precious bread and every other staple of the Lebanese diet. If his mission was not successful, his family would face certain starvation.

The boy had struggled to walk with eight grown men up and down two rugged mountains to come to this rich valley. It was backbreaking, tedious, and dangerous work for the frightened group, and even more so for the young boy. They carefully stayed out of sight from the army patrols by staying low to the ground, and stopping at the slightest sound, their eyes darting side to side.

The Bekaa Valley was warmer than his village, so Iskandar took off his tattered sweater. The late morning sun was high in the clear sky. He was hot and tired, and his legs ached from crouching down for several hours within the remaining wheat stalks. Until now, his powerful feelings of determination had kept him going. He looked at his small hands. He saw that the men could collect so much more grain with their large cupped hands. There was only a slight cooling breeze in his face as he looked up. For hours, he felt mixed emotions of concern and pride at helping his mother. He was afraid of being

6   B E Y O N D   T H E   C E D A R S

caught, yet excited by the adventure of being so far from home. He knew he was on a critical mission to bring home the precious wheat.

This adventure was now becoming a frightening experience for the boy.

Iskandar realized that his pride and sense of responsibility had gotten him into this dangerous situation...beyond what he could deal with...and it would take all his determination, physical strength, and faith to overcome it. He remembered how difficult it was to get to the valley. And he now realized he had to climb back with his load of wheat.

In the village, he was always admonished to "get down from that cedar tree," or "get off that roof, don't take such chances, son." But those adventures were strengths, a vital part of Iskandar's life. He was always testing fate and his own capabilities. And he usually found a solution.

Iskandar, being the smaller of two sons, was always seeking to prove himself. He became the smartest in school classes, told jokes to have fun, took chances, and was an adventurer. He was a loving son and dear to his mother. He always felt loved, protected, and he totally returned that love. His mother taught him those lessons that would prepare him for life: *to love, be loved, accept love, work hard, and be resilient, tenacious and determined. "Have faith in the Lord. He will watch over you,"* his mother often told him.

There was a dichotomy in his young life. At home in Douma, everyone knew everyone else. Cousins, aunts and uncles were often surrogate parents. And, while he felt loved in that small, intimate, somewhat isolated village, the outside forces of the harsh Turkish occupation, and the barren hills left few options in life. Locusts and other unforeseen catastrophes seemed to invade the region beyond the norm. So, even in his early, formative years, the boy had to find a way to enjoy each day. Yet, watching his father struggle and his mother make-do with little taught him that his life soon would be his own responsibility, that life could be hard, that one should never give up. His family had endured many hardships in this region of high rugged mountains, barren with the loss over the centuries of most of its lush, majestic, ancient cedar trees. Only small scattered forests nearby were left.

During the four-year famine from 1912 to 1916, the Turks were trying to starve out the mountain people of northern Lebanon. The region was too rugged for the army to penetrate or occupy. A few fruit trees and grapes grew on the ancient stone-wall terraced slopes, gnarled olive trees hundreds of years old produced their bounty in the valley below the village. Most of the land was too steep and the soil too filled with rocks to grow wheat to make bread, pilaf, and *bulgur* staples of their Middle Eastern diet.

Their favorite food, *tabouleh*, a rich, traditional salad made of chopped parsley, *bulgur,* diced tomatoes, onions, olive oil, and lemon juice, didn't have quite the same taste or feel without the *bulgur,* which grew mostly in the Bekaa Valley. There were no roads to the Bekaa, and the Turks had stationed army patrols near the mountain trails. They would arrest anyone they could capture, especially young Christian men they could conscript into their army; in 1902 the Turkish government had changed the law, now requiring Christians to serve.

As a result, the only way the men of the village could get wheat in the valley was to climb over the two rocky and steep, treeless mountains, with heights up to 7,000 feet down to the rich valley. The entire time they traveled, they had to hide from the Turkish army patrols behind rock outcroppings. It was harrowing and physically exhausting for everyone. After climbing the first ridge, then descending into the valley to cross the full-flowing river at *Farhilda*, they had to climb the worn, tortuously narrow, curving path up the second range of mountains. From there they could look down with parochial pride on the warm, fertile Bekaa, Lebanon's "bread basket."

It was late autumn, 1913. Wheat harvest season in the Bekaa Valley was complete. The farmers had left their fields. Most of the Turkish army had gone to the port cities of Tyre and Sidon on the southern coast for the winter. Several deeply concerned men of Douma decided they were going to have to walk over the mountains forty miles east to the Bekaa Valley to survive that winter. Overhearing their plans, ten-year-old Iskandar jumped at the chance to go. It would be an adventure. As he listened to the men talk, crouched behind a large stone in the *souk*, he made his plans. He would take a burlap sack made of goat's hair and fill it with wheat for his mother. He knew he was really too young to make the trip but he desperately wanted to help his mother. His father, searching for a better life for his family, was in America with his sister, hoping to send for all of them soon. His brother, Milhelm, had gone down the mountain to the port city of Tripoli seeking fish. So, he decided to do his share although he was just a boy.

Early the next cold, dark morning, the men gathered together as Iskandar sneaked out of his house to join them.

"I'm going too," exclaimed Iskandar to the group. "I have my sack." He was known in the village as precocious, but loyal to his family. He always seemed to be challenging his older, wiser and more stable brother, Milhelm.

"You are too small, my cousin. It is very difficult and dangerous," said one of the men.

"Stay here with your mother," said another as he brushed Iskandar aside.

That last remark convinced him he *had* to go. Iskandar was determined and stubborn. He also knew that the men were going to gather wheat for their own families. He too would be providing for his family, and since Milhelm was not here to take advantage of these plans, he also would prove his ability despite his youth to help provide for his family.

The men knew that Iskandar would follow them anyway, so they reluctantly allowed him to join them in this dangerous journey.

The small group began their struggle up the mountain path before daybreak. It was very cold but the steep climb kept them warm in their worn sweaters. The massive rock outcroppings of the barren, stone-filled slopes made the climb all the more difficult. It was late that night before they reached the 7,000-foot crest of the second mountain range. As they reached the top, they could feel that the air was growing much colder. They slept, sat and rested until dawn. A couple of the men, more tired than the others, lay down on the stony patch of soil. Iskandar, not wanting to convey that he was already growing tired, crouched against a stone outcropping. But in time he slept curled up in a fetal position.

Before the first warm rays of the morning sun appeared across the eastern horizon, Nicola, their determined leader, shook the men, one at a time. "Get up quickly," he said. "We must get down to the Bekaa Valley immediately. I don't like the weather signs up here. It may get colder, but I hope that there will be no snow."

They spent four more hours walking down the difficult winding mountain path to the valley floor. Once there, one by one, they selected their areas and, on their knees, quickly began sweeping the ground with their bare, cupped hands, collecting the remnants of the harvest, and filling their sacks and bags. It was a slow, frustrating, but necessary process.

Nicola, hearing voices in the distance, alerted the others once again. "Watch out for the Turkish soldiers!" he said in a loud whisper.

In order to collect the remnant grains, they had to spread out and search the ground for loose wheat cut and left by the farmers. In this way, they wouldn't follow one another and inadvertently seek the same morsels. The wheat stalks were stiff, brittle, thick, and hard to move around, making their efforts even more difficult. It took several hours to collect the scattered unharvested wheat, and fill their bags, sometimes with as much soil as wheat kernels. It was a backbreaking, tiresome, but successful six-hour "harvest."

When they were finished, they needed to rest. They laid down in a small circle on the soft soil and slept in the fields for an hour, using their filled sacks as pillows. They all felt the soreness and painful cramps in their backs and legs from bending over, kneeling, and crawling along the ground.

"My God," complained one, stretching his pained back, "how much we must go through for so little wheat."

After nearly an hour, Nicola spoke to his tired group, "Our sacks are full, thank God. We must begin our return to the village. The clouds are building on the mountains. It will be dark soon. *Yallah*."

Knowing the return walk home would be difficult and treacherous, they gathered their belongings, heaved the heavy sacks over their shoulders, and began their trek back to the village. It was painfully difficult for most of them, but especially for the young boy, even though they all had very strong legs developed from climbing up and down the rugged mountains to visit neighbors, and tend to their goats, fruit trees and terraced vineyards. The walk up the mountain itself was exhausting and painful. For young Iskandar, it was an enormous test of his strength and youthful determination. Though he was very tired, he silently promised himself he would not let the men see him weaken. *I cannot let myself cry from the pain. I will not let that happen,* he told himself. It was much tougher than he could have imagined it would be.

Nicola glanced back at Iskandar and watched him struggle. "Are you able to continue, boy?"

Iskandar stifled a breathless grunt, and replied, "Yes, sir. I am fine," while praying the leader would tell them to stop and rest. His body was giving way to exhaustion and he was afraid he might not be able to keep up with the men. But he forced himself onward.

One spoke to his neighbor, "Sometimes these mountains can be your friends, but other times, like now, they can be your enemy."

Breathing hard, and feeling the weight of their heavy sacks, the group finally reached the crest of the first mountain.

The leader raised his arm to stop the stretched caravan of men. "We will rest here."

Without any hesitation, they gratefully dropped their heavy sacks on the ground at their feet, using them for back rests. They sat in a circle and drank water from their sheepskin pouches, breathed easier, and stretched their sore legs.

One man, feeling sorry for Iskandar, offered water to him from his pouch. The boy drank readily. It felt wonderful flowing down his parched throat, refreshing his small body. He could hardly straighten his legs. His whole body was so sore. Even though it was cooler in the mountains, he could feel his body dripping with perspiration. Yet, he dared not let the men see his tired face as he turned and winced with great effort, wiping a tear from his cheek.

One villager said, "My God, that was difficult. I am so tired. And yet, we have so far to go."

"Yes, *khali*, but look down to the valley and see how far we have come. And we have wheat for the winter."

Another spoke, "Yes, we must be grateful to God we have full sacks for our children. I feel good that we are safe up here and we have once again cheated those damned Turks."

"Did you hear any birds while we were in the valley?"

"No, I didn't. I'll bet the soldiers shot them all. It is so bad that the whole world is in such a state of war. And we are but a small part of the craziness. But this winter we will not see our children starve to death at the hands of the Turks!"

To Iskandar, after what seemed to be only a few minutes, the leader led them down the mountain as they resumed their arduous trek on the steep trail down the mountain to the river where they could refresh themselves in the cool mountain waters. Each stride was painful. Their thighs ached with every step as they constantly shifted their sacks of wheat from one side then the other.

"One more mountain and we'll be home, men," said Nicola, venturing a smile of impending success, and seeking to encourage his weary group. "Stay close, Iskandar. I don't like the weather signs. The clouds from the sea are getting darker."

As they slowly climbed up the last mountain, the sacks of wheat seemed to get heavier and heavier, more cumbersome, and more unwieldy.

One yelled back, "Iskandar, keep up with us."

Another complained, "I knew he shouldn't have come along. He is too young...too small. I told him so."

"But his family needs wheat too," interjected another villager. "And he said he would keep up with us."

Iskandar was in great pain and began to lag farther behind the group. His legs felt like logs. His thighs began to cramp. His muscles cried out for rest. His body dripped with perspiration. But he was determined. He would not complain nor would he ask the men to go slower. Every step was a test of his will. He would keep up until he collapsed. This was his nature. Besides, he knew his family would starve this winter without his bag of wheat.

"Die here on this mountain if you quit, or join your family in your home if you continue," the leader encouraged the weary group.

I cannot shame my father. I must not stop. I must keep up, Iskandar repeated to himself.

They pressed on. Finally, they reached the 6,500-foot second crest. Now they could look down the mountain at their village, about 3,000 feet below.

Nicola exclaimed, "Oh, my God, I see snow ahead."

A second man pointed down and shouted, "There must have been a surprise snowfall up here during the night. It looks at least a foot deep on the crest."

Snow had fallen on the mountain while they were gathering wheat in the valley and it had accumulated quickly.

Another looked up and yelled, "Oh, my God, look, here comes more snow from the sea!"

The approaching, freak snowstorm was their worst nightmare. In minutes, the wet, heavy snow quickly deepened on the ground as the moisture-laden dark-gray clouds blowing east from the sea unleashed this potential disaster. They knew that snow had sometimes accumulated more than twenty feet on this mountain. They had to hurry. The wind-driven snow stung their bare faces and hands. The men had not brought the adequate warm caps, boots, stockings or heavy coats and gloves they needed. Their legs were wrapped in rags. During these times of desperation and starvation, everyone in the impoverished village existed with only the barest necessities.

Iskandar was not at all prepared. His only thoughts were to surprise his mother with a supply of precious wheat. He was very cold; his face, hands and feet were freezing.

They trudged through the deepening snowdrifts along the crest, leaning into the wind and blowing snow, covering their faces as best they could as they shifted their sacks. Their feet grew even colder.

Iskandar now walked with only stockings on his feet. His feet were so numb that he did not realize that he had stepped out of his shoes, leaving them behind on the snowy trail.

After nearly an hour of walking through nearly knee-deep snow, Iskandar, stumbling with great difficulty, and more stubborn than wise, was straggling behind the men. Each step was a major effort. With frozen tears around his eyes and nose, in great pain and totally exhausted, he finally collapsed and fell face down in the snow.

A man nearest him saw him fall and, alarmed, yelled ahead to the others, "Give me a hand, the boy has fallen down." Iskandar's feet felt like ice to the village man. They were hard as stone.

"We must take shelter and build a fire. Some of us, Iskandar for sure, cannot go on in this deep snow. There!" Nicola pointed to a large overhanging stone, "We can find refuge for the boy under that."

Iskandar, shivering from the cold, did not say a word as they carried his limp body. He was in great pain, embarrassed, frightened and exhausted. He closed his eyes and silently prayed, *Dear Lord, please save me.*

The small group worked their way under the large rock protruding from the mountain and quickly stacked their wheat-filled sacks, making a low makeshift barrier to protect them from the wind and blowing snow. They quickly gathered sticks and built a small fire. As they huddled together for warmth, the men placed their bodies next to the boy to warm him. It was bitter cold for all of them.

"Put the boy's feet near the fire to try to get them warm and cover his shoulders," yelled Nicola, taking charge. "He is freezing. I will go down to the village and get Milhelm. He is young and strong, and will come here to take his brother home. He isn't called *Markab el Bar* for nothing." His strength, size and endurance were well known in the province and had earned him the nickname "Ship of the Land." That day, he would have to call on all of his strength to save his brother's life.

Milhelm was in the *souk* in the middle of the village when the man came running to him. He stumbled, dropping his bag of wheat on the ground, and breathing hard as he bent over, hands on his knees.

"Come, Milhelm, come now." Waving his arm frantically, and gasping for air, he pointed to the mountain. "Your brother is in trouble. His feet are frozen and he cannot walk. He is weak and cannot carry his wheat down the mountain. He has been brave, but he is just a boy."

"Damn! We have been looking for that boy for two days, Where is he? Take me to him now. I'll get a blanket at the house and tell Mother that I'll return soon, but we can't tell her about Iskandar yet."

Milhelm and the neighbor ran down the village dirt road toward the mountain slope. Their hurried climb took nearly two hours instead of the normal three. They finally reached the group by the small fire.

"Iskandar, what has happened?" Milhelm asked his frightened brother.

"My feet are frozen, Milhelm," he cried out. "They are turning black. What is going to happen to me, *khai-yi*, my brother? Am I going to die?" Tears were flowing down his young cheeks.

Alarmed, Milhelm spoke. "I will take you home now, Iskandar. Here," he called to the others, "put him on my back. Someone wrap his feet and cover him. We have to go immediately."

With both his brother and the sack of wheat on his back, fifteen-year-old Milhelm had a double load, but he knew he could manage. Even though he had almost run up the steep 3,500-feet of mountain path to rescue his brother, he had not climbed the mountains as had these men the past two days. The snow on the crest was deep and getting deeper. Milhelm had to hurry along the crest, then down the slope. It would take nearly another two hours.

He loved his brother as he loved his own life. Their relationship was extraordinarily close. His parents always told him to watch out for his young brother. "You are the wiser, the strong one. Iskandar is born to explore, to test his fate. You must protect him, Milhelm, sometimes from himself."

Milhelm prayed for God's help during the entire difficult trek back to the village He nearly ran down the mountain with his brother on his back, slipping and falling several times, shifting his brother and his sack of wheat.

Finally, nearly exhausted, Milhelm slammed his muscular body against the heavy, wooden door to enter his family's crude, dirt-floored hovel, *biet Chalhoub*, home of Chalhoub. It was warm and dry inside and there was a fire going. His mother always kept a small fire in the house during the cold winter. He carried his brother and the sack of wheat inside and gently placed Iskandar on the small carpet by the fire. Iskandar, now more like a whipped puppy, happily lay near the fire getting warm, looked at his mother with sheepish eyes. "Mama, I..."

"Aieee," shrieked Katrina. "What is wrong?" She placed her hands over her mouth, frightened at the sight. Her eyes were wide open as she surveyed the scene. Her children were obviously in great trouble.

"His feet are frozen," exclaimed Milhelm to his mother, nearly out of breath. "Iskandar went to the Bekaa with the village men to gather wheat for the winter. The men were surprised by a sudden snowfall on the mountain, and Iskandar lost his shoes in the deep snow. I think he was embarrassed and scared. He knew he should not have gone." Milhelm caught his breath and paused, "He thought the men would be angry with him, so he never complained. He just stubbornly kept walking in the snow still carrying the sack of wheat without saying anything to anyone. You know how determined he is, *Imei*."

"Milhelm, run for the *khoury*, the priest," Katrina cried out. "I'm sure he is at the church. And find the doctor... even if you have to go to Tripoli!" she commanded her son, pointing to the door.

She put more water in a kettle over the fire and began to heat a pot of olive oil, the miracle from God. She began soaking rags in the warm water and carefully wrapping the boy's feet as he lay on the carpet near the fire.

Finally, after what seemed like hours, she heard voices outside the door. "Milhelm! Come in here, *ta ha la hawn*. Is the doctor with you? The *khoury*?"

The doctor knelt by the boy, one knee on the rug, and quickly did those things rural doctors did in those austere, difficult times of 1913. He felt the boy's temperature at his forehead, and then his chest. He checked his pulse and looked into the boy's eyes. Then he turned to his legs and feet. Iskandar's toes were already hard and turning black. The doctor silently frowned. They were frostbitten.

With a serious look on his face, he turned to Katrina and said, "We must watch the boy's feet for a few days. I will send to Beirut for another doctor. Keep him warm, and wrap his feet with warm, not hot, blessed olive oil. Be very careful. Hot wrappings will make the pain he will experience even worse, almost unbearable. This will not be a pleasant experience for the boy." He thought for a moment, and looking into her eyes, added, "It will be very difficult for you both."

Collecting his thoughts, Milhelm spoke, "*Imei*, I couldn't find the priest. But I will." Milhelm knew his mother would want the *khoury* to come and comfort her and the boy.

The doctor returned in two days. He and his colleague silently studied Iskandar's feet. With a sharp pin, they carefully poked his calves, ankles, feet, and toes. There had been no positive change. After a careful examination, the doctors stepped to the side inside the bare one-room house, away from the boy near the fire, and began conferring in whispers, gesturing as they spoke.

"What is it? Tell me!" exclaimed Katrina in a whisper as she stepped toward them, away from her son. "What shall I do?" She bowed her head and wrung her hands.

The doctor softy put his hands on her shoulders, looked into her eyes with great sadness, then whispered, "Katrina, I am so sorry to tell you, but your boy's feet are frostbitten. They are dead. They must be cut off immediately to save his life."

"No!" she hissed in a loud whisper as she stiffly squared her shoulders and turned her body, rejecting that statement. Outraged, tears already flowing in desperation, her narrowed eyes piercing the doctor's. "Never! You will not cut off his feet! You may as well cut his throat! How can this boy live without feet?" She pointed to her young son. "Should he be a beggar in the *souk*? Impossible. Never! With God's love and guidance, I will save his feet and his life. Tell me what to do!"

Iskandar, frightened, huddled by the fire and could only hear whispers, wondering what was being said. He felt sadness as his eyes filled with tears and he stifled a need to cry, knowing it wasn't good news.

"*Imei...*" Iskandar cried out, reaching for his mother with both arms.

What Katrina had to do was a monumental task only a loving and totally dedicated mother could endure. That very day, she began a two-year regimen that would tax her, while bringing her and her son even closer together. Twice a day, day after day, by the fire, Katrina lovingly massaged Iskandar's feet with warm olive oil. She completely devoted herself to saving her son's feet. When Iskandar would jerk away from the terrible pain with tears in his eyes yelping, "Oowww..." his mother would comfort him with a kiss as she touched his face gently. Only after many months, into the summer, the pain began to lessen. "You are a brave young man," Katrina would whisper to him as she rubbed his feet. "I know it is difficult. If I could take the pain instead of you, my son, I would gladly bear it for you."

"Oh, *Imei*, I'm so sorry I worried you. Please forgive..."

"Shhh, my little one, be still. It is alright," she would interrupt him.

Meanwhile, Milhelm would call on their neighbors' homes and borrow olive oil when she had no more. In the late summer, he made more oil from their olive trees by harvesting, then carrying the *zeytoon* to the village's olive presses. The whole village came to their assistance, aiding this family throughout the crisis. Cousins and friends brought to Katrina whatever food they could spare. After all, Ibrahim, their father, had been a leader of the village, the stonemason, builder, and cultural pillar of his church and the village, but now, and for more than a year, he was across the sea in America, and his wife was without her husband and his sons were without their father.

When two years were over, Katrina had saved Iskandar's feet and his life. Everyone in the village celebrated at mass in the churches of Douma as he gingerly took his first steps. They all had faith in God and believed in Katrina's love and devotion and were grateful for his healing. His feet had recovered, but they would remain very dark, nearly black, for the rest of his life.

During his recovery, his mother had gently rubbed his feet in her lap with the warm oil, speaking to him with loving tenderness, almost in a whisper, all those many days. She spoke to Iskandar of his father's courage, the difficulties he had had to overcome, his mastery at building homes for his neighbors, his strength and his principles. "He built this very house with his bare hands. He gathered each stone from the mountain and placed it with loving care. Then he cut the limbs of the olive trees for the door lintels and the ceiling. He placed the stones and soil on the limbs to make our roof, and brought the heavy, ancient Roman marble column section and rolled the roof each day to keep us dry. He never gave up, *habibi*, never. And we must not ever give up. We must stay strong," she would tell him. "Remember these things I tell you, Iskandar."

"Yes, *Imei*, I will. I will always remember."

She told him the stories of his ancient heritage, of how their family forebears, six brothers Chalhoub: Hanna, Eassa, Maloof, Bashir, Simaan, and Ayoub had settled in this very place before the Greeks, long before Christ, and how there were on these mountains, in those times, thousands of cedar trees that harbored bear and deer. Some even said lions lived in the mountains when they were blanketed with cedar trees. She taught him about his Phoenician heritage and how he must be brave like them and follow God. "You must have faith, Iskandar," she whispered to him, "because your faith is your destiny." She told him all these things from her heart. She told him of all the difficulties his family and all the Lebanese had endured over the centuries. "From the Greeks, Romans, the Europeans, and the Turks, it has been Lebanon's destiny to be where everyone wants to be, to provide the great cedar wood, plentiful water, food, labor, ingenuity for the world. Our people have always been resilient and come back from adversity." He listened intently. There had always been a deep, loving bond between mother and her youngest child. And these two years brought them even closer. She was so beautiful to Iskandar, so gentle and loving. She was perfect.

All his life, Iskandar would remember what his mother had spoken to him during these two years when he was young. He deeply felt and appreciated his heritage and all that it meant as he witnessed his mother's total dedication and commitment to her family.

Yet, he knew that the people of the village were impoverished, powerless in the face of the Turkish Occupation They had no freedom under siege, and because of the locust infestation which lasted four years, they had little or no food. It caused him great pain to know his father had to sacrifice by leaving his family to go far away to America to provide a better life for them all.

Thirteen-year-old Leila had gone to America with her father to care for him, as was the custom.

They would be separated until Katrina and her sons could join them. Iskandar knew his mother terribly missed his father and sister and yet she never complained.

*I nearly lost my feet, my very life, because we had no food. With no food we have nothing. We have no freedom, no father, and my mother is without her husband and only daughter. When I get older...*he promised himself, *I will never be hungry again and I will always have food for everyone. That is my vow.*

Three years after his frostbite, during the severe famine and Turkish blockade, his mother died of malnutrition in his arms. He loved her so much. Now, after years of her gentle touch and endearing affection, she was gone. Her death left an enormous void in his life. He grew more determined to go to America where he would have the opportunity to make his fortune. He did not know how he would fill the void of his lost mother's love. But, he believed God would provide him with someone to love, someone who would love him as deeply as he wanted to love her. Iskandar would never forget those terrible and painful days of his youth. He would never, ever forget his mother's love.

CHAPTER 2

*K*atrina Azar, whose family too had lived in the village of Douma for centuries, was considered one of the more beautiful women in the region. Fair-skinned, with her auburn hair fashioned in the style of the day, she was one of the village's favorites. As a teenager in 1895, like many young women from the mountains, she moved to Beirut to live with her cousins. Beirut was Lebanon's major and most cosmopolitan city where marital prospects were better. It was there she married Albert Azar, a distant cousin, and a young, hard-working fisherman who ventured out to sea each day to provide the merchants with the most wonderful, most succulent *Sultan Brahim* fish, a Beiruti delicacy in the finest restaurants.

Sadly for Katrina, she was widowed at twenty-four when Albert was overtaken by a storm and lost at sea.

After the proper mourning period, Katrina's brother Nicola, who had married Sara Chalhoub Thomé of Douma, suggested that she meet Ibrahim, Sara's brother, a young man of good standing in the village. Younger than Katrina by three years, he was tall at six feet and two inches and formidable with strong shoulders and arms developed from years of stone masonry. His family was already deemed acceptable. He was of the same Antiochan Orthodox religion, and he was responsible, ambitious and ready to settle down. "After all," he told his sister, "I am now old enough and I make good money. It is time for me to have my own family."

When Katrina came to the village for a visit, Ibrahim was invited to his sister's home to be introduced. It was a Sunday afternoon after church, so they were dressed in their best.

Katrina's years in Beirut had treated her well. No longer a simple mountain girl, she had a flair about her, a panache that Ibrahim found irresistible. She laughed at his jokes, and was clearly the nurturing type of woman he found magnetic. Yes, she was older, quite mature, and with her city exposure, was tantalizing. She too found him very handsome and appealing.

When he asked if he could visit her again, she lowered her eyelids coquettishly, looked up into his eyes modestly and nodded, not speaking, fearing she might sound too eager. She was, after all, a beautiful widow. To behave with modesty and reluctance, she was taught by her sister-in-law, was "the only proper thing to do, and will make my romantic brother fall all over himself to come back and see you again."

Katrina, though young, was often too selective which sometimes made her seem like a spoiled daughter. She had already turned down several potential suitors with "It's too soon, I think," or "I don't find him attractive," or "I want to stay in Lebanon. This is my home and he wants to live in France, so, no, thank you. I'll see what awaits me in Douma."

In the summer of 1897, after months of chaperoned courting, and conversations between just the two of them, Ibrahim Chalhoub Thomé and Katrina Azar excited the entire village by getting betrothed. Within three months of both families' involvement in the joyous planning, they were married in Douma in the "Chalhoub Church" with most of the tiny, delighted village in attendance. They were to live near their cousins, sisters and brothers. Ibrahim, considered a young leader in the community, had already selected a portion of the family's land on which to build his home, his gift to his young bride. In a matter of weeks after their marriage, they entered the door of the small stone house with its thick walls and hard packed dirt floor. The roof was built of eighteen inches of collected soil mixed with stones on top of a layer of cut olive tree limbs. It was crude and Spartan, but functional, like most homes in the village. It was shelter. And it gave an opportunity to Katrina to decorate, to make it her home. When Ibrahim carried her through the doorway for the first time, before family and friends, happily laughing, she followed custom and slapped a handful of bread dough against the jamb beside the doorway for good luck. "Be happy, my love," she whispered to her new husband as she hugged his neck. "I will do my best to make your every day a happy one. I will care for you and our children and teach them for you. I do love you Ibrahim and I will love you forever. This home will be filled with love. I promise you." She was grateful for a second chance at marriage and family.

As he set Katrina's feet to the floor, he took her in his arms, and looking into her blue eyes exclaimed, "I am the happiest man in the world! And you are the most beautiful woman in the world! Our families have been in this place for ages, Katrina, and here we shall stay long into the future...you and I and our sons and daughters." They lovingly embraced and kissed.

Katrina eagerly accepted her new place in Douma as the wife of a church leader. Together, she and Ibrahim were often seen at the village *souk* strolling hand-in-hand. They expected to build a family and live long lives together in the village with their children and grandchildren nearby.

"I love this place, Katrina," Ibrahim said as he looked first across the vendor booths in the *souk*. Then, turning his head, he swept his strong arms over the mountains above and the valley below. "Look how beautiful is the valley below filled with ancient olive trees. These are my people and now they are yours."

As they both had hoped, less than a year after their marriage, Katrina bore Ibrahim a son. "We will name him Milhelm *Ibn* Ibrahim Simaan Eassa for my father, Thomé, Eassa, Chalhoub," he said proudly as he held his healthy son for the first time. "He will grow tall and strong and help me build houses in our village."

Within two years, the popular couple added a baby girl to the family. Katrina, lying in her bed, caressing her newborn daughter, said, "My husband, we have a daughter to care for us in our old age. We will call her Leila, after my grandmother. She will learn all she can in the home to help me cook the meals, tend to the goats, and make clothes. I am so happy, Ibrahim."

But they were not finished. Within two more years, Katrina bore Ibrahim a second son.

Ibrahim, raising his newborn baby above his head with both arms, said, "His name shall be Iskandar Thomé Simaan Chalhoub, like Alexander, the leader of the Greeks. He will be the smartest boy in the village."

Katrina was a very happy, contented wife and mother to her growing family. "Two sons and a beautiful daughter," she would remind herself nearly every day. "And I have the best husband, a hard worker and loving man. I am as happy as a person could be." She prayed daily at the Orthodox church, near the Catholic church. The small village had four churches with a total seating capacity of nearly the entire village. This village had placed great priority on regular church attendance over the years, as had so many similar villages in the mountains of northern Lebanon, the *Shimal*. Katrina was grateful, spiritual, loving and happy. The future looked bright, and while poor, they expected to be fruitful and grow old together in this nurturing village.

Ibrahim and Katrina could not know that events and decisions taking place far away would have significant impact on their dreams, their plans. They could not know that one day their youngest son would leave Lebanon to join his father and sister in America.

CHAPTER 3

skandar stood alone at the rail of the passenger ship, a converted rusting old World War I Turkish freighter, still tied up at the Beirut pier. His eyes impatiently searched the milling crowd on the docks below, looking for his older brother Milhelm, who was staying in Lebanon, and his Uncle Elias. "Where could they be?" he asked himself. "I have to see them before the ship departs." Anxiously, he swept his eyes through the crowds standing on the pier waving vigorously. He could see the faces of most of the people waving to their departing loved ones, his fellow passengers. The older men and women were wearing *kiffeyehs* and *afeyehs*, loose, flowing cotton gowns, the traditional clothing of the Arab Middle East. Younger men wore western European pants and shirts acknowledging the influence of the French occupation following the war. Some of the men still wore the Turkish pants with the loose-fitting waist, balloon-like upper legs and tight-fitting calves, and the Turkish fez or flat, wound turbans on their heads. A few businessmen wore fedoras, European-styled brimmed hats, worn by the more sophisticated and well-traveled.

Iskandar wore the more European style of clothing, a close-fitting blouse that caressed his strong physique and emphasized his youthful virility, and long double-pleated, cuffed pants in the French tradition that concealed his athletic and strong legs. A cousin in Beirut had introduced him to the more contemporary look and bought him clothes imported from France. His mustache was part of the Lebanese culture, and something Iskandar was proud to wear. The stark contrast of tradition and the introduction of European influence were obvious everywhere in Beirut.

The 400-year Turkish Occupation with its Muslim influence still had its followers, thought Iskandar. *I wonder what I will wear in America?*

Early in 1912, Iskandar's father, Ibrahim, had gone to America. Since then, the war, the locusts, and the four-year famine of Lebanon had all come and gone. Ibrahim had settled in some place called Florida. The family had waited for him to save enough money to pay for his trip back to Lebanon to bring his wife and two sons to America. But his earnings were so meager, even though he saved every penny, it took much longer than he had hoped. Then came World War I, which had, together with his inadequate funds, prevented Ibrahim from coming back to Lebanon to have his entire family in America. Now, eight years later, Ibrahim, currently owner and operator of a small dry goods store near Orlando, would not be reunited with his late beloved wife and his eldest son. Even though he had sent money by telegraph to Elias to purchase two tickets, only Iskandar was now on the ship.

More than one hundred-fifty other Lebanese, mostly young men like himself, were on board leaning at the railings looking at the crowds on the pier, each of them thinking anxiously of their conflicting emotions in leaving their villages, their families, cousins, all things familiar and treasured, and the contrasting mystery and wonder of what their new lives would be like. Some were nervous and eager. Others were frightened. Some silently wondered if they were doing the right thing leaving their beloved homeland: Lebanon, "jewel" of the Middle East, leaving their heritage, and for some, they thought, their very souls. There were many on board who still had doubts that they were doing the right thing. They were all poor and had endured the difficult years of foreign occupation, famine, little work or income, and were willing to risk anything for a better future.

The ship stirred as the boarding-ramp was removed. It acted as a reminder to them that it was now too late to change their minds. They were on board, and all their belongings were down below in the hold. The visits and good-byes with relatives were complete.

"Am I doing the right thing? Should I have tried harder to bring Milhelm with me? Will I see ever him again?" murmured Iskandar to himself.

How wonderful it will be to see my father again. I have missed him so much. It has been so very long...eight years...I was just a boy of ten. I climbed trees and played in the village when he was here. I wonder what my father looks like. He was such a good father to us all to Imei, Milhelm, Leila, myself and to the people in the village. We all missed him so much. Imei was so healthy and beautiful. And now she is gone, he thought sadly as he looked toward the city, feeling that now familiar emptiness in his gut.

And Leila, how my sister must have changed after these eight years. She was my playmate everyday. She has surely changed! She is now twenty-one, married and living in Orlando with her husband and their two young children. But with the war, the locusts and the Turkish army, who could know; there was so little communication. And I have changed. Will they recognize me? After all, I was so young when they last saw me, just a child. That terrible Turkish Occupation...

His thoughts continued as he stood at the ship's handrail, looking at the beloved, rugged, ochre-colored stone-filled mountains of Lebanon beyond the city of Beirut. It was a beautiful and exciting city, but for several years the mountain people were not permitted to venture out of their villages alone because of the Turkish army presence. Beirut especially was prohibited by the Douma elders after Uncle Salim, two years older than Iskandar, was taken prisoner by the army just three years earlier. Beirut was then under martial law enforced by the dreaded Turks where they captured young Lebanese men and either conscripted or imprisoned them.

The entire village was stunned with what had happened to Uncle Salim. Only seventeen years old, he was already a popular singer, and *oud* player in a Beirut nightclub. What haunting, lyrical sounds emanated from his *oud*, a bowl-shaped guitar, as he strummed its strings. His voice charmed the people of Beirut society, where he drew attention to himself as the most popular young singer of Arabic poetry and love songs in the city. Salim was just an entertainer—why should the Turkish army want him?

But they did.

One late night, in the early morning hours, as Salim was leaving the bistro after closing, the neighborhood army patrol, which he usually was very careful to avoid, came out of the early morning fog at an unexpected moment and stopped him in the narrow, shadowy alley behind the night club. They were looking for any young Christian men of Beirut they could arrest.

"Halt!" shouted the mustached patrol leader.

Salim could feel nervous tension spread throughout his body. His body stiffened as he raised his hands, his *oud* in one, the other empty. He was very afraid. He felt beads of sweat quickly emerge onto his forehead. *What to do but obey? I have no choice. But what is to become of me? This cannot be happening! The Turks are cruel. There is no way out. God, I hate the occupation. It is so terrible, so humiliating. And I have done nothing. I just play my oud and sing. Why don't they go home and leave us alone? They are doing the same thing to us they did to the Armenians. And we too are a peaceful people unable to protect ourselves. We only want to be free.*

He clenched his empty hand into a fist as he pressed his body against the wall. *I have nowhere to turn. What am I going to do? I am lost!*

"Stay where you are!" sneered the army leader.

Salim, a singer and poet, not a fighter, a son of the mountains, not a city boy, stayed frozen in place, hoping he would not be arrested. "What do you want of me? I'm just a singer."

As he kept his arms above his head into the cool night air, he was alarmed and frightened. What was he to do? He felt the perspiration spread all over his body. The night air was cool, but he was sweating!

"No matter what you do for a living," the Turk told Salim, pressing a gun into his chest. "You are the enemy and would kill any one of us if you had the chance. Come with us. Now!"

Salim braced himself as one of the soldiers shoved him hard in the back with the butt of his rifle. "*Y'hara deen bladuk!* May your country burn in hell," he muttered under his breath so he couldn't be heard. *Allah! When will these horrible foreigners leave our country? When will the day come when we can live in peace? Would I of all people have to go to prison for walking home from work in my own country? They could kill me this very night. No one would ever know.*

Salim was forced to march down the dark alley onto the cobblestone street within the cluster of Turkish soldiers to a waiting flat bed wagon pulled by two horses, where he was pushed to join the half dozen other young Lebanese men the patrols had captured. They were quickly driven outside the city to the south where there was an army encampment. Jostling in the back of the wagon, the young men were convinced they would either die that night or be taken to Turkey and put into the army.

The following anxious days in the outdoor barbed wire stockade prison went very slowly for these imprisoned young males, some having hardly reached their teens. All were victims of the last years of World War I, and the Ottoman Empire occupation of this freedom-loving, heritage-rich population in this beautiful God-blessed country. The Turks were under siege by the Allies, and they were preparing for their final rear guard battles.

In less than a month, the prison commander received orders from his superior to "get rid of your prisoners."

"I have so many prisoners. Must I kill them all?" asked the commandant.

"Get rid of them," was the brusque response.

As a result, the commander immediately began a systematic process of random executions. He didn't like this duty. "Commanding a stockade in Lebanon is not going to further my career, and my talents are being wasted here," he wrote to his wife back in Turkey. "I hate this war. I hate the killing. I really want to get out of this land."

Each day, several young prisoners were lined up and shot by the firing squad, without a trial, without recourse, and without any hope of rescue. Many were as young as twelve years old. They were simply *born* in the wrong place, *stayed* in the wrong place, and *ventured* one day or night into the wrong place, although, *always in their own city, in their own country,* a country that was always being conquered and occupied by some nation, it seemed. For more than four hundred years, the Turks ruled Lebanon as a province of Syria. Before them, the Western "Crusaders," the conquering Europeans. And before them, the Muslim hordes. And before them the Romans, the Greeks and the Egyptians. Would it ever end?

Salim's story was told by the villagers many times. Iskandar had memorized every detail.

Each evening Salim was imprisoned, he would entertain his fellow prisoners by playing his magical *oud*, and singing to his attentive, melancholy fellow prisoners the beautiful folk songs of Lebanon, and his own poetry. The young men would clap their hands in unison with the happy, vibrant songs, and find their eyes filling with tears as he sang poignant, romantic songs of love. They would enjoy these songs for hours every evening as Salim serenaded them. Singing was his passion. It was his escape from the reality of the Occupation. Out of desperation, during the last few years, many Lebanese adopted a sense of fatalism, putting their lives faithfully and completely in the hands of God...*Allah*...believing there would be a better place, but not in this life. Salim believed his voice and talent were given to him by God, and therefore, to please God, he would sing and play, even in the face of terrible adversity, as his gift back to God. He would use his feather from the eagle to strum the strings, as the fingers of his left hand would slide up and down the tapered bent neck of the *oud*, pressing the strings firmly, resting the rounded bowl-shaped guitar on his thigh.

During each interminable day, the youthful, depressed prisoners would nervously pace back and forth endlessly within the fenced area, waiting for their turn to be shot to death.

One day, after several weeks of killings and nervous waiting, it became Salim's turn. Two soldiers came into the fenced area, marched to him and grabbed both arms, one of which continued to grip his *oud*. Brusquely, they took him to the camp commander's office.

"Aren't you the young man whose voice I hear singing to the prisoners at night?" asked the commander, looking up from his papers.

"*Na'am*, yes, I am," responded Salim, nervously, head bowed obsequiously. "That is what I do for God, I sing."

"You have a gift of *Allah*," the Muslim Turk responded, nodding kindly. "You have a magnificent voice, young man. And, although I am ordered to shoot every prisoner, I cannot kill your voice." He paused, thought for a moment as he looked at Salim's sad eyes, and, in a firm, angry tone, said, "I will not do that." He slammed his hand on the desk, then calmed his voice almost to a whisper. "I will propose an exchange for you. Tonight I will have you brought to my office where you will sing for me. If you sing to me the way you sing to your fellow prisoners, I promise I will set you free." The Turk waved his hand toward the door, impatiently, thinking to himself, *I hate this job.* "Go now. I will send for you later."

Salim was astonished, yet unsure if the commander would keep his word. "Praise God," he whispered as he was walked back to the enclosure. "Oh, please, God, let it be so."

Iskandar recalled how his uncle with the wonderful singing voice, his romantic poetry, and *oud*-playing ability was saved.

Salim did sing for the commander that night. He sang his heart out knowing it was for his very life. His voice filled with the emotion and purity that was his reputation. He sang with all the warmth and sensitivity God had bestowed on him. He sang and sang, watching the commander's face, sensing what he enjoyed the most. The Turkish officer, with his eyes closed, thinking of his home and family, listened intently, sometimes swaying his head to the music.

True to his word, that night, the commander gave Salim a Turkish uniform and had him taken to the railroad station where he caught a train north to the seaport of Tripoli, about twenty miles north of Beirut. Once in Tripoli the next morning, Salim was almost home. In his hated used army uniform, with his *oud* in his hand, he nearly ran the remaining thirty miles up the winding gravel and dirt mountain road to his family's village. Within that day, he was back in his home and safe in the haven of the mountains where he stayed for the remainder of the war.

Thereafter, he and Iskandar spent many days and evenings gratefully playing *towleh* (backgammon), laughing, shouting, sometimes cursing under their breath as the other got a *shaish-baish* (six-five), roll. They grew together like twin brothers.

Salim, called Sam in America, was now in Boston, Iskandar remembered, smiling at his memories of his days with Salim as he moved along the ship's railing, gazing back at the city and the mountains. And Iskandar swore he would find him.

His thoughts returned to his place on the ship's deck. His eyes looked to his left up the northern coast to the port of Jounieh, then, beyond, where Tripoli is situated. His eyes then returned to Beirut and swept the city with its predominant four-story buildings, some of brick, most coated in mottled grey stucco. There were scattered tall pine trees in the city, and parks and the grottos to the north of Beirut. He continued absorbing his last views of unique Beirut, the dock area's shops, then, looking more nearby, his eyes searched the crowded pier.

"There! There is Uncle Elias and Milhelm. Wonderful." He stuck his hand into the air over his head, waved vigorously, and happily yelled, "Here! Here! Milhelm! Here I am, look here!" He *had* to make eye contact with his older brother. He was leaving Lebanon for a new life and he must connect with his beloved *khai-yi* before he could leave. He stared at his brother's face. Milhelm, who, at six feet three inches tall, stood out of the crowd. He was lean and muscular with thick dark hair like Iskandar's. At age twenty-three, he was an imposing man. His hands and arms were twice as large as Iskandar's, even though Iskandar looked a lot like his brother—he was nearly four inches shorter than his brother—Milhelm's endurance and strength were legendary and for good reasons his nickname was *Markab el Bar.* Iskandar was so proud of his older, kind *khai-yi.*

There! Eye contact. He could see Milhelm waving to him. He knew that he was yelling to Iskandar, "*Allah ma'ak! Allah ma'ak! Khai-yi!* Go with God. Be with God. Good-bye my brother. Until we meet again." Milhelm had been planning to go to America with Iskandar mainly to take care of him as he had all his life. But at the last minute, he changed his mind. He simply could not leave Lebanon now that World War I, "The War to End All Wars," was finally over. The hated Turks had been forced to leave Syria and its western province of Lebanon three years earlier, and the French government had become its "protector" under the League of Nations settlement. Another, although friendlier occupier, Iskandar whispered to himself. As a result, life in Lebanon was much better. And Milhelm, ever the gentle mountain man, and not as daring as Iskandar, had decided to stay.

But Iskandar was convinced that his life would be better and expanded in America, the "Land of Opportunity." That was more than he could ever hope for in Lebanon. He prayed simply for the right to be free in a land that offered opportunity to a young man with no money and no prominent family connections, but armed with a tenacious, determined attitude honed in his youth in the rugged mountains of northern Lebanon. Few obstacles would deter him. He would join his father and learn the American ways. Then, as soon as possible, begin his new life with his own business. He would not work for someone else. He would marry and have a family. He would be *free.* The Turkish Occupation had molded his thinking, as had his very heritage of Lebanese entrepreneurs and adventurers. He had had enough of life where someone else tells him what to do, where to go, and where not to go.

Iskandar felt the tears well up in his eyes as he vigorously waved to his brother and uncle, but especially to his close brother.

Suddenly he felt the steel floor under his feet shudder as the ship's engines groaned, gained power and the ship's rudders turned, directing the ship away from the dock. His hands gripped the iron railings even tighter, not from fear of falling, but from the strong emotions he was feeling as he realized he was actually leaving his homeland of Lebanon, for America, without any concept of what awaited him. He reached inside his blouse and gripped the precious gold crucifix which hung against his chest. He made the Orthodox sign of the cross; forehead, heart, right shoulder, left shoulder, heart. "Lord, be with me, protect me." He looked at his right hand. The tips of his thumb, forefinger and second fingers touched each other in the Trinity fashion of the Orthodox Christians. He felt a sense of family with the passengers since ninety percent of all Syrians and Lebanese migrating to America were Antiochan Orthodox Christians.

"Goodbye, my Lebanon," he whispered.

His eyes moved back to Milhelm and then once again to the skyline of Beirut—ancient Beirut—home of the Canaanites, home of the Phoenicians. Iskandar knew his heritage well and was proud of it. He remembered many things: that it was his ancestors who invented the alphabet, and who were navigators who explored, traded and settled in far off lands. He knew the stories of how the adventurous Phoenicians in ancient times had traveled throughout the Mediterranean Sea in their sailing ships out of the small natural ports of Sidon to the south and Byblos just north of Beirut, to all parts of the then unknown world. Carthage, now Tunis, on the northern coast of Africa, was one of the Phoenician trading settlements they founded back in the 9th century B.C. He knew the legends of their survival in the storms that caught sailors at sea. Their exploits were legendary and made all Lebanese proud of their ancestors. Some even believed the Phoenicians were the first to discover the Americas, centuries before Christ, after circumventing the enormous continent of Africa. So too would Iskandar travel and seek his new life with a sense of adventure and confidence. And like his forebears who sought to trade even as far away as Britain two thousand years before Christ, so too would Iskandar become a successful trader and business-man like the free Phoenicians. He would live, work and prosper in America under their customs and laws and not seek change. Lebanese emigrants eschewed politics for entrepreneurism. He *would* succeed, he was certain. He *must* succeed.

He felt passengers now bumping into him slightly as more and more people came also to stand at the rail and call to their families. "Excuse me," they spoke to him time and again, he nodding in return. It was becoming crowded and much noisier. His fellow passengers were getting caught up in the moment, waving, calling out, and moving around for better views. "*Allah ma'ak*," they yelled to families below on the pier. "God be with you!"

His eyes again swept the rugged mountains of Lebanon where snows fell up to twelve meters in the higher mountains of Mount Lebanon protecting Beirut on the east. He could see the ochre-colored sandstone mountains with the sunset rays to his back striking the mountaintops and outcroppings, turning the beige sandstone to a beautiful, bright rose-pink glow. Lebanon's mountains are its trademarks and what he would most remember. *I shall miss these beautiful mountains. I wonder if there are mountains like this in America?* he wondered. And yet, the warm, clear waters of the Mediterranean, for centuries, were the west protectors of Beirut. He could never forget Lebanon with its vital city of Beirut, its moisture-laden mountains and the fertile, almost sub-tropical, narrow, prolific plain that ran along its southern coast bordering the eastern Mediterranean Sea.

He knew well too, the fertile, rich soil and the wildlife-filled ponds of the water-rich Bekaa Valley that ran nearly the length of Lebanon, between the two mountain ranges, even though he was a mountain son who was born in the *Shimal*, the North.

His village, Douma, the loveliest in all Lebanon it was said, was, at 3,000 feet elevation, a day's walk or donkey ride north of Beirut. It was an old Christian village of fewer than eight hundred people and six churches, predominantly Antioch Orthodox, Melkite, and Maronite Catholic. Iskandar's ancestors first settled there, he was told, in 350 B.C. Nearly everyone in the villages of northern Lebanon was Christian and, in some way, everyone was a "cousin" in the customary "extended family" culture of the Mediterranean. Most cousins were of light olive complexion, like Iskandar. Some were light skinned and some were even blonde and blue-eyed like his mother. His country, Lebanon, was the envy of the entire Middle East, and the second country to convert to Christianity after Palestine, although Armenia was the first to establish Christianity as its state religion. It had been conquered and occupied over the centuries by sixteen civilizations. As a result, its people would have obvious mixes of residual physical and cultural characteristics of the occupiers from the Canaanites, Assyrians, the Egyptians, Greeks, Romans and the Arabs and the European "Crusaders," called the "Western Invaders" by the Arabs, and who stayed for two hundred years during the eleventh and twelfth centuries.

As Iskandar and his fellow passengers stood at the railing, the ship set sail west into the setting sun and the city grew smaller behind the ship. He felt a smile form on his face as he remembered the favorite teenage joke, "Your mother is probably descended from a blue-eyed European knight who came here during the Crusades. That's how your cousins got blue eyes," the other teenagers would say as they teased him.

With a smile, he turned his head at the thought, scanning the people nearby to see how many were fair-haired, blue-eyed, and fair-skinned. There were a few, but most were dark haired, to be sure, and most men wore the customary mustache as did he.

His deep brown eyes scanned the coastline of Beirut. He focused on the famous Pigeon Rocks barely offshore, a landmark viewed from the Corniche that stretched along the top of the high palisade at the edge of the sea and strolled daily by the constant stream of visitors and residents. He brushed his thick, wavy, full head of dark brown hair from his forehead and squinted his eyes to focus as the coastline grew smaller and smaller.

As he watched the crowds on the deck, his thoughts turned to his mother. She was fair, with dark blue eyes and auburn hair. She was beautiful, loving, gentle and kind. She would tell her son, "*Habibi*, dear one, you have your father's light olive complexion and dark hair, but you have my nose, my smile and my sense of beauty and adventure." But, sometimes, she would admonish him, "You are too adventurous and sometimes take risks you shouldn't."

He had enjoyed many childhood adventures, like climbing the large olive trees before he was seven years old. He had also loved the challenges of the rugged mountains and the enormous cedar trees, and would venture up the winding mountain trail to the top, a 6,000 foot elevation, where the villagers had fruit orchards. *"Figarie"* it was called. There, the extraordinarily large apples, Lebanon's finest, and succulent plums grew near the remaining patches of groves of cedar trees that had barely survived the invaders over the centuries—the Phoenicians, the Egyptians, the Greeks, the Romans, the Crusaders, and the Turks—who had cut down and removed most of these majestic, ancient trees because of their need for this hard, yet workable wood for their temples, ships, and war wagons. Some of the scattered trees were now more than 4,000 years old, but most were much younger. One huge, triangular shaped cedar tree north of Douma in the village of Bsharre was said to be over 6,000 years old. The cedars of Lebanon have always been considered the symbol of the resilience, tenacity and endurance of the Lebanese people. The hard wood of the cedars made them coveted by all who came and took them. The Phoenicians and Romans cut the trees and made their hearty ships of the wood. The Egyptians cut and took back to Egypt the wood for their temples and homes. Solomon's Temple in Jerusalem was said to be made of the cedar trees by artisans from Iskandar's village who still to this day fashion beautiful works of all kinds of wood into furniture, statuettes and moldings.

Iskandar especially loved the cedar trees. They symbolized his visceral heritage. He would climb the giants with their outstretched limbs to the top to see in the distance the clear blue waters of the Mediterranean Sea, sometimes cerulean blue near the shallows and beaches, sometimes dark cobalt blue in the deeper waters always glistening like diamonds, reflecting the setting sun.

"Come up here, Milhelm," ten-year-old Iskandar would yell to his older and more reluctant fifteen-year-old brother. "What a beautiful view of the sea!"

He remembered that Milhelm once yelled, *"Imei* wants you down here before you hurt yourself. Come down, *khai-yi*, slowly, not like last year when you were showing off and came down too fast and broke your arm!"

He recalled this event with a sigh, knowing he would be scolded when Milhelm reported the day's activities to his mother. "What am I going to do with you, Iskandar? Be more careful," she would say.

Abruptly, the ship lurched as it hit a swell. He caught himself remembering his childhood adventures. Iskandar felt his eyes moisten as he remembered his brother and mother. He was absorbed in his thoughts as he stepped from the rear to the starboard rail of the ship, still watching the mountains of Lebanon rising above Beirut. The ship was now too far at sea to make out anything but the northern high mountains and soon, they too would disappear into the eastern horizon. He knew this was his last view of Lebanon.

CHAPTER 4

"Iskandar! Come join us below! We are having a *hafli*. We will dance and celebrate our new beginnings!"

Iskandar recognized his new friend Butrus, and while his call disturbed his thoughts of America as he stood at the rail, watching the sunset, this first night at sea, he knew there would be plenty of time to think of America later.

The party was already in full swing when Iskandar and Butrus finally arrived three staircases below, at the steerage level, the lowest and least expensive deck of the ship, literally the bottom of the ship, only inches of steel plate from the sea. Most of the Lebanese emigrants were hearty, young men; hardly anyone was past the age of thirty. Almost all were very poor but happy as they envisioned their new lives. A group of ten men, arms interlocked in a semi-circle, were dancing the *debkeh*. Two men were playing the *defs*, hand-held drums; a third was shaking and hitting with his other hand a *darbuka*, the tambourine, and a fourth was playing the clarinet, emphasizing the sharps of their favorite songs. All were participating in the favorite Lebanese recreational group pastime. They were dancing, singing and laughing. There were a few women on the voyage—mostly young wives, sisters, and several young brides sitting together in clusters along the cold, steel bulkheads.

None had an accurate picture of what life would be like in America. Most didn't even know exactly where America was. In fact, many actually thought of America as the entire Western Hemisphere. Yet they were excited about going to freedom. Some, after they were established there and earning an income, would return to Lebanon and marry a "good Syrian girl." Or, with luck, find a young Lebanese or Syrian bride in America, hopefully of a good family of the same religion.

"Here Iskandar, have some *arak*," shouted Butrus, so he could be heard above the rhythmic hand clapping, the drums and the occasionally loud outbursts from the dancers. Iskandar smiled and eagerly reached for the cup, quickly sipping the clear anisette liquor. "Ahhh!' he exclaimed. "The Greeks knew what they were doing when they created their ouzo, Butrus, but I like our *arak* even better." Iskandar, of course knew about this favorite beverage of the men.

A moment later Iskandar again sipped the very alcoholic beverage from the small cup. He smiled at Butrus. "*Shookrun, sahbi*, thank you, my friend!"

Everyone was as happy as they could be in spite of the meager provisions and lack of any furnishings in the cold and barren steerage class area. It was depressing to stay there for too long. Banks of bare, incandescent light bulbs along the cold, gray steel walls at the ceiling were fully bright eighteen hours a day. "It's for security" the crew responded officiously when asked later in the voyage if they could be darkened during the day so some could makeup for their sleepless nights. Along the side bulkheads, hung on the walls, were canvas-stretched hammocks stacked four layers high for them to sleep on. There were just two feet of vertical space between each bunk. Certainly not luxury, but welcomed. The conditions were greatly improved since his father had traveled to America. In 1912, the steerage passengers had to sleep in small groups on the floor using each other's bodies for pillows and for warmth.

Soon, each of the group thought as they clapped their hands and sang together, *we will be in a new land, free of occupation by a foreign country... a land where any man could become rich if he is willing to work hard. Yes, it would take time...but soon.*

Like Iskandar, most had at least a cousin, father, brother or friends already in America who would make it easier for them to get started. The Syrian/Lebanese people had been emigrating to America since 1850 and many were already established in cities across the Americas from New York to California, from Montreal, Canada south to Buenos Aires, Argentina. But the massive emigration actually began in 1902 when word came that the Turks had enacted their laws requiring Christians to be conscripted into their army.

Iskandar knew that Boston was already home for a large constituency, and where his father's cousins were already located. Even his *Khali* Salim, whom he loved so dearly, now lived there. He asked himself, does he still sing so beautifully? I wonder if he can still beat me at *towleh*? I cannot wait to see him. Brooklyn was home to another large Syrian neighborhood. These two cities were settled by the first immigrants because they were at the East Coast ports of entry and jobs could be found. So too, were there large established communities in Cuba and other islands of the Caribbean, Brazil and Honduras. Many Middle Eastern and Mediterranean immigrants found themselves in Caribbean countries, instead of the United States, mostly because of America's 2% immigration limitations, a national policy to keep the population proportionately the same as it already was; mostly Western and Northern European. Since there were already so few Syrian/Lebanese, Italian or Greek U.S. citizens, those like Iskandar and Butrus who were approved to enter the United States considered themselves extremely fortunate. As a result, for the first time in their lives, they would be a minority in a society to which they would have to adjust. To some people, they would be "different." The United States, to be sure, was the favored destination, although some preferred the smaller villages and new frontiers of the Caribbean and South America to the larger cities of America. Still, they were all justifiably excited and optimistic about seeking their new lives in America, the "Land of Milk and Honey."

Iskandar recalled that those were the same words used by God to Moses in the books of Exodus and Deuteronomy as he described the "Land of Milk and Honey" to the Israelites as they came out of Egypt to settle in the land of Canaan.

He smiled to himself and thought, *But Canaan, including Lebanon, was his homeland.*

Now, he and his friends would live in a new "Promised Land," a new "Land of Milk and Honey."

After sipping more of his *arak*, Iskandar became a little light-headed, left his nostalgia of remembering his family, and joined his fellow travelers in dancing. He was an energetic *debkeh* dancer, stomping his left foot as he crossed his shin with his right foot while he hopped into the air a few inches, keeping in rhythm, double stepping so expertly with his happy compatriots. It was a joyful time. Those not dancing were laughing and watching as they happily clapped their hands in unison to the infectious rhythms.

Butrus joined the end of the line, while Iskandar boldly stepped over and took the lead place in the dancing line. It was the place where, while his left arm was interlocked with the person's arm next in line, his right hand would twirl a rolled, twisted kerchief above his head. As leader, he could be creative in his dance steps. He was really happy now, shouting out exclamations like *yeh!* or *yih!*, jumping, slapping his elevated foot, some steps and movements like Greek dancers, spinning under his now-unlocked right arm while holding his neighbor's right hand with his out-stretched left hand. He was now showing off for the crowd, smiling and laughing. They loved his display and began clapping louder and louder in rhythm. The drumbeats got louder and more pulsating. Suddenly, captured by emotion and joy, the *darbuka* player stepped off the box he had been sitting on, stood tall, and shouted, "Dance, Iskandar, dance like you are a reborn man! We are going to America, Iskandar!" Now, he was shaking the tambourine over his head, making as much noise as he could, staying in rhythm with the drums. The laughter, chanting, singing and clapping of the musicians and more than one hundred young people with their joyous excitement vibrated loudly off the steel walls of the large, cavernous room, and were intoxicating and infectious. Everyone was clapping and feeling great joy. The *arak* was having an effect on Iskandar now, making him more daring in his steps. The drumbeats grew louder as more and more of the group were beginning to feel the affects of the *arak* and the rhythm of the drumbeats. The dancers were exciting all their energies in high-stepping movements. They were feeling so happy! So free! Finally, in time, as the song ended, the dancers laughingly stumbled to the edge of the dance area and hugged their fellow travelers. Some sat down. Some bent over, perspiring and spent from exhaustion. And some, laughing like drunks, fell down and lay on the floor laughing out loud. Iskandar found Butrus and wrapped his arm around his young friend's shorter and heavier shoulders.

"We are going to America, Butrus! We are going to America!" Iskandar repeated excitedly, exuberant from dancing, with a hint of slurring in his speech. "How lucky we are, *sahbi!*"

"We are fortunate, Iskandar. We will be in America. Imagine! If we work hard, we can be anything we want. Not like in Lebanon under the Turks."

They walked to the side of the room and, together, slumped to the floor and leaned against the ship's steel wall. They were winded from the dance, but happy. Each eagerly finished their cup of *arak*. With a flourish, Butrus, who always somehow was able to find just what was needed, reached to his left into his bag beside him, and pulled out a sack of natural pistachios, offering the open sack top to Iskandar.

"Aah, heaven," he smiled to Butrus. "*Arak* and *fistok!*...after the *debkeh*. I feel so complete!"

"I think you were showing off for the ladies," laughed Butrus.

Iskandar winked, "I love to dance, Butrus. Back in Douma, I would lead the dance, but there, everyone was my cousin. Here, for the first time, I am dancing with people from all over Lebanon. You are from Zahle. Hassan and his brothers are from Sidon. Ibrahim from Tyre, Paul from Baalbek, and Michael from Beirut. Until now, everyone I knew was a cousin and we all lived in the mountains."

It was the same for all of them in the group. Most were not allowed by the Turkish army to travel far from their towns and villages where they could make new friends. Until the end of the war, all Lebanese had to stay in their regions.

Butrus and Paul were from farming families who likely lived for many generations in the Bekaa Valley, by far Lebanon's largest and richest agricultural region; a valley measuring seventy-five miles north to south, an average of ten miles wide. Located about thirty miles east of Beirut on the coast, the fertile valley is bounded by the Lebanon Mountains to the west and the Anti-Lebanon Mountains to the east, the ridge boundary between Lebanon and Syria. Until 1946, when Lebanon declared its independence, Lebanon was a province of Syria populated mostly by Christians.

The Bekaa, Lebanon's breadbasket today as it was for the Eastern Roman Empire, is rich in soil, fruit orchards, hay and wheat producing pasture lands in the northern portion and, in the southern reaches, because of more rainfall and sunshine, abundant crops of all kinds, including corn, potatoes, vegetables, tomatoes, vineyards of Chardonnay and other types of grapes. For thousands of years, the Bekaa, a major part of the famous "Fertile Crescent," produced food stuffs for the entire eastern Mediterranean region and, with its historical Roman and Omayyad monuments still present, added a high sense of pride to those who lived in the valley. The Bekaa is steeped in history with ruins from as early as the Phoenician presence at least two thousand years before Christ. The myriad temples in Baalbek, mostly of the Roman era, celebrated the god of Baal with temples to Jupiter and to Baachus, reflecting the presence of prolific vineyards even in that era. When Emperor Constantine converted to Christianity in the third century, all symbols of Baal were removed on his orders.

The two major rivers are the Orontes (Asi) which originates in the Valley and flows north into Syria, and the Litani which flows southward from Zahle through the Valley and turns west in the southern reaches of Lebanon before flowing into the sea a few miles from its southern border. The southern Valley, south of its major city of Zahle where Butrus lived, is rich in water, with lakes, ponds and streams, contradicting stereotypes of the region as consisting of sand deserts and barren images.

Butrus loved the Bekaa Valley as Iskandar loved the mountains. "Anything and everything grows in the Bekaa," Butrus would say proudly. Butrus and Paul, leaving this rich heritage, hoped the area to which they were emigrating would be at least as prolific a region to farm as they had in the Bekaa. Paul would join his father in the Los Angeles area where cattle ranching and potato farming were very successful. Butrus's father was now located in Stockton, California, finding the San Joaquin Valley very much like the Bekaa, with its rich soil, plentiful water, good weather, and vineyards growing in the north. While Butrus would miss Zahle, the ancient Roman and Greek ruins, the Omayyad dynasty arches and the Roman temples, he was happily destined for California.

"I will miss the lakes and ponds too," Butrus reminisced. "What a beautiful place to grow up. But now, like you, Iskandar, I am joining my father in America. You are eighteen years old, but I am just sixteen. So, I will tag along with you for it is said: 'one who is even one hour older is wiser. Listen to Him.' There is so much I don't understand, Iskandar. Everything is new to me."

"Everything is new to me too, Butrus," he replied, laughing, "but as long as you can find *arak* and *fistok*, you can be close to me, *sahbi*!" They were both rural innocents about to experience for the first time unbelievable new sights and cultures.

As the trip slowly continued at sea, every day was like the day before. During the twelve-day voyage to Marseille, when they weren't seasick, many passengers slept late, and walked the outer deck as often as possible to view the open sea. The days were long and boring, with only the sound of the passing sea beneath them.

Sometimes, as the ship sailed near to the Mediterranean islands, they would get excited and talk among themselves of their heritage. For many, like Iskandar, these were the first islands they had ever seen. First came Cyprus, then Rhodes, both former Phoenician trading settlements, and then, near the tip of Italy's boot, they passed ancient Sicily on the starboard. As they turned north, Sardinia was passed on the left. These were large islands and could easily be mistaken for the mainland of Greece or France.

In the evenings, each would find his own hammock, collect their handbags and place them under their heads for comfort and security.

Iskandar, too, located his handbag and placed his head on his arm as he lay on his right side, his favorite position. As he lay in his hammock on this voyage, the first time in his life away from Douma, he thought of his father in America, and then about his mother and how much he missed her. His thoughts always returned to his small village of Douma, the only life he had ever known. As was his habit, he fondled the gold crucifix resting on his lean chest, hanging by an almost pure gold chain. Holding it in his hand somehow helped him fall asleep easier. How he loved his gold cross. It was so special when his mother draped the chain over his head that Sunday at St. Mary's church just a few yards down the road from their home. He was twelve years old. It was his Confirmation Day at church when he took on the responsibility of leading his life spiritually. *This cross was his most valuable and treasured possession.*

This gift from his mother was even more treasured now that she was gone. He found himself fondling it often, rubbing it between his fingers every day when he thought about his mother, whom he loved so much. He recalled when his mother had had Iskandar's aunt, Ibrahim's sister Sara go to Beirut to have it made especially for him by a cousin who was a gold merchant and goldsmith. It seemed like almost every Lebanese or Syrian family had a gold merchant for a cousin. Discounts and fair negotiating were assumed between seller and buyer, and business volume depended on "word of mouth."

This particular 20-karat gold cross was designed to reflect the characteristics of the Antiochan Orthodox church, St. Paul's first church, his mother told him. It was beautiful and unique. It always reminded him of his mother's love. As Iskandar remembered her, he brought the cross to his lips and kissed it. This night, he gripped the cross, asked God for a safe voyage, then fell asleep on his cot remembering that winter day four years earlier, when his mother was so very sick.

"Quickly, Iskandar, get me some soup from the kettle so I can feed your mother," shouted Aunt Sara.

"Katrina, how could you go so long without telling me, your own husband's sister, that you were ill?" Then, shaking her head, Sara asked, "I am like your sister. Haven't we known each other all our lives? Wasn't I there when you and Ibrahim were married in St. Mary's church? And wasn't it I who helped you bring Milhelm, Leila, and Iskandar into this world? And wasn't I the one you came to when you were lonely after Ibrahim left for America? I was the one who went to Beirut to have the special gold crucifix made for Iskandar's 12th birthday. Now, my dear cousin, you are very sick. And I am here. Thank God Iskandar came to me and asked me to come to you. You are terribly ill. When was the last time you ate decent food? The locusts and those bastard Turks! They are determined to kill us all."

Sara carefully brought the spoonful of soup to Katrina's lips, angry and frightened at what she saw. Katrina tried to eat, but she had not eaten much beyond broth for weeks, saving the bulk of their food for her growing sons. She was actually becoming unable to eat and did not feel the need for food.

"Eat, eat, my sons," she would scold. "You are growing and you are young. Eat."

"But what about you, *Imei*? When will you eat?"

"Don't worry about me, Milhelm," she would reply, smiling softly, hiding her pain. "I eat while you and Iskandar are out during the day. I am fine." But she was not fine, looking tired and worn all the time, getting thinner and thinner, and having less energy each day.

The boys had no idea their mother was so sick and was actually dying. They could see she was sad most of the time, not as hopeful for them as before. It was only when she began coughing...hacking deeply, that they felt something was very wrong. Already, more than two hundred people in Douma had died of malnutrition or pneumonia during the past year. Those were terrible, agonizing days for the people of the mountains.

It had only been a dozen years since the cruel decimation of the Armenian people to the north by the Turks. Nearly all two million Armenians had been systematically killed in the holocaust. Those who could escaped to Syria, then to Lebanon, exacerbating Lebanon's social problems. But since the Armenians were mostly Orthodox Christians, the Lebanese welcomed them even though it would be difficult. Culturally, they were the same peoples. And now, since the Turks could not move their armies across the steep northern Lebanese Mountains, and especially could not cross the *Wadi Kadeesha*, "Valley of Passion," that deep narrow rift that runs north and south through the north half of central Lebanon which is so steep it cannot be traversed, the

Turkish Army chose simply to starve the Lebanese to death by blockading all routes into and out of the mountains.

And now, lovely Katrina would become another of their casualties.

That day, in their one-room stone home, Katrina was wearily lying in her bed covered in blankets. She waved her hand to her son as she spoke in a soft whisper, "Iskandar, come sit beside me. I want to speak with you. It is very important that you understand what I am going to tell you." She paused as he sat beside her. "You are a strong young man now. You must know how much I love you, my son, more than life itself. You are my very heart."

She reached for his hands, tears welling in her eyes. "From the moment you were born, you were different. You were special. Of course, I love Milhelm and Leila too. I would give my life for any of you, Iskandar. And perhaps I have. But it is right, and it is good." She paused to breathe, her eyes deep with sadness. "I want you to know your father and I are so very proud of you, how bright you are and how you have grown into a fine, handsome, good man. You, your brother and sister are gifts from God and have made us so proud of you."

Iskandar became frightened, listening to her as his eyes became moist too. He interrupted her, "*Imei*, please, you are tired. I…I…don't understand. You make me sad. You have always been the strong one." He reached out to her.

"Even though we know you and Milhelm are different, you both make us happy." She smiled wanly, then continued. "He is very strong. He loves you as he loves God. I know you love me and that you know how to love completely. In the lessons of life, you have excelled." She breathed deeply, sighing, "Milhelm will always stay here in Lebanon. He is not like you. He will never leave these mountains." She tightened his hand for emphasis as tears began to overflow on Iskandar's cheeks. She focused deeply on his eyes, summoning all her strength, and, in a higher pitched voice, firmly said, "But you, Iskandar, you *must* go to America."

"But I want him and you to go with me," he cried, pleading, tears now flowing from his eyes.

Katrina paused slightly for a moment, gathering her thoughts, "You have been especially bright in school. You are the smartest in class. I remember the day you stood on your teacher's desk, where he put you for your examinations, and you made no error in your French, history, mathematics, or writing abilities. Iskandar, you have always been confident, adventurous and daring. Your missionary teacher told me you even speak his native Russian very well, but that you are best in mathematics and French. You will do very well in America. You will be very successful and strong."

"You belong in America where there is opportunity. As long as the hated Turks stay in Lebanon, there is nothing for you here. It is too difficult simply to live, especially for you, my son. You must be free or you will have no life."

She was pleading now, her hands on his hands as he knelt beside his mother to get closer to her face. "Your father saw that. I know you love these mountains, that you enjoy the ancient cedars, our beautiful but poor village, and our way of life. But, it is not enough for you to thrive. You cannot not stay here to meet your true destiny, Iskandar. Your heart is where you are free, where your talents will thrive. Your future is in America. You must promise me, my beloved Iskandar. You must tell me now, for I am very sick. Promise me that you will go to America and seek fulfillment of your dreams. *You are someone who loves totally. For us, true love never dies.* Find a good woman, be a fine husband, and love her as your father and I love each other. Go join your father."

As she spoke, she caressed Iskandar's hands. He felt the tears steadily slip down his cheeks as he brought his face to hers, touching her moist cheek with his. Impulsively, he hugged her tightly with both arms, both now crying silently but openly.

Iskandar had watched intently as his mother spoke to him. He was choked, unable to speak. He kept shaking his head, and whispered, "No, *Imei*, please. No! You must go with me."

Only now did he realize she was truly very ill. But he still did not know how seriously. He became more frightened by her words, portending something he wasn't prepared to face. He could see tears in her eyes. Yet, he could also see her smile of pride in her son. Katrina had twice given Iskandar his life. She had saved his feet and his life only four years earlier. And now she spoke to him with her final advice and hopes. She knew it would be for the last time.

When she finished speaking to him, they embraced and kissed each other's cheeks. He cupped his hand under her chin, and he kissed her cheek again. They gently looked into each other's eyes and saw their tears overflow. He lovingly stroked her hair, clinging to her, not willing to accept her sense of finality, unable to let her go.

"*Imei*, I love you so much. I cannot bear to leave you. I will stay with you forever. I will protect you."

"No, *Imei*," Katrina replied, addressing her son with his name for her in the customary way, "You must promise me one day soon you will leave this place for a new life of opportunity. Seek your adventures in America, not here. Promise me, *Imei*, this minute. I must hear your words so that I may sleep in peace tonight knowing you will fulfill my dreams for you. Speak the words, my son, so that I may sleep now. Promise me, Iskandar, you will leave these mountains and go...go *beyond the cedars.*"

His tears were now welling again, greater than he could hold back.

"Yes, *Imei*, I promise you, but you must be with me," he sighed sadly.

"Remember, Iskandar, my beloved son, I will always be with you."

Her head turned on the pillow toward him as her eyes closed and she whispered, "You have made me happy, my son. Thank you and God bless you." He pressed his open hand in hers and held it there, not wanting to let go.

That night Katrina peacefully fell asleep for the last time.

CHAPTER 5

The ship lurched harshly and awakened Iskandar from his sleep. He felt the tears flowing down his cheeks.

"Get up, Iskandar, we are arriving in Marseille! The ship will soon dock at the pier. Get up. Join us, we are all going on the outside deck. It's so exciting, *sahbi*. Let's go see."

Iskandar shook off his emotional dream and joined Butrus. They stood with the other passengers at the starboard rail as the ship neared Marseille from the southeast, gazing on a coastline of high, steep ridges and scattered rocky islands offshore. They were glad to be outside and eager for the voyage to end.

"It's very different from Lebanon," exclaimed Butrus, pointing to the shore. "Our mountains are at least a mile, maybe two, from the sea. These are right at the sea. We grow bananas and tomatoes along our coast, I don't think they can grow anything along this French coast!"

"I wonder what this place is?" asked Iskandar, sweeping his arm across the view of the French coastline.

They were sailing past *Les Calanques*, the white-faced steep cliffs that climb as high as 500 feet above the sea. They watched as many coves and secluded beaches nestled in the meandering water's edge passed by. Some people were actually walking along the crests, others were coming out of the coves in fishing boats, and still others were sunning on the stones at the shore.

"Well, it *is* Saturday, so maybe the people of Marseille come here on weekends," decided Paul, standing nearby.

"Weekends we go to the Litani River near Zahle," replied Butrus proudly.

"Well, I'm from Mount Lebanon, so I'm feeling pretty good about seeing these cliffs and mountains. They are special, aren't they?" Iskandar reminded them with a smile.

"It's beautiful!" yelled Butrus. "I can't believe these cliffs and those secluded coves. See the people sunning on the rocks, some swimming. And over there on the other side of the ship, all those islands offshore. Marseille is incredible! So different."

"Butrus," Iskandar responded to his young friend and the others nearby, waving his arm across the shoreline, "I think Marseille will offer a whole new life for us while we are here."

He couldn't have known how prescient was his statement.

As the ship neared Marseille, the cliffs became rounded hills and gave way to scattered buildings along the shore as the city came into view. The hills along the shore were now less steep and rounded. The first large structure they could see near the city was the magnificent mansion called *Jardin du Pharo.*

As they slowly approached the port, the two fortresses on either side of the entrance to the Old Port, *Vieux Port*, became prominently visible.

"What are those?" yelled Butrus, as he pointed. "They look like they are protecting the city from invaders."

Butrus and the other excited passengers were viewing the massive Fort Saint-Jean and Fort Saint-Nicolas on opposite sides of the Old Port entrance. Remarkably, both were built to keep the Marseille citizens from *exiting* the city when parochial and wealthy residents of Marseille were battling the royals of Paris during the rule of Louis XIV in the seventeenth century.

But the passenger ship was not to enter the Old Port. Instead, it would dock at the newer, larger docks in the Bassin de la Grande Joliette where seagoing ships following World War I could be accommodated. *Vieux Port* was now used primarily for docking small fishing boats and those wealthy enough to have private boats. The city was huge, spreading over many hills. But these Lebanese travelers were fortunate because their destination would be the *Panier* District, "the Basket." For centuries, *Le Panier* had been known as the place where immigrants and the poor who came to Marseille would reside, at least temporarily. It was also located just across the road from the Joliette docks, very nearby their disembarkation dock, and conveniently near the railway station.

The ship pulled slowly and unsteadily to the dock at the western portion of the city, where the crew, under the watchful eyes of the captain, raced to and fro tying the ship's lines to the large mooring piers.

As his hands gripped the top rail, Iskandar's eyes swept the large city's earth-toned brick buildings...strange, but in many ways similar to Beirut's. Rail yards and hills were in the background. It was late afternoon as he watched the longshoremen busily loading and unloading the ships at the piers. The sun bounced off the light ochre buildings and glistened on the clear blue waters. The sky was mostly clear with a few puffy clouds and a light breeze drifting across the anxious passengers' faces. The pleasant weather was a good omen.

Iskandar took in all of the busy sights as the ship slowly completed its ponderous chore of docking and tying up. With his right hand, he brushed back his thick, wavy hair. He had a smile of excitement on his face, anticipating his next several weeks in this exciting city of Marseille, his major stopover before sailing for New York. He was more than ready to get off the ship.

"It really is something, Butrus. Look at all the people!"

"Let's go, Iskandar. Let's get our feet onto the soil of France. Isn't this just about the most exciting day of your life?"

The dock area was a fabulous human beehive of activity, and Iskandar took it all in. This had been a long, uncomfortable, exhausting trip made even worse by frequent bouts of seasickness. But the adventure of seeing this magnificent city of France for the first time was something he knew he would always remember.

From the moment their feet stepped onto the Joliette pier at the west corner of the port, the passengers, most from poor and small, remote villages, admired this busy city of Marseille. They had seen Beirut, but Beirut did not have the bustle, the vibrant shipping activity, and certainly not the overwhelming French presence. France's national and regional flags fluttered in the breeze. Everyone was in awe of the enormous port and its activity. Groups clustered on the pier seeking directions, looking for waiting relatives, gaping at the busy port.

Iskandar and Butrus were no exception. Their eyes searched the area, simply taking in this great city that had seen throughout its amazing history, centuries of travelers making this their port of call. During the Crusades of the eleventh and twelfth centuries, tens of thousands of Europeans en route to "the Holy Land" passed through Marseille. Immigrants from Palestine, Sardinia, Italy and other Mediterranean lands arrived over the centuries seeking to locate in Europe, using the city's excellent transportation facilities. The railroads, near *Le Panier* and the docks, absorbed travelers bound for Paris, Le Havre and other major European cities. Others simply found safe haven there.

The city was a hubbub of commercial activity. Energy pervaded the vendors, shopkeepers, and the people of the city, hawking their wares to any passerby who would listen, and seeking eye contact.

There was especially much happening in the enormous area of the docks and rail yards…ships coming and going…supply ships and trains unloading goods from the farms and industries of France, then to be shipped by rail or barge down the rivers of France to the Saône River that flows southward to the port of Marseille.

In turn, agricultural products from North Africa and other countries of the Mediterranean were being unloaded: oranges and other citrus products from Jaffa, Palestine and Sardinia, bananas from coastal Lebanon, Egyptian cotton from Alexandria, silk, cloth, olives and cork from Spain, and Eastern spices, olives and wheat shipped from Latakia, Syria's major port.

Dockworkers were seen hauling freight and luggage. The French workers were busy with their wagons and carts, some pulled by horses, some pushed by hand. The larger transfer cranes and machinery were mechanized. It was now only two years after World War I and its devastation of Europe, especially France, so the dockworkers were either those too young or too old to have served in the army. Marseille was clearly one of the most active, entertaining, and, in a word, the wildest city on the Mediterranean coastline. It was an open city with an attitude of *laissez-faire* in nearly everything. The mood was driven by the postwar relief and carefree attitude that spread across most of Europe, except Germany, which was bankrupt by the Draconian provisions of The Versailles Treaty, "the spoils to the victor" agreement that would come back to haunt Europe and especially France, in less than two decades. Germany would soon suffer from terrible inflation that would bring starvation to the German people. Soon, in less than a decade, the Great Depression would come to all of Europe and, later, America.

But for now, and for the next ten years, both Europe and America, and especially Marseille, were determined to enjoy "the Roaring Twenties" which were now beginning. This was an era unequalled in its euphoric consumption of nearly everything, especially anything that made one "feel good." Those tastes and demands especially included copious consumption of France's more than ample supply of wine and its companions, women and song. The spring weather was temperately cool, but comfortable, with a late afternoon light breeze off the sea.

Bistros, cafes and outdoor restaurants, with their ubiquitous sidewalk tables, lined the dock area streets that included rows of brick and stucco buildings typical of the Mediterranean coastline. Booths and shops of every specialty filled the spaces along the streets, with offices and apartments occupying the upper three floors of the typical four-story buildings. The offices and apartments had many windows with wooden shutters that were open most of the year and closed only during the few coldest winter months. There were people everywhere: working, driving, walking, shopping, dining, visiting, with some simply sitting, watching the ships arrive in port, bringing even more immigrants from French colonies, some nearby and some far-flung, including Indonesia or South America.

Businessmen, merchants, and vendors of everything anyone could possibly wish for were "hustling" each other. Everything, it seemed, was available in Marseille at excellent prices, especially near the port. Hawkers carrying their goods walked among the newcomers shouting out prices of their myriad variety of wares—always with a smile and ready for bargaining, the culture of the Mediterranean merchant.

"Look, Iskandar," exclaimed Butrus as they began hurrying through the jostling population, "look at the shops, the buildings, the people. This is so exciting," he called out as he stumbled on the cobblestone quay, while looking up and not watching his step.

There were many small specialty shops. One sold mosaic boxes, backgammon games and tables. Another displayed colorful fabrics of wool. Still another shop was full of all things brass and copper. Different sized trays were displayed and pots hung from hooks above and around the entrance, dangling in their shiny hand-tooled shapes and sizes.

Iskandar and Butrus scanned the shop fronts in amazement.

"There is so much to see," yelled Butrus over the noise of the hundreds of shoppers in the immediate area.

"You are right, Butrus! This is wonderful. Shops are everywhere. It would be nice to have money to buy these things, but, unhappily, we don't," Iskandar reminded his younger, slightly shorter friend.

"Let's have a quick look anyway."

They spotted a small, narrow shop, reminiscent of Beirut's *souk*, crammed with barrels of nuts in front of the shop and on either side of a small passage into the store. Each wooden barrel, about three feet tall, was filled with individual kinds of nuts with a scoop atop the mound. Paper bags were stacked near by. The mustached shopkeeper was smiling and beckoning with his hands to each shopper. "Five francs! Only five francs for a bag of the finest almonds, and pistachios! One bag free if you buy two! Come here, *ta ha la hawn.*"

"I knew he'd have *fistok*, Butrus. Let's have a look!"

Butrus grinned happily. "They do, they do! And they have almonds from Jordan and Syria too! And next to him, the *zeytoon* shop. They must have a dozen kinds of olives! Their barrels are full."

All along the promenade, the city had provided spaces located especially for the shopkeepers, so every day of the week they might sell their goods to disembarking passengers from all ports of call along the shores of the Mediterranean Sea. Ships were continuously arriving from every port in the world, such as Zanzibar and Saigon where the French had established their colonies in the South Pacific, and from Uruguay, Brazil, and even Chile which shipped its rich and abundant copper.

Marseille was indeed a principal European port for goods and passengers from all over the world and the city's merchants rolled out the red carpet with their eager smiles, to make sure they collected as much money as possible quickly from the passengers of every ship arriving at the docks.

"We'd better be going now, Butrus. We'll go crazy here with no money to spend. Let's go find my Uncle Hanna at *Place de Liban*. The French call it *Place de Lenche*. That's where Uncle Elias told me I'd find the *mushthamah Libnani*…in the *Panier* District. He said that there's been a Lebanese colony in Marseille since the Phoenicians, and I should go there to find my Uncle Hanna. I'm certain he can provide us with a room because he's a wealthy businessman here who owns many buildings."

"*Yallah!* Let's go, Iskandar, I'm ready. I'm sixteen years old…in France… and soon will be in America." Smiling mischievously, he added, "And now I want to see the pretty French girls. *Yallah!* I am ready!"

The day was wonderful. The skies were clear and the air cool, very comfortable for the two excited teenagers seeing Marseille for the first time. As they walked to the boulevard from the pier they felt the soft, cool breeze while at the same time the warmth of the bright sunshine fell on their faces. Scattered tall sycamore trees in a row along the *Rue de l'Evêché* added a natural softness to the stark rows of storefronts and brick buildings. These carefully spaced trees were planted in and along the cobblestone sidewalks, and because it was late spring, there were young, pale green leaves sprouting everywhere in the trees. They eagerly spotted pretty French girls everywhere.

The two of them soon blended in with the flow of other disembarking travelers. As these young, "in transit" passengers took to the streets, they were all just as excited as Butrus and Iskandar. They all rushed to experience walking on the firm ground of France. After twelve days at sea reeling of seasickness they had to find their balance on land, shedding their unfamiliar "sea legs" which they had constantly braced against the ship's rocking movements. Now, seeing this free city for the first time, most would also find themselves in the "Lebanese Quarter" in minutes.

"Just think, Iskandar," laughed Butrus, "if Marseille is this exciting, imagine what America will be like! But I'm glad we are staying here for a few weeks until our ship to New York arrives. So many others are going to take the train to Paris and to Le Havre to get to New York faster."

He turned to watch a cluster of teenage girls walk nearby. "Now I *know* I want to stay here for awhile," he added with a wink.

Watching the girls, Iskandar happily nodded in agreement and then continued, "I think we're going to like being in Marseille for awhile. I mean, you never know who might come into your life in a city like this…I don't think there's another city like it! There's so much to see…."

Some of the group they knew would indeed leave by train to Le Havre within a week to board a ship there that would take them to America along the "North Sea route" and get them to Canada and the United States faster. Iskandar and Butrus knew they would remain in Marseille for several weeks before boarding their passenger ship bound for America via the "South Atlantic route." Some of their fellow voyagers would end up in New York, while many would disembark in the Caribbean islands, or in Central America or the South American countries of Brazil, Argentina or Chile.

Iskandar recalled his father's wishes that he not take the train to Le Havre, but wait in Marseille as long as necessary before sailing to America. The southern route was safer he had said. In February 1912, Ibrahim, his father, and Leila, his sister, arrived in Marseille, and like the others had the same choice: stay in Marseille and wait several weeks for a ship that would take them across the southern route or board the train for Le Havre. "It is a faster trip to America from Le Havre," they had been told. His father's passage ticket could have included the train, but he decided to stay in Marseille and not go to Le Havre. This was lucky for him and Leila. The ship boarded by those who went to Le Havre en route to New York was the Titanic, then on its ill-fated maiden voyage. Almost all of those Lebanese émigrés were in steerage with the equally poor Irish. Most of them perished at sea, although a few did survive to tell the story of the horror of that night.

But Ibrahim and Leila, with others who chose to wait, were spared, and with grateful thanks for their good fortune, thanked the Lord everyday in America.

So, rather than tempt fate to hurry to America, Iskandar was following his father's wishes and waiting in Marseille for the next ship to America in accordance with his scheduled arrival in New York where his father would be waiting for him.

That decision would be of enormous importance to him for the rest of his life. For during his lengthy stopover in Marseille, he would meet his first love, the beautiful and captivating Madeleine DuBois.

CHAPTER 6

*T*here is a policeman, Iskandar," Butrus exclaimed, pointing. "Let's ask him how to get to *Place de Lenche* before we get lost."

"*Pardon*, monsieur," Iskandar raised his arm and called out in fluent French as he approached the uniformed *gendarme* who was walking toward him with a smart gait. "*Gendarme, s'il vous plaît*, can you tell us where 216 *Place de Lenche* is located?"

"*Oui*, I can," responded the friendly policeman, quite accustomed to requests for directions from incoming passengers from other ports. "It is here in the *Panier* District and very near by." He continued, pointing with his arm, "Follow *Rue de l'Evêché* straightaway. You will come to a stone stairway on your left. It is wide, and perhaps a climb of only three meters. At the top is *Place de Lenche*. It is quite beautiful. It is what you are looking for, I am sure. It is where the Lebanese community congregates, and where most coming from Beirut meet with their relatives and friends. You cannot miss it. It has many trees and is surrounded by handsome apartment buildings, cafes and restaurants."

"Let's go, Butrus. We're nearly there!"

In moments, the two found the steps leading to the plaza.

Place de Lenche plaza was an intimate courtyard less than one hundred meters square. From the plaza, they could see on a hill in the distance a huge church with the figure of St. Mary on the top coated in pure gold. The tables were already being set under the big sycamore shade trees. There were *towleh* sets on many of the tables, with some men already occupied playing the game. They could smell food cooking.

"I can smell dinner being prepared. I can tell they are baking lamb. I'll bet they're baking *kibbee*, *tabouleh*, *koosa*, and *imjadara ma' roz*...I love beans and rice! We have found the right place!" exclaimed Butrus. As he turned to look around at the shops that lined three sides of the park, he caught his foot on a cobblestone edge and tumbled to the ground. Laughing at his clumsiness, he added, "And pastries, don't forget the desserts! I can't wait for some fresh baklava! It's been a longer ride on that ship than I thought!" He laughed at himself. "I can hardly walk."

"You have to slow down, Butrus."

Iskandar and Butrus found the four-story row building along the south side of the square-shaped plaza as the *gendarme* had instructed. They looked at the number over the entry door carefully, verified his uncle's offices on the directory, entered the doorway into the small alcove, climbed the fourteen well-worn unpainted wooden steps to the second floor and walked into the hallway.

"Ah, 216. Here it is, Butrus. Why don't you go down to the plaza and look for something to do while I speak with my uncle and get us a room? Meet me at the restaurant downstairs later this evening. Alright?"

"Sure. I won't get lost. It'll be fun!"

After Butrus left, Islander turned to the paneled door and knocked on the door anxiously.

"*Entrée, s'il vous plaît,*" spoke the man's accented deep voice behind the door. Iskandar reached for the door handle, turned it, pushed the wooden door open and confidently stepped into the small, sparsely furnished office, looking around the room. Money was spent on the home, not the office in those days. Behind the wooden, unpolished desk, sat a handsome mid-fortyish man with a friendly smile. His dark hair was stylishly combed straight back with a part in the middle. It looked wet to Iskandar. He was stocky and about Iskandar's height. He had the familiar full mustache and olive complexion of most Lebanese men. They both had the same deep brown eyes and strong straight noses. *Hanna is well manicured and meticulously groomed*, thought Iskandar. *He must be very successful.*

"Monsieur Hanna Chalhoub?" Iskandar asked tentatively.

"*Oui*, I am Hanna. And you must be Iskandar! *Ahlen wa sahlen!* Welcome, cousin! Welcome! Look at you!" Hanna exclaimed his welcome as he stepped around the desk and, with out-stretched arms, fully embraced Iskandar with a bear hug. They customarily kissed each other on both cheeks, stepped back after a moment and, each holding the other's shoulders, smiled warmly.

"Ah, *habibi*," he said endearingly, "Elias telegraphed you would arrive today. Coffee, juice, tea? You will love the juice from the fabulous Jaffa orange. We'll have wine later," he smiled.

"*Shookrun*, thank you, Uncle Hanna. It is so wonderful to be here. I have been looking forward to this meeting for a long time. Marseille is so friendly. Even the *gendarme* who directed me to your office." He was excited now, and eager to converse with Hanna, who was not really his uncle but was his father's cousin, part of his extended family. He leaned forward. "Let us talk. I need your assistance. Can you help me? My friend Butrus and I need a place to stay." Iskandar spoke very fast, nervously.

"I was told you are an impetuous young man." Hanna smiled as he gestured to one of the two oak chairs opposite his desk. "Of course, but first, calm down, sit and be comfortable, my son. It is better to visit first." As he looked carefully at Iskandar's face, he spoke, "You look just like your father. I cannot believe it. But you have your mother's smile. So, tell me Iskandar, how is your brother Milhelm? Is he well? Why is he not here with you? He was supposed to arrive at the same time... Elias wrote me with the details weeks ago."

"*La'a*, no, *Khali* Hanna," Iskandar shrugged and turned his body away, showing a bit of disappointment. "Milhelm decided at the last moment to remain in Lebanon. He simply could not leave. His heart was too heavy at the thought he might not ever see Lebanon again." Iskandar paused as he watched Hanna's eyes. "So, I am here alone." Now his eyes widened and a smile came over his young face as he continued, "And I am to stay in Marseille for the next six weeks until my ship arrives to take me to America."

"And Uncle Elias. How is his health?"

"*Na'am*, he is in very good health and his businesses are going well in Beirut." *Hanna is so wise and elegant. I want to be successful like him*, thought Iskandar as he watched every move of his distant relative. He was glad he had come here to wait for the next ship. He looked around the office and noticed everything. A picture of the cedars of Lebanon covered in snow hung on the side wall which was painted off-white like the others. The wood floor was serviceable and plain, like the hallway. The ceiling was made of wooden planks painted white. `A large backgammon in mosaic on a table to the side with two chairs was set to play. On a small stand behind Hanna's chair was a large journal at least two inches thick. *It must be his record book of rents and costs. Hanna is so confident, so pleasant, yet I bet he can be tough and strong when necessary.* He smiled back at Hanna who was quickly becoming his mentor.

Window dressings were not necessary because of all the tall shade trees outside and the hinged outdoor shutters that could be drawn closed if necessary but usually were left open.

"And the family? Is everyone in Douma in good health?"

"Yes, *Khali* Hanna, everyone in Douma is doing better now that the war is over and the Turks are finally gone. There are a few more jobs now, and the *zeytoon* (olives) are flourishing; the *areeshi* are full and lush now in the vineyards of the productive Bekaa Valley, and Beirut's businesses are getting stronger. It took several years for the vineyards, olives, and the farms to come back in Douma after the locusts. That was a terrible time. No food, no jobs, no medicines, no money—those evil Turkish army patrols. I love Lebanon, but I hated life there. It is so difficult. All our freedoms were taken from us. Everyone was so poor."

Hanna, nodding somberly and murmuring as Iskandar spoke, understood. He had heard of the difficulties, but he was safely away in Marseille.

Iskandar caught his breath, boldly stood and took a few steps around the office as he thought. Then turning back to Hanna said, "The men slowly lost their confidence and dignity. Some could hardly face their children. They helplessly watched their families grow sick, and many died. Life was mostly filled with fear and a loss of hope. You cannot imagine how meaningless life became. And you know, those very things took our mother from us."

"Ahhh, beautiful Katrina. *Ya'haram*, poor thing. How it broke my heart to learn that she had died. She was so kind, so sweet, so beautiful. How I always wished she had seen me first! Your father was a very lucky man. I might have been your father, Iskandar," he laughed aloud, extending both arms out in front of him, gesturing. "And that would have been good for me, for I have watched from a distance as you, your sister and your brother have grown into fine young people. You have always made your mother and father so proud of their children."

Hanna, now standing at the tall, wood-framed window that came within twelve inches of the floor and ceiling, turned, gesturing back to one of the chairs opposite his own. "And now Iskandar, let me tell you about Marseille and the room I have provided for you and your friend Butrus right here at *Place de Lenche* or *Place de Liban*, the name given in deference to the main plaza of our Lebanese community. Even the French have adopted our name although Monsieur Lenche was quite famous. We Lebanese are quite active here in Marseille. Most of our immigrant community is here in the *Panier* near the docks and railroad yards. There is so much history here. And our people love being near to each other. Those who have the ability to do so, live in other parts of the city. I myself live on the hill overlooking the harbor. I have lived in Marseille for many years, almost twenty-six now. You know, it is the second largest city in France, Iskandar. Only Paris is larger. But our city is growing fast. It is one of the most active ports on the Mediterranean. It brings good business and has been a stopover for Lebanese and Syrians bound for America since the mid-1800s, more than seventy years." He paused to catch his breath, then resumed, "Although the Greeks claim to have first settled here in 600 BC when they fought the Roman armies for this land, we Lebanese love to say, 'Yes, that is true, but the Phoenicians were here first, way back around 2,000 BC, but they decided to travel to more distant lands including Britain which they called 'The Land of Tin.'" His proud smile showed his prominent gold tooth.

Iskandar laughed with his uncle. "I am told you own many apartments near the docks. Isn't this so?"

"Yes, *habibi*, I do. They have been good investments for me. Lots of trouble sometimes, but like all of our family, I believe in owning land and buildings. I don't trust the bankers, you know. I bought most of my holdings during the Great War when the French were selling their properties…almost giving away everything they had of value. I think, as Lebanese, we have had such a history of being conquered that we do not let mere war deter us from investing." He laughed at his joke. "After all, we have learned that even the conquerors need people in business. We have a sense of history. We have had to learn the hard way, since it seems Lebanon has always been occupied by someone. Of course, we never conquered anybody's lands. And this is a good lesson for you. *Y'eini*, always have cash when others do not. Have faith in the future. If you truly believe, God will watch over you and your faith is what makes all things happen. Then life will be good." He smiled confidently. "But this is most true if you work like hell as you are waiting," he laughed aloud.

"And if you are free, Uncle Hanna." Iskandar interrupted him, remembering his village.

Hanna, focusing on Iskandar's eyes, nodded, "Yes, to be sure." He stood up, feeling an emotional need to be Iskandar's "Dutch Uncle." He was now exuberant in his advice to his youthful, distant cousin who might have been his own son and admonished him saying, "That is true, my son. Use your brain that God gave you and your faith, and buy when others sell. Sell when everyone else is buying. It is good business. Listen to your own mind. Seek advice, yes, but decide for yourself. You must hide your cash until it is needed. Many people spend their cash on silly things. I do not. But, *y'eini*, you will have a good life in America. Remember, this is your only life. Make the most of it." Waving his finger upward, he continued, "This is a good lesson you must understand. Ah, but now I have rushed to become your teacher. You see, I have no children of my own." He shrugged, "Perhaps I have spoken too much so soon, my son." He smiled as he put his hands on Iskandar's shoulders. "But, I am very happy to see you."

After a moment of thought, Hanna walked back around his desk to his chair. Taking a deep breath, he leaned back comfortably into his soft leather chair.

He continued, "I do have a room for you, Iskandar. It is on the third floor of this very building, *Place de Liban* is where our working people love to visit, congregate, and entertain their friends. As the end of the day approaches, you will see many men at their tables down there playing cards, *towleh*, or dominoes. The women visit here also. They often knit in groups under the trees. The favorite pastime for the men is playing *towleh* and smoking *aguilas*, water pipes. If you are anything like your father, you must be very good at the game!"

"I love to play, and sometimes," Iskandar smiled in modesty, "I win my share."

Hanna laughed and slapped his thigh. "I bet you do, my son."

"But my father can beat anyone. He taught me well," responded Iskandar, smiling.

Hanna rose from his chair, walked to the window again and called the young man to his side. They both looked down on the plaza. He affectionately put his arm over Iskandar's shoulder as they both looked out the window. "See how beautiful our plaza is? Say, my boy, have you eaten today?"

Iskandar shook his head.

"Then let's go down and have something. Do you want a *shawarma*, a sandwich, or would you like to visit with me over a cluster of assorted appetizers, a *mezza* of *jibneh*, *hummus*, *kibbee*, and *tabouleh*? The French insist I drink their wine," he chuckled, "but I do enjoy my daily glass of *arak*."

Iskandar took an instant liking to his uncle and became convinced that he must know many people in Marseille. It would be a good thing to be close to this man. After all, the city was large and very different from anything Iskandar had ever seen. And Iskandar was certainly new to all the activity in this hectic port city. His tiny village was very quiet and without visitors. The contrasts were bewildering and challenging. He thought, *I will be in Marseille six weeks. I should make the best of it while I am here.*

Hanna moved away from the window and, using both hands, carefully placed his burgundy-colored, flat-topped, tasseled fez on his head, one of the many Turkish customs the Syrians adopted during the years of occupation. As he turned to the side to look at his reflection in the mirror, he smiled with pleasure as he shifted the fez to the correct angle. *Some habits never die,* Hanna thought.

"Follow me, Iskandar," said Hanna as he waved his arm and led him to the door, down the stairs and to the plaza below. They strolled among the tables and afternoon pedestrians, across the open, shaded cobblestone park to the opposite side. Hanna pointed as he described everything to Iskandar and they slowly walked the more than two hundred feet across the plaza. Iskandar listened, learned, saw it all and asked questions. They also discussed Lebanon's travails, Beirut, the family, Katrina, and what Iskandar would do with his future.

Hanna smiled proudly. "This city is known as the most exciting city in France, Iskandar. That is especially true these days, *habibi*. We are now just two years after the terrible war throughout Europe, and the French people are euphoric with peace; yet, there is still a struggle. So many young Frenchmen were killed by the Germans that there are many, many young women for every man. Many still look for work. They are poor. Germany too is very poor, as are other lands in Europe. This city, especially near the docks, has bistros, cafes, restaurants and, yes, prostitutes. Everyone wants to enjoy themselves, even though there is difficulty everywhere in Europe. The immigrants and travelers like you attract the "ladies of the night," and the risqué "can-can" is a favorite entertainment for the men. You must be careful with what little money you have, my son. Everyone wants your money because they have so little. They will know you are new to the city and that you are naive. It is good you are fluent in French. At least you will understand what you hear, although your accent signals you are from Lebanon."

As he looked around, Iskandar laughed at Hanna's reference to money, something of which his family had had very little. He noted the old four-story buildings on the three sides of the plaza with their varied fronts. The fourth side was open and offered a magnificent view of the port. The structures were somewhat similar to Beirut's: mostly brick, some of old stucco and in need of paint. The windows all had wooden shutters that hung on either side, many painted colorfully in turquoise, deep red or yellow.

As if reading Iskandar's observations, Hanna commented, "These buildings have been here a long time. You know, Iskandar, the *Panier* has been the favored place for all immigrants from the days of the Crusades when tens of thousands came to Marseille to find transportation to the Holy Land." He laughed. "Some of these buildings look like they were here even then," he laughed. "But while old, they were mostly built in the past century. They just need some paint, don't they?"

Iskandar laughed and nodded as he continued to observe the waiters scurrying around from table to table, covering them with white cloths, silverware and napkins, readying them for customers. There must have been a hundred tables grouped throughout the stone plaza. The plaza was now quickly filling as shadows deepened with the approach of evening. It was an interesting but understandable observation by Iskandar that French was spoken by most people. Only once in a while did he hear Arabic spoken in conversation by the older people. *This is so different from Beirut.*

Pulling out his pocket watch on a gold chain, Hanna flipped open the cap. Looking up, he smiled, surprised, "My God, it's six o'clock already, Iskandar. The dock and rail workers are finished for the day and getting ready for their evening. There will be much activity for several hours. Around ten o'clock, prostitutes and single men, mostly travelers, will be on the streets. For now, we will go over there to the *Café Liban* for a glass of *arak*, some *fistok* and *hummus*."

Pointing his arm toward the port, Iskandar asked, "What is that beautiful building in the distance? Over there on the hill. It looks like an old church."

"That, my son," Hanna stated with formality, "is the Notre-Dame-de-la-Garde. It is Marseille's proudest landmark. And on top is the magnificent gold statue of the Madonna. The church is more than one hundred years old, very young for French cathedrals, but very beautiful and very important. They say the sunsets from that hill are the best in Europe. It is magnificent, is it not? All citizens of Marseille revere Notre-Dame-de-la-Garde, Iskandar. It is visible throughout the region and far at sea."

They quickened their pace as they dodged others striding across the crowded plaza. These two men, one very distinguished in his late forties, the other, a naïve, handsome teenager from a small mountain village, walked slowly, conversing and gesturing. Hanna was a most friendly man with a broad smile that he shared with the many passersby. He acknowledged his many acquaintances and friends with a cheery nod. But Iskandar knew that when it came to business, he would be like any other successful Lebanese businessman: pleasant but not hesitant while bargaining, friendly yet expecting to be well paid for his services. He would not spend his money freely, nor would he waste his time in fruitless conversation. His hard-earned wealth did not come easily, and he would not let someone else have it without a more than fair "*quid pro quo.*" He relied on his experiences and instincts for guidance. However, Hanna, like many successful Lebanese men, knew the benefits of the "good life." He knew how to play, how to enjoy himself, and how to make his woman happy.

"Over there, Iskandar," Hanna pointed with his hand, "several blocks away from the sea and near the east end of *Vieux Port* is the *Canebière*, the main shopping boulevard. You may want to see it. The stores are popular and busy. They are also expensive. I have a dear lady friend whom you will meet later tonight who owns a popular ladies' boutique there. Several parks with fountains are nearby, good for relaxation." Pausing, he motioned to the left, "There is the infamous street named 'the street where women never sleep alone.' That's where the prostitutes gather. It's very near to 'the street of forgiveness,' where the prostitutes and their customers go later for confession at the small church that has been there serving the same vital mission with its nuns for more than five hundred years." Hanna laughed at his description. "Ah, no matter when, there is always a need for both. It is famous they are together, eh?" He smiled at his rhetorical question.

Iskandar was coming to realize that Marseille must be the most carefree city in Europe, and a far cry from Beirut. Certainly it was beyond anything he had imagined. For a moment, he felt a sense of concern, wondering if he could adjust to such a city as Marseille. For a moment, he longed for the familiarity of home.

As he listened to Hanna, Iskandar's hand went to the gold crucifix at his chest. Needing comfort for his thoughts, he gripped the treasured gift from his mother.

"If you would like to be with a woman some evening, contact me, I have a friend who has many associates and she will provide for you. But you must see me first. There are other kinds of pretty girls and prostitutes on the streets. They are not for you or me, my son."

Iskandar watched the people in the plaza and thought they all looked somewhat familiar. *Are they Lebanese? Are they Syrians? It seems the Lebanese look like Frenchmen, and they look like the Greeks. The Spanish and Italians probably resemble me too! Everyone has occupied each other's lands for centuries and we all seem to look like each other. Will America be like this?*

As Hanna spoke, they strolled under the tall leafy sycamore trees across the plaza.

"Here we are, Iskandar. This is *Café Liban*. Let us sit down. I am hungry and it is time to rest." They found a typical four-legged wooden table covered in a white cloth surrounded by four wooden chairs in front of the café, and took their seats.

Hanna signaled to a waiter in black pants, white shirt and red vest with a white towel apron and called out their order in French, "*Garçon, s'il vous plaît, arak, deux. Et hummus. Nous sommes très faim.*"

They looked around and Hanna recognized a familiar Lebanese face.

"George! *Mon ami,* meet my nephew, Iskandar. He is just in from Beirut. He is eighteen years old and will go to America in a few weeks."

George was very similar to Iskandar in appearance. He too was nearly six feet tall, well-built, about one hundred and seventy pounds, and had dark brown, almost black, wavy hair. Both were attractive young men, handsome, most would say. Their most distinguishing traits were in their faces—the olive skin, straight prominent noses, deep thoughtful brown eyes, and the affectation of the customary mustache.

"*Mahrharbahr,* welcome, Iskandar," smiled George as he offered his hand to Iskandar's and welcomed the fresh-faced newcomer in the typical Arabic way, with an embrace. "And what is the news from Beirut?" he asked, making conversation.

George was sitting at an adjoining smaller table for two, smoking a cigarette and sipping his *arak* as he watched the strollers pass by. "I love to come here each day at this time. Many interesting people to watch, Iskandar," George commented to his new friend. "I am from Zahle in the Bekaa, and Marseille has been very exciting for me. There are so many beautiful French women, and so few French men. It is a good time for us to be here, Iskandar," he grinned.

They both glanced around, watching men and women, some young and pretty, some carrying babies or holding hands with their young children as they crossed the plaza, conversing as the waiters rushed to tend to their tables.

Iskandar laughed at George, "Is there nothing to do in Marseille but look at pretty girls and work at the docks?" As Iskandar looked at George, he noted his stylish tight-fitting clothes; his shoes were French and *au courant.*

George was in his late twenties, Iskandar reckoned, worldly and more confident than he, and looked like quite the ladies' man. A friendly sort with a ready, almost cocky, smile who should not be underestimated, he thought to himself. Iskandar looked out of the corner of his eye and tacitly asked Hanna if he was correct. Hanna caught his glance, smiled and nodded his head acknowledging that his nephew was judging George exactly right…he would like him, enjoy him, but know he has his own plans that may not be the same as yours. "Another lesson, my son," Hanna quietly told Iskandar. "You are learning; you are a smart young man."

"What more can most men do?" responded George with a knowing smile and a shrug of confidence. "This is the good life, the war is over and the French people have been through hell. They want to have fun now, and they will. So, who am I to try to stop them?" he chuckled, as he shrugged his shoulders and spread his arms, questioning.

"Well, I am not interested in being with just any girl," replied Iskandar as his eyes widened above a warm smile. He was so serious, idealistic, and naively romantic. "I want to be with someone I love. And I will know her when I see her."

"Well," spoke George dubiously, "maybe we can sit here until she comes by, looks at you and says '*Bon jour,* will you come home with me?'" He rolled his fingers as if signaling someone to come to him and laughed out loud at his clever response to this young innocent. *This boy is young and inexperienced,* George thought, *but I like him.*

"Perhaps that is too much to expect, George," Iskandar shrugged, feeling a bit embarrassed, "but it is a wonderful way for me to think. Remember, all my life I have been surrounded by relatives who loved me, especially my mother. So, how am I to think differently now? I have faith. And when she enters my life, I will know it. Don't you think so, uncle?"

Hanna nodded, as he watched the growing numbers of strollers, while not really following the conversation. He was busy consuming a dip of *hummus* on pita bread. After a moment of chewing and a sip of *arak*, he told Iskandar, "Have your dreams, son, follow your heart. Be patient, and wait for God. He will provide for you, Iskandar." He spoke with an uncle's affection and sincerity. Iskandar smiled and reached for the pistachios in the small bowl.

"How about a game of *towleh*, Iskandar?" asked George, testing his new friend while raising an eyebrow and waving his hand to the table. "Pull up a chair Iskandar and let us challenge each other."

"Yes, let us play *towleh*! But I must keep an eye out for my friend, Butrus."

Iskandar stood up and stepped from the larger round table he and his uncle had been sharing to sit opposite George at his table where the backgammon game was already set to play.

"Roll your die, Iskandar, let us play," extolled George as he threw his die on the board to determine who would be the coveted first to roll the dice. They began their game. George threw a five to Iskandar's four and looked confidently into Iskandar's eyes and said, "My roll."

"Next time I will lead," said Iskandar to George with a confident smile.

"Next time, perhaps, my new friend, but not this time. This time I am first," responded George with a confident smile. "Be on your guard and do your best, because I am going to win this game."

Iskandar narrowed his eyes as he studied George's first moves and quickly determined his strategy. *It all depends on the roll of the dice*, he remembered, *but I must be prepared. Perhaps I'll play defense this game*, he thought as he rested his chin on his closed hand, focusing on the game.

And, as George had boasted, he did win the first game. But Iskandar was very good too and George was impressed.

"Another," demanded Iskandar with determined confidence, lightly slamming his open hand on the table. "Let us play another," he challenged George as he took a small sip from his glass of *arak* and then confidently swept a dollop of *hummus* on his wedge of bread and brought it to his lips.

After an hour, Iskandar had won two games and George had won three.

Hanna exclaimed, waving his arm with a slight sense of importance, "Iskandar, come back to my table, it is time to talk and enjoy our dinner. Join me. I have something to tell you."

Iskandar stood up, stretched and nodded to George who laughingly taunted, "Come back and let's play another time." He stepped over to his uncle's table and sat down. "Yes, *Khali* Hanna?"

"You are a good player, *habibi*," Hanna spoke softly, touching Iskandar's shoulder affectionately, "and you are making a good friend in George. It is good you did not beat him too much too early. You don't want to anger him. *Y'eini*, you will be in Marseille many days before you leave for America. And George is popular. You want him to enjoy being your friend. This is a good lesson in life, *habibi*. Listen to your Uncle Hanna, Iskandar." Somehow, Hanna felt a fatherly need to mentor Iskandar and continued to advise him, surprising himself because he knew he was always focused on his business. But with no children of his own...

Interrupting Hanna's thought, Iskandar nodded and whispered, "I understand. Thank you for your counsel."

"Iskandar, I told you I have a small apartment for you and your friend Butrus in this very building, on the third floor above the restaurant. Here is the key. It is number 3-A. Now, go to the restaurant door, take the stairs on the right, and climb to the third floor with your bag. Then return to me here. I have a lady friend, lovely Madame DuBois, coming to visit with us. She is my lady, and will be here any minute with a surprise for you. So, go now, wash your face, change your shirt and return here. Do not tarry. I promise you a delicious meal and warm fellowship. *Yallah*, Iskandar!"

He hurried up the stairs, two at a time, and entered the sparse room. There were two small cots with mattresses. *It was a much better situation than on the boat*, thought Iskandar happily with a smile as he sat on his cot.

After a quick face wash and shave, Iskandar looked around the room, saw again the bowl on the wooden commode with a small mirror above hanging from a nail in the wall. He went to the window overlooking the street below and saw the now even busier plaza filling with people. The apartment was perfect, nicer than his own humble home. The bathtub and toilet were located in a communal bathroom at the end of the hall. In the village, his modest stone home had no plumbing and a thick roof composed of a mixture of packed earth and rocks. There, he slept on a leaf-filled wool cloth bag on a hard, earthen soil floor, and washed his face in a bowl near the fire. His toilet was an outhouse, a humble *shishmeh*. His entire one-room home in Douma was not much larger than this room. So, Iskandar was very happy with his good fortune. *This is my home for the next six weeks*, he thought with pride as he looked around the room, sweeping it with his eyes. And with a smile of excitement, he pulled on his other shirt and his only coat, smoothed the front and checked his buttons. He turned, opened the door and stepped out into the hall. Remembering Hanna's words of caution, he pulled the door closed firmly, carefully turned the key in the lock, and walked to the staircase.

By the time Iskandar returned, primped with his wet hair neatly combed close to his head, the plaza was almost filled with nearly three hundred diners, visitors, and game players. The volume of voices loudly overcoming the rest seemed to have doubled in less than an hour.

"It's perfect, *Khali* Hanna. Thank you so much. It's more than I could have hoped for. You are very kind."

"It is my pleasure, the least I can do for you. Enjoy the room, Iskandar!"

Then, at the same moment they both heard a young man's voice over the growing crowd. Butrus, a young sixteen, excited by the newness of Marseille and eager to explore, was urgent in his movements and always using his hands as he spoke. Stocky, with a full head of black wavy hair, tousled striped shirt, and dark gray pants, he seemed to be dodging people as he approached the table with one arm up and a happy smile as he excitedly yelled out, nearly stumbling, "Iskandar, there you are." He came to the table quickly, and too out of breath to speak softly said, "I am glad I found you. This is exciting. My neck is sore from trying to see all I can see, and all the pretty girls. What a wonderful, busy city," he exclaimed, both arms spread out.

"Ah, Butrus, meet *Khali* Hanna." Iskandar quickly introduced Peter to Hanna. Butrus, calming down, politely extended his hand to Hanna. "He has provided us with an apartment." Reaching out to Butrus, he handed him the key. "Here is the key. It is room 3-A on the third floor. Go see it."

Iskandar gestured to his uncle and then, for Butrus, pointed to the window of their room. "I will be here having dinner with my uncle this evening and will join you later.

As Butrus left, Iskandar turned to Hanna and, as he swept his shirt with both hands, said, "Do I look appropriate to meet Madame DuBois? I am wearing my best shirt. I have only two," Iskandar spoke in nearly a whisper because he didn't want to embarrass his uncle.

"You look very nice, *habibi*. Daniella is a very beautiful and kind lady and I think she will be most impressed by you. Her husband François was a good man and my friend. But, sadly, he was killed in the war. It is so unfortunate."

"Oh, killed...that is very sad."

Hanna's voice softened as he spoke endearingly, "I try to help her and her charming daughter as much as I can. I think our friendship is of great comfort to both of us. She is a popular seamstress for the wealthy ladies of Marseille. She owns a boutique where she and her daughter design and custom make fine clothing. She does very well, and although she receives a check from the French government for the loss of her husband, it is very little. Still, she is a magnificent woman. She is well read and makes her own beautiful and, I must say, quite stylish clothes and those of her delightful daughter who is learning the same trade, as an apprentice, from her mother. I am certain you are going to like my friend, Daniella, and, I think you will enjoy her surprise for you," said Hanna with his easy smile. "Her daughter, Madeleine, is such a charming, delightful, young lady. We shall have a lovely evening, *habibi*, the four of us."

They both smiled, enjoying the early evening cool air, the slight breeze off the sea, the birds chirping in the sycamore canopy above. Small wrens were hopping on the ground near the tables picking at particles of food on the plaza stone. Hanna, lifting his glass of *arak*, gestured to Iskandar. "A toast then, Iskandar, to the wonders of what this evening might bring to us."

Madeleine was just twelve years old when her father had to go off to war to fight the Germans and to protect France, "to protect our Madeleine," her mother had told her so often.

"But why must Papa go away?" Madeleine had cried. "I will miss him terribly. I love Papa. I love to sit in his lap, to have him hug me and tease me. I need Papa, *Maman*."

"I know, *ma chérie*, I know. I will miss him too. But, we must continue. Soon he will return to us," Daniella said to her young daughter that difficult day when he left, trying to comfort her. "We both love papa, and we need him with us. Soon, *chéri*, he will return to us so he can take care of you and love us, like before."

But François did not return. "The War to End All Wars" took François forever. He died protecting them, but he left an enormous pain of loss, especially with the little girl, an emptiness where there had been such joy, laughter and love. She had so much love to give because she was a child of love and affection from her father and her mother. There was a very special bond between father and daughter. Nearly every day during his absence, Madeleine would sit alone by the window, hugging her pillow to her chest, fondling the gold ring her father had given her as he left. She would stare out the window at the street and the short walk to their front door wishing, hoping to see his face, remembering his laughing face as he would pick her up off the ground when she would run from the house to greet him, shouting, "Papa, Papa, you're home!" She was the fulfillment of his dreams. She had so much love to give, and longed to give her love to a man like her father. Her mother tried to be both parents, but could not.

This is the Madeleine into whose life Iskandar appeared that evening. Now sixteen years old, she was blossoming into a beautiful, sensitive young woman.

CHAPTER 7

A h, Daniella, there you are." Hanna, standing up as she stepped toward the table, smiled and welcomed her with outstretched arms. "Come sit with us."

"Hanna, *bonsoir, mon ami*," replied the voice of Daniella, emerging from the crowd of strolling pedestrians.

Iskandar looked to his left and saw her, a tall, beautiful woman in a fashionable close-fitting sleeveless, chemise dress that flowed to her knees over her sensuously slender body that reflected her every movement as she walked toward them. A silk scarf was draped around her long slender neck and the ends fluttered in the breeze. Her broad smile revealed exquisitely perfect rows of teeth that matched her clear, unblemished white skin. Daniella DuBois was indeed a strikingly attractive woman with dark hair shaped in a chignon at the nape of her neck, in the fashion of the day. Her lips were crimson, and her arched eyebrows perfectly defined her blue eyes. She had long shapely legs and slender arms, and was carrying a small purse in her left hand. She looked very self-assured and seemed so friendly. Her daughter was a step behind, to her side. She looked very pretty and turned Iskandar's head. *She is so lovely*, he thought to himself as he saw Madeleine for the first time. *She looks so much like her mother*, he mused. She wore a loose fitting peasant blouse, while her full skirt was snug at her trim waist. His eyes swept over her face, her smooth, bare shoulders, and her beautiful dark, almost black, hair pulled back with a large white ribbon tied in a bow on top of her head. The strands of the ribbon draped down over her long, straight hair as it flowed down her back to her small waist.

As Iskandar and Hanna quickly arose in unison from their chairs to greet Daniella, a young boy seemed to come out of nowhere and jostled Daniella and, even more so, her daughter. Caught off balance abruptly, Madeleine's shoe caught on the uneven cobblestones and she stumbled and fell to her knees. In a blur, Iskandar rushed to her, leaned down and reached out with both arms to help her to her feet. She looked up at Iskandar with an embarrassed smile, and with eyelids lowered in slight hesitation, offered him her right hand for assistance. Facing her, he gripped her hand with his right hand and placed his left hand on her small waist. As she felt his strong but gentle grip on her waist, she put her left arm on his shoulder for support and allowed him to pull her up. She felt secure with his strength and chivalrous reaction to her dilemma. As they stood now, very close together, face to face, their eyes met for the first time. She was only slightly shorter than he. Suddenly he felt warm as he looked down into her deep blue, almond-shaped eyes. Her face was stunning, with natural rose-colored lips, arched eyebrows, and clear white skin. He noticed every detail of her smiling face. For a second he stopped breathing. *That face...she's the most beautiful girl I've ever seen! I think I've met the ideal of my dreams!*

She looked at his handsome face, then stared into his dark brown, sensual, almost liquid eyes. She felt a surge of warmth and a tingling sensation spread throughout her young body. She lowered her eyelids and blushed from her unexpected emotions of attraction. Then, as her eyes remained frozen on his, she smiled with the loveliest curl of her full lips and whispered to him, "*Merci, merci beaucoup.*" Her knees were weak, but not from the fall.

His knees buckled too as his libido responded. Her voice was so soft. Her fair, flawless skin was like silk, and her sensuous, penetrating eyes, outlined with long, delicate eyelashes, were pools of femininity, the likes he had never seen. He was aware that he was feeling incredibly excited and, in a way, thought his whole body was melting.

Gathering his composure, Iskandar finally stammered, a bit embarrassed with his redundancy. "Hello, my name is Iskandar. Uncle Hanna is my uncle."

"*Bonsoir,*" she whispered. "I am Madeleine, Daniella's daughter." Then, nodding slightly to him, "I am so happy to meet you."

As he continued looking into her eyes, Iskandar became unaware of the activities and movement of all the people in the plaza. He no longer noticed the waiters rushing around serving their customers. Suddenly, the chatter of the people dining, playing table games, the loud discussions nearby...all became mere background to the arrival of Madeleine.

As she spoke to him softly, Madeleine smiled her innocent wide smile and continued to look into his moist eyes. She could not help but be struck by the handsome features of his face—his strong cheekbones, straight nose, soft full lips. *He seems so gentle, yet strong, and so kind. He must be a good man... he's the favorite nephew of my mother's dear friend.* She instantly felt safe with Iskandar.

She too had become unaware of her mother and Uncle Hanna beckoning to them. After a long poignant moment of intimacy and touching, her hands were still on his shoulders and he was still holding her small waist. If they had not been standing in front of his uncle and her mother, they might not have loosed their embrace for a long time. They both lost all sense of time and the world around them, and after what seemed like an hour, they finally looked to their table and attempted to begin a semblance of *savoir-faire.*

Iskandar gently continued to support Madeleine's arm, not wanting to lose his contact with her, as he guided her carefully toward her chair.

As Iskandar and Madeleine moved toward the table and their empty chairs, he looked at his uncle for guidance...wanting to joyously shout out "I am in love!" and "Help" at the same time.

Daniella watched her daughter, suddenly taken by Iskandar, Hanna's nephew. She appeared to have been rescued and was not in pain. She reached her hand to Madeleine's and said, *"Tut'es fait mal, chérie,* did you hurt yourself, my darling?"

"*Merci, Maman,* I am fine. My knee is a bit scratched, but I am fine," she replied standing as she pulled up her dress to her thigh and brushed her knee with her hand, allowing Iskandar to see her long, shapely legs. She turned her head from her mother and looked at Iskandar as he watched.

Now smitten and a bit unsure, he offered, "Please sit down, Madeleine. May I help you?"

Nodding, she gracefully sat down, smoothing her dress beneath her. Iskandar took his seat next to her at the table. She was utterly a dream come true to Iskandar. He knew he was already in love with this enchanting young woman and was embarrassed at how obvious his behavior might be. He felt at that moment that she liked him too, as she, to her surprise, turned to him and conveyed her affection for him by looking in his eyes and smiling once again. They shared a golden moment that might have been fleeting, but they consciously continued as spontaneous warmth overcame both of them. Each was mesmerized by the other's gentleness, sensitivity and the response to the other that compounded the sensual excitement they felt.

Incredibly, meeting Madeleine had changed his view of life. And he knew he could never let her go.

CHAPTER 8

After dinner, Madeleine and her mother left for the night and Iskandar went to his small apartment deep in thought, remembering every moment of the evening...Madeleine's enchanting smile, the suddenness of his almost overwhelming feelings, her reciprocation that had given him confidence and daring. Butrus was already asleep, probably dreaming of America, thought Iskandar. But he could not sleep. His thoughts were only of Madeleine...enchanting Madeleine.

I have met my love, he thought to himself as he lay on his cot. *I have to see her again...and very soon. She is so beautiful, so perfect. She likes me too! I cannot sleep. I do not want to sleep.*

Butrus was snoring lightly so he couldn't share his newfound excitement with his friend. Iskandar was experiencing that exciting, tingling rite of passage, "first love." To anyone, it is a fabulous experience, but at eighteen, every emotion is magnified. Love! What other word could describe what Iskandar was feeling?

After a long time lying on his back in bed, remembering every moment of his encounter with Madeleine, he finally drifted off to sleep, dreaming of her.

Early the next morning, Butrus was awake first. He chided gleefully, "Wake up, Iskandar! Let's go, yallah! We must see the city."

"*Na'am.* Yes, Butrus, let's go see Marseille. But first, I must go and visit Uncle Hanna. Then, I must go to see Madeleine's mother's shop to see her too! I've met my dream. It's amazing! She's so beautiful, Butrus. I believe I'm in love!" Iskandar could not stop thinking or talking of Madeleine.

"Madeleine? Who is she? Is she very pretty? Is she Lebanese? Or is she French? What is she like? In love so soon, Iskandar?" Then, standing with his arms folded across his chest, he laughed, "You are a lucky man! Maybe you are crazy too!" Butrus was excited for Iskandar and couldn't stop his inquiry. They were both young and experiencing a new world.

"Maybe I am crazy, but I don't care! I can't wait for you to meet her,

Butrus. She looks Lebanese, although she is French. She has the bluest, loveliest eyes. Like my mother's. Her voice is like a soft breeze, her skin like silk. Her hair is so pretty. She dazzles me!"

"Iskandar, you are speaking so fast. Slow down, *sahbi*."

"You are right. Let's go have some breakfast, Butrus. Then after I will visit with my uncle."

They quickly washed their faces, carefully combed their hair, dressed, and hurried out.

"Good morning, *habibi*. I am glad to see you," welcomed Hanna from his chair behind the desk. "Sit down, have coffee with me and tell me how you find Marseille. Is it to your liking?"

"Oh yes, *khali*. I love Marseille." He was overcome with excitement. "The people seem very friendly. I especially enjoyed meeting your lady friend Daniella last night..." Iskandar felt a bit embarrassed.

"And Madeleine?" inquired Hanna, with a knowing smile. "How did you like meeting Madeleine? It seemed to Madame DuBois and me that you lost your appetite and could do nothing but look on Madeleine all evening."

"She is lovely don't you think, *Khali* Hanna?"

"Indeed she is, just as alluring as her mother." Captured by Iskandar's enthusiasm, he thought for a moment and replied, "Would you like me to arrange another meeting, perhaps dinner another evening, say next week?" Hanna was teasing Iskandar.

"Next week? How could I wait that long? You are playing with me. Why not tonight? Why not this minute?"

"Actually," Hanna responded laughing, "I spoke with Daniella this morning. She told me Madeleine did not sleep at all last night, and she did not eat her breakfast this morning. Daniella had a difficult time getting her to even go to work this morning. I believe she is thinking only of you, *habibi*."

"Oh, *Khali* Hanna. That is how I feel toward Madeleine. I'm captured by her. I'm stunned! I can think of no one or anything else."

"Well, that's nice, *habibi*," replied Hanna, trying to calm his nephew by not joining in his exuberance. "I'm glad you are happy. I'll arrange another meeting this very night. Meanwhile, Iskandar, go join your friend Butrus and see some of Marseille. There are many pretty girls here and so few men. There is a very nice park nearby, or the fish market along *Vieux Port* where people go to stroll, shop or meet friends. I suggest you go to the park near the *Aix Marseille*, the University, at midday when it's busy. There is another gathering place where young men play football (soccer) a block or two beyond the *Canebière*." Hanna's mind was exploring all things and places these two teenaged boys might enjoy. "But I think you will have a good day simply seeing the city, the busy docks, and the people. Perhaps you would like to meet me at the same restaurant as last night. You and I can meet earlier, say six o'clock, before we are joined at seven by Daniella and Madeleine, d'accord?"

"*Khali*, I will be there, even before the appointed time. I will not be late." He paused, thinking. "Now, I must go join Butrus before he grows too impatient. Until six o'clock, then. *Allah ma'ak.*"

Iskandar, filled with energy, bounded from his chair and went to the door, waving as he quickly left the office.

Ah, youth, Hanna said to himself with a smile. *It's a pleasure to watch… sometimes*, he laughed.

After a busy, adventurous day of touring the city, Iskandar and Butrus were able to locate *Place de Liban* again and return to their apartment at four o'clock. They refreshed themselves and lay down on their cots to rest and recapture the day with each other.

"Isn't this wonderful, Iskandar? Here we are in Marseille, France, on our own, in our own apartment. And you, my dear friend, have fallen in love! How lucky you are! Maybe I will find someone too, *mon ami.*"

"I am so lucky, Butrus. Imagine meeting the most beautiful girl in my life…here in Marseille. I suppose everyone creates an ideal in his own mind. I have, and she is that person. Her face is perfect. Her smile is perfect. She smells so good. Her eyes drive me mad, especially when she looks at me out of the corner of her eyes. Do girls do that deliberately? It surely works on me! I want to see her everyday. All the time! I hope she wants to see me the same way. If she doesn't, I think I'll die."

"But remember, Iskandar, we leave for America in six weeks."

"Don't remind me, Butrus."

"Why don't you take her for a walk up to the cathedral? There is a beautiful park near there. You could be alone. I can keep myself busy if you like. There is much to see."

Iskandar was daydreaming, lying on his back on his cot, hands under his head, thinking of this dream who had come into his life, and whom he would be with shortly. He was in heaven. Iskandar would surely remember Marseille and his time here for the rest of his life. He was nervous, energized, and bewildered all at the same time. After a while of lying down, he could not be still any longer.

Lifting his head and looking at Butrus, he spoke, "It's time for me to go now, Butrus."

Iskandar stood, sprinkled water on his face, perfunctorily wiped his face with a small towel, dressed quickly, and satisfied with his appearance went to the door, waved good-bye to his roommate, locked the door and walked to the stairs. He hurriedly bounded down the stairs, two steps at a time, to the street and walked to the nearby restaurant.

At exactly six o'clock, Iskandar sat at the same table outside the restaurant as the evening before, deliberately sitting in the very chair that was occupied by Madeleine. It felt good.

The waiters were busily setting tables, pouring water into glasses and scurrying around taking orders. There were abundant outdoor dining chairs and tables, with many tables already taken by men playing games, drinking, laughing, shouting, and generally, enjoying the end of the day.

Lots of Lebanese were playing cards at several tables, *towleh* at others, and dominoes at still others. Most of the men were in their forties, fifties, and older. As they played their afternoon games, some smoked elaborate *aguilas* with the mouthpiece attached to the long narrow hose that reached to the top of the bottle of water sitting on the walk beside them. Others were smoking Turkish cigarettes. As time passed, the *aguila* smoker would stir the charcoals in the top pan and place new tobacco on the glowing red coals to keep the pipe operating. Sometimes, hashish would be placed on the hot coals, sometimes apple slivers.

As he anxiously looked around at the arrivals filling the plaza, searching for Madeleine's arrival, he shuffled the table's cards nervously. *I think I'll burst when I see her. But I must act natural. Slow down, Iskandar, calm down*, he told himself.

It was difficult for him to think of anything or anyone but Madeleine. *I hope she likes me. But I must not make a fool of myself! After all, I am eighteen years old and becoming a man of the world; she is but sixteen. What can happen? I am going on to America. Oh, my Lord? What can I do?* What a dilemma he felt. He was already debating with himself as he sat impatiently waiting, reshuffling the cards again and again.

As they approached the table, he looked up, "Oh, Madeleine, there you are. *Bonjour!* And Madame DuBois. How nice to see you." Iskandar smiled as he stood, nearly tipping over his chair as he stood.

"*Allo*, Iskandar. Where is Hanna?" replied Daniella, looking around the plaza. "Is he not here?"

"He'll be with us in a moment. He just stepped into the café. Please sit down."

Iskandar stood and helped first Daniella, then Madeleine to their chairs. "How is your knee, Madeleine? Is it feeling better now?"

Madeleine lowered her face and blushed from a bit of embarrassment, not wanting to draw attention to herself. "It is fine, *merci, mon ami*. I am so embarrassed that I fell down; that was most unusual for me. I am very grateful that you came to my rescue. *Merci*." She thought to herself, *He is so handsome and so thoughtful. Mon Dieu.*

"But that boy running through the people bumped you. Don't be embarrassed; it couldn't be helped. It could have happened to anyone!" he shrugged. "I was happy to help you." He caught himself as he almost used the word eager instead of happy!

"*Est-ce que tu aime Marseille?* she asked, looking at him with her blue eyes wide open.

"*Oui*, Marseille is very exciting. I have found the people very friendly, and the city very busy. I want to see more while I am here before I leave for America."

"Oh? When do you leave?" inquired Daniella, surprised at his comment.

"I will be here for six weeks, I believe. My father is to meet me in New York." He smiled, remembering his mother's words. "I must find and fulfill my destiny in America..." The words were hardly out of his mouth when he suddenly felt enormous conflict and wanted to take them back.

"Oh," whispered Madeleine as she lowered her eyes in disappointment. "Just six weeks then?"

"Yes, but I have begun to wonder if I should stay in Marseille. I have felt wonderful since last evening."

"I have enjoyed meeting you also, Iskandar."

Tempting fate, and looking directly at Madeleine, he softly said, "Perhaps I could enjoy Marseille more if I had someone show me the city." Then, remembering Butrus' suggestion, he added, "I would like to see as much as possible. Do you think we could see the Notre-Dame-de-la-Garde together?"

"That would be very nice I think. May I, *Maman*? It is the spiritual symbol of our city," she added with a flourish of pride.

"Perhaps," Daniella responded with a smile.

Iskandar, hoping she would say yes, tried as much as he could not to gaze on Madeleine, but he couldn't take his eyes from her. "May I come by your shop tomorrow?"

"*Oui*, that would be nice." Turning to her mother, she asked "What time, *Maman*?"

Daniella lifted her head as to assert her concern, then discreetly whispered to her daughter so Iskandar could not hear, "Perhaps we should speak about this later, Madeleine."

"*Allo*, Daniella, "greeted Hanna with a smile and his arms reaching out to his lady friend as he came to the table, interrupting their thoughts. "I apologize for not being prompt. I was detained and could not arrive sooner. Please forgive me, *mon amie*."

"We are comfortable," responded Daniella with a smile, acknowledging Iskandar's presence, while remaining seated as she offered her hand to Hanna's. "We have been speaking with Iskandar. He tells us he will be here for only six weeks before he must travel to America."

"Yes," interrupted Madeleine, with widened eyes, "and he has asked me to show him parts of Marseille."

"Ahh!" Hanna whispered aside to Madeleine, "He is happy to meet you Madeleine. Perhaps you both will become good friends. We would like that, wouldn't we, Daniella?"

"Well, I think that would be nice," replied Daniella, a bit reluctantly. "They can become good friends, and yes, they should enjoy themselves. Life is short, as I have learned." Turning to Iskandar, she noted with a smile, "Madeleine is adventurous. I hope you can keep up with her, Iskandar. She loves to see everything and has more energy than most."

Daniella held a reserve inside, concerned for her impetuous daughter, noticing that Iskandar had already turned her head, yet in six short weeks he'd be gone.

Hanna turned to Daniella, "Well then, I will bring Iskandar to your shop on the Canabière tomorrow? At noontime, *n'est pas?*" Now, he spoke as the host of the group. "*t'Fuduloo*, let us dine," easily switching from French to his native Arabic.

Throughout the evening there was laughter, good feelings, and free-flowing, animated conversation in French. Iskandar told of his life in the village, his mother and brother, his voyage from Beirut, and was already clearly anxious about the next day's events. Madeleine was interested in his every description, and showed her carefree spirit. She smiled at Iskandar most of the evening. She also was a bit anxious, yet felt very comfortable with her new handsome friend. She looked up to him. She was innocent, vulnerable, yet free of inhibitions. After all, she was just sixteen years old. She had never felt like this before. She couldn't really explain what she was feeling. But she knew she liked what she was feeling. She felt warm, happy and pleased with herself.

Iskandar turned his head from side to side as he listened to Hanna speak with Daniella while they suggested places to go, to see. But Madeleine, while listening was making her own plans. She wanted to show Iskandar the city. Maybe go to the park, she thought, but their suggestions of museums and the university were *not* high on her list. She was thinking of showing him *Les Calanques* with friends in a boat, and walking the Corniche overlooking the sea, visiting seaside *les jardins* along the way.

It was a lovely, cheery evening for everyone. When it drew to a close, more than an hour after dinner, Daniella spoke, "*Pardon, s'il vous plait.* We must return home now. And we shall see you gentlemen tomorrow at twelve o'clock at my shop?" Her tone of voice indicated that the question was actually confirming a definite arrangement.

Hanna turned to Daniella and said, "You and I should meet for dinner tomorrow evening on the *Canebière* and let them make their way. *Ça va bien*, is that acceptable?"

"*Oui*, I believe so," nodded Daniella. "Perhaps tomorrow at noon we can determine where we will dine, so that Madeleine and Iskandar can decide if they wish to come join us." Then, standing and moving her head toward Hanna to receive a kiss on her cheek from him, Daniella nodded to Iskandar and, turning, said with her warm gracious smile, "*Alors, bonsoir, mon amis.*"

Iskandar rose from the table with them. "*Bonsoir*, Madeleine," Iskandar said, wishing the evening would not end so early. He kissed the back of Madeleine's extended hand for the first time, emulating his uncle's gesture.

"*Bonne nuit*, Iskandar. I will see you tomorrow," whispered Madeleine as she reluctantly followed her mother

As they walked away, Madeleine exclaimed to her mother excitedly, "Isn't he wonderful, *Maman*? He is so gentle, so kind, so handsome. I like him very much."

"*Oui, chérie*. I can tell. He is special to you, isn't he?"

"And I believe he likes me very much too! Don't you agree? *Maman*, I feel so good. I am happy. It is wonderful to meet Iskandar. I feel so alive. I've never felt like this before. It is good isn't it, mama? Tell me it is good, please."

"*Ma chérie*, I love you so much. The one thing a Mother desires is that her child be happy, carefree and lively."

When they arrived at their home, Daniella sat on the sofa in the parlor and, with Madeleine sitting beside her, they held each other's hands. They spoke into the night; Daniella vicariously enjoying her daughter's excitement and feelings of first love.

"Madeleine, you must understand that Iskandar will be here only a short time. Be good friends, yes, but be careful with your heart. Please understand that he will be gone in six weeks. I'm a bit worried for you."

She continued, looking lovingly into her daughter's eyes, "You know, don't you, that I was just one year older than you are when I fell in love with your father. We were so happy, and you were born of the love we shared so deeply. And even though your father is no longer with us, I am grateful for the time we had together. But remember, *chérie*, your father was not leaving Marseille."

"But," Madeleine interrupted, "Papa did leave for the army. And he didn't come back, yet you're happy you fell in love and married him, aren't you?"

"Yes, I believe it is better to feel the excitement and deep caring of true friendship and love even for a short while than it is to let it pass by. So, *ma chérie*, follow your heart. I have never seen you like this. It is a treasure in my heart to be with you and see you this way. God works in strange ways. Perhaps your meeting was meant to be. I could feel as he spoke that he loved his mother deeply. And that is a good sign. He will treat you well and with respect. And," she reminded her, "he is Hanna's nephew. And I know how you feel about Hanna who is a very good man. Iskandar does seem to like you very much. So, enjoy tomorrow, and sleep well tonight."

With her mother's concerned, yet supportive comments, Madeleine did indeed sleep very well.

～ℰ～ℐ～

After the ladies had left the *Café Liban*, Iskandar and Hanna stayed at the table speaking with each other for some time as Iskandar gathered in the energy of his mostly fellow Lebanese all around him, making him feel all the more comfortable. He and Hanna played several games of *towleh*, and visited with Hanna's friends who passed by on their evening ritual. Butrus then stopped by their table by ten o'clock and excitedly told Iskandar of his day.

"Six weeks in Marseille! Iskandar, in Beirut, I thought I would die if I had to wait so long before sailing to America. It seemed that too much time would be wasted. But I have met so many nice people here from Lebanon. And the French girls are so pretty. It's a good thing I have so little money. The prostitutes are everywhere, and so enticing. I would gladly have spent all I have," he said with a grin.

Iskandar, thinking about that but not interested in "girls," responded, "I too thought six weeks would be much too long to wait. I even thought that maybe I would go immediately on to Le Havre, but for my father's schedule. But now, after meeting the most wonderful girl in the world, *sahbi*, I wish I was going to stay in Marseille for a long time, years maybe," he laughed. "I'm going to see her again tomorrow, Butrus!" He thought for a moment, looked at Hanna, then back to Peter. "I want to see her all the time, everyday. Is that crazy, *Khali* Hanna?"

"Yes, Iskandar, it is crazy," responded Hanna with a smile. "But life is short, and one never knows what tomorrow will bring. Enjoy your young life. I think Madeleine likes you very much. She will be a good friend." Looking at Iskandar, he explained, "You know, her father was a good man, a devoted father and husband. But his life was cut short by the war." Hanna remembered all the sadness. "The war changed our ways of thinking. Daniella was only eighteen when Madeleine was born. And Madeleine was just thirteen when her father was killed. I respected him very much, and I waited two years after the sad news before I asked Daniella to share just a dinner with me. And even then, we were with her friends. But now, I can say to you, I consider her my love. She feels the same way. We do many things together. I have watched with pride as Madeleine has grown from a child. Daniella and I have even spoken about marriage one day. I believe, Iskandar, life is a gift from God, and what you do with your precious time is your gift to God. And God is Love, we are told. So what better gift can you give but love? The French people, especially these days, remember how the war took so many young people of France, destroying lives, families, hopes and dreams. Perhaps that is why we treasure each moment, each day, for tomorrow could be painful."

"So, my young nephew, follow your heart. And be grateful for each day. It cannot be retrieved. I know you are smitten with Madeleine. And why not? She is lovely, she is sweet and kind. A fine young woman. But Iskandar, you know you must go to America in six weeks. You must be honest with her... treating her kindly. What will be will be."

CHAPTER 9

For young Iskandar, the next day and the days following were filled with the pleasure of Madeleine's company. Sometimes they sat together in the *jardins* of Marseille watching the people. She would pack a lunch and a blanket and they would eat in the shade by the sea, always laughing, touching, sometimes holding each other's hand.

Iskandar was filled with affection for Madeleine, his lovely companion, and at the same time felt a longing memory for the love he had had in his home. He was ready to meet someone to love. She also looked to find some man to fill the void left by her father's death.

One day, as they sat on the blanket in a city park near the river, Iskandar began thinking of his family, his village, and his youth. He looked at Madeleine, took her hand, and looked into her eyes. "I would like to tell you more about my village, Douma, and my family. Would you like to hear about them?"

She quickly responded, nodding her head anxiously and smiling warmly as their eyes met, "*Oui*, Iskandar. I would like very much to hear about your family." She gripped his hand affectionately with one of her own and placed the other one on top of his. Madeleine found herself drawn to this young man from the mountains who had come into her life, giving her a new interest beyond her girlfriends, helping her mother, and attending church. She felt comfortable holding his hand, wanting to touch him and nurture him.

Iskandar began…"Douma is a tiny, but beautiful little mountain village high in the northern mountains of Lebanon, a blessed country, but the village is so poor. There is little money. There is very little of anything there, and with the four-year locust infestation, the shortage of food, and the Turkish army everywhere, life has been too difficult for kind people. Yet, my family has survived there for hundreds of years—the Greeks came, then the Romans, and on and on. My people, my family endured in poverty. I already miss them very much, Madeleine. My cousins and playmates, and Antony Bashir…my favorite," he said as their faces flashed in his mind.

His voice trailed off as he remembered his beloved mother's love and dedication to her children. He told Madeleine of the mountains, the goatherds, the village, the orchards, the olive groves, and the incredible vistas. He smiled as he recalled his youth, climbing his treasured cedar trees, and, when looking west from his perch in the trees, seeing the same Mediterranean Sea that Madeleine had seen all her life.

Then, gazing out over the sea, he thought in silence. After a few moments he turned to her. "Let me tell you the story of a small boy just ten years old trying to be a man too soon. But first, let me show you something."

He reached to his feet and began removing his thick, smooth black shoes and white socks. "Look at my feet," he said to Madeleine.

"Why are your toes so dark? They are almost black," she exclaimed, pointing at his feet.

He frowned, as he had every time he looked at his feet. He knew they would be visible, lifelong reminders of the severe poverty of his youth. "They turned black after I suffered terrible frostbite in an unexpected snowstorm. I nearly lost them." He paused, recalling that terrible experience high in the snowy mountains. "We had no food to eat. Now, I will tell you."

"I want to hear, dear Iskandar. Is this your own story? When you were a little boy?"

"Yes," he responded in a whisper. He looked around to see if passersby would overhear, feeling the sun's warmth as it came from behind the scattered clouds. He could hear the reassuring joyous songs of the small birds in the trees fluttering from limb to limb. He was relaxed with her, but became more tense as he began. "This is what happened." Iskandar cleared his throat, closed his eyes, leaned forward and thought in silence for a moment. Then, using his hands as he spoke, he told Madeleine the entire story of sneaking from the house early that late autumn morning to go to the Bekaa Valley with the group of grown men. He told her of the near starvation he and the village faced. He spoke in passionate detail as he described the exhausting climb up the two mountain ranges, admitting to her that he was very scared as he hid from the army patrols, crouching in the wheat field, and carrying the sack of wheat he had swept from the valley soil with his small hands. He was a bit embarrassed and had trouble describing to her how exhausting was his journey, how he had to be so stubborn not to quit on the mountain. He spoke of the frightening sudden snowstorm along the mountain crest, the shelter under the outcropping stone, and how his brother Milhelm came up the mountain to save him. Somehow, he felt safe telling Madeleine of his most harrowing experience. He realized of all people, he could somehow trust Madeleine with his most personal feelings; secrets he would not be able to share easily.

Taking a deep breath, he paused to make certain he had not forgotten any of the traumatic experience before he lay back and said with a strong statement as he looked into her eyes, "Madeleine, my mother saved my feet and my life." He paused, remembering, and after remaining quiet for a few minutes, he looked up to the sky, silently thanked God, sat up again and continued the story by telling her of his mother's commitment to him those two painful and difficult years of rubbing his feet every day with warm olive oil.

Throughout, Madeleine was silent, listening, stunned at his honesty and candor at what he had gone through. She began feeling even greater warmth toward Iskandar. As he completed the story, she saw his fluid brown eyes fill with tears. He wiped his face.

"You loved your mother very much, didn't you, Iskandar?" Madeleine asked in a warm, soft whisper, looking into his eyes.

Iskandar, hearing her voice and loving her presence as he had loved his mother's touch, replied softly, "More than my life itself, Madeleine. I still treasure her deep in my heart. I revere her. I always will. She was everything to me. Can you understand? And now, she is gone." Pausing, reflecting, he lay back on the grass.

Madeleine, touched by Iskandar's story, his descriptions of his "scorpion-shaped" village as seen from the high mountain road above the town, deep in the rugged, steep mountains, the village *souk*, and his childhood playmates. She listened quietly as he spoke almost in a whisper of his father, his mother, sister and brother. She could sense that he was a passionate young man of tenderness, empathy, courage, and determination, with an enormous capacity to love. She wanted to embrace him, to hold him. Then, without restraining herself, she moved close, to lie next to him, pressing her side against his, drew her face to his and kissed him gently on his cheek, consoling him with her embrace and affection. She was overwhelmed with warmth, wanting to hold him near to her to comfort him. It was a magical moment for him, and a natural, nurturing and loving moment for her that only brought them even closer together. Madeleine began to feel emotions toward Iskandar that had very quickly gone far beyond mere friendship. This was the first young man to enter her life, and she felt fortunate that he was so sensitive, so poetic in his words, and so respectful of his family, especially of his mother. She had often heard ladies in the shop speak of young men seeking their daughters. "Watch how they treat their mothers and you'll see how they will treat their wives." She listened as he spoke in his rhythmic voice, watched the way he moved his hands as he described his life, and noticed the way he walked. She focused on everything Iskandar did and said.

After the fourth week of being together nearly every day and evening, they agreed to meet in the early morning to spend an entire Saturday together.

They started very early in the morning at the fresh fish market along the east side of the *Vieux Port*, opposite the *Panier*, soon after the last of the small fishing boats returned to port. They walked to the lines of booths along the pier where men were selling all kinds of fish from their morning catch. It was not far past the *Canebière*.

"This place, Iskandar, is where the fishermen of Marseille return from their excursions in the sea. Sometimes they are gone for several days. They bring their bounty here where it is sold in these booths along the Corniche. Every restaurant owner comes early to select the most succulent fish for their specialties. My mother shops here at least three times a week. You know, Iskandar," she said, smiling while she held his hand as they walked from booth to booth, "bouillabaisse is the trademark of all foods in Marseille. The finest is made here! My mother makes it with four different fish when we have friends over, the same as in the best restaurants."

"Bouillabaisse?" asked Iskandar.

"Yes," she replied. "It is a delicious fish broth. It is best served with several tasty types of fish. They say the best in the world is made in Marseille," she added in a light, playful boast.

He laughed at her as she smiled at him, still holding his hand as they walked, enthusiastically speaking almost non-stop, pointing at each wooden stall, stopping to ask about the specialty of that particular vendor. One booth showed hundreds of snails crawling up the sides of the buckets. Others displayed on their sloped table tops numerous freshly caught fish, some smaller ones he recognized as similar to those in Tripoli. Another stall sold only fresh squid.

"And the escargot, are they all fresh today?" she asked, pointing at the nearly full buckets of squirming, slow-moving snails.

"*Oui*, of course," the fisherman laughed, "my boat is just there." He pointed at the small sailboat nearby.

After spending the morning at the bustling fish market with hundreds of other shoppers, the pair continued along the *Quai de Rive* to tour Fort Nicholas, built by Louis XIV and located at the port entrance on the way to the *Jardin du Pharo*.

After Madeleine led Iskandar through the old fortress, he announced that he was hungry for lunch.

She laughed. "Let's go back to the market, get a basket of food, some bread and wine, and have a picnic."

"Wonderful," Iskandar replied with a smile, and loving her exuberance, he grabbed her hand as they nearly ran back, not wanting to waste any time. *This is all very fascinating. The fish market was fun. The fortress was not so interesting, but she wants to show me everything. And I'd rather be with her no matter where. As long as she holds my hand, I don't mind where she takes me. But alas, my stay here is so short.*

"I want to see everything you can show me, Madeleine. Marseille is unbelievable, but mostly because I am with you!"

Slightly embarrassed, she gripped his hand and brought her face near his. Kissing his cheek, she whispered, *"Merci beaucoup, mon ami.* I believe you can see that I feel the same way." Then, she pulled him along quickly as they returned to the northern end of the *quai,* back to a stand where she could purchase the bread, wine, and cheese for their picnic.

"Grapes?" she asked as they stood at a stall by the boats. "Do you like grapes?"

"Oui, of course. I love grapes," he replied as he imagined placing one in her mouth at their picnic.

"I have a wonderful idea, Iskandar!" she exclaimed, pointing to the pier where there were small excursion boats loading passengers. "My girlfriends and I have taken one of those boats to the coves along *Les Calanques.* Let's do that. It will be fun. We can picnic on a beach."

"Yes," he eagerly responded. "That sounds exciting. I've never been on a beach. I'm from the mountains, you know," he laughed.

Holding hands, not wanting to let go of each other, they ran to the pier where the boats waited. Each had an innocence and vulnerability, yet both dared to want each other. They touched hands at every chance. She felt safe and comfortable in his presence and wanted him near to her. In turn, he found her *joie de vivre* intoxicating. Her coquettish glances at him made his knees weak. He longed to feel her body pressed against him.

"There, Iskandar, look up at the hill at the beautiful *Jardin du Pharo* and the huge mansion there on the left," Madeleine said to him as they stood at the bow of the boat's deck with a group of perhaps twenty young people.

He felt so good being with Madeleine. He wondered how it would feel to actually kiss her on the lips. She smelled wonderful each time they kissed on their cheeks. She was so soft, so gentle. While he looked at her as she pointed first to the cliffs on the left, then to the small rocky islands offshore on the right, his urge to hold her grew and grew. Finally, as she turned to him, her face close, he embraced her for the first time. It was magical.

Emboldened, and willing to express his inner feelings, he said to her, "Oh, Madeleine, it feels so good to hold you. I think I am in love with you. Can we find a place to be alone?"

"Oui, Iskandar," she giggled. "I was hoping you wanted to be alone because I feel the same way. We'll find a cove and go to a beach. After our picnic, we can climb to a grassy spot and be alone to look at the sea together."

After they sat on the small secluded beach enjoying their picnic near the water's edge, they could see couples pairing off to be alone. Some found large secluded rocks near the water, and some climbed the hill to the plateaus much higher overlooking the sea. And still others climbed more than three hundred feet to the top of the palisades. There were well-worn paths in every direction. *Les Calanques* were a very popular place to explore for the young people of Marseille.

"Let's go there, Iskandar. I'll bring the basket and the blanket," Madeleine suggested, pointing to the slope of the hills. "We can be alone for awhile. Is that what you want too?"

"*Oui*, absolutely," he responded quickly.

They gathered their possessions and headed for the cliff. After climbing up the path, they soon found a private grassy plateau.

It would become their favorite spot overlooking the glistening sea below. The sea breezes brushed their faces gently causing Madeleine's hair to lift and flow with her movements. As she faced the sea's breeze, her hair streamed behind her. She was a goddess to Iskandar who was gazing on her every movement. Madeleine spread their blanket on the lush, soft grass and sat down. He fell to the blanket next to her. For quite a while, they sat together, arms around their knees, quietly looking at the sea, appreciating their being by themselves on this lush grass overlooking the sea.

She turned and smiled at him. "Isn't this the most beautiful place in the world, Iskandar? This is our special place. It now belongs to us," she giggled happily.

He turned to her and watched her long, beautiful dark hair blow in the wind despite her ribbon and her futile efforts to pull it back. Iskandar playfully reached to help her and, for the first time, felt her silken tresses against her slender back. He thought to himself, *she is so magnificent. And such a free spirit!* She shifted her body and, inadvertently, a breeze blew the soft folds of her dress above her knees. He felt a sense of electricity streaking throughout his body as he looked at her long, shapely legs. He was spellbound, and grew more excited. He moved his hand to the nape of her neck and caressed her gently. After several electric moments of feeling his strong fingers resting gently on her neck, his arm against her shoulder, she reached for his hand and slowly moved it across her shoulders and lightly brushed her breasts, inviting him. She was deliciously sensitive to his touch. She turned to him longingly, bringing her face to his. Iskandar pulled her to him, feeling raw sensual emotions rushing through his body.

"Oh, Iskandar, I have wanted you ever since I fell into your arms that first night weeks ago. And it's only gotten better and stronger every time we are together. You have been so good for me," she whispered as she lowered her eyelids demurely.

He leaned to her and, with the smell of early summer and the sea in the air, he lightly, tentatively kissed her. Their lips touched softly, with the delicacy of a butterfly, like a soft wisp of a breeze. He felt her eyelashes brush his cheeks. Their first kiss expressed the bond of two young lovers venturing where they had never been before. Neither spoke. Both felt their hearts and emotions yielding their bodies to each other.

She lay back and gently rested her head on the blanket and gazed up into his eyes. Drawn to her, he lay close and kissed her full lips that opened...asking. Madeleine melted against him as he pulled her close to him, embracing her completely for the first time and feeling her entire body pressing against his.

To their right, the golden setting sun, a willing participant and observer, spread its last rays of the day, creating millions of diamonds of reflections on the surface of the sea, casting a soft pastel hue across Madeleine's face enhancing her beauty. The sun slowly became a magnificent, exaggerated, red-orange ball silently slipping into the sea. Shadows lengthened and crossed their entwined bodies, exciting Iskandar even more and magnifying their youthful sense of secrecy and adventure. They were in a moment of full, young love and happiness, sharing thoughts and sensations neither had ever felt before.

"This place is so beautiful, Madeleine. Almost as beautiful as you," Iskandar whispered, gazing into her eyes.

They were young and innocent, yet old enough to respond to their desire to love, and these afternoon hours together were almost joyously overpowering. They became willing prisoners of their sensual yearning for each other. Iskandar could not constrain himself any longer. Slowly, his hand reached inside Madeleine's dress, caressing her firm young breasts gently as he kissed her deeper this time, his tongue exploring her delicious mouth, blending with her searching tongue. She quivered as she felt her nipples harden. With his other hand, he stroked her thighs, moving higher and higher. She responded with a shiver of excitement, savoring every sensation as she yielded to him. She reached to his hand and gently guided him to her hard nipples. As he fondled her, sometimes circling her nipples with his fingers, tantalizing her, teasing her as he carefully avoided, for the moment, actually touching her now hypersensitive nipples. She gasped a deep breath as an incredible tingling sensation flowed downward to between her legs.

"Oh, Iskandar, oh..." she moaned softly.

It was good. It was exciting. It was natural. He too felt his loins swell and grow very hard. He was even more excited now. She tentatively explored his thighs, touching and stroking the inside of them. Responding, he took her hand in his and guided it higher on his thigh, then upward. She felt him becoming very hard and firm beneath her hand as she gently stroked him. His eyes fluttered as he felt sensations he had never known before. She groaned, looked into his eyes, then closed hers, as a lover asking him to guide her more, yielding, wanting him to consummate their love...on this spot...at this moment...here...at their place overlooking the Mediterranean Sea. She anxiously moved his hand beneath her dress to her quivering thighs and directed him to where he must go.

She whispered, "I am yours, Iskandar. I love you."

"Oh, Madeleine, let our souls become one. I love you so much too."

He gently rolled onto her and, with her guiding hand, entered her. As he did, she muffled a cry of pain and ecstasy. Her body trembled and her breathing became heavy with emotion. As he boldly thrust himself against her, they began to vigorously move together rhythmically with abandon, seeking to increase the already intense, nearly overpowering electric feelings of sensuality, enraptured by his penetrating movements as their bodies blended and became one. His body shuddered as he finally exploded inside of her, throbbing and pulsating. She moaned as tremors of ecstasy flowed throughout her body as she climaxed with him. They had experienced the consummation of their love, savoring every moment.

They lay spent for a long time, holding each other, never wanting to let go. He embraced her tightly as he raised his head to look at her lovely face and again kissed her inviting lips softly, expressing his total love for her. *"Mon amour."*

Madeleine felt emotions she had never known before. She whispered, "Oh, Iskandar, you are very romantic. I love that in you. I love that we loved each other here today. I give myself to you completely. You are my life."

After a few moments of lingering pleasure, Iskandar looked at her protectively. He loved her so and wanted her to have his most valuable possession. "As a symbol of my love and my lifetime commitment to you, Madeleine, I want you to have my gold cross." He carefully removed it from his neck. "It was given to me by my beloved mother when I was twelve years old. I have never taken it from my neck. It is the most valuable thing I own. I want you to wear it always as a reminder of my love for you. It is my treasure and should be around your beautiful neck." He reached to put the chain over her head. "Please accept this as a remembrance of this day, of our becoming one in deepest love. I promise you, Madeleine, you will never leave my heart. Only you, my love, only you...forever."

Madeleine, her eyes welling with tears from emotion and sincere love, pulled back her long hair as he carefully placed the chain around her neck, carefully placing the cross between her firm breasts.

"And for you, Iskandar," she whispered, "I give you this ring from my finger. My father gave it to me the day he left to go to the war. I have worn it always as a reminder of his love for me and my love for him. Now, I give you my treasure. I commit my heart and my love to you Iskandar, forever and ever, for my whole life. I have found you and I will never stop loving you. Know that…and believe that…forever." She placed the gold ring on the smallest finger of his right hand. It fit perfectly.

"I promise, my love, this ring will never leave my finger. I will be reminded of your beautiful face, your eyes, your love, every day for the rest of my life. You will always be my love, forever, Madeleine. I promise you."

At that moment, almost as a signal blessing their union, the bells of Notre-Dame-de-la-Garde began their evening chime. They looked to the church high on the hill overlooking the city, smiled gratefully and embraced, feeling their union had indeed been blessed.

They lay back together for a little longer, savoring moments of their love, their eyes returning to the other's.

The sun was still setting as a full moon began to rise from in the east. They believed the sunset and now the moonrise were God's signs of joy. They were filled with love. They were complete.

"This truly is the most wonderful, most beautiful place on earth, Madeleine. And yes, this is our place. It will be ours forever. We will come back here together."

"I will always remember this day, Iskandar. It is our day. This is our place."

CHAPTER 10

Iskandar and Madeleine remained inseparable each day. The last two weeks of his stay in Marseille raced by. They both knew that Iskandar had to go on to America.

Sometimes as they spoke, one or the other would think of his leaving and become sad. Madeleine or Iskandar would feel a tear overflow on their cheeks as they embraced so often. They knew the day would come all too soon. But they both knew that their lives were in God's hands and that they should savor each moment with gratitude of their time together, although short. They tried to believe that there would be no regrets. Yet they both felt sadness as they attempted to hide their innermost fears and feelings from one another.

She knew he had to find his future in America, yet she also knew she would never have room in her heart for another.

He, too, could not imagine anyone else in his life, but was obliged to meet his father in New York.

"I *will* come back for you, Madeleine. One day, when I am able, I'll come back for you so that we can be together again. I promise, I'll never love another as we have loved. *I'll find you wherever you are.*"

"And I *will* wait for you too, Iskandar. I cannot love another as I love you. I'll fondle your...my cross...your mother's gift each day...and I'll want you beside me each day. *I am yours forever.*"

Despite the private hopes and wishes of Madeleine and Iskandar, all too soon the day of his departure arrived. They had avoided the subject as they spent each day together, painfully knowing that the ship taking him from her would slip away from the pier on the next at evening tide...sunset.

Very early that morning, Iskandar had a light breakfast with Hanna in the tree-shaded plaza at the café.

"I'm not very hungry, Uncle Hanna. I'm very sad."

Reluctantly, Iskandar had packed his meager belongings the night before after being with Madeleine all that day and into the evening. He had avoided any preparations, hoping against hope it wasn't true that he must leave her. Perhaps something would delay his departure. They had spent several more days together on the promontory above the beach, their favored place. His heart ached as he faced the truth that his father awaited him in New York and he must leave Marseille and his love, Madeleine. He knew he had no choice. Or did he? What a terrible dilemma. Over and over he asked himself, *Should I stay here with Madeleine instead? What am I to do?*

As he and Hanna sat at their favorite table, Iskandar's eyes searched the plaza, remembering the many evenings he had waited for Madeleine and the moments they had shared together...the familiar store fronts, the scattered tables, the lush sycamores with their colorful trunks spreading their full limbs overhead, the neighbors simply sitting and sharing their free time over coffee. His eyes swept across the opening looking north, and there, between the two buildings that formed the east and west boundaries of *Place de Liban*, through the open north end, he focused on the magnificent cathedral, Notre-Dame-de-la-Garde, and the golden pinnacle of Saint Mary atop the high dome, some four hundred feet above sea level and he prayed for guidance.

"Uncle Hanna," he said softly, "I am going to miss her desperately. Look! Look at Notre-Dame-de-la-Garde, how beautiful she is, the symbol of Marseille. Madeleine took me there many times. How am I going to deal with this, uncle? How? What should I do? How can I leave Madeleine? I love her so much."

Hanna's eyes looked down as he rubbed his forehead with his hand. "My son, you are a very sensitive, and yes, a very romantic young man. You feel with your heart, like your mother. And certainly, Madeleine is very special."

"But, Uncle Hanna," Iskandar interrupted, not wanting to hear anything but encouragement.

Hanna waved his hand and continued, "I love her as if she were my own daughter. So I am biased. She is in pain too. But neither I nor anyone else can tell you what you should do. You have a full life to live yet, and," he paused, reaching for Iskandar's shoulder, "you alone must decide. America is the hope of so many Lebanese, in fact, the world over. Your father awaits you. You will have opportunities there that do not exist here these days. To be sure, you have a most difficult decision to deal with. If you continue your journey to America and do well, then perhaps you can return to Marseille and Madeleine." Then, looking directly into his eyes, Hanna, sensing this young man's dilemma, asked, "My son, when you consider all things, even at your young and inexperienced age, you will make the correct decision. I do believe completely that Madeleine loves you with all her heart and that no one ever will replace you. These painful conflicts are what make life fascinating and challenging. And none of us knows what the future holds. Trust God."

Smiling sympathetically, he raised his demitasse cup of strong Turkish coffee, inviting Iskandar to do likewise. They touched cups as Hanna, looking now directly into Iskandar's moist eyes, said, *"Bon courage*, Iskandar, *bon courage."*

Iskandar replied, "And to you, my Uncle Hanna, *bonne santé."*

After picking at his breakfast, he eagerly went to Daniella's shop to be with Madeleine one last time.

"She is not here, Iskandar, she is in her room. She is very sad today. We both hate that you must leave."

"But I must see her. I must be with her."

Daniella embraced Iskandar and spoke softly to him, "We all knew this day would come, Iskandar. She and I spoke of it many times. *C'est la vie* is a way we French people have had to learn to think, accepting our fate. She is so sad today; I know this to be true, because she loves you with her whole heart. You are her love, her friend. Your soul has bonded with hers. I bless your beautiful love, Iskandar. Be happy and come back soon. She wants to see you, I am certain. But she needed to be alone for awhile. Why don't you come back at twelve o'clock? Your ship departs at six o'clock, isn't that so?"

"Yes, six o'clock. But I want to be with her this day, Madame DuBois."

"Come back then, Iskandar, at twelve o'clock. I will see that she is here for you."

Frowning, Iskandar left, disappointed and saddened, but accepting. *This is a most terrible day*, he said to himself. *I have to leave Marseille. But it is a day when I begin another journey to my destiny in America. How can I do both? How can I stay with Madeleine here in Marseille and fulfill my destiny? How can I not? I will come back for her. I know it! My destiny must include Madeleine!*

After spending the next few hours alone walking along the *Vieux Port* quays, recalling their times together in this same place, he returned to Daniella's shop at twelve o'clock.

"Madame DuBois," he asked, "is Madeleine..."

"Allo, chéri," interrupted Madeleine with a sad smile, reaching out her hands to him. "Please forgive me, Iskandar, this is a difficult day for me."

"It is difficult for me also, *chérie*. My heart is exploding with sadness. I truly do not know what I must do. I am so torn by this. How can I leave you? But how can I stay? I have nothing; I have no way to earn a living here. My father is in America. I am to go there. But it is an impossible conflict for me. You must be with me today, Madeleine. Come let us go to our favorite place until I have to go to the ship."

That day, their last in Marseille together would once again be filled with emotions. They went to their favorite place on the promontory above the beach. They both were aware that this could be their last time together, and that their future was not in their hands. They had known this from the very first day. But in the ways of the young, they chose to live in the present, convinced their future would be wonderful. This was their moment. These two young lovers, feeling so close to each other with a sense of belonging and yet, with sadness, walked hand in hand to the hill overlooking the sea. With their blanket on the grass, they sat close together. Holding hands, they felt their bodies touching, while looking at the sea together, perhaps for the last time. They embraced longingly, and kissed deeply, several times. They simply could not pull themselves apart.

Iskandar held her face close to his as he whispered, "This is a terribly difficult thing for me to leave you and go to America without you, but I am without any money at all. My father will look for me in New York and I must go. I hope that you understand because we've spoken about it so many times. Yet, I will be empty without you and will think of you every day, wishing you were with me." Then looking into her eyes, he whispered, *"I promise... I'll return for you someday."*

Madeleine, holding him tightly, whispered to Iskandar, "I am so grateful that we met as we did and that we love each other so deeply. I will treasure every moment we shared together for as long as I live. These weeks have been heaven on earth. I'll never forget you. I will treasure also the beautiful cross you gave me."

He felt the same way as he fondled her ring on his finger, the reminder of her love.

As she finished, he stood up, looked down to her and reached out, helping her up. "Let's go now." They stood together and, looking into each other's eyes, kissed each other deeply, embracing each other as close as they could, lingering.

They arrived just in time at the docks. Holding hands as he stepped toward the ship, they reached for each other's outstretched hand until he stepped completely away from her reach. She turned her downcast head toward him as he walked to the ramp, tears filling her eyes. He reluctantly walked up the sloped ramp and boarded the ship while she stood on the dock.

In time, she saw him at the railing of the ship. Waving, she called out to him with her beautiful, wide smile, "Iskandar! Remember that I love you. I will wait for you forever."

He could barely see her through his tears as he vigorously waved his arms to her, watching her stand on the pier below. "I love you, Madeleine," he shouted. *I feel as though my heart has been ripped from my chest. I'm empty. I ache all over.*

"I am so sad," Madeleine whispered. "I am lost without him. How will I live?"

The engines of the ship increased their roar as the ship shuddered and began to slowly pull away from the docks. As Madeleine watched from the pier, the ship moved west away from the port toward the sea, carrying her love far away... to America. She wrapped her arms around her breasts, not moving her eyes from her beloved who was still at the stern's railing. The ship grew smaller and smaller until she could no longer make out his form. Then, finally, the ship disappeared into the sea's last reflections of the golden sunset.

Iskandar stood at the ship's railing; his tearful eyes focused only on Madeleine until he could see her no longer. His heart was heavy, yearning to hold her in his arms. *What am I doing? Why must I always lose the ones I love so much? It is because I am poor that I cannot stay. I will succeed in America, never be poor again, and I will return to my love. This is my promise.*

He remembered how being poor had cost him so much in his young life—separation from his father, loss of his mother, near loss of his feet, separation from his beloved village and brother. And now, he must leave the young woman who had filled his heart, his first true love. He would always remember the sight of her as she waved to him, standing at the edge of the pier, eyes fixed on her beloved, tears flowing down her cheeks. They both felt enormous loss and experienced that awful sense of emptiness of separation.

As the ship pulled away, she whispered to herself, trying to be brave, "How fortunate we are to have met each other, even for a short time, and to have found a love so real, so good. And yet, I am having difficulty accepting this, his leaving me for America. I pray he is always safe, and finds his father. I know he loves his father and his sister as I love the memory of my father, and I understand. But I miss him terribly already. I will think of him everyday until the wonderful moment when he returns to me and embraces me, holds me close to him and makes love to me again."

She watched as the ship sailed away toward the setting, blazing, orange sun, carrying her beloved. She saw Iskandar wave again with both arms as he shouted something she could not hear.

She wiped the tears streaming down her face before she turned from the sea and walked away, thinking of her love now on the high seas. *How long,* she wondered. *How long before I see my Iskandar again.* She felt a tingle deep in her abdomen as she fondled his cross, her hands brushing her breasts. She knew. Somehow she knew that this sensation meant that she would bear a child... Iskandar's child.

Remembering the joy and complete happiness of their moment of beautiful and fervent lovemaking, she paused and looked up over her shoulder to her right to the hill above the beach. The trees stood as guardians of Iskandar and Madeleine's place of love, overlooking the sea. Madeleine, recalling their magnificent union there on the lush grass, hugged herself, smiled broadly and looked up at the sky with scattered pink and lavender clouds reflecting the setting sun. Birds flitted overhead; a sea breeze gently ruffled her hair.

I am happy. I am complete. Now I am a woman. I have found my love. I have given myself to him. He has given me his love and his seed. And that makes me very happy. Life goes on and he is my life.

She reached inside her blouse again to feel the gold cross. Rubbing it with her fingers, she lifted her head, straightened her shoulders, stood tall, and confidently walked away from the pier back toward the city and the *Canebière*.

Iskandar could not leave the deck railing at the stern of the ship for hours.

"Come, *sahbi*, come, walk with me," said Butrus as he put his arm around his friend's shoulders, interrupting his preoccupation with Madeleine. "I know you are feeling great sadness, leaving your beloved Madeleine. But you have beautiful memories. I know you will never forget her. And she will always remember you. But now you must focus on your future and how you will soon be able to return for her."

Iskandar again found her ring with his thumb and rubbed it as he had all day. "You are right, Butrus. I ached when I had to leave Milhelm, and, I am torn to pieces having to leave Madeleine. But somehow, I must now turn my thoughts to America. Yet, it is so painful for me. I must find a way somehow to come back to Madeleine. I will work hard, save my money, and come to her." He kept rubbing her ring on his finger, thinking of that day on the hill.

Later, below on their bunk beds, Iskandar asked, "Butrus, I need paper and a pen. Can you help me find these things? I must write to Madeleine and tell her how I am feeling, if I can."

The ship sailed west to Malta for refueling and supplies before stopping in the Azores for replenishments before it turned its course for New York.

The trip was long—nearly a month. Iskandar had a miserable voyage, as did many of the passengers: nausea, seasickness, unfamiliar food, sleepless nights. Steerage class was awful for them. There would be no joyous dancing like before. It was a voyage to endure, not to enjoy. He had said good-bye to his homeland, to his beloved mother and to the only other woman he ever loved, and now, like so many immigrants before him, would begin a life so different, so strange, that he could not possibly imagine what awaited him. With the others in steerage accommodations, their trip was hard. Mixed emotions filled the hearts and minds of the new immigrants daily as they remembered their pasts and pondered their futures.

During this seemingly endless journey, Iskandar wrote six letters to Madeleine, telling her about events on the ship, his love and loneliness for her, and how he missed her desperately and would work hard and return to her. He would post them in New York.

Day after day Iskandar and Butrus would stand on the deck at the railing. Butrus would put his arm around Iskandar's shoulder as they stood together watching the sea.

"How vast is the sea, Butrus? How great is the distance between my Madeleine and me? It is so enormous. Yet, I must find a way to come back for her after I am able. I must work hard and commit myself to my work. I must succeed, save enough money and return to my Madeleine. I swear I will not rest until I have accomplished that mission."

"Iskandar," Butrus spoke to his friend, "that is a good goal. But we must also live in the present. Let us enjoy the beauty of the sea, the sky, and think of the new life that we will have in America."

CHAPTER 11

New York

"Look, Iskandar, look!" shouted Butrus above the din of the ship's engines. "See the Statue of Liberty? She is holding the torch of freedom, lighting our way to America. Isn't she beautiful! And look at the buildings! I've never seen such tall buildings before! What a city! What a country! I can't believe what I am seeing! We are free!"

Iskandar wept with joy. "God has watched over us. Thank you, Lord. Now we must find our fathers and begin our new lives. Butrus, even though you will be in California and I will be in Florida, we must stay friends."

Their initial excitement of arriving in America soon gave way to the difficult process that lay ahead. Most of the day was spent going through the frustrating, bureaucratic, officious immigration process on Ellis Island. They filled out forms, stood in lines, endured humiliating medical examinations, and the other unpleasant procedures required of all immigrants coming to America in the early years of the twentieth century.

Iskandar was impatient with the delays and turmoil of the process. The rooms were crowded with hundreds of new immigrants mostly from his ship pushing and shoving. No one could understand the English signs or shouting of the immigration officers. After all, they spoke only French or Arabic. They were guided only by hand signals and interpreters who led them to their physical examinations which were so impersonal and embarrassing. The interpreters shouted aloud to them, "Hand me your medical records...let me see your eyes...disrobe and let me examine your body...here, sprinkle this cleansing powder on your body...you cannot enter America unless you are healthy."

The process is demeaning and crude, but I must endure this shame, he repeated to himself. *I have to complete this terrible experience. My father did it, and now I must go through this, as awful as it is. The Turks did this to Salim,* he remembered. *Well, Salim and my father have lived through it and so will I.* He straightened his shoulders with resolve.

Finally, after what seemed like hours of humiliation and being treated like an animal, he was directed to a large room where he stood in line for a long time, papers in hand stamped "Approved for Entry," and his passport. The line slowly moved forward until it was almost his turn. He looked around the room at the others, also in endless lines, and searched with his eyes until he spotted Butrus in another line. "Butrus! Here Butrus!" he yelled in Arabic, "You made it too! *Shookrun, Allah!* I will see you outside!"

"What is your name? Where is your passport?" asked the immigration officer gruffly in English with an Irish accent.

"My name is Iskandar Chalhoub Thomé, *Ibn* Ibrahim." He handed his papers to the official.

"What? Let me see your passport. Uh-huh, mustache, dark hair, five feet, ten inches tall, your number, everything is in order, but you must have an American name. Let's look in the book. Iskandar is Alexander; *Ibn* is the son of...Abraham Thomé. Hmm, that can be Tomay or Tomei," said the officer, frowning, searching for a phonetic sounding name. "Or, many named Thomé take the name of Thomas. So, will you? How about Alexander Abraham Thomas?"

"*Ma Bakar,* I don't know," responded Iskandar thoughtfully with a quizzical look on his face, not fully understanding the man's question. *Iskandar is to be Alexander, and Abraham is my father's name, so Alexander Abraham Thomas is fine. I think Thomas is a good name. So be it. My American name will be Alexander Abraham Thomas,* he thought, then nodded yes in acceptance.

Iskandar, who had lived under Turkish authority for so long, was relieved to be given a bit of a welcomed option to agree with, but not *required* to do. It seemed refreshingly hopeful.

The officer thrust the official papers back into Alexander's hands and he was finally permitted to enter America.

"Go through that door to find your family if they are waiting for you," ordered the officer. By this time, Alexander would have agreed to most anything if it meant he could leave the building.

"There! There is my father." He pointed and waved when he recognized Abraham waiting in the crowd of relatives anxiously searching for their loved ones. Iskandar thought, *He hasn't changed much. Still taller than most, his hair is a bit thinner and grayer, but he looks the same as I remember him when I was a boy of ten...always standing so straight and proud. His skin is darker, maybe from working outdoors. And his smile of pride is still encouraging. Oh, I love this man.* "Biyee!" he waved and yelled. "Here! Here I am!" He pressed through the crowd, turning his shoulders as he moved between people, his eyes never leaving his father's face.

"Iskandar, come to me," Abraham beckoned and shouted loudly so to be recognized above the din of the noisy, jostling crowd. He opened both arms wide, excited to see his son for the first time in eight years. "Here, my son! Come to me!"

They stood facing each other with outstretched arms, tears of joy pouring out of the eyes of father and son as they embraced, repeatedly kissing each other's cheeks, displaying affection in the custom of their homeland.

"Thank God," he murmured as his father's strong arms wrapped around him, smelling his father's familiar scent while absorbing this wonderful moment.

"Eight years! Eight years! So long, my son! How you have grown! You are as tall as me now! I am so happy to see you, Iskandar." Abraham proudly tousled Iskandar's thick hair.

"*Biyee*, you look so good. You are still so strong! What joy to be here with you. Oh, how I wish *Imei* was here with us today."

"And Milhelm too," responded Abraham. His large hands swept Alexander's shoulders and the side of his face as he smiled broadly with pride. "Let me look at you. Your shoulders are strong. You look very healthy and handsome, my son! Come now, bring your belongings. I will help you. We will go now and be together."

He paused and thought, *It's been so long since I've seen my boy...so many years of living alone, wondering, remembering my family so far away...finally realizing I'd never hold dear Katrina again, or watch my sons grow up...all because we were so poor and I couldn't afford to bring them with me or go get them sooner. If only...*Tears began to well up.

Iskandar interrupted his father's thoughts, "Father, let me look at you."

Slowly they separated, joyous yet sensing the emotions of sadness too as both father and son couldn't escape the questions of why they were separated for so long.

They stood facing each other, "Son, there is so much to tell you. And there is so much for you to tell me. Your sister Leila could not be with us, for she is with child, her third, and the journey would have been too difficult for her. We will see her in due time. She sends her love. Now, are you hungry? Let us eat before we begin our journey."

"Forgive me, Father, my legs are still a bit weak from the journey on the seas. I must walk a bit slowly for a while. I was sick on the ship so much! But yes, *Biyee*, I am hungry. I am hungry for food, for you, for your love, and for my new life in America. I met a wonderful girl in Marseille, *Biyee*. I want to tell you all about her. And *Khali* Hanna sends his love to you as well." Alexander spoke fast and excitedly to his father. He had so much to say.

The moment Alexander and Abraham stepped outside, they were struck by the enormity of the city. The buildings were so tall, and there were so many people and so much traffic. But the sky was clear and blue, a good sign for the young man's arrival. The light winds off the sea were refreshing.

Abraham grabbed Alexander's arm and moved them through the crowd toward the bus stand. "Come, Iskandar, we must go to the train station. It is on the island over there. It is called Manhattan. Here is the bus. Let us go."

By 1920, New York had more than three million people. Most were recent immigrants or first generations. It was the largest city in America, and much larger than Beirut and even Marseille.

He could hardly restrain himself. "Oh, *Biyee*, what a big city! So many people! Is it like this where we are going? Is this the way America is everywhere? Everything is so full, so fast, so big, so tall. Everyone is walking fast...so many buses with overhead power wires, cars and trucks in the street. Everyone seems so free, so happy. It's exciting!"

He whispered to himself, "Alexander...Alexander Thomas. Everything is so strange and new. I wonder how I will get used to this new world." He was bewildered by everything that was so different...the black cars and trolleys zooming in the streets...the people dressed so differently.

He muttered to himself, "My God, village life was so simple." Thoughts raced quickly through his mind. *I feel dizzy from the amazing change, almost like being in a dream. Thank God my father is here. We both traveled so far to finally be together. What a wonderful father I have. Without him I would be lost. I can barely imagine what he had to go through just to get here eight years ago.*

"Iskandar, New York is different from everywhere else in America. There is only one New York," Abraham said to his son, interrupting his thoughts, still using his Arabic name. "I would rather live in a village where I know everyone and everyone knows me. I feel safer there than here. Everyone is an immigrant here in New York, speaking his own language until some of them go on to other places. Their young go to school to learn English, but the older people do not. That is why they live in separate places. Brooklyn, in New York, has many Syrians. You can purchase any kind of foods from Syria you wish: *bulgar, fistok, jibneh, zeytoon*, herbs and spices. Everything is there. The same is true for the Irish, the Greeks, the Jews, the Italians and others. Most Armenians are with the Lebanese. New York is a big place with many kinds of people. Somehow, in America, they all get along without wars. That is the miracle of America. Now, we must eat something."

They went to a restaurant near the terminal building that was quickly filling with new immigrants and their welcoming families, speaking to each other in their native Arabic. They found an empty table and sat down to wait to place an order.

Abraham spoke in his native language to his son across the table, "Rest, my son. You have had a very long journey. And today was difficult. But it will get easier and less confusing in time. You will find it much simpler after you have learned to speak and read English. English is a hard language, Iskandar.

I have not yet learned to speak it well. But you are young and must learn as soon as possible. I have arranged a speaking tutor for you in Florida, and you must attend school there to learn the customs as well, and make friends. There is so much to talk about. We will speak more about these things later."

Then, looking into his son's dancing eyes, he said lovingly, "Oh, I am so happy you are finally here with me, my son." Pausing, he decided he must discuss his plans with Iskandar. "We will have a long journey, my son. America is a large country. Our village in Florida is fifteen hundred miles away. That is nearly ten times the length of Lebanon. A new frontier, so they say, far to the south where it is warm all year. But before we go there, I think we should go see your cousins, my brothers and your Uncle Salim and Uncle Mike. They wait for you. So, after we eat, we will go to the station and take a train to Boston."

Throughout the entire seven-hour train ride, seated on a wooden bench, they had the windows open, wind rushing to their faces. Alexander, eagerly sitting next to the window, kept pointing at fascinating new scenic views. His eyes rarely left the sights whizzing by. The two, father and son, spoke in their native tongue and exchanged banter and recollections. It seemed a bit strange to be with his father for the first time in eight years.

"You were just a boy of ten, my son, when I had to leave you or face being taken into the Turkish army. *I had no choice.* Like so many other Lebanese and Syrian men, there was no hope for us under the Ottomans."

Alexander, remembering the separation, his mother's sense of loss, and his trials following the freak snow storm, recalled to his father, "*Biyee*, it was so awful without you. *Imei* missed you so much, but she took good care of Milhelm and me. She never was careful of her own health, but worried about us…too much…and now…" he ended in a sad whisper, tears welling up.

"But now, we must turn to the future, Iskandar. We must remember her and love her. She would want more than anything that you are happy in America."

CHAPTER 12

*A*hlen *wa sahlen!"* exclaimed Uncle Mike, Abraham's brother, with both arms outstretched, welcoming his nephew with a big smile and a strong embrace.

"Come in, come in. We are so happy to see you. Ah, Iskandar, you are a young man now. Eighteen, eh? You were just a boy when last we saw you in Douma during the winter of 1911. We all came to say goodbye to your mother, and her sons. Milhelm was then fifteen and tall, strong and muscular, and so kind, like your mother. It was so sad for us to learn of her passing. Beautiful Katrina. She was everyone's favorite. And now, Milhelm remains in the village, and you're in America," Uncle Mike exclaimed in happiness to see his young nephew. "Please sit, rest, and have coffee. We have food for you both. How was your voyage?"

Alexander, smiling from joy at being with his family, simply said, "It was difficult." He didn't feel much like talking yet. He was just excited to see everyone.

Mike turned to Abraham. "And, *khai-yi*, how good to see you. It's been too long. How are you, my brother? Our voyage was very difficult too, eh?" They laughed and embraced, two men in their fifties, affectionately kissing both cheeks. They all sat around their room on chairs, the couch, even getting additional chairs from the dining table, for a long moment, gazing at each other, savoring their reunion, loving the sight of each other, and all speaking at the same time.

"This is like the end of the Prodigal Son parable that Jesus spoke of in the Bible, isn't it, Abraham? We must dine on the fatted calf, rejoice and be happy for your son who has come to you after so many years."

"I am so happy, Mike," replied Abraham sitting with Alexander, and with a broad smile, his hand never leaving his son's arm. "I am rejoicing the whole time. Yet, I must confess, I am also sad. My son Milhelm is not here. And my beautiful Katrina can only be with us in spirit. I miss her so much. You cannot believe how much." As he spoke remembering their years together, thinking of his lovely bride, with joy at the birth of each child, Abraham's eyes welled up. He reached to embrace his youngest son, so grateful for his arrival. "I love you so much, Iskandar," he whispered. "You have your mother's eyes and her smile. This is a wonderful, but bittersweet day for me, my son."

As the family gathered around the room, Alexander described his trip in a few sentences, not elaborating. He knew each of them had made the same unpleasant, humbling, seemingly endless voyage. There were no exciting stories to tell the gathering. He was not yet about to relate his times with Madeleine in Marseille to his family. It would have caused serious glances —or worse, it would have been dismissed as "puppy love," nothing to be taken seriously, of course, since Alexander, like every young person in this immigrant family, was expected, without question, to marry a fellow Syrian Orthodox Christian.

So, with emotions of joy from seeing his father, Uncle Mike and Uncle Salim, and happiness because his experiences at sea were over and he was now in America, he had to put aside for today the conflict between his heart's desire to be with Madeleine and the reality of his heritage and family expectations. To the family, his responsibilities were to diligently work with and obey his father, save his money, and, in the end, marry someone acceptable to the family.

I hope someone changes the subject, Alexander thought to himself.

Uncle Mike read his thoughts and said, "My wife, Sara, and I own a store. We sell clothing, shoes, and notions to our community. We have worked hard together, and now we own our building. It takes time, yes, but we think in terms of family, not just ourselves. Everything is possible in America. We look to the future for our children. Our son, Edward, is in school now, and one day wants to be a teacher. He is very smart, like you, Iskandar, and will do well. He studies every evening, and wants to go to college, *inshallah*, if it be God's will."

Mike continued, now elaborating to the gathering as much as to Alexander, describing life in America for the immigrants, and how many had dealt with it in their new country. "We have a large Syrian community here in Boston, one of the oldest in America. There are many of us here. Like the Irish, the Jews, and the Italians, we formed our own neighborhoods. In that way, we know all our neighbors, go to the same churches, speak the same language, eat the same foods, and live the same traditions. Some have shops. Others work in the mills. It is good. Still, one-by-one, some leave for other places in America. One cousin started as a peddler in Dakota, out west, selling to the Indians. He now has a store. Another took the train to California near Los Angeles. They came from the Bekaa Valley, and are now doing very well farming and growing potatoes. Most are clothing shopkeepers or food merchants. We are everywhere... in small towns or villages in other states like Texas, Louisiana, Ohio, Mississippi, Georgia, Illinois, and Michigan. Some even left here to go to Cuba, Puerto Rico, Honduras and still others to Canada. We are all over America, even though there are not so many of us. But more are coming now that the war is over. It has not been easy for any immigrants. But we survive as we must." He paused, and now looking directly at Alexander, pointed and said, "And so will you, Iskandar, so will you. It is your destiny to succeed here in America."

Abraham then added, "Soon, too, perhaps Milhelm will join us."

Alexander never moved from his place on the couch next to his father. He loved his touch on his arm, listening to his deep, authoritative voice. Later, during the evening, he would wrap his arm around his father's shoulders, showing respect, and his father would, in turn, wrap his large arm around his son's shoulders, expressing his love. Both were on the edge of tears all evening, filled with gratitude and love. There were moments during lulls in the conversation when Alexander would surreptitiously rub the gold ring on his finger. His thoughts wandered and he found himself remembering Madeleine and Marseille.

Finally, Alexander could no longer hold back, so he spoke of Marseille. "*Khali* Hanna asked me to give you his warmest wishes, *Biyee*. He treated me very well. We visited many times. He gave me the use of an apartment for six weeks and my new friend Butrus and I shared the room. *Khali* Hanna is so nice. He has a beautiful lady friend named Daniella." Tentatively, he ventured to the precipice. "She has a beautiful daughter whose name is Madeleine." Pausing in thought, sensing no positive response, he felt he could go no further.

"Butrus met his father in New York as I met you, and his plan is to go to California where his father has established a small farm in some valley there. He told me it is very fertile like the Bekaa."

"That would be the San Joaquin Valley; it is very productive," spoke young Edward, the teacher-to-be. "They feed most of the western communities from there."

"That's the name Butrus said. 'San Wakeen,' or something like that," responded Alexander with a smile. "I must learn English as fast as I can, otherwise it will be so difficult for me. Going through immigration was a nightmare," he explained, still speaking in Arabic.

"Sara," Mike directed to his wife, "send one of the boys to get Salim. Tell him Iskandar is here and to come visit with us."

Mike turned to Alexander, "Iskandar, Salim has been anxiously awaiting your arrival. Since he arrived two years ago, he has been eager for you to come. He wants to introduce you to his lady friend. She's such a nice girl. Her name is Julia. We are all very happy. She's from a good Orthodox Syrian family like us. They arrived in Boston in 1903 from Damascus. She has many sisters. Perhaps one of them is for you." Mike laughed as he put his hand on

Alexander's shoulder.

Alexander felt the conflict in his stomach. He felt more certain than ever that they would never understand his love for Madeleine.

"Salim works in the shop downstairs. He should be here in a few minutes. Now we will eat, *fudulou.*"

The group moved to the dining room table, some carrying their chairs. A blessing of thanks was said, and the first plates of the *mezza* were passed around. They all continued to discuss Alexander's arrival, the family still in Douma, the joy of the family's happenings, and Abraham's news of the Florida frontier.

After their dinner of lamb meat on a skewer, *laha mishweh*, beans and rice, *lubya oo riz*, and of course, *tabouleh, zeytoon*, olives, and khoubas, pita-like bread in which they wrapped almost everything instead of using forks and knives, the women cleared the dishes and gathered with the rest of the family to visit and relax in the living room. The men sipped their *arak* and exchanged stories late into the night. This was a time of re-bonding. They were family. Cousins came and went all afternoon and evening. The house was crowded for hours. It was very much like home in Douma where everyone's friends were relatives—an extended family reunion where everyone had a turn to speak, even the children. *It is so wonderful*, thought Alexander. Family was paramount in their lives.

"*Mahrharbahr,* Iskandar!" Salim almost shouted in happiness as he entered the room with arms wide open to hug his young nephew. "How good it is to see you here. I have waited for this day for a long time. Let me see you! You have grown so much!

Alexander smiled. "Ah, I hear you have a lady friend. Wonderful! Her name is Julia Shaheen?" He silently thought to himself, *I too have a love— a lovely young girl in Marseille.* Alexander glanced at his right hand and realized he was rubbing the gold ring on his little finger.

"Now then," replied Salim, not registering what Alexander just said, "we must spend some time together here in Boston while you are here. I want you to meet Julia. You will like her. She is wonderful, the eldest of seven children, four sisters and two brothers. One of her sisters, Helene, could turn your eye. She is just fifteen, but she's a beauty and will soon become the right age for marriage."

"I will be happy to go with you to meet Julia, Salim, but I must go to Florida with my father in less than a week."

Their almost brotherly closeness resumed, and they promised to visit each day as often as they could. Perhaps, they agreed, Alexander would return to Boston during the hot summer months in Florida. During the seven days following, they spent every day together. Each night during their week's stay, Salim entertained the family playing his *oud*, singing his romantic songs of love. Alexander savored them even more having met the girl Salim intended to marry. Evenings were devoted to family gatherings filled with singing, dining, and dancing. It was a joyous reunion for Alexander.

On the next day, a Sunday, they all went to church together. That morning Alexander first met pretty, fair-haired, Syrian, English-fluent, 15-year-old, Helene Shaheen.

"*Ahlar har bahr*," spoke Alexander as he looked at the pretty, blue-eyed, shy teenager.

"*Ahlein*, hello," was her smiling response to this handsome 18-year-old who had just arrived from the Lebanese mountains.

"He's kind of cute," Helene confided to her sisters later, "but he is dressed like a country bumpkin. He's okay, I guess. I *do* like his eyes. And he *is* nice."

Forgetting that Madeleine was sixteen, Alexander later whispered to his uncle, "She's very nice, Salim, but she's so young. She's only fifteen years old, and I am on my way to Florida. I don't know when I will be back to Boston. Maybe a year. We will see. *Inshallah*."

"I think Helene likes you, Iskandar," responded Salim as they walked back home from church later that evening. "In fact, I think her whole family likes you. Of course, it helps that you are my nephew," he smiled, slapping Alexander on his shoulder. "And you're not ugly!" Sam laughed at his own joke.

"How could I be ugly and also be your nephew, Salim? Helene is pretty and nice. We shall see. There is a lot of work to be done before I can take care of someone else beside me. I have no money, no home, no job, nothing. I am not able to think about a serious relationship at this time. Besides…" he stopped himself before he spoke further about Madeleine. He realized even more that he must not now bring up the subject of Madeleine, Marseille, and his love experience. That would only go from Salim to Julia to Helene and to her parents. They wouldn't want to have anything to do with him if they learned of his liaison with Madeleine. So, he had to change the subject and not mention these things. But he was constantly reminded of that beautiful evening on the hill overlooking the Mediterranean Sea—gazing down at Madeleine's lovely face as they lay on the soft grass…remembering how her beautiful, long hair caressed her shoulders and flowed onto the lush green grass around her head…remembering her passion as they made love. He constantly caught himself rubbing her ring with his thumb as it circled the small finger on his right hand. He smiled for a moment…thinking…staring into space, remembering.

"Iskandar! You haven't heard a word I said. Where is your mind? You almost walked into that lamppost! Are you blind?" Sam gripped Alexander's arm as he abruptly pulled him to his side. "Where are you, Iskandar?"

"Oh, Salim, I am so sorry. My mind was somewhere else. It's not important. I was just thinking," he replied with an embarrassed smile.

"Well, you had better look while you are thinking, my friend. And now, we are nearly home. What do you think? Do you want to go to the picture show with us? It would be good for me. I cannot take Julia alone. If you go too, then Helene can go, and the four of us can have a good day. Maybe even ice cream after. Would you like that?"

"What is ice cream, Salim?"

"Oh, Alexander, you have so much to learn about America. You will love ice cream. And you will love America!"

After an active and tiring week in Boston visiting cousins, Abraham and his son anxiously boarded the train for Florida. *"Allah ma'ak*, 'Brahim. *Allah ma'ak*, Iskandar. Come back soon. We will miss you!"

Uncle Mike, Uncle Salim, Julia, Helene, and at least a dozen cousins, aunts and uncles were at the train station that Monday morning as Alexander and his father stepped onto the metal steps leading up to the open air rail car that would be their home via New York City, Atlanta, Tampa, and finally Kissimmee.

CHAPTER 13

$\mathcal{T}$he trip south to Kissimmee, Florida was long; yet, the sights were unbelievable to Alexander. "This is my new land. It is so different, so big, *Baba*," he exclaimed to his father sitting on the aisle seat next to him on the train's wooden bench. The 2,000 miles of cities, towns, and thick forests whizzed by. Traveling day and night, the train ride took nearly a week. It was early summer, and some flowering trees were still in bloom. Alexander marveled at the lushness of the rolling, wooded American countryside, its beauty, and the size of his New World. He stared out the window all day, everyday. The early summer weather was beautiful; cool air blew into the train through the open windows onto his face, blowing his hair to the side. Sometimes, Alexander would stretch his arms and head outside to feel the wind as the train moved along the tracks, "clickety-clack, clickety-clack," at twenty miles an hour. So fast, thought the young immigrant. His father, sitting beside him, watching Alexander's youthful enthusiasm, enjoyed the trip even more than he dreamed he would...because his son was with him.

Alexander told his father the story of the snowstorm on the mountain, Milhelm's rescue, Katrina's rubbing his feet with olive oil for many days, the villagers' suffering, the capture and release of Salim, the starvation, the locusts, the end of the war, and finally, the freedom under the French after the war. He wondered if he should ask the question he and Milhelm had asked themselves many times: "Why didn't you come for us sooner when *Imei* was still alive?" But he felt that it was too soon to ask and would be insulting and too painful for his father to discuss.

Abraham, in his deep, resonant voice, used all the evenings to tell his son of his life in America.

"I decided there would be more opportunity in the southern frontier of Florida, not Boston which is industrial and most of our people work in the mills. It gets very cold there in the winter too. I preferred a smaller village, and fewer people where it is warm much of the year. They say it is healthier there for many people who must leave the cold in the north because they suffer from consumption or pains in their bodies like arthritis. The winters are very mild and pleasant. I like it in Florida."

Wondering about his father's life, Alexander asked, "How did you find enough people to sell your goods? How did you do all this, *Biyee*? You had no family, no friends."

"It has not been easy, son. For several years, until only three years ago, every week, I rode the train eighty miles to Tampa and Tarpon Springs with my suitcase of notions our cousins in Boston sent to me. Then I walked back along the railroad tracks, selling at each house along the rail route, sometimes miles apart. It was exhausting and difficult because I could not speak English. I was embarrassed too much to speak." He stopped for a moment, thinking, and continued with, "I still speak English badly. I wish I could sometimes speak to my customers in my native language, but there is no one here who will understand me. That's what was so nice to be in Boston on this trip, so we could speak in Arabic. It was so easy," he smiled.

Then, thinking of the days behind him, wanting his son to know, he said, "I would open my suitcase to display my goods. When the people chose something they liked, I would show with my fingers the cost. Ten fingers was ten cents, one finger was one cent. As long as I sold something during the days I walked, I was happy. I always tried to make sure the people liked me. I am a large man speaking a foreign language, so I think I scared some of the children in the beginning. I am a stone mason, but it is important to make sure everyone is comfortable. I loved to dance, laugh, play cards and *towleh* back home. But, of course, it is not easy to do that here. Your sister's father-in-law is nice, but except for him, I am alone. I prefer to be with other people. So, in Kissimmee, I am sometimes called a 'gentle giant' because I am so friendly with everyone. I argue with no one, Iskandar. That is good advice, for we are strangers here. And some think of us as 'different.' That will be a new and maybe painful experience for you. It is a strange feeling to be thought of as different."

Then, he continued, "Some days I only sold enough to earn ten cents. The suitcase was heavy, but I had to do what I had to do. I had no money, but I believed in myself. I endured whatever I had to do to save enough money to bring you, your mother, and Milhelm to join me."

"I walked ninety miles each trip. It took me several days. And when it was dark, I slept on the tracks, using the rail as my pillow so I could hear if a train was coming. That way I wouldn't get lost. People were friendly, but since they couldn't understand my language, I could not sleep in their homes. Of course there were no public rooms, and I had little money. Sometimes I sold notions to the Indians near the swamps, and sometimes, the cattlemen would buy my goods. I slept in the village under a house many times to stay warm in the winter, and to be safe. But, of course, there were animals everywhere, and mosquitoes. My God, the mosquitoes were so thick that I had to cover myself with rags." Gesturing with his hands, he exclaimed, "Sometimes I had to chase a snake from my sleeping area."

Alexander listened intently to the stories with respect and wonder. He felt sad as he listened to his father's sacrifice and hardships. It seemed to him that his father's life was more difficult here than it would have been in Lebanon.

"*Biyee*, did it ever get better for you?" he asked.

His father explained, "When the war in Europe grew to involve America, I could not come back to Lebanon, but business got better; so much was needed. In 1916, during the war, I used my savings to buy a house in Kissimmee for $400. I paid for it over the years. I added a few rooms on the second floor, and that's where we will live. It is a good home situated near the railroad, an excellent location. I opened my store on the first floor at the street and named it A. Thomas Company. Maybe now I will change the name to A. Thomas and Son. What do you think?" he asked his bewildered son, rhetorically.

"Before the war ended," he continued, "I purchased another building, then another, and I now have three buildings. I rent and collect money from my tenants. That is an important lesson, Iskandar. Save your money and buy land. I choose not to give my earnings to the bankers. This way, I can see and touch what I own. Money does not come easily. I also own a vacant parcel of land where I bury my extra money. They call it 'banking in the field.' It is safe there because no one knows where it is. Soon I will show you."

Alexander listened carefully to his father's words, feeling enormous pride at what his father had accomplished under incredibly difficult conditions, taking them all in, and thinking eagerly how to begin his new life in America.

Abraham continued his counsel in Arabic, "It was only this year that I saved enough money to send for you and Milhelm. I can never forgive myself for not finding a way to send earlier for you boys and your mother, Iskandar. My son, for several years it was almost too difficult for me. I nearly went back to Boston to be with family. I am not a young man anymore, and I had hoped I would be able to send for you, Milhelm and your mother much, much sooner, but it was not possible. I was heartbroken when I received word from Elias that your mother, my beloved Katrina had died. I could not eat for days. I cried alone in my shack, missing all of you. Only later did I learn of the famine, the horrible locusts, the war, and those terrible Turks. I had no way of knowing what was happening to you and everyone in Douma during those days. Very few in Douma are accustomed to writing letters. Even so, there was nothing I could do. I felt so helpless. It was so painful and lonely for me." Pausing, he looked up and continued, "God helped me through those terrible days. And now you are here with me. But not Milhelm. When will I see Milhelm again?" Looking up, he sighed, "Only God knows."

Abraham and his son grew closer during the trip. There was so much to say, so much to describe. They talked late into each night, sleeping with their heads resting where they could, snoring together or listening to the snores of the other passengers. There were many stops along the way...Philadelphia, Charlotte, Atlanta, Jacksonville, then, finally...

"Last stop, Tampa!" yelled the conductor. "Time to get off, Mr. Thomas." He shook Abraham's shoulder to awaken the man and his son.

Abraham wiped his face, leaned back, stretched, and looked out the window. He spoke to Alexander who was just waking up to the warmth of coastal west Florida. "There is a large Greek community near Tampa, my son, called Tarpon Springs where we can get a room at the Inn. They have good places to eat, and a fine church we can attend. The Greeks are known for their large fishing fleet. They dive for sponges here and are the best sponge divers in the offshore waters. Tampa is a much bigger city than Kissimmee, with a busy port where large ships come from all over. There are many Cubans there. Cattlemen from Kissimmee, Bartow, and other towns near where I live, drive their herds here to Tampa, and ship their cattle to the markets in Cuba."

Getting off the train with their bags, Alexander eagerly looked around, fascinated by the sights, and the strange mixture of languages spoken —Spanish, Greek, English. He smiled at the newness, the unfamiliar, not understanding a single thing. His father pointed the way, saying, "It has been a long, tiresome journey, *Biyee*. Let us go find something to eat at a restaurant I know."

They arrived at the Aegean Sea Restaurant owned and operated by Stanos Demetriades and his wife Lydia, Greek immigrants and friends.

"Ah, Stanos!" exclaimed Abraham. "Meet my son, Iskandar. He has just arrived."

Stanos, setting the table near the front door, wiped his hands on his white apron, smiled and extended his hand. "Well, Iskandar, we have been waiting for you. Your father speaks of you all the time. Welcome! You must call me Stanos, Iskandar."

Alexander, returning Stanos' welcoming smile, reached out to shake hands.

Abraham interjected, "And now that he is in America, his new name is Alexander."

"Then you are both welcome here, Iskandar and Alexander." He laughed at his own joke. "Come inside. I will set a place for you. We have many foods you may find familiar, perhaps just slightly different from in Lebanon, but very much the same. Would you like rolled grape leaves in olive oil? I know you will enjoy Lydia's baklavah!" he said, smiling.

After their early meal, Alexander, relishing the new sights and wanting to walk around, wandered along the dirt road where hundreds of round, light brown sponges hung in huge stretched nets to dry. They are beautiful, but so strange, thought Alexander. What do they do with them? he wondered. He was fascinated by his first view of the turquoise waters of the broad Gulf of Mexico, the sponge and fishing boats, and the nets strung out to dry.

"We will come back here often," Abraham said to Alexander. "They are just like we are—Greeks and Syrians eat the same food, dance the same, and attend the same church and pray the same. I feel at home here with Stanos and his family. They are our kind."

Iskandar thought, *At home, everyone is our kind. It seems strange to hear my father say these things.*

After his first night in Florida, Alexander and Abraham left Tampa early the next day, taking the small gauge train to Kissimmee, nearly three hours to the east. It was a warm, sunny day in May, but heavy, dark clouds were building in the south, signaling the start of the summer rainy season. Evaporation from the Everglades and swamps to the south created their seasonal cycle of pounding heavy rains, winds, and then, evaporation by the hot sun providing more clouds, then rainfall for the miles and miles of grassy pastures. And the cycle continues.

As Alexander rode the train eastward from Tampa, he spent most of the ride still gazing out the window, watching the flat grasslands and pine forests of Central Florida flash by him. Nothing he saw reminded him of anything he had ever seen in his entire life. It was all so different, so flat, so green. Mile after mile was mostly piney woods, palmetto fields, grasslands, and, occasionally, swamp lands and a gently rolling countryside.

They could see thousands of small cattle grazing in the open pastures and men on horseback. "The men are rounding up the scattered cows," said Abraham. "This land is filled with cattle. There are so many, they say, that it is one of the largest producers of beef in America. We are in the middle of a new American frontier that has a wonderful future. People are moving here from the cold winters in the north. Already, since I came here in 1912, the population of Kissimmee has tripled! Yes, even here there were natives, "Indians" they call them, the first Americans."

My father walked all this way all the time for years! With these thoughts, Alexander appreciated all the more what his father endured, hoping to earn enough to send for him, his brother, and his mother.

As Alexander gazed over the open countryside, he said aloud to his father, "What a great, large country. I want to find my destiny here. I will seize every opportunity to better myself. I am anxious, *Baba,* to get started, to fulfill my destiny of success, adventure, and wealth. I want to learn all I can from you. I don't ever want us to be poor again!" And, he added, "I want to prove to you how much I appreciate what you had to endure to save enough money to bring me to America."

"Iskandar, our faith is our destiny. You must believe that with God's guidance, it will come true. So, my son, believe it, have faith, and it will happen. But be patient, especially with yourself. It doesn't come easy. It requires hard work, very hard work. And you must be careful, for there are those who will try to take what you have."

"As I told you in when you first arrived, I have arranged for you to be taught by a tutor so that you can learn the English language, to speak it well, to write it, and to *learn to think* in English. That way, you will have an easier life than mine. That is my hope, my dream for you. I do not want you to be embarrassed or feel like an outsider, different from the other people, as I have had to feel. This is very important, my son. Each generation must make it easier for the next, as you will do for your sons one day."

True to his nature, Alexander's head was full of emotional eagerness to get started. He felt like a young horse who wants to run across the field, yet is being held back. *I will learn from my English lessons and I will listen to others, especially my father. And soon I will be on my own.*

Alexander felt his weight shift, leaning slightly forward as the train began to slow down, signaling the approach to the Kissimmee railway station. "Kissimmee!" shouted the conductor in his dark blue wool suit with a railroad badge on his breast, and small brimmed cap walking briskly down the center aisle of the passenger car. They could feel the train buckle and sway as the arched steel brakes began to press against the smooth steel wheels. The train finally stopped abruptly in the middle of Broadway, the town's main street.

Abraham, still speaking in Arabic, looked at his son and said, "We must leave the train now. We'll go to our store over there."

Alexander liked the sound of "our store." As they reached the end of the car and stepped down onto the dirt road, Alexander turned his head and looked back at the railroad car and smiled. *I am here Madeleine! I am finally home. Now I must find a way back to you.* He rubbed her ring on his little finger, silently imagining she heard him announce his arrival in Florida…America.

CHAPTER 14

By 1920, Kissimmee was an active frontier cattle town located in Central Florida on the north shore of huge Lake Tohopekaliga which fed into the Kissimmee River, a majestic winding, fast-flowing, large river that meandered southward across the flatlands, through hundreds of thousands of acres of pastureland and piney woods, to Lake Okeechobee to the Caloosahatchee River, southwest to Fort Myers, finally emptying into the Gulf of Mexico. At the city's lake shoreline were busy docks where supplies were brought in by small steamboats up from the Gulf of Mexico. Because of its location, Kissimmee was one of the busier Florida towns of the late 1800's and early 1900's. Henry Plant, a former Standard Oil partner, had brought his railroad from Jacksonville to Tampa with a spur to Kissimmee by 1883, at least ten years before Henry Flagler, a fellow Standard Oil executive, under the same franchise agreement with the state of Florida built his rail line south from Jacksonville along the east coast to Palm Beach and, later, Miami and the Keys.

Broadway, the main commercial, dirt street was vibrant by 1920, lined on both sides with mostly two-story red brick or earth tone stucco shops with apartments above. There were also scattered wood framed clapboard single story homes and white pinewood frame two-story buildings with shops. Plant Railroad tracks ran down the middle of the street. The population was 2,700, nearly three times that of Douma, and growing.

Cattlemen had been part of the area since the early 1800's. Most of the Kissimmee families had relocated from the southern states of Georgia, the Carolinas, Tennessee, and Alabama after the Civil War. Deep-seated southern traditions and prejudices remained since most of North Florida, "Dixie" in culture, consisted of plantations of cotton, and pine forests with black slave owners. Florida had been part of the Confederacy, so its northern tier had been occupied by Federal troops after the Civil War. Northern and Central Florida were still very segregated and "Southern" in character.

"This is a nice, small village," Abraham pointed out to his son as they stepped along earthen Broadway toward his shop. "I like its size, and I like most of the people. Most are friendly," he smiled, recalling a few faces, "and,

I must say, a few are not very tolerant of newcomers, Alexander, especially new immigrants like us." Lines appeared on his forehead as he recognized one of those unfriendly "locals" riding horses just ahead. "Watch out for some of those rough young men on their horses, Alexander. They can be rude and insulting. But," he admonished, "try to avoid any trouble. This is their country, and we are new here. We must find ways to get along with everyone."

Abraham's eight years in the area, first as a very poor, itinerant rail peddler, now as a small vendor-shopkeeper, had humbled him. And while he was not intimidated by the rough and wild cattlemen who descended on this cattle town on weekends at the end of their cattle drives, he found his life more pleasant by staying away from them.

Ironically, while Kissimmee was deeply imbued with the southern culture, nearby St. Cloud on "Little Lake Tohopekaliga," only five miles away, was settled by retired "Yankee" Civil War veterans from places like Illinois, Ohio and Michigan, creating sharp and interesting contrasts between the citizens' behavior of both neighboring communities. While they tended to get along, they each had their loyalties and did not really mix.

Kissimmee was a key community during Florida's Indian Wars that ended in 1858. Cattle ranching was big business in Central Florida, and Kissimmee was the central "cattle town." In 1884, only thirty-six years before, Florida's Governor Bloxham contracted with Philadelphia heir Hamilton Disston to drain the swampland of central and southwest Florida, including making the waters navigable from Kissimmee to the Gulf of Mexico in exchange for an option to buy four million acres for twenty-five cents per acre. Bloxham's goals included draining much of the land to attract new settlers and farmers to Southwest Florida to buy his lands at a handsome profit. Even into the middle of the twentieth century and beyond, the region of Central Florida was second only to Texas in cattle production because of its enormous, uninhabited pasturelands. Thousands of these wild, roaming cattle were mostly descended from the small, spindly Spanish cattle deposited hundreds of years earlier in St. Augustine, that "fountain of youth" discovered by Ponce de Leon, about one hundred-fifty miles away on the northeast coast of Florida and those left by Hernando De Soto in the mid-1500s. They were tended by rugged cowmen all over open ranged Central Florida. It was a hard, but adventurous way of life for these men, mostly in their teens and early twenties.

Because of the "Confederate" heritage of most cattlemen and their "cowmen," rarely, if ever, did the major ranchers of Central Florida ship their cattle to northern markets, preferring Cuban markets to the "Yankees," particularly after the end of the Civil War in 1865 and during the years of Reconstruction. There was still a lot of simmering anger and frustration over the Federal occupation during those Reconstruction years.

For decades, the cowmen continued to be free spirits, living on the range, branding, herding and moving the cattle. Even in 1920 when Alexander arrived, their cattle drives ended in Kissimmee as they herded hundreds of cattle down Broadway to the rail yards for loading and shipment. When they did, most would show up on their horses—pistols on their hips, rifles in their saddle holsters, lariats and leather whips tied to their saddle, and horn, and spurs on their boot heels—on Broadway, the main street of Kissimmee, to have raucous fun in town at the local hotels, brothels, and saloons.

"Sometimes, son, those cattlemen get too drunk, shoot into the sky, yell into the night, and frighten everyone with their fights and guns."

The open range cattle industry was huge, independent, and powerful. It brought great wealth to the region and had for many years. In contrast, a few miles to the east, on the north-south ridgeline, Haines City, St. Cloud and other nearby towns were becoming major citrus-growing regions due to their citrus-friendly sandy soil and scattered lakes. Cattlemen stayed to the west and south on their prairies.

In even sharper contrast, two-hundred miles away, Southeast Florida, over in Miami and Palm Beach, on the eastern edge of the wet Everglades, did not attract new settlers until after 1894 when Henry Flagler's railroad finally reached Palm Beach, fully eleven years after the Plant railroad reached Bartow in Polk County, south of Kissimmee, in 1883. Flagler's railroad did not reach the swampy, mostly water-covered region of Miami until 1896.

By 1920, much of Southeast Florida was still mostly swampland, but growing fast. Central Florida, north of Lake Okeechobee, near Kissimmee, was higher and dry, even though the winding, serpentine Kissimmee River overflowed every year during the rainy season. Interestingly, Orange County, now including Orlando, and Osceola County were created by the state by splitting Mosquito County. Mosquitoes were very prevalent but the leaders felt its name was hardly attractive to visitors, so they changed it. In the early days, before tourism and marketing in the area became important, Mosquito County seemed well-named.

This is what Abraham Thomé-Thomas Chalhoub, Alexander's father, found when he arrived in Kissimmee in 1912—an area in transition from a single dirt road, remote frontier cattle village to a town with promise of better things to come.

By 1920, Kissimmee was a bustling town with sharply contrasting activities. Yet, it was still very much a cattle town. Osceola and Polk Counties to the south were vital cattle producing areas also. But the town of Kissimmee was quickly becoming the mercantile center, with its rail access, main commercial street, hotels, and busy river port. On weekends, the cattlemen who worked the cattle herds on the surrounding ranges came into town.

"You will find many kind and friendly people all around Kissimmee," Abraham explained as the two stepped into the store. "There are many young people here too, and because it is much easier for older people to live in Florida, in time, I think more and more people from the cold North will relocate here. Iskandar, so many people keep coming here, one day we may have to expand our store. Business all over town keeps increasing each year," he added.

Abraham told his son the history of the area. He knew that cattle and citrus groves to the east near St. Cloud, and in Orange County to the north were increasing in importance and were becoming the twin economic engines of the area. Hundreds of thousands of head of cattle had roamed the open ranges throughout the 19th century and into the 1900s. But by the 1920s, automobiles were hitting so many free-roaming cattle on the expanding roadway system of the region that "No Cows on the Roads" became the cause, since drivers were liable to have to pay for or replace the "prime" bull or cow the cattleman would claim had been killed. Even so, the cattlemen continued to drive hundreds of herds of cattle right down the middle of Broadway to bring them either to the rail spur for loading and transporting to the port in Tampa, or to the boat docks for shipment south to Cuba via the Kissimmee and Caloosahatchee Rivers to Ft. Myers. These were the new and strange sights and sounds Alexander would grow accustomed to as he, just like the other store keepers, stood in front of their shops on the wooden sidewalk to watch the horsemen move their herds down the center of Kissimmee's commercial main street. They created excitement, activity, and enormous amounts of flying dirt and strong odors of wild cattle and their "droppings."

The region was so expansive, wide open to everyone, so attractive for cattle raising, that by 1920, a few ranchers individually owned, or claimed to own, as much as an astounding 150,000 acres of open lands—part palmetto, huge groves of thick pine trees, and part grasslands—on which, they found, they could raise one head for each ten acres. These were huge land owners and powerful individuals. "Big John" Sommerland was among the largest, most successful and most respected ranchers. He owned more than 160,000 acres of pastureland, and 16,000 head of cattle. Even more interesting, but true, though Jim Crow still reigned, one north Florida African ex-slave, Isaiah Johnston, was said to own more than 90,000 acres, having accumulated his land and cattle since the Civil War.

By the early 1920s, the wild Saturday night cattlemen parties, fights and drunkenness began giving way to the sedate tourist trade of the winter months. The cattlemen unhappily were becoming more constrained by the growing population, improved law enforcement, influence of residents, storekeepers, citizen-built churches and the voices of their preachers. The presence of finely dressed ladies caused them to gravitate to more remote places to the south like tiny Holopaw, Yee Haw Junction, and Keenansville with its two-story white stucco Heartbreak Hotel. Its hitching post and stories of wild shootouts in front of that hotel were legendary well into the 1930s.

Cattle ranching had been big business in the Kissimmee area for more than seventy-five years, and beef was "king." But, by 1920 there was no question that times were changing.

Settlers were moving in, investors were beginning to buy up available tracts of land, new roads were being built by the state, and downtown Kissimmee, in the middle of this growing state, was active with the newest automobiles. Horse drawn carriages and wagons were giving way to mechanized cars and trucks. The pace was picking up, and business was getting better than ever. It was a good time to own land, to operate a business, and to have holdings.

This world was so different from the only places Iskandar knew. In his tiny, impoverished village of Douma, everyone he knew and loved was "family"—cousins, uncles, aunts or extended relatives. But here, he began to realize, *no one* except his father was "family." Then, of course, there was Beirut, the big city of Lebanon. Some new people had arrived there, mostly Armenian refugees via Syria, but all spoke Arabic and were "like him." In Beirut, there were yet to be automobiles, mechanized trucks, and machines. Those would not begin to arrive until 1926 when Mr. Chrysler brought his first two trucks to Beirut to introduce his products to the Arab world.

Alexander had seen some cars and trucks in Marseille, but that city and Kissimmee could in no way be compared.

"This is my world now, *Baba*, with you. I have nothing without you, and I promise to you I will work as hard as I can and do nothing that will make you less than proud of me. I am grateful more now than ever for what you have done so that I may have an easier time than you did. Oh, *Baba*," he whispered as he embraced his father, "I am so proud of you and will do my best so that you will be proud of me. I only wish Milhelm and *Imei* were here with us."

Looking into his son's thoughtful eyes, he replied, "But I *am* proud of you, my son. I have always been proud of you. And I, too, wish they were here...more than I can tell you."

This was the world Alexander found when he arrived in Kissimmee in 1920—a city whose transition from a wild cattle-driven frontier village to a twentieth century city was well under way, and he and his father were exquisitely placed to share in that prosperity. And they both sensed that.

As Abraham had described, tourism was rapidly becoming an important economic source of income as Northerners were attracted more and more to the warmer climes, especially from December to April. Henry Plant's impressive hotels along his rail line in Tampa, Kissimmee, Haines City, and

Ft. Myers were magnets for tourists from the North. Central Florida towns like St. Cloud, Haines City, and new Lake Placid, named after Lake Placid, N.Y., Kissimmee, and even Orlando to the north were beneficiaries of the powerful demographic forces of rapidly increasing economic growth. New investments, growing wealth, new state roads providing accessibility, and the desire of more and more Northerners to relocate to warm Florida brought fresh money, shoppers, and simply more people to this climate-friendly, sparsely populated frontier...pleasing almost everyone, except for some of the cowmen who wanted it to stay the same.

"I'm gittin' tired of all these newcomers and their ways," complained many a cowman.

By 1922, these new visitors and settlers had begun to invest heavily n land, significantly driving up prices. St. Cloud, immediately to the east, had begun to be settled in 1909 by retired northern Civil War veterans and was attracting more and more settlers. At auction in New Jersey, for $50 they could buy a downtown lot, plus, an option on the adjacent lot, *and* a five-acre parcel in the country. By 1924, those $50 lots and five acres unbelievably were worth over $10,000. "Yankees" were eager to flee the harsh winters in the north in hopes life could be easier, and they would overcome their "consumption" as their doctors described the various bronchial diseases.

They also wanted to be in on the growing wealth of Florida and buy a "piece of the action," part of a cycle that would occur over and over again in Florida through the rest of the century and into the 21st century. The weather was pleasant, sometimes cold, but only for a few days in January or February, and regrettably, very hot in the summer, with the air filled with not only gentle breezes, but with millions of penetrating, stinging, maddening mosquitoes, horseflies, and gnats. There were lots of other creatures unfamiliar to the newcomers, like scorpions, poisonous snakes, cougars, foxes, bears, alligators and, gratefully, wild turkeys, pigs, and deer to hunt. Certainly, to Alexander, the terrain was an extreme contrast to north Lebanon. Here there were no 7,000-foot mountains, no olive groves, no deep winter snows, and no ancient cedar trees. It was very strange. Nothing was familiar, and the people seemed to respond to him differently from those in his village. Even in *laissez-faire* Marseille, he felt very comfortable, as he could speak their language. But, he thought, maybe that was because Hanna and Madeleine, in her youthful exuberance, embraced him instantly and completely.

But in America, there was freedom and opportunity. In this strange new environment, Alexander was convinced he could succeed and thrive. Here, the shopkeepers' faces were relaxed, without the fear that was so visible on the Lebanese under the Ottoman's rule. Here, he could believe that he would never go hungry again. Here, he could save enough money to return to Marseille and his love, Madeleine.

CHAPTER 15

A lexander looked around the plain, yet functional shop that first morning after his arrival, studying every shelf, every wall, the ceiling. The floor and ceiling were made of wood paneling. Sparse lighting fixtures hung from the high ceiling. There were shelves along the white plaster walls layered with notions, and stacks of bedding, towels, and bolts of cloth for making clothes on tables in the middle of the store. On the counter, near the front door, were candies in glass containers, and the store's books and a hand crank cash register that contained the money that was collected from the shoppers before they left the store.

Within an hour of their arrival that morning, an attractive middle-aged woman entered the store. She was fashionably dressed in a long cotton print dress with a full skirt flowing to her ankles, and long, full sleeves. Her hair was pulled up under a cloth bonnet with a large brim in the front to protect her eyes from the bright Florida sun. It was early June, and Central Florida was already very warm. The winter tourists had returned to their homes in the North, and Kissimmee was left to its year-round residents—cattlemen, farmers, and a few new emboldened settlers.

Cattlemen spent the slow summer months tending their herds on the open range while their cattle ate the grasses, put on weight and became large enough to market. Those with citrus groves worked their land, fertilizing, weeding, and tending their wagons and equipment. Shops, busiest before noon, were empty of customers many hours of the long, hot afternoons.

Women tended their homes and families, fanning themselves all day with palmetto branches or store-bought fans. Those who could spent afternoons cooling at nearby Lake Tohopekaliga with its covered pier and pavilion. Umbrellas were a necessity during the intense heat for many of the ladies, and this lady who now entered their store was no exception. Once inside the store, she folded her parasol.

"My, Mr. Thomas, it surely is getting warm these days," she exclaimed, smiling as she fanned her face with a paper accordion fan. "Do you have new goods from your trip?" She stood in the middle of the small store by a table laden with bolts of various fabrics, lifting the bolts with one hand, while holding the hand of her child in the other. "You promised me you would be bringing a surprise with you. What do you have for us?"

"My son is my surprise, Mrs. Andrews," said Abraham, smiling, speaking in his broken, heavily accented English and gesturing toward Alexander. "He just arrived with me from New York." Holding up three fingers, he said, "Three months from our village in Lebanon to Kissimmee. And, I have new goods for you to see. In a few minutes I will have them ready for you to see."

He turned to Alexander, motioning with his hand and speaking to Alexander in Arabic, "Iskandar, help me with these rolls of fabric and these boxes."

After Mrs. Andrews viewed the goods and selected several yards of the new cotton cloth from one of the bolts, she reached across the counter to pay Abraham. "It's nice you are back, Mr. Thomas," she smiled warmly. "I will tell my friends of your new lovely things." Looking at Alexander, she said, "And I am sure your son will be popular here, especially with the young ladies." She whispered as she bent toward him, "My, he certainly is handsome! Bless you, Mr. Thomas. Perhaps we will see you both in church on Sunday?"

"We will do our best, Mrs. Andrews. Thank you," he smiled, almost saying, *Shookrun*, as he watched her walk to the door.

Mrs. Andrews stopped and turned back to speak over her shoulder after considering Alexander, "Oh! I nearly forgot. I looked into finding a proper tutor for your son, Mr. Thomas. I believe I have someone who would be perfect," she exclaimed, keeping her small daughter in tow, while glancing at Alexander across the store. Then, smiling, she said, "Abigail Sommerland has returned for the summer from FSWC, you know, the Florida State Women's College. It's in Tallahassee."

Abraham turned and spoke in Arabic to his son, "Tallahassee, another Indian name, is where the government is located, in the north. It is also where young women go to the university." *I assumed his tutor would be an older woman or man, not a young girl.*

"I was just telling Alexander what you said, Mrs. Andrews. Please continue," he encouraged her, waving his hand in a cupping motion.

"Well," she responded, enthusiastically, "Abigail has been studying French and Home Economics at the college for three years and just arrived last week. Next year she will graduate and receive her Bachelor of Science degree. She's very smart; she makes all her own clothing, teaches cooking, and home bookkeeping. I am certain she would be very good at teaching English to young Alexander. Since she knows Florida so well, perhaps she can also teach him about our cattle country and citrus industry, so he can learn about our ways in Florida and America. She can ride a horse as well as anyone too! Does Alexander ride a horse?"

Abraham, watching her lips while trying to understand all she said, listened intently. It was difficult, but Mrs. Andrews had learned over the years to speak slowly to Abraham.

"Well, Mrs. Andrews," said Abraham as he struggled with his English, "I have not seen Iskandar—uh, Alexander—since he was ten years old, but he cared for the goat herds, and I am certain he can ride a horse—he was always adventurous. I do know that he was good in mathematics in school, and I am sure he will be a good student in English. Please tell Miss Sommerland that Alexander is eager to learn, and will be ready to meet with her as soon as possible. I am prepared to pay her what you asked, five lessons for one dollar each week. Thank you, Mrs. Andrews," Abraham confirmed as he bent at the waist in sincere respect.

"Perhaps, if you both come to church on the Sabbath, you will meet Miss Sommerland. Would you like that, Alexander?"

Not understanding a single word of the conversation, and too embarrassed to say anything, Alexander simply smiled and nodded his head at Mrs. Andrews as he watched her speak to Abraham, nodding to him while walking to the door.

"Sunday then. Good day, Mr. Thomas."

Turning to his father, Alexander said, in his native Arabic, "*Biyee*, I am useless without understanding what people say. I want to learn English as quickly as possible. It is so embarrassing, so strange. I feel like I'm not even part of the world here."

"You will be tutored this summer and begin attending the town school in a few months."

Near sunset, at the end of his first bewildering day, Alexander went upstairs with his father to his own almost barren room, and unpacked his meager personal belongings: an extra shirt and pants, a gift for his father of a carved piece of cedar wood from an ancient tree near the village, the mountain stone in his pocket, and his treasured sling from his suitcase. He delicately grasped the sling, pulled each of the two strands of leather, each a meter in length tied to the leather pouch in the middle, and set them on the cabinet next to the stone. The small stone was his reminder of his village and his youth. His tasks completed, he lay down on his small bed. For the few minutes before he fell into deep sleep, he fondled his gold ring, the ring Madeleine gave him that night on the hill overlooking Marseille. *Was it a dream? Is this ring a dream? Was I really in Marseille? It seems so long ago, so far away. Yet, something wonderful happened in Marseille. I fell in love with the most beautiful girl in the world. And she is in love with me. How much I have thought about you, Madeleine. Everyday, every night. Holding you. Kissing your beautiful full lips, feeling your face against mine. Oh, Madeleine! I like it here, but should I have stayed with you in Marseille? Did I do the right thing? When will I hold you again, my dear Madeleine? Soon we will be together again.* He dreamed and dreamed...of Madeleine.

"Come, Iskandar, it is late. I am sure you are hungry." His father was standing in the bedroom doorway, relishing his son's presence after so many years of living alone. "You slept well, son. It is morning now. Come be with me. You were very tired from your long trip so I let you rest. Let us eat, *Baba*."

He rubbed his eyes with his hands and replied, "Huh? Uh, yes, *Biyee*, of course. It's time to begin my first full day of my new life." He pulled on his pants and buttoned them, pulled on his white, full-sleeved shirt, stretched his suspenders, and buttoned his sleeves at the wrists. Then, he stepped into his only pair of leather shoes. He washed his face in the porcelain commode, and joined his father in the modest kitchen.

"Sit down, son. I have bread, cheese, olives, and yogurt from Stanos. I don't know how Americans can start the day without *jibneh*, *zeytoon*, and *laban*," he smiled.

After they opened the store for the day, Alexander wanted to take a walk and see his new surroundings. He decided to walk down the main street to get familiar with the town of Kissimmee. The sun was already casting its warmth, making everything bright. The sky was blue with lavender clouds hanging low in the western sky, typical of the early summer mornings. The street was bustling with the beginning of the day's activities. He saw the shopkeepers across Broadway opening their stores, sweeping their walks, and hoping for their first customers of the day. The street was busy on both sides. It was much busier and bigger than the *souk* in Douma, he thought as he watched people walking along the wooden sidewalks in front of the stores. He crossed the street, being careful of the noisy, unpredictable automobile traffic, and looked back at his father's store where he saw the name above. Although it said A. Thomas Company in large letters, and beneath the name it said: Dry Goods, Hats, Shoes and Notions, Alexander found the lettering totally foreign to him. Even though he could read French, it was too different for him to understand.

Another reminder, he said to himself, *I really have to learn English, or I am helpless.* As he walked the streets and wooden sidewalks, all he could do was look around. He could see the frame buildings, often separated by vacant sandy lots and scattered pine trees. They were mostly two stories tall with overhanging roofs. People were people coming and going. The women were friendly to him, and as the ladies would walk past him, he could sense the pleasant fragrances of perfume and talcum powder. Their fragrant smell reminded him of Marseille and Madeleine. Their dresses were ankle-length, wide at the bottom, with long sleeves, formfitting at the waist, and high-neck collars. Fashions were different from Marseille, he noted. Some carried parasols to block the sun. A few would smile at Alexander, returning his happy smile with a friendly "hello." He then said to each, with a slight bow of his head, using his French, *"Bonjour,"* or *"Allo,"* as he began to overcome his shyness. Men slightly nodded their head or tipped their hat brims, most neither speaking nor smiling, but acknowledging this unfamiliar young man. He began to feel better about his new home and the people he would get to know in time. His emotions took off. *I am free! I can be! I am home! In America!*

Many of the men wore their business suits, high-necked shirts with starched collars, ties, and straw skimmer hats. Others wore overalls or jeans and work shirts.

It's so warm here, he thought, *yet the men wear such tight-fitting, heavy clothes. I think it would be smarter the wear the loose-fitting abeyeh gowns men wore in Lebanon, with the sun-shielding cloth kifeyehs on their heads. If I wore that, I would really be different. But I must dress like everyone else, no matter how uncomfortable I am.*

After he had walked past the five blocks of buildings in the busy center of town, Alexander looked around and saw in the near distance a few scattered white wooden one- and two-story homes with sandy yards and shrubs. There were a few shade trees, but mostly pines around the downtown area. *So different,* thought Alexander. Between and beyond the houses was open land, and in the far distance, he saw cattle grazing on the lush grasses of the open pastures and in the piney woods. The strong pungent odor of the cattle pervaded the town, and their droppings were a clear message to him that there were hundreds of cattle everywhere in the area. He ventured down the dirt road even further until it became a path of wagon wheel grooves in the dirt leading into the grassy open lands.

As he walked into the unfenced pastureland and near the trees, he felt as if he were in a totally different world. So flat, so open, such a big sky.

His dark pants, suspenders, and long-sleeved white shirt were typical of a shopkeeper. There was a nice breeze on his face. Suddenly he saw the man on horseback galloping toward him and noted the contrast between his clothes and those of the rider who was wearing high-heeled boots with spurs at the heels, blue faded jeans and shirt with a red kerchief around his neck, and a wide-brimmed felt Stetson hat. Alexander focused on the man's eyes as he got closer and closer. Then, too close. The horse brushed against Alexander, knocking him down. As he got up, brushing off his pants, he glared at the rider. He noted the man's deeply sun-tanned face with his prominent, straight nose, the scar on his left cheek, the demeaning scowl on his lips, and his long brown hair that emerged from behind the large-rimmed hat and fell down the back of his neck. *I will remember everything about him. And I will remember this day,* thought Alexander, frustrated that he could not respond in English. *Yet I'd better be still and patient.* He watched the rider turn the horse and walk him back to Alexander so that the horse's head bumped Alexander. He was not afraid, for Alexander feared no man. And he was now free in America. Not wanting to get in trouble his first day, and yet, determined to protect himself with knowledge about such things, he quickly reached to the bridle and tightly grabbed the reins, now taking control of the horse's movements.

"Hey, storekeep'," said the surly rider. "You're a little outside your place, ain't ya?"

The sneer on his face deepened the knife scar on his cheek. He was obviously not friendly like the others in town. Alexander, not understanding, was so surprised by the man's actions that he could only stare back at him. He refused to speak, and could tell the man was deliberately being insulting. He acted like a Turkish soldier.

"Better git outta here, storekeep', before you git hurt. These cows will go anywhere. And so does my horse," he laughed at his lie. He jerked the reins but Alexander tightened his grip and his shoulder muscles, keeping the horse's head in spite of the rider's efforts. He noticed Alexander's strange clothes and haircut.

"This is the place for cowmen, not storekeepers. You don't belong here, you foreigner," he hissed. "Git now," the cattleman said as he waved his arm, pointed back to town and dug his spurs into the sides of the horse, causing Alexander to lose his grip, this time brushing hard against Alexander. The horse leaped, and then the cattleman rode off, laughing as he looked back at Alexander to make sure the intruder was on his way. Alexander watched, befuddled, angered and startled at the cowman's unfriendly behavior. He thought about his sling in his pocket. I could defend myself, but I'd better avoid trouble, at least for now, he said to himself. He took notice of the coiled black leather whip tied to the saddle, the black pistol and holster tied to the rider's right thigh with bullets in his gun belt. The horse had a brand on its hip: TJ.

As Alexander watched the cowman ride away, he was fascinated by this exchange. Not afraid, just unpleasantly surprised. The man certainly talked different, looked different, and, he supposed, because he lived on the range and rarely bathed, smelled different. He smelled like *khuda*, manure, Alexander smiled to himself. Still, he was struck by the strange aggressive nature and appearance of this man up close, the twang of his speech, so different from the others' he had heard speak in town. The whip. And the gun. *I guess he has to whip or shoot wolves that may attack his animals like we had to fight off in the mountains when they came to attack the goats. But only the Turks used guns. We never owned or used guns. We used the sling.* "I'll bring my sling with me next time in case he does that again," he said out loud to himself as he shrugged and turned, and walked back to town.

"You've been gone sometime, where did you go, Iskandar?" asked his father in Arabic as he entered the store.

"I walked down the street and to where I saw those animals we saw on the train. Out that way," he replied, pointing. "I met a man on a horse who wasn't very friendly. He spoke differently than the people in the town, Father, and he smelled different, too."

His father laughed and his face became a broad smile. "They are with the animals all the time; some even become like the animals. They sleep with them in the fields. I don't know when they bathe, but to me, they smell like *khudda*. I'd forget him. Most everyone here is kind. Don't worry about him. His kind are just rough people."

Alexander laughed again remembering his own similar thought. "He smelled bad and he was not nice. He acted like he was a Turkish soldier," he replied to his father. "I saw he had a rifle, a whip, and wore a pistol on his hip. Do they need guns here? Are there many bad animals around here?"

Abraham nodded and explained as best as he could, "There are some wild animals here and big poisonous snakes too. Actually, there are many kinds of animals—panther, foxes, deer, bears, and in the wet areas, there are even wild pigs and large alligators. So, guns are sometimes necessary for them, Iskandar. But, there are times when the young men drink too much and shoot their pistols while they race down the street. Sometimes, they even shoot their guns at each other. It can get dangerous. You have to be careful. Some of those men are crazy."

"Do I need one?"

"A gun? Not these days. If you stay in town, you will not need one. Certainly I do not want you to wear a gun on your hip in town."

"Well, I brought my sling. I think I will carry it with me, and even practice later out in the field. I'm pretty good with the sling. I'll show you."

He soon forgot about his encounter with the cowboy, as he had more important things to think about...like learning English.

During the next several days, from dawn until dark, Alexander diligently tended the shop with his father. Some slow days they stayed in the shop until late into the night waiting for one last purchaser, while constantly folding and refolding the cloths and rearranging their goods. When he got bored, he would venture into the fields and practice throwing his sling. He could swiftly hit a rodent from 50 feet without a sound except the soft whirring of the rotating pouch overhead. He always held one end of the thin leather lanyard in his right hand by pinching it with his largest right ring and small finger against the heel pad of his hand. He then would pinch the opposite end of the other thin lanyard between his index finger and his thumb. With a stone or marble in the small pouch in the middle of the two lanyards, he would then quickly whirl the pouch over his head three times, taking careful aim, and release the single lanyard between his index finger and thumb. The three feet of lanyards would reach a very high speed at release. The stone could actually kill small animals, like rodents, snakes or rabbits. It could also kill large animals like deer or pigs when it hit the animal's head.

Alexander was expert with the sling and could probably beat another man with a gun if they competed. He hit his target every time.

Wilbur McCray, whose family came to America from Scotland during the 1700s, was a kind soul, a friendly, self-assured popular young man in his early twenties who had no problem bridging the cowman-shopkeeper cultural gap. "I want a life that lets me be me," he would say. "Free to ride the range, sleep under the stars, and someday have my own herd."

One day, Wilbur, lean and muscular, rode his horse up to the hitching rail in front of the store. While he was in the store looking around for kerchiefs, he suggested to Abraham, "Mr. Thomas, you should stock Stetson hats here. There are a lot of people who would buy them. Right now, we have to buy 'em way down in Polk County in Bartow, because there's no place in Kissimmee to buy a new Stetson. I think you ought to try them."

"*Shookrun*, thank you, Mr. McCray, that's a good idea. I'll look into that and see if I can find a supplier."

Wilbur turned to Alexander, thinking they were about the same age. "Is this your son, Mr. Thomas?"

"Yes, his name is Iskandar, uh, Alexander, and he just arrived from Lebanon. He doesn't speak English yet, but he will."

"I've got some time. I'll show him around," he responded with a friendly smile. He was wearing a wide-brimmed felt hat, and jeans like the other cowman Alexander had run into, but his face was kinder. His hair was light brown, and, Alexander noticed, he also was wearing those same kind of spurs on his boots' heels, and a gun belt on his waist with the pistol's holster tied to his right thigh.

Wilbur beckoned to Alexander, "Come on, Alexander. Let's ride."

In the days that followed, Wilbur would come by the store, wave to Alexander to come outside, hook his arm under Alexander's and swing him up onto the horse behind him. The two of them rode around the lakeshore into the open areas and into the piney woods around the town, sometimes at a gallop, sometimes just walking, passing the hot, lazy summer days with Wilbur McCray playing the friendly tour guide. He became a weekly visitor to the store and showed Alexander the area by the lake and river, the boats, and the docks. He rode Alexander into the cattle pastures and taught him many things of local life. For reasons that were simple, Wilbur liked making friends with young Alexander. His grandparents were immigrants too, and he was well aware of the difficulties Abraham and his own father had faced. He was happy to find a young man his age, a newcomer to Kissimmee who wasn't a cowman but looked strong. He soon became a good and reliable friend to Alexander who grew to look forward to his visits. Alexander, who watched everything, noticed everything, and listened as best he could, became familiar with the area because of Wilbur, his first new friend in America. He came to look on Wilbur as a brother...a more knowledgeable brother, especially of his new world...perhaps even as a surrogate Milhelm: a young cowman his age who was friendly, spoke good English though with a Southern twang, and as a result, he was completely relaxed with Wilbur and willing to trust him. Wilbur, basically a good man who loved the freedom of the open range and sleeping under the stars, was self-assured and happy with his roots and his life. Consequently, he was willing to share all that with this new immigrant who apparently had talents but surely needed a friend to find his way in this very unfamiliar country.

"Want me to show you how to handle a pistol, Alexander?" Wilbur said to his new friend, standing in the piney grove, showing his gun to Alexander. "Lemme show you how to aim it and hit that stump over there. Think you can do it?" he asked as he pointed to a rotting pine stump.

After trying unsuccessfully several times to aim the gun, frustrated but still confident, Alexander pulled his sling out of his pocket, placed a stone in the pouch and after three fast turns over his head, let the stone fly in a blur. Smack! The stone drove into the stump.

"Wow! That was something, Alexander. You sure make that stone fly. How'd you do that so quick?"

Alexander just smiled and shrugged his shoulders. He really could understand so little of what people said to him. But his friendly smile seemed to be adequate, maybe infectious, at least for now. Even though his new friend was good to him, Alexander still felt embarrassed that he could not yet converse with Wilbur. Much of their "conversation" was through hand signals, not speaking.

Then, Wilbur pulled his coiled whip from his saddle strap and swung it over his head. With a quick jerk, the whip tip reversed on itself and made a loud report: CRACK! Alexander simply stood and watched as Wilbur cracked his whip several times. "That's how we get the cows to move out of the pine trees, Alexander. If you don't git a cow out of the pines, they'll just circle a tree for hours until you give up. That's why we all carry whips. And that's why they call us 'crackers'." He laughed at his own comment.

One afternoon, Alexander bought a few handfuls of marbles from the hardware store next door, put a handful in his pocket, and left a handful in a dish on his father's store's counter. When Wilbur came by, he was ready.

They rode Wilbur's horse out to the piney woods by the stump. With hand signals, Alexander challenger Wilbur to see who could hit the stump the fastest. With Wilbur's hand hanging by his hip ready to draw his gun, Alexander likewise held the lanyards of his sling beside his leg. "Go," said Wilbur as he reached for his gun. At the same moment, Alexander whirled the lanyard. The bullet struck the stump just as Alexander's marble reached the same stump.

"What the hell? How'd you do that?" exclaimed Wilbur. "Damn! You're fast!" He slapped his thigh and bent over with laughter.

All Alexander could do was smile as he placed another marble in the pouch of his sling. *Just let T.J. try to mess with me,* he thought to himself with a smile.

CHAPTER 16

$\mathcal{T}$hat next Sunday morning, Abraham and his son walked to church. Alexander was wearing his good white shirt buttoned up to his neck, and a new coat his father bought for him during the week from a friend's shop on Broadway.

"Good morning, Mr. Thomas. Good morning, Alexander. I'm so glad to see you here at church. And isn't it a beautiful day? But it certainly is warm," Mrs. Andrews said as she fanned herself and wiped her forehead with her white kerchief.

Alexander smiled and nodded in response.

Mrs. Andrews was dressed in her pretty "Sunday" dress; the bodice was decorated with delicate lace, with cuffs similar to her high-necked collar, and the skirt that flowed to her ankles was patterned in blue pastel flowers. A cloth bonnet with a ribbon tied under her chin covered her hair. Scanning the faces of the exiting congregation, she turned, smiled broadly, and said, "Just a moment, I see Abigail Sommerland now." She stepped a few feet away and waved her hand while calling out, "Yoo-hoo, Abigail!"

Alexander watched as she spoke to a very pretty young lady who had briefly caught his eye in church as the only person in the congregation of his age. She had on the same style of dress and bonnet as Mrs. Andrews, but was tall and slender, just a bit shorter than he, but taller than Mrs. Andrews. She had a very nice smile, and focused on Mrs. Andrews' eyes as she politely listened. She glanced over her shoulder at Alexander and smiled broadly, nodding her head as she listened intently and watched Mrs. Andrews tilt her head toward Alexander. "I mustn't point," she whispered. Alexander, uplifted by her response and attracted to her friendliness, returned her smile with a courteous European nod of his head. Mrs. Andrews, acknowledging the tacit reaction between Abigail and Alexander, pulled Abigail's hand as they both walked to Alexander and Abraham. *Wow*, he wondered, *who is this?*

Abigail Sommerland, at twenty-one, was a perfectly beautiful young woman about to enter her fourth and final year at the women's college in Tallahassee. The only daughter of one of the region's largest ranchers, she was adventurous, self-assured, and creatively independent-minded. Her panache attracted the glances of every young man in the area and she knew the power she had over them when she decided on rare occasions to be flirtatious.

However, she was not willing to relinquish her self-control when it came to men. Her father's reputation and protectiveness strongly influenced her behavior. As a result, she was very particular and reticent. While loyal to her family, she was fun loving, passionate about life, playful, and jealously guarded her individuality. Although she had grown up as a tomboy, riding her horse as fast and expertly as any cowman, she was comfortable in social surroundings, having been groomed by her mother who had come from Philadelphia to Kissimmee as a young woman twenty-four years earlier. Her family was prominent, wealthy, and a part of Philadelphia society. She was cultured, and, in spite of their frontier life, was determined to teach her only daughter the finer things of life and the best manners.

It was difficult at first for Abigail's mother to leave her family in the upper society life for a frontier cattle town. She had met young John Sommerland through family friends that glorious summer when John had visited his cousins living on the Main Line outside Philadelphia. Surprising herself as much as her girlfriends, she had fallen in love with this tall, strong, independent rancher up from that "new frontier of Florida" as it was called, a "place of unbelievable rewards for the young and adventurous."

Born in their fine home nearly two years after leaving Philadelphia, Abigail grew up on the family ranch in Kissimmee, and, adhering to her mother's tutelage, dutifully fulfilled her mother's goals of being a lady schooled in the social graces. At the same time, she learned from her father, lovingly nicknamed "Big John" by her mother, how to ride a horse, cut cattle, and hunt and fish in the nearby rivers and lakes. She had made the family very proud over the years. She always knew she was loved, probably spoiled a bit, and yet very kind to her friends. Her mother made sure their home was always open to her playmates, and that Abigail shared her childhood toys, then her horses with her friends. "Always share, darling. Never be selfish. We have so much, remember that."

Abigail was game for any new adventure, so when she had an opportunity to teach English to a new young immigrant, although at first reluctant, she quickly decided it would be a new and unusual experience and would help fill the hot, quiet summer months at home before leaving for her final year of college.

"Good morning, Mr. Thomas," Abigail spoke with a very sincere smile as she gracefully extended her hand to Abraham. Then, tilting her head toward his son in a slightly flirtatious manner, continued, "And you must be Alexander." She smiled again, extending her soft hand, palm down, looking into his eyes.

"*Bon matin, enchanté,*" Alexander responded, in French, returning her smile.

Surprised and impressed, Abigail responded with an even wider smile, "Oh my, you speak French. *Merci.*"

Mrs. Andrews interjected with a smile, "Alexander, I am pleased to introduce you to Miss Abigail Sommerland. She has agreed to be your English tutor for the summer, until she returns to school in September. Isn't that nice? It so happens that she has studied French at FSCW and that should be helpful to you both."

"Shall I call you Alexander?" Abigail demurred softly in French, looking teasingly into Alexander's eyes.

"*Oui*, mademoiselle," he replied, a bit nervous, catching only his name, as he returned her smile, looking into her large brown eyes fringed with long dark lashes, her face framed by long, wavy brown hair. Her high cheekbones gave her an exotic look, favorably compared to the other older women in town.

"When can you begin?" she inquired. "Tomorrow?"

Seeing his father nod, he replied, "*Oui.*" *As soon as possible*, he thought, looking at the prettiest girl he had seen since arriving in Kissimmee. *And I thought my tutor would be a man, not a lovely young woman!*

"Early tomorrow then," she said. "It is cooler in the morning." Turning to Abraham, she queried, "Can he come to my home at nine o'clock, Mr. Thomas?"

Abraham responded, "Absolutely, Miss Sommerland, he will be there. He is very anxious to get started on his English lessons. He is a good student, and will, I am sure, progress rapidly, especially learning from you. You are very kind to do this for Alexander."

"It will be my pleasure, Mr. Thomas. He looks like a fine, young man, and will make a wonderful addition to our community. I am also sure the young ladies in Kissimmee will be happy to meet such a handsome young man. I will do my best." Then turning back to Alexander, she smiled directly at him and continued in French, "Soon you will be speaking excellent English. Tomorrow then, Alexander," "I will expect you at nine o'clock in the morning. You know my father's home, don't you, Mr. Thomas?"

"Yes, I do. I will show him today. And thank you, Mrs. Andrews," Abraham said, looking to his friend with a slight bow.

"*Au revoir,* mademoiselle," smiled Alexander to Abigail as she, now flattered, stepped away with Mrs. Andrews.

"She is a very pretty, young woman, wouldn't you say, Alexander?"

"She's very nice," responded Alexander as he fondled his ring, remembering Madeleine's beautiful wide smile, longing to receive her letters. *I miss you so much, Madeleine. I think I'll go home and write you another letter and tell you of my new home, and how hard I will work on my lessons and in my work so that I can save enough money to send for you.*

He knew he would not write of meeting Abigail. It was so complicated, he thought. *Then, he calculated...it's been six weeks since I left Marseille. My letters surely have arrived by now. Soon, I should be receiving letters from Madeleine.*

CHAPTER 17

"Good morning, Alexander," Abigail welcomed him at her door as he walked up the steps to her porch and front door, trying out her stilted French to impress Alexander. "You are here exactly at nine o'clock." Smiling, she said, returning more comfortably to her native English, and with a hopeless grin and shrug, "I'm glad you are not late, and I'm glad you didn't come too early. Ladies are never supposed to be ready too soon," she smiled sweetly. "It makes them look anxious." She spoke now as the teacher of social graces. Cupping her hand to her mouth, she laughed, while comfortably educating her student. "Oh, I think I gave you a secret. Do come in. We will sit in the dining room and begin. I have books, paper, and pencils."

Not understanding her words, but interpreting her friendliness and directions, Alexander followed Abigail up the few steps into the beautiful Sommerland home. He had never seen such a home in his life. It was larger than any home Alexander had ever seen. He marveled at its size and beautiful furnishings. It was modest in its design, having white clapboard siding, a large open wrap around porch, large windows, and two stories with dormers providing light to the bedrooms on the second floor. It was also well-shaded by tall oak trees. *Someday*, he thought to himself as he gazed up at the big house, his eyes sweeping across the entire property, *maybe*.

His stone, one-room home in Douma, his uncle's rooms in Marseille, and his father's rooms above the store were so sparse and humble. Now he had a reality to dream about and hope for.

During the first bewildering but challenging week, Alexander met with Abigail at her home for his basic English lessons. Five mornings each week thereafter, Alexander diligently arrived promptly at nine o'clock, and sat down at the dining room table opposite her. They both were very intent and focused. The lessons consumed a full hour devoted to elementary steps in learning the alphabet, then on to identifying pictures and words, or simple phrases like: "see the horse, house, store, street." The early conversations were stilted, clumsy and difficult, but when he stumbled, she would smile to minimize his embarrassment. Sometimes, upset with himself, he would blurt out something in Arabic or French, causing her to laugh. He appreciated her sense of humor and her patience. It helped him from becoming too frustrated.

Alexander was intent on learning as fast as he could and so he listened to her every word. But there was no boy-girl connection. His growing respect for Abigail just seemed to accelerate his learning process. He liked it when she tilted her head and when she would look at him out of the corners of her beautiful eyes, sometimes cheering him, happily applauding with her hands, and sometimes showing a quizzical look when he erred. Her patience was always accompanied by an open, friendly smile. She liked Alexander and found herself enjoying her new summer teaching job.

"Good morning, Alexander. Today, the beginning of our third week, we'll review all that you have learned."

"*Bon*," Alexander quickly replied, pulling from the stack of elementary books the one with names matching pictures of structures, animals, fauna, and just about everything printed that Abigail had gotten for him from the library.

"I'll point at pictures, and then you say the correct word. Okay?"

It was very much an exercise that first and second graders repeated day after day in the public school, but the recitation accelerated since Alexander had already studied diligently the night before. He had completed his schooling in Douma, though in Arabic and some Russian as he was taught by the missionary from Russia.

As the lessons progressed, they began spending more time together. Abigail, enjoying her teaching and Alexander's eagerness, extended the lessons to two hours. So concentrated on the subject matter were the two, now sitting side by side, that the sessions began to stretch to noon.

The repetitious exchange of Abigail pointing and Alexander responding became a pleasant game for the two young adults. They easily laughed together as Alexander might occasionally mix-up or confuse the words.

"*Towleh*, er, table," he said as she pointed.

She laughed. "No, Alexander. That's a chair. *This* is a table," pointing to the opposite page.

"Oh. *Shookrun*...uh...sorry."

"How about this?"

He hesitated for a moment. "That's a bicycle."

"*Oui*, yes! Exactly right!" She laughed as she patted his hand, becoming friendlier and more familiar each day.

"You are making good progress, Alexander. But let's stop now. We've been at this for three hours. Time for us to take a break," she declared, looking at the wall clock about to chime twelve o'clock.

"Excuse me," Mrs. Sommerland interrupted with a smile as she stepped into the room, wiping her apron with both hands, "would you two like to have lunch?"

At welcomed breaks like these, Abigail would speak to Alexander, first in French, and later, more and more, slowly in English.

"You are going to help me improve my French, Alexander, as much as I help you speak English." As she laughed, Alexander felt himself noticing how really pleasant and kind she was. And beautiful too. He couldn't help but grow to like her very much. They were becoming good friends as the weeks passed by. Sometimes, they would take breaks and walk in the gardens behind the house. They strolled together so Abigail could point at the trees, flowers, houses, and automobiles in the street—teaching Alexander the names of everything in sight, trying to expand his vocabulary.

One day after a lesson, Abigail decided to change her approach. She spread a blanket on the grass in the garden and opened a picnic basket of chicken salad sandwiches, fruit, and lemonade. They sat next to each other, almost touching, and as they enjoyed lunch, speaking in French, Abigail told Alexander all about her life at Florida State College for Women in Tallahassee. She spoke of the campus and the fact that only girls attended there. "Boys can attend the University of Florida in Gainesville," she remarked. "Imagine all those girls in Tallahassee, and all those boys so far away, yet so close. Sometimes," she laughed, "some of the boys drive over in packed cars and come to our campus to meet new girls. They come on Saturdays and take girls out dancing. It's a lot of fun," she laughed. "Don't tell my parents, but sometimes I go out on Saturday nights with a group of girls so we can see the boys, and dance." She hastened to add, "I never was alone with a boy. That wouldn't be right, would it? Only with groups." She turned and looked into Alexander's eyes as she placed her hand on his, making him a bit nervous. She knew it would tempt him to find her even more attractive. Alexander was surprised to find a growing sense of jealousy as Abigail laughed about the boys driving over to see her and her friends.

Abigail, twenty-one years old, nearly three years older than he, knew much more about flirtation than Alexander, and was much more grown-up than he. But, Alexander was not as innocent as she may have thought.

Carefully choosing his words to make a sentence, he spoke haltingly in

English, "I am glad...you are my tutor...Abigail...and I am glad...we are... becoming friends...you are a wonderful...mademoiselle," he said as he clasped her hand and looked in her eyes, surprising her and himself, and becoming aware of how appealing touching her felt to him. He also noticed that Abigail, at first indifferent to his touch, was now responding warmly, sometimes smiling demurely, sometimes even turning her head toward him, realizing she was enjoying his touch. There was a growing sense of physical attraction that slowly began to replace the purely platonic initial relationship.

"*Merci,* Alexander," she quickly responded, feeling his hand grip hers. "And you are a fine, handsome young man any girl would be proud to be with. I too am glad we're becoming close friends."

She quickly turned her head away from his deep, sensual eyes, sensing increasingly warm feelings of affection for him. She thought to herself, *after all, Kissimmee is not filled with internationally cultured, handsome young men like Alexander, even if I am older than he. Hmmm, I am really beginning to enjoy being with him...let's see where this leads.* Her leg somehow leaned firmly against his. She knew she was flirting and was pleased with herself.

As they sat snacking on the sandwiches, Abigail stretched her arm to him, "Apple?" she smiled at her double entendre, enjoying her flirtatious biblical temptation.

He glanced at the apple and watched her other hand polish another apple on her dress that covered her leg. She brought the shiny apple to her lips and smiled at him as she gently bit into it, juices tantalizingly dripping from the corners of her mouth onto her chin. He watched her eyes, noting that as she looked at him, her eyes lowered seductively. He then noticed for the first time that Abigail's dress, normally falling below her knees, was now draped with the hem forming a line across her smooth, firm thighs. He felt a warmth in his thighs as he gazed at her shapely legs tapering down to small ankles, her skin unblemished and tanned bronze from the warm Florida sun.

Abigail, now looking out the corner of her eyes, slyly glanced and caught Alexander staring at her legs, and smiled as she teasingly licked her lower lip. She didn't immediately pull her dress lower. *I wondered when he would notice,* she thought to herself. *He's not at all like those eager boys from Gainesville. I'm beginning to like teasing him. He's such an innocent. He tries not to notice. Maybe I'll have to teach him about life, about women, about college girls,* she thought to herself mischievously as she smiled confidently. She tempted by flipping her hem lower as she watched his eyes. After a few minutes, finished with lunch, she lazily stretched, then stood.

"Would you like to go for a ride on horseback, Alexander? I can show you some of the area around Kissimmee. We have nice open pastures, piney woods, rolling hills, and some beautiful lakes."

"I would like that very much, Abigail," he replied, not realizing she was anxious to ride right then. "Can we do it after my English lessons one day?"

"What a wonderful idea," she diplomatically responded. Disappointed and foiled, she thought maybe he had to get back to the store. So she gave him the credit for not seeming too eager, something smart women do to men. "I'll make a picnic basket, and after your lessons, we'll have two horses saddled, and ride over to Lake Joyce. It will be fun. Next week, Alexander, how about Monday?"

"Yes," he responded eagerly, looking forward to just the two of them riding alone.

That weekend, Alexander wrote another long letter to Madeleine describing his lessons, and how much he was enjoying his new life. While his letters were in French, he wrote a few words in English, hoping to impress Madeleine with his new knowledge. Each letter always ended with the words, *je t'aime, mon amour.*"

> *My dearest Madeleine, my life here is getting better each day. I work at the store from daybreak preparing for the day, learning all I can about our inventory and business from my father. Then, always just before nine, I walk to the Sommerland home for my English lessons. Miss Sommerland, who is older than I, is a really good teacher. I work hard those three hours, and study in my room at night. There is little to do here in this small village, so I have most evenings to prepare for my instruction. My father goes to bed right after dinner, depending on what time we close the store.*
>
> *The Sommerlands are big ranchers, and the whole family works hard.*
>
> *I miss you, chérie, and hope soon I will receive your letters. Je t'aime, mon amour.*"

CHAPTER 18

*C*hat's enough English for today," Abigail exclaimed, already dressed in jeans, boots, and faded blue shirt. "It's Monday, and I promised you we'd go riding together today," Abigail smiled. "It's time for you to learn to ride a horse if you're going to live in Kissimmee! I've had two horses saddled up for us. I'll ride the bay, and you can ride the Appaloosa—she'll treat you right."

"I can ride a horse. Let's go look."

Alexander's first ride in a western saddle was really exciting. Back home in his village, he had, on occasion, ridden a horse up and down the mountain path, but his horse, "Toufeh," was an older, slower Arabian, and knew the path well. Those days, he rode on a makeshift saddle of wood similar to those used on camels, or, sometimes, bareback with only a blanket thrown over the horse's back.

Abigail spent the afternoon happily riding with Alexander, at a walk at first, teaching him, and coaxing her new friend. "Hold the reins lightly. Let her go." She led them from the family stables through the piney woods, out onto the pasture about three miles, then down the gentle grassy slope to the lake on the family farm.

"Now, let's sit over there by the lake for awhile, Alexander," she told him while she pointed to the shoreline. "We'll take a rest."

He was concentrating on guiding the mare with his thighs and the reins, so he just smiled and laughed, as he was concentrating, hoping to learn rapidly how to ride in a western saddle for the first time. He enjoyed riding horseback with Abigail, and wanted more opportunities to be with her, and to learn every American way he could.

Each morning when Alexander would arrive on Abigail's front porch precisely at nine o'clock, she would meet him at the door with her lovely smile and greet him in deliberate English, "Good morning, Alexander. And how are you feeling today?"

"I feel good, Abigail," he would reply with a smile, more confident and bold in the English greeting she had taught him, as she opened the screen door, inviting him in.

She would lead him by his hand into the parlor where they could sit opposite each other—he on the fine armchair with the high back, she on the settee. They would go through verbal lessons for the first hour.

"Come sit by me, Alexander. We must now read together for awhile." She patted the settee next to her. He was always a bit shy and nervous to sit so close to her, but when he did, their hips might accidentally touch, sending an electric feeling through his strong, firm body. And if she brushed his hand with her delicate, smooth, soft hand, he would almost faint from the warmth and sensual feelings. These were feelings he had only at Abigail's lessons. Yet, he knew he could not move toward her. He was shy and inexperienced. He had been with Madeleine, but that was different. She was younger than he. But Abigail was older. Even as he felt aroused by Abigail, and complimented that a 21-year-old woman student from a university found him attractive, he was also aware of the sense of guilt, as though he was betraying Madeleine's trust. He was daily being caught up in a constant dilemma: He liked Abigail who was here, but he had a sense of near betrothal to Madeleine, six weeks away by rail and ship, and from whom not one letter had been received in all the weeks since he left Marseille. He was torn every day.

Alexander's English abilities improved more and more, and everyday his confidence increased. *Soon, I won't be embarrassed to speak to anyone in Kissimmee. Soon, I will be a real American, not different.*

After reading together, the tutor and student would move to the den and sit at her father's desk where, again, they would sit next to each other in separate chairs to practice writing, at first the alphabet, then names, then sentences. Alexander laughed with a sense of great accomplishment when Abigail taught him to print, then write in script his own name. He wrote his name twenty times, looked at the paper, put the pen down, sat back and smiled. "Thank you, Abigail. You have brought me to a wonderful place. Look! That is my name. Now, I will show you how I write my name in Arabic. Watch."

"Oh, Alexander, your Arabic lettering is beautiful. And you write right to left. Isn't that interesting! And with French, you can now write in three languages!"

There were times like this when Alexander's background would enter their conversation. He would tell Abigail of his village, his ancient heritage, his mother, and how important these things were to him.

One day he wanted to tell her of his ancestry. "The Phoenicians, my ancestors, traded and settled throughout the huge Mediterranean Sea, Abigail. All the way past Gibraltar, even to Britain. Imagine. Sailing ships 2,000 years before Christ. Even Hannibal of Carthage was of Phoenician heritage. He defeated the Romans, you know. And though I am an immigrant here in America, I have an ancestry equal to any. And I am just like them. I am willing to become like other people here, to work hard, and become a successful American. That is my destiny. That is why God brought me here." He smiled as he proudly explained his heritage.

She reached out to touch his hand, smiled warmly at Alexander, leaned over and kissed him on his cheek. "I am so proud of you, Alexander. You have done very well with your lessons, and it has only been, let's see, eight weeks. Goodness, how time has flown by! Only four more weeks and I must leave Kissimmee to return to school." She frowned. "There are so many more things I want to teach you." With that, she smiled and looked at him coquettishly out of the corner of her eyes.

He scowled at her news. Yet, that look of hers was so enticing to him. He reached to his cheek and touched his fingers where she had kissed him. As he looked into Abigail's eyes, returning her stare, he wanted to hold her close. But he knew he couldn't. She was everything he could want. Her slender figure called for him as he held back the urge to touch her. Every time Abigail touched him or looked at him with her eyelids heavy or out of the corners of her eyes, or smiled warmly at him, his body would get warm and the hormones would begin to rage throughout his body, and his self-esteem would become reinforced. Somehow, he was able to permit himself to feel these attractions to Abigail but as soon as he returned to the store or to his room, he would feel badly, as he resumed thinking about Madeleine and how much he missed her. *One letter. Just one letter is what I need. Where are they?*

He knew Abigail liked him, but he was an immigrant, different, and she was so desirable, so cultured, so accepted everywhere. She was from a prominent and important family. As a consequence, he was awkward and reluctant to make any advances. *Better to avoid the possibility of rejection. What if she were to draw away and not want to teach me anymore?*

Sometimes, when Abigail's mother would interrupt with sandwiches, or to announce noontime, he would have those same contradictory emotions. He enjoyed sitting with Abigail each day while doing his lessons, and yet, he knew he had to leave soon and work at his father's store until dark.

During the slow summer months, on some days, he and his father might have realized only a dollar in sales. But unless it was needed for food, it was deposited in their "bank in the field."

Alexander's days all that summer were spent with Abigail in the mornings, and afternoons and evenings with his father in the store where he worked long hours, and then studied his lessons into the late hours of the night. He knew that, working at the store with his father gave him a sense of purpose, slow as it seemed, to an independent person such as he was.

Abigail and Alexander were becoming very close and enjoying each other's company before she returned to FSCW in September for her senior year. After the lessons, they shared lunch, sometimes on the back lawn. Horseback riding became part of their daily activity. He was becoming a very good horseman thanks to Abigail's advice and encouragement.

She was bright, independent, and extraordinarily adventurous…a very exciting young lady. She could ride a horse as well as any cowman in the region. When she wanted to ride fast, she would dig her heels into the horse's sides, rise up off the Western saddle and, with bent knees, stand in the stirrups and lean forward. She loved the sense of liberation, of freedom as the wind blew on her face with her long brown hair flowing behind her. She showed him how to rope a calf, tie it up, and cut cattle from the herd. She would yell to Alexander, "Watch me and do as I do!"

"You are so good!" he would exclaim with pride.

Alexander couldn't help but be fascinated by this lovely creature. And although her father was one of the wealthiest ranchers in Florida, and he was a poor, inexperienced immigrant, they were becoming very important to each other. She was so kind and patient with him. Her gentleness inspired him in many ways. He was determined not to disappoint her, studying his lessons diligently every night in his room, so that before she completed their summer, he would be fluent in English. And with her lack of any perceptible, albeit slight southern accent, he too would lose his accent of "broken English" with a Middle Eastern emphasis. For example, he learned to pronounce the letter P instead of using the letter B like many of his countrymen. They would say, "Look at the beeble" instead of "look at the people."

He was inspired to become "American," as his father always told him. "We are in America. Be an American." So he was learning the new customs, greetings, slang, and behavior as he studiously watched Abigail's gestures and listened carefully to her every word. He learned to sit properly at a table, keep his elbows off the table, and utilize the fork instead of wrapping food in bread, as was the custom in the Near East. He learned so much from Abigail, and if it weren't for Madeleine, he would have found himself drawn romantically to this lovely, intelligent woman.

Each of them grew very fond of the other, as they eagerly spent so much time together. They would laugh at his "almost English," and his falling off the horse trying to get down after his first try at lassoing a calf.

"You are becoming quite the cowman, Alexander!"

"Because of you, Abigail, because of you," he smiled.

She too was drawn to his warmth, his strong desire to learn, and his kindness toward her and her mother. Especially, she found this handsome, young, hard-working dedicated immigrant from Lebanon worldly, almost exotic, and his sensual eyes magnetic. Even though he was three years younger than she, she was enticed to affection, but held back. He was certainly different from the boys at the University of Florida who would drive over to Tallahassee on weekends, get drunk, and try to get their arms around her. "They're so childish. Not like you, Alexander." And he was really different from the common young men of Central Florida who would seek her out. They were so rough-edged, so crude. And, in spite of his meager income now, she believed without doubt Alexander would have a prosperous future. He was so determined. His father, though a shopkeeper and not at all in her social circles, was hard working, with a reputation for honesty, integrity, and ambition...and Alexander was becoming known to be the same.

One day, late in August, Abigail raced Alexander on horseback across the wide pasture, through the piney woods to the largest lake on the family's ranch outside of Kissimmee. She laughed all the way, waving to him and yelling, "Catch me, Alexander! Catch me!" And while Alexander laughed as he trailed behind, trying to catch her, her bay was just too fast. The wind was cool on their faces on this typically hot afternoon. The sky was overcast with large gray rain clouds building, causing a strong cooling breeze ahead of the rain.

Abigail, now keenly aware her time together with Alexander was drawing short, realized she likely wouldn't see him until Thanksgiving, and then only for a day or two. They would not again have all these days together, she knew, as she would graduate next year, and then what? These thoughts drove Abigail to become more anxious to express her feelings for this young man more boldly than she might have if she was not leaving Kissimmee very soon. She became very candid and emboldened.

They finally reached the lake and dismounted. Together, they flopped down on the grass, resting, touching slightly, and laughing together as they lay back side by side looking into each other's eyes, her light brown hair cascading over her shoulder onto the grass.

"That was fun, Alexander. It's always fun being with you. You have become my very best friend. You Lebanese...Phoenician!" She laughed aloud at her candor and smiled warmly as she reached for his hand. "You are a wonderful, kind young man. I'm glad we have become such close friends. Most American men have difficulty being a friend of a pretty girl. I'm glad you are not that way. I like being with you and want us always to be best friends."

"Abigail, you are so good to me. I cannot express to you how happy I am hearing your words. America is such a wonderful free country, and I have so much to learn. You have taught me how to become an American, and how to speak English properly. I want us to be close all our lives. You must know that I am determined to be successful here, and maybe soon own my own land, raise my own cattle, and establish myself. I need friends and help to get there. And so, I am grateful to you. You are my best friend!"

She listened intently to his message, wanting to help him even more. She felt a sense of exhilaration looking up at the expansive blue sky, feeling the wind blow across them. Then she felt his hand on hers, saw the olive complexion of his skin next to her pale white hand, and felt drawn to him, Abigail reached out to hold his hand. Then, with an urge to be closer, she reached to touch Alexander's face, then slowly leaned toward him and gently kissed him on his lips.

It was such an electric moment, a wonderful surprise for Alexander, lying in the grass next to this beautiful young woman. When she gripped his hand tighter, he felt that unfamiliar warmth that he had known only with Madeleine now surge throughout his body. He felt himself grow firm being so close to Abigail, sensing she wanted to be closer to him. He almost desperately wanted her near him. But he was so shy and intimidated that he did nothing but look at her lovely face and smile. Her delicate kiss was like a soft breeze whispering past his lips, barely touching his with hers. And as she kissed him, their eyes met each other's, transfixed. He would never dare to kiss her in return. His thoughts raced, thinking of all the reasons *not* to pursue her. He was too afraid. And, she was older; she was his tutor. Her father was one of the most powerful men in the region, and he was a young immigrant with a modest life. And always, in the recesses of his mind was Madeleine. He was always in conflict as he experienced his growing fondness for Abigail. But his heart would not let him go further with her. He continually reminded himself that he would return to Marseille to Madeleine one day, and he could not allow himself to fall in love with Abigail. Friends, he cautioned himself over and over, I want her to be my best friend. Abigail was wonderful and very magnetic for Alexander. He adored her. But she was not Madeleine.

So, he did nothing. He didn't move, but he didn't want her to pull away either. He just kept looking at her and gripped her hand slightly. When she kissed him again, he got nervous, and while he kept his gaze on her face, he realized he wanted her so much.

Then he spoke, "Your kiss was so wonderful, Abigail. It's difficult just lying here next to you. I am growing warm all over. You are so beautiful and I am helpless beside you." He dared to touch her cheek with his hand, and reached over and kissed both her cheeks. "I think I had better stand up and walk a little." He was overcome with mixed emotions and reticence.

As he rose, she reached her hand to him and said, "You are so dear, Alexander. Go for your walk, but don't be long. Come back and we'll lie here together some more."

He nodded and slowly walked away, looking back at Abigail, with a wondering look on his face. She had risen on her elbow and followed him with her eyes. She felt good; glad she had kissed this handsome, sweet young man with the deep brown eyes. She watched his every move, becoming more and more enamored, realizing she was treading farther than she should.

As she watched Alexander stroll through the tall grass along the lake's shore, she sat up, reached to her feet and pulled off her boots and socks. She loved the feel of the cool grass between her toes as she slid her feet through the grass, then lay back, arms outstretched. Her feet almost reached the lake's shoreline filled with tall, thick grasses. They moved closer to the water's edge. Too close.

She watched Alexander, now perhaps thirty feet away near the water's edge, as she slid her toes back and forth in the grass. Alexander searched around and found a gathering of stones. He grabbed a handful and put them in his pocket. Then he pulled his sling from his back pocket and pulled the leather strands together. As he wrapped one strand around his last two fingers on his right hand and pinched the end of the other strand between his thumb and forefinger, he placed a stone into the pouch. The weighted pouch by his side hung nearly to the ground.

He spotted a ripple in the lake, quickly whirled the pouch over his head three times, and let the stone fly. Almost in an instant, the stone struck the water's surface exactly at the ripple. He smiled at his accuracy.

"Nice shot, Alexander," Abigail called to him. "How do you do that so fast?"

He laughed, accepting the compliment. "I have been using the sling since I was five years old," he called back. "When I watched over the goats in the mountains, I had to protect them from predators. I could hit a hawk in flight when I was fifteen," he boasted.

As he turned to walk back toward where Abigail was sitting, near the water's edge, feet outstretched nearly to the rushes, wiggling her toes in the cool grasses, his eyes searched the area for another target.

The deadly cottonmouth moccasin snake watched with its beady eyes as the bare pink toes wiggled before it in the grass. With a flash of its forked tongue, the viper sensed flesh. Its keen eyes dripping from the lake's waters as it emerged, slithering through the grassy rushes in the shallows onto the harder shore line, now focused on the movement of Abigail's slender toes. The snake had found its meal, its prey. It slowly moved onto the higher ground, never moving its head from its target, its entire body pressing against the grasses, moving inexorably toward its nourishment. As it drew within striking distance, mere inches from Abigail's bare toes, it began its coil by bringing its entire body directly behind its tapered head.

The snake's forked tongue silently, rhythmically, flicked again and again, searching the air for the scent of its very tempting target. Hardly a leaf of grass moved as the mature moccasin slinked along the ground. The forked tongue flicked one last time as the entire five feet of sinew and muscle, held together by a series of bone and ligament, was poised to lash forward in an instant. It would engulf its prey in its hyper-extended mouth, sinking its fangs filled with deadly poisonous venom into flesh not of a young rodent, but of Abigail's toes.

"Don't move, Abigail!" Alexander suddenly yelled, interrupting her reverie. He quickly placed a stone in the pouch and almost as a blur, whirled the pouch over his head, again, three times, and with a whirl let the stone fly. Thud! The stone flew true to its target, as he knew it would, striking the viper in the head, instantly killing the reptile only a few inches from Abigail's feet. He ran toward her.

"Oh, my God!" Abigail screamed, staring at the very large, lethal snake. She leaped up and ran to him, frightened, with both arms outstretched. "You saved my life! That was a big and dangerous cottonmouth. You are my hero!"

She embraced him tightly, wrapping both her arms around his neck, shaking at the realization of what might have happened. "Oh, my God, Alexander. That was so awful. Hold me." Now, more emboldened and yet still very frightened, Abigail spontaneously kissed him on his lips. It was an impulsive, explosive reaction to what he had done for her and how she truly felt about him. She suddenly felt safe in his arms and realized she liked kissing him so much. Then, pulling her head back, she cupped his face in her hands and brought her face to his. She could not help herself as she kissed him deliberately and firmly on his lips. He held her and enjoyed her lips on his, but could not return the kiss.

After a few minutes, she stepped back, and more calmly said, "Wait until I tell my father what you did. He will love this story, Alexander. You are my protector. I love you!" She was still shaking as she exclaimed her gratitude.

He was stunned by her demonstrative affection. They spent a few minutes looking down at the now immobile, dead five-foot reptile.

"I think we should ride back to my house now, Alexander. I'm a little nervous," she whispered in his ear as she hugged him once again.

They rode their horses side by side, first walking the horses, then breaking into a canter for awhile. Smiling at him affectionately, she pulled up close to him, reached over and clasped his hand while mouthing the words, 'thank you, Alexander.'

Alexander, trying to better understand all that had taken place, sat tall in his saddle, proud that his mastery of the sling from his homeland had saved his best friend from certain severe pain, if not death. He recalled Abigail's response, her embrace and genuine affection. The thoughts empowered

Alexander. This was a big day, an important day in both their lives, and they both understood the strength of the affectionate bonding that brought them closer than ever before.

⚜

"Mother, I've never seen anything like it!" she exclaimed after they arrived at her house. "I think that with his sling, he could beat any cowman in Osceola County with a pistol. He is so sure of himself in his modest way, and yet, he never misses his target. I felt so safe with Alexander, Mother."

"Oh dear, I worry so much when you go out into the country."

⚜

Alexander was working at the store the next afternoon, rearranging goods on the table at the front of the store, when he heard someone calling his name.

"Alexander, I want to talk to you, son." The deep, masculine voice came from a tall, muscular, middle-aged man standing in the shop doorway. He was wearing a large grey Stetson hat low over his face, deeply creased and tanned from the harsh Florida sun. His faded blue shirt was wide open at the neck, unbuttoned at the collar; sweat marks under his armpits. On his hip was a silver pistol in a black holster. His jeans were well-worn, faded Levi's as were the jeans of most cattlemen. His wide leather belt with an embellished large, tooled oval silver buckle stood out against the deep blue of the jeans. Alexander surveyed the man in snakeskin boots still wrapped by the spur straps at the ankles. He knew who was standing there in the doorway, and he knew he had to be absolutely respectful to this man, a recognized man of power and wealth.

"Yes, sir, Mr. Sommerland."

"Big John, son. All my friends call me Big John. C'mere, son. Let's talk."

Alexander walked toward this big man, a few inches taller than he and likely forty pounds heavier than his own one hundred-ninety pounds. He had a broad chest that filled the shirt, and a slight pouch that hung over his buckle.

"What you did for my daughter, Abigail, is right important to me." He spoke firmly in a deep Southern drawl as he reached out and put his large hand on Alexander's shoulder. "I appreciate yer killin' that danged cottonmouth. That's a bad ass snake that coulda killed her. I do believe you saved her life, son, and for that, I'm mighty grateful."

Alexander was immediately overwhelmed. He shrugged, nodded and said modestly, "Yes, sir. But all I did was watch out for her."

Big John stared into Alexander's eyes, the same way he was known to stare into another man's eyes so he held that person's total attention to hear his every word. 'Big John' was not known to repeat himself. And while he was respected throughout the region, folks said of him, "He's a good, honest man, but he can be damned tough. Don't ever cross Big John. While he'll give you the shirt off his back if he likes you, just don't make him mad. He has a long memory. And he worships his wife and daughter, Abigail."

Big John's face was now very serious, to make sure Alexander fully understood his message. "Young man, if you ever need anythin,' and I mean anythin,' you jest come over and ask. You jest come on over t' the house and see me sometime, y'hear?"

Alexander stammered, "Yessir, Abigail's my best friend, sir, and she has taught me so much. I would do anything for her."

"Well, son, from what she says about you, the feelin' is mutual. You know, she's mah girl, mah only daughter and she's right important to me. Nah, she's *the* most important thing in my life. And I am so grateful. D'ya understands what I'm trying to tell you, son? You gotta good dad, Alexander. I like him a lot. You both are good people, and we need good people here. So, I'm tellin' ya, come see me, son. You know where we live. Mrs. Sommerland told me to tell ya, don't be a stranger. An' don't let me down, y'hear?"

"Yessir. Abigail is giving me lessons tomorrow, so maybe I can see you then."

"Right, then," he replied as he turned to walk out of the store. As he did, he perfunctorily raised his right hand above his shoulder, not looking back, as to conclude the visit. That was his style.

CHAPTER 19

$\mathcal{A}$ bigail left for college in Tallahassee three weeks later. The same week, Alexander was required to enroll in the first grade in the local town school just a few blocks down the main street.

"Do I really have to go to school with six year olds, Father?"

"That's the law, son. Just do your best," his father shrugged. "Maybe you'll learn English faster that way."

"Aw..." Alexander complained.

Within eight weeks, he attended the first grade through the eighth grade in the same building. The teachers were understanding and realized it was futile to hold him back. He didn't enjoy school very much, since he was much older and bigger than his classmates... at nearly six feet tall, he had nothing in common with his classmates who were mostly under the age of twelve. He had learned excellent English from Abigail all summer, and since he had already attended twelve years of schooling in Lebanon, the only education he lacked was English, American history, American government, and a few other subjects like biology. He was advanced in mathematics.

In a very brief period, he grew bored, especially since he was no longer spending his days with Abigail. He was ready to venture out before Christmas. It's my time to begin he decided.

"I want to go out on my own, Father. Will you help me?"

"So soon, son? What will you do?"

"I want to open my own store before the winter season and sell goods you do not sell. I believe I can do well with furniture, clothes for cowmen, shoes, hats and jewelry for the ladies." Remembering all that he had seen while riding with Abigail through her father's lands and massive herds of cattle, he added, "One day I want to own some land and raise cattle like Big John Sommerland. Boldly, he asked, "Will you lend me $500 to get started?"

"You are in a hurry, aren't you, son?"

"Yes, sir, I am! And I am your son, aren't I?" he smiled.

By Christmas, Alexander had opened his small store on Broadway, and spread the word at the hotels, the docks, and at the cattle corrals. By then, tourists had begun arriving by train from northern cities, and the streets began to fill with more shoppers, including ladies in their latest fashions from New York, Philadelphia, Pittsburgh, and Boston. Dress hemlines were beginning to rise to mid-calf so sales were picking up as women wanted to be fashionable and not wear the Victorian floor length cotton dresses of the past. The ladies needed fashionable sun umbrellas, and the men liked his inventory of hats. While Alexander initially ordered from his father's suppliers, more and more traveling salesmen and manufacturers' representatives stopped by his shop with their catalogs. Alexander eagerly reviewed the catalogs, looking into new opportunities, and ordered on consignment all that the companies would permit. He ventured into ladies' shoes, which, he found, were a bonanza. It seemed every lady needed at least several pairs of shoes while men would wear the same boots or shoes for more than two years. He stayed open from seven in the morning until nearly midnight six days a week. He worked very hard, and studied at night, but he was intoxicated by his opportunities, his freedom, and his mission to save enough money to somehow return to Madeleine. Still, almost everyday the absence of a letter from her gnawed at his stomach. When he looked to the postman with sorrowful eyes and watched him shake his head, he almost felt sick. *It's been five months!* It was awful.

During that autumn season of 1920, both Alexander's and his father's store prospered. They deposited their growing earnings in their "bank in the field." With their Spartan lifestyle, it cost little or nothing for them to live. Their expenses were rent on his store, ethnic foods, biweekly train rides to Tampa to see friends or to Orlando to visit Alexander's sister. There was little else. There were no taxes to pay, no insurance premiums, no gasoline, for they did not yet own an automobile. So, except for their meager personal expenses, and paying for their goods for sale, their income was saved and deposited every Saturday night after closing. The immigrant's visceral, almost personal, concern for security was too difficult to set aside. "When you come from the poorest, oppressed land to make a new life, son, you cannot forget ever that it can all be taken away in an instant. An immigrant remembers always...everyday...every minute, that there is no one to help if he fails. He cannot afford to fall. All depends on his willingness to take responsibility for his life and his family's life. He must try harder than others, save more, not waste any time, and not spend his money on foolishness. Abraham often spoke to his son of his near obsession with his frugality and sense of financial insecurity.

"You must never look back and say I wish I had worked harder."

"But Father, we work as hard as we can," Alexander interrupted, almost frightened at his father's words.

"You must save everything you can. I knew bringing your mother, you and your brother would always be up to me. No one else. There are no cousins here…no one to help. So I saved every penny. I spent nothing on myself. Sometimes, I gave a little something to your sister to help her. But I waited too long for you and your mother, Iskandar, and I am so sad I did."

"Why did you wait so long, Father? Why?" he pleaded when he could, hoping for an explanation that would salve his wounds.

"I did the best I could, my son. Still, my heart aches. You must work very hard, have a better life than mine, and make certain your children have a better life than yours. Do you understand, my son, what I am telling you?"

Alexander understood to be sure. And he would remember. As he thought about his father's predicament and remembered he could not bring his own wife whom he deeply loved to America, Alexander wondered, *how then can I think I can bring Madeleine here? Is it impossible? Must I return to Marseille then? But where are her letters?*

Abigail returned to Kissimmee at Thanksgiving and, a few weeks later, for the Christmas holidays. For her senior year gift, at Thanksgiving, her father bought a new 1921 Ford Model A coupe. It was considered the "hottest," "the cats meow," the best car for young people in America. Of course it was black, like all Fords back then. When Abigail drove into Kissimmee mid-December, she stopped first at the sidewalk in front of Alexander's store where she hopped out of the car sporting a scarf around her neck, a ribbon in her hair, and stepped onto the wooden sidewalk. With a great big smile, she shouted into the store, "Hi ya, Alexander! Whatcha' doin'?" She spoke like she was still at college with her girlfriends.

Alexander was on a stepladder reaching for the Stetson hats he kept on the high shelves with the ladies bonnets. He turned at her welcoming voice. "Hi, Abigail!" he shouted, releasing one hand to wave to her and, almost losing his balance and falling off the ladder. "Be right down." When his feet touched the floor, Abigail noticed a familiar clicking sound.

"Are you wearing boots, Alexander? You rascal!" She laughed out loud. "Come here and give me a hug. It's Christmas, Alexander!"

"It's so good to see you, Abigail! You look wonderful." He smiled, feeling his affection for this lovely creature, his pretty friend. "I've really missed you," he nearly shouted with pleasure.

"Listen, Alexander, I just drove in from Tallahassee. I haven't even been home yet, but I wanted to see you so bad! So, why don't I go on home, and if you don't have any plans, come over to the house for dinner with my momma, Big John and me." Then rushing out, she called out over her shoulder, "See you at 6:30. Okay? I'd better get home now. Momma's waiting."

Alexander eagerly closed his shop early, went home, still above his father's store, freshened up, and combed his hair in the middle the way all the young men did that year. He put his straw skimmer on top of his head, and stuck his head in the store downstairs to see his father.

"Hello, *Biyee*. How do I look? I'm going over to see Abigail. She invited me to supper."

His father, smiling with pride, said, "Go see your friend, son, and have a good time." Then Abraham thought, *This is the first time you or I have been invited to dinner in a home of someone so prominent.* In times like these, Abraham wished he too was young again, with his thoughts turning to his pretty bride, Katrina.

"Come on in, son," said Big John as he sat in his favorite chair on the porch. "Abigail's gittin' ready for supper."

It was a wonderful evening for Alexander. Abigail's parents were very warm to him. He loved being in the big house, and Abigail was so full of life, so excited, and now only a semester from graduation. She was pretty as ever, and her slim figure, large animated eyes, and enthusiasm made for a happy evening. They saw each other nearly every day during the rest of her vacation.

"My daddy wants you to come over on Christmas Eve after church. He says he wants to talk business with you. I think you should say yes, Alexander. Besides, I'd love to have you be with me on my favorite evening, Alexander. So please come for dinner."

At seven o'clock on Christmas Eve, arriving early as requested, Alexander stopped at the walkway to the Sommerland home and looked at the magnificent two-story wooden, Victorian home with its broad shingle-covered porch and large oak trees on either side of the walkway. He could see the brightly decorated Christmas tree through the large living room windows. Abigail was in her holiday dress with red and green ribbons in her hair. *She's so beautiful, and I'm just an immigrant, younger than she,* he thought to himself, still carrying that burden in his mind. *But I am as good as anyone, and one day I too will have a grand house like this.* As he considered his plans, he smiled and stepped onto the stone walkway to the steps that would lead him to the large front door with that familiar oval vertical window framed by dark oak.

He swung the doorknocker with its clack-clack and waited as he had so many mornings all summer.

Now it was Christmas Eve, and Abigail had invited her "special friend" to join her, her mother and Big John for dinner.

With anticipation, Alexander waited at the door, carrying a wrapped gift for Mrs. Sommerland and wondering what Big John wanted to say to him. He was happy tonight. He and his father planned to go to Orlando—the next morning Christmas—is for family but tonight he was excited about Abigail's invitation. Tomorrow, Christmas morning, they would take the train to Orlando and see his sister, nephew, and niece, and his boastful brother-in-law.

Alexander couldn't believe his ears that Christmas Eve. Big John asked him outside to sit on the front porch in the rocking chair facing him. Alexander mused, *Here we are, two men, a nineteen-year-old immigrant, and a prominent, seasoned rancher, a native of Florida and very wealthy, sitting alone together on the porch in the cool December air.* He was very excited with his good fortune to be here.

With his pale blue, almost transparent, eyes, Big John leaned forward toward Alexander and placed his hands on his knees.

"Son," he spoke slowly in his drawl, as though there was no one else in the world. "I'll get right to the point; I don't like wastin' time." Quickly moving on, he looked straight into Alexander's eyes, a tad intimidating, and continued, "I owe you, and I want to do something for you."

Alexander, drawn to this man with great respect, leaned forward so not to miss a word.

"I like your daddy, and I like you. And I know my daughter likes you a lot. I'd also like to see you stay in Kissimmee." Then pausing, sitting back with a serious look on his face, he announced, "Here's my proposition."

Alexander looked into Big John's eyes and listened intently, having no idea where this conversation was going. Big John was very focused, and Abigail had urged him to accept whatever her father was proposing.

Lowering his voice, he spoke softly, "Mrs. Sommerland and Abigail are very important to me, and I'm obliged to you for saving Abigail's life. I know what a cottonmouth can do to someone, and I've seen the pain their bite can bring."

"Now it's Christmas Eve, a time when we all feel good. I like your dad. I've seen how hard he has worked since he came here. He's honest, and his word is gold. I admire what your daddy has accomplished here in Kissimmee. An' I've watched you, son. You are the same way. You work harder than any young man I've seen. And you're important to Abigail. I do believe you are her best friend, and I want you to stay her best friend. I think you and she should be close for a long time."

Big John continued, leaning toward Alexander as he described his family's life in Kissimmee since the Civil War, and how he had bought his first land from Hamilton Disston, had amassed 160,000 acres of pasture lands, more than 16,000 head of cattle, and 5,000 acres of citrus land over at St. Cloud just five miles to the east.

"That Mr. Disston, now he knew how to do business. He got the Governor to hire him to drain all the swamps in this part of Florida back in 1884. Disston connected Lake Tohopekaliga with East Lake Tohopekaliga over in St. Cloud." He laughed. "I hear that when he opened the gate, East Lake Tohopekaliga dropped eight feet! Scared the hell outta everybody, too, I'll tell ya. And then, he went down and opened up the Caloosahatchee River down in Fort Myers; that made shipping cattle to Cuba easier and opened up a helluva lot of pastureland too. Why, if truth be told, Hamilton Disston made Florida's cattle industry. That man got an option from the state to buy four million acres for twenty-five cents each. With a little help, I bought my first 10,000 acres from him in 1895 for fifty cents an acre."

Alexander watched Big John's lips carefully, trying to understand his words, picking out most of the familiar sounds.

"That's the price I'm going to charge you, Alexander. Here's my deal. I'm offering to sell you 5,000 acres at my cost price, and I'm throwing' in five hundred head of cattle too. Now, that oughta get you started, son. And I believe Abigail will give you a hand when you need it."

By the time Mrs. Sommerland stepped onto the porch announcing dinner, Big John had completed his offer to Alexander. Both men were smiling broadly. Big John reached for Alexander's hand to shake on the deal.

It took Alexander a pregnant moment to fully understand what had just taken place and he had difficulty disguising his surprise. He was amazed such a generous offer would ever come his way, especially after having to work so very hard for every penny. To be certain he fully understood what was being offered, he memorized the figures so he could write everything down on paper when he got back home. He was thrilled at his good fortune. *Five hundred cows and bulls! We will never be hungry again!*

Noting Abigail's smiling face in the window as she nodded her head urging him to accept, Alexander, overwhelmed, but without hesitation reached out his right hand with a nervous smile and said, "Big John, I can't refuse your excellent offer, so my answer is yes, sir, and thank you very much. But I think I'll need a few years to pay you, and I'll need your guidance. I'm really new at this. But you have offered me a wonderful opportunity. I accept, and I'll do what ever I must to earn your confidence, sir."

"Good. Take two or three years, son. I'm in no hurry. What with those politicians up in Tallahassee, I expect I'll have to start payin' taxes on all this land anyway. Looks like the days of the open range will soon be over. My cows are all over three counties now. Too many cows gittin' hit by them dang automobiles. So, it won't be long before we'll have to fence our grazing lands. In a way, you're doin' me a favor." He smiled. "I'll git you a survey of what you're buyin', and by spring, we'll have it fenced for you. You can pay me back for the cost of the fence. By then, you better have a man run the operation for ya and git you a brand registered. Wilbur McCray is a good man; I'll let you hire him from me."

"I like Wilbur very much, sir. He's my good friend," Alexander interjected, smiling and nodding as he listened to Big John describe his generosity.

"Good, son. But I'd stay away from T.J. Hatfield and cowmen like him. T.J. is always angry it seems. He's a bad one. His family came from to America from Germany, I think. They have good solid character, but I wouldn't trust him if I was you. He doesn't take kindly to immigrants. His family was involved in the Native Party back in the late 1800s when they fought...and I mean fought...hard to keep out immigrants. They want America to themselves. So be real careful of T.J. and his family, Alexander. Now," he continued after a thought, putting his hand on Alexander's shoulder, leading him to the door, "let's not keep the ladies waitin.'"

"I'll stay away from that man. I already learned that. I don't want any trouble."

Abigail met Alexander at the doorway to the dining room with a warm, happy embrace. "Merry Christmas, Alexander. I'm so happy you are here tonight. Let's sit down for dinner and drink a toast to your new ranch!" She had known exactly what her father was going to do, and that made her very happy.

All through dinner, although it was delicious and smelled so good to him, Alexander could hardly eat. He was startled at his good fortune while also sharing this evening with such a prominent family.

After dinner, they visited awhile before the ladies started cleaning up. Alexander could hardly restrain himself. He nearly ran to his home to tell his father what had happened.

"Five thousand acres and five hundred head of cattle, *Biyee*! I will pay him $2,500 over two, maybe three years. Can you imagine what this means to our lives in America, *Biyee*? I love America!" Then, thinking of his mother and Douma, his terrible hunger as a child, he exclaimed, "I will make sure we are never hungry again." *Oh, how I wish Imei and Milhelm were here!*

Abraham embraced his son and whispered, "Merry Christmas, Iskandar. Your mother and I always believed you would have a special future. God has blessed you, my son. The Sommerland family is very generous and good. They care." Then he became silent for a moment, mulling over what had just happened, and unable to suppress his immigrant's sense of caution and fear, continued, "Now you will have to protect and care for God's gift to you. It will be a big responsibility, and there will be others who will want what you have. They will be jealous and angry. So, be cautious and safeguard your new treasure."

Not totaling understanding, and perhaps a bit naïve, he considered his father's admonition. Then, Alexander looked at his father with utter respect and pride. "This would not have happened, *Biyee*, were it not for who you are and what you have taught me. Mr. Sommerland has great respect for you, *Baba*. We are so fortunate."

"*Baba*," Abraham responded, "what we are and how we live determines what happens in our lives. You have a long and good heritage. Be proud, and someday you will be able to help someone as Mr. Sommerland has helped you." Father and son embraced warmly, having been struck deeply by the good fortune that had come their way.

Alexander, looking around their sparse and humble home, noticing the simple pinewood dining table, two ladder pine chairs, and a single reading lamp, began considering what all this could mean to them. *Perhaps one day we might have our own home, like true Americans. Maybe even as grand as Big John's house.*

They both prayed with thanks that night, grateful for the blessings they were receiving.

CHAPTER 20

In early 1924, the people of Kissimmee, like those throughout southern Florida, began witnessing the second year of the most incredible real estate "Land Boom" in Florida's history. Open pasture land and pine forest land valued at fifty cents an acre until 1915, and 75 cents per acre in 1920 had shot up to an incredible $20 per acre by 1924. Alexander had never experienced anything like this turn of events. Neither, to be sure, had his father. Ownership of land never changed hands in their village. It always stayed in each family for hundreds of years. Now they were startled to watch lands being bought and sold several times in a week! It was against their culture to sell land. Although they were tempted, they .watched as others began to sell theirs. They always were philosophical about land, intending to hold on to it for generations.

Some Florida tracts, even into 1925, were bought and sold several times in one day! "America is amazing," they would tell each other as they watched. These were heady days when Alexander stood at the door of the shop and watched the frenzy of speculators on Broadway negotiating hurriedly, buying and selling. He was both befuddled and excited...torn between being amazed at what he saw...and wanting youthfully and anxiously to join in it.

During the early years of the post-war "Roaring Twenties," consumers were buying everything in sight...automobiles, furniture, and expensive trendy fashions. Lavish spending and irrational investing exuberance swept the nation after "The Great War, The War to End All Wars." Kissimmee, Central Florida and South Florida experienced incredible, even absurd price increases for vacant lands as well as developed real estate. The large landowners, mostly ranchers, were not selling much, so speculators were chasing each other to buy what little land was actually available for purchase. Developers scooped up all lands they could, driving prices up exponentially each day. Streets were built on raw lands almost daily. Utility infrastructure and sidewalks were installed by cities and counties trying to keep up. Demand and speculation far exceeded the supply of accessible land available for purchase, even inaccessible, submerged land. On the East Coast of Palm Beach to Miami, land values went from $30 per acre along the oceanfront to

$20,000 per acre in less than three years. Money, credit and debt were plentiful with most purchases based on five percent equity, and 95% promissory notes, just as with the booming stock market. Developed homesites selling in the morning for $5,000, were available at noon for $10,000, and by the end of the day, the same parcel was selling for $50,000. Speculation was as rampant as a fever. Speculators and brokers formed long lines in the streets seeking to record their purchases at the land abstract desks so they could go out and buy and sell more real estate. Auctions produced prices far in excess of asking prices.

Tampa and all Central Florida experienced the same kind of rapid inflation in property values. In the same year, Abraham was offered $20,000, then $40,000, and then $100,000 for each of the buildings he purchased in 1916 for only $400 each. These were amazing times. Young, eager Alexander, now twenty-two years old, shop owner and relatively small rancher of by now 600 head of cattle on 5,000 acres of land, was sorely tempted nearly every day to buy more property as prices skyrocketed. But his more conservative father, with wisdom built over years of hard work, frugality, and a deep sense of insecurity, would advise him almost daily saying, "Do not speculate, my son. This fever cannot last long."

"But *Biyee...*" Alexander would plea day after day for two years as the frenzy continued.

Abraham had devoted himself to saving every penny and working more than twelve hours each day. With an awareness that these times could not continue, he sought to temper Alexander's youthful impulsiveness. Using Arabic when he spoke as father to son, he continued to caution him nearly every night over the dinner table, "No, Iskandar, we will not take the money from our savings. It will remain. We will not buy when all others are buying. I'm glad we did buy those other buildings right after you arrived in 1920, but no more, not now."

"But, *Biyee*," Alexander invariably protested, "the prices continue to skyrocket. I want to buy something."

It took all of Abraham's adamance to constrain Alexander from risking everything on skyrocketing land values. In keeping with his cultural heritage, Alexander reluctantly adhered to his father's admonitions.

"You have enough now, Iskandar. You have cattle, 5,000 acres of land, a few lakes, your store...I'm glad you bought that building when you did. But now, son, it's time for you to forget about getting into this craziness. Be patient. It is now time for you to consider getting married and having a family. You need to think about this."

Abraham's verbal wish for Alexander to get married caused tension in Alexander's stomach. Instinctively, Alexander's fingers went to Madeleine's... his...ring. *Where is she?* he thought to himself sadly. *Every month I write, yet no response. Is she still alive? Has she completely forgotten me? I will never forget her. How can I marry another woman? Yet, how can I not get married? Of course, I have wanted to be married and have children. I have wanted to be with my true love, Madeleine, since we met four years ago. Four years! But where is her love now? Where are her letters? Yes, I am ready but she is not here. And I don't even know where she is.* His mind raced, riding the emotional roller-coaster that always came when he had to confront his seemingly unsolvable dilemma.

Abraham beckoned to his son as he sat in a chair at the table. "Sit with me, son."

He couldn't expect his father to understand. He knew that from all their conversations that his father, whose expectations he couldn't deny, would not understand. He knew he was expected to marry *the right girl*, a Syrian of Orthodox Christian faith, from a good family. This put him in conflict emotionally not only with his father, but his sister too, and the wishes of his entire extended family.

"Iskandar, you know I only want what is best for you. Your mother and I hoped our children would have happy lives one day with their own families. If we were still in Douma, it would be easier to understand. I believe completely that you will have a happy life if you choose to marry someone of our kind…a Syrian girl."

"*Biyee*, I know you only want what is best for me, but I fell in love with a wonderful French girl in Marseille and I want to marry *her*!"

"Iskandar, listen to me. I'm sure your friend in France is nice. But it is better that you marry in the same religion, the same culture, so you will avoid the difficulties that you will face if you do otherwise. And while I am also sure Abigail is a kind and beautiful girl, she too will be advised by her mother the same way you are by me. I am certain Abigail's parents want what is best for their only daughter. Even though they respect us and are grateful to you for saving her life, they want her to marry her own kind also. It is best. As the Bible says, '*Always seek to be in equal yoke with your partner.*' You will see."

Interrupting, Alexander blurted, "But I have not said I want to marry Abigail, although I think she would be a perfect wife for me…" his voice trailed off as he rolled his "Douma stone" in his fingers, something he always seemed to do nervously when he and his father talked about his personal life and his views of America.

"We are immigrants, Iskandar. We are considered different. Be aware of that. The Sommerlands are more understanding about this than most people, but still, they too want the best for their daughter as I do for you." Abraham, watching Alexander fondle his ring, looked up, paused, caught his breath and spoke firmly. "Iskandar, it is for your own good that I *insist* you marry a good

Syrian girl of our religion. She will bring you healthy children, cook for you, love you, and support you." Then looking around his Spartan apartment, Abraham swept his arm in a circle before him and admonished, "Look at our house. It is bare; it is not what an American woman can accept. We accept it because we came from less than this, but want more. A Syrian girl will understand. She will make it pretty, warm and comfortable just as your beloved mother did in that small stone home I built for her. Marry someone like your mother, Iskandar. We can find one like her in Boston. Of this I am certain. Forget this infatuation with a girl in France."

Those final words struck Alexander right in his young, romantic heart. Yes, he thought, *I haven't received any letters from Madeleine. Yes, Uncle Salim's wife has a younger, pretty sister. Yes, she was also Antiochan Orthodox Christian too. Yes, I owe my father my total loyalty and honor just as the Bible says. And yes, I have grown older and more realistic. But it is so impossible to forget Madeleine. How can I forget my love?* he cried out rhetorically to himself.

"What is happening here, my son? Listen to me. Do what is right. You can learn to love the proper woman."

"But, Father..."

Alexander stood and stepped away from the table where he had listened to his father's plans for him and went across the small room, his back to his father who stayed seated, watching his son pull away, not willing to be convinced that this proposed marriage arrangement was in his best interests.

And that's how the evening discussion ended, neither convinced of the other's desires and, to be sure, their deep rooted needs. It was a painful moment for both of them, a confrontation between father and son that neither would be able to fully put aside for a long time.

Over the next several weeks, Alexander's personal future became a preoccupation for him and his father, to the point of creating significant tension between them. Their body language became more separated, almost adversarial.

CHAPTER 21

$\mathcal{D}$uring the remaining semester of Abigail's college career, she became more involved with classmates, her courses, and friendships. Like most attractive girls at Florida State School for Women, she was invited to weekend events and parties with boys at Gainesville's University of Florida for Men. Ultimately, she began seeing a student one year older than she who was enrolled in law school at the university. He met all the criteria for a prospective husband her mother had laid down that summer day when Abigail had initially expressed that she favored young Alexander, the shopkeeping newcomer to America.

G. Hamilton Smythe III was the perfect model that she was sure her mother would approve. "Ham" ("Ugh," she would say when his buddies called him that) was a football player. He was rugged looking with a strong chin, sculptured cheekbones, a wicked sensual smile, and an abundance of confidence, bordering on cockiness and arrogance. He intended to graduate from the University of Florida School of Law, become an attorney in Tampa, and maybe even one day be elected governor.

Yet, when Abigail would return to Kissimmee, she would fill her days with helping her father at their ranch, visiting with Alexander, often riding her horse alongside his as they would spend hours together inspecting his growing herd. They were bonding more and more as best of friends. Each time there was even a hint of romance from Abigail, Alexander would feel a mixture of guilt and apprehension which would lead him to subconsciously fondle Madeleine's ring, still on his little finger.

"I'm so glad you're my best friend in the whole world, Alexander," she would exclaim nearly every week.

"And you're *my* best friend, Abigail! I can't imagine being happy in America if you hadn't come into my life. I'm so lucky! You taught me so much, and your family has been very good to me. I've learned how to be an American by watching you and learning the ways of the cultured society." Smiling at her while tipping his new Stetson hat, then a sweep of his hand, he turned to her, "And look at my cattle...all because of you and your father and mother. I owe you so much."

He did his best to make clear his feelings for her and likely, deep down, she understood. But she was a romantic, very bright, popular and quite attractive. To be sure, Abigail had been his very fortunate introduction to the cultures of America, very different from what Alexander knew in the tiny village of Douma. And for that he was grateful. He also felt that he had to honor his father's counsel, and even more, his father's insistence that his choice for a mate could not be Abigail. Most of all, he felt deeply that his destiny could only be fulfilled with Madeleine. These emotional pulls kept Alexander in a constant state of turmoil that he would somehow have to resolve or "turn it over to God," as his mother would have advised him.

And so when Abigail came to him after her graduation to tell him she had become engaged to a man from Tampa she had met in college, fulfilling her mother's demands, he felt at once a sense of joy for her, and yet jealousy and a great sadness. Although they remained good friends and spent a good deal of time together that summer, Alexander knew that was as much as they would ever be—best friends. And he made himself be comfortable with that.

As a result, he was surprised when only a week before her wedding, she came to his store in her car one evening after dark and asked him to "get in and come be with me tonight."

"Sure," he replied, always yielding to her, unsure of what she meant by her firm request as he closed the shop. She drove them out of the downtown to the same lake where Alexander had killed the cottonmouth. He searched her face, looking for a clue to her mood, as she stared straight ahead, driving the automobile along the double rutted dirt road, twisting through the pine thicket, past the clumps of palmetto and down the grassy slope of pasture to the lakeside. She parked the car, pulled the brake, and began to softly talk to him. Turning in her seat, she looked squarely at Alexander with a loving smile, and spoke of her life at the university, her deepest emotions, their important and close friendship, and of her fiancé. "I'm not so sure I love him, but I'm now twenty-four. He is handsome, comes from a wealthy Tampa family, plans to be a lawyer, and is very popular at the University of Florida." Her eyes and chin lowered as her voice drifted off. She seemed less than certain she was doing the right thing.

"Alexander," she whispered as she reached for his hand, "you are my dearest friend. There is no way I will ever forget how much I care for you, and how in many ways I do love you." She paused, reluctantly remembering her mother's counsel, "But for reasons I don't fully understand or agree with, it seems we will not marry."

Abigail was torn deeply at having to finally face the decision she knew would come ever since her mother strongly cautioned her when she first expressed her warmth and affection toward Alexander after that incredible day at the lake shore when Alexander was so brave and loving. "Abigail," she had said firmly and motherly, as she placed both hands on Abigail's shoulders, "yes, Alexander is a fine, hard-working, honest, good person. That is true, but you should find an 'American boy' who is going to be a doctor or lawyer, someone whose background is the same as yours. 'Birds of a feather' has a lot of truth in it. Besides, you are accustomed to a life that requires a good deal of cultural status and financial stability. You'll be happier, Abigail, if you stay with your own kind."

Although Abigail had felt anger at her mother's description at the time and had wanted to defend her friend, she ultimately acquiesced, acknowledging in her heart it may probably be true. Rarely could a young girl in those years go patently against her parents' wishes, especially those with social standing. Taking those kinds of risks were unheard of.

Now sitting in the car with Alexander, her eyes were moist, but she did not cry. She had something to say and perhaps silently was hoping he would pull her from the edge by embracing her and responding with his own marriage proposal.

Alexander," she whispered, gripping his hand, looking directly in his eyes, "I want you to know this. I do not want to marry anyone else before you make love to me. I want you to make love to me tonight. I need you to be with me, Alexander. *Please. Tonight.*"

He was stunned. His eyes grew large as his forehead furrowed from surprise. Suddenly his brow grew wet. His hands moistened, and his heart pounded in his chest. He was bewildered with this incredible turn of events. *How can I keep from saying 'no' to dear Abigail? What am I to do*? he asked himself, worried what to say. This would never happen in Lebanon. He was out of his element. It was more than a special friendship...even a love that he shared with her. She was very dear to him and he had always found her so desirable, but he had never allowed his feelings to advance to the romantic and emotional intimacy that he had felt with Madeleine. In fact, he had always felt a sense of betrayal toward Madeleine when Abigail got romantic. Because of Madeleine still being in his heart, intimacy with Abigail could never become an option for him. It was a painful and awkward dilemma. He found it difficult to breathe.

The silence and his lack of immediate response was almost deafening to Abigail.

He was torn apart at the thought that Abigail was getting married to another man. *"A rich American. Damn!" And now, she wants me to be her first love. But I'm not good enough to marry! Oh, Madeleine, where are you?* He struggled silently, wishing he had the right answer, but knowing he didn't. Seeking a break in the palpable tension of the very strained moment that lingered, he reached for the door handle and nervously pulled it to open the door. Stepping outside, he kicked the ground as he walked around the car to Abigail's door, opening it for her. *She is so lovely...*

As she came out, reaching for his extended hand, she leaned into him, hoping he would seek her, take her down to the grass and make love to her with a mix of overpowering tenderness, passion, and lust, yet, with the respect they had always had for each other. She was bolder than he, and she was seeking to somehow let him solve her own dilemma, loving Alexander but trying to understand and accept her life's destiny in marriage.

But he could not hold her close as with Madeleine. He remained very still as the whistling whippoorwills in the trees morphed into absolute silence. Taking a deep breath, he held her face in his hands. "Abigail, you know how I love you so very much. You know you are my dearest friend. And I want more than anything that we stay very, very close. I do love you and I want to do whatever you ask me to do. But my heart won't let me make love with you tonight. You belong to another. And, maybe I am a fool, but I think this is best for both of us. I want us always to be friends." He bowed his head, not wanting her to see the pain in his eyes any longer. He knew by saying this that their closeness and wonderful relationship might never be the same and it agonized him terribly.

"You do understand, don't you, Abigail?' he said softly, "You know I'll always be here for you. I cannot bear the thought of something like this destroying our friendship."

As he finished his struggling response to her longing, he hoped he was doing the right thing. He stepped backwards and began nervously fondling Madeleine's ring with his left hand, not knowing what to do, what to say. Then, wanting to bring the tension to a close, he added, "We'd better get back to town now, Abigail."

She watched his eyes, understanding what she had asked of him and sadly whispered, "Yes, I suppose you are right, Alexander. Funny, maybe because of our deep friendship, I'm not all that embarrassed somehow." She kissed his cheek. "Thank you, Alexander, for your understanding. I'll always be there for you too, my love, my friend. Yes, I guess we'd better go now."

Neither ever spoke of that evening again, letting it be safely protected in their hearts forever.

CHAPTER 22

*W*ith his personal life in shambles and too confusing, and with no word from Madeleine, Alexander became totally committed to his work. Fortunately, the area was booming in so many ways, keeping him very busy. Sales at both Thomas stores increased substantially; their earnings multiplied as they did for most of the other merchants in the region. Alexander's life, beyond his personal longings which caused him so much uncertainty, was liberating and prosperous.

They continued to deposit their growing profits in their bank in the field. Demand for beef and prices for cattle doubled in three years. The Texas fever tick of 1920 had done its damage, but was now under control, and ranchers were once again making *a lot* of money. "Prosperity for Everyone," the nation's press headlined.

By 1924, wealthy investors and Northerners looking for opportunities flooded the region. In nearby Lake Wales in Polk County, Blue Mountain Development Co. began building a resort of homes. Amazingly, beyond anyone's wildest imagination, minimum investments required proof that at least $250,000 had been spent on each home. These amounts were unbelievable when compared to just two years earlier.

"It's plain crazy what's goin' on, Mr. Thomas," Big John Sommerland said to Abraham one day on the sidewalk in front of the store. "Everybody's gone plumb crazy, I tell ya."

"It can't last, Mr. Sommerland, it can't last. But it's getting tempting to sell something, isn't it?"

Claims that "they aren't making land anymore," and that "the stock market has no top" were actually being proven daily in every respect. Certainly, everyone's perception seemed to believe it, and that attitude just compounded on itself. Values and accumulated national debt were becoming irrationally, extraordinarily high, yet everyone thought the trend acceptable because asset values went up daily. But so did debt. *Lots and lots of debt.*

Alexander devoted most of his waking hours to his store, his cattle, and his land. As Big John had urged, he hired Wilbur McCray, and while Wilbur was put in charge of the cattle and the pastures, Alexander found he couldn't simply stay in the store six days (it was never open on Sundays) each week wondering what Wilbur was doing, what problems he was facing daily. Especially, he felt that if he stayed in the store everyday, he couldn't learn the cattle business which he believed he had to do. As a result, he decided to close his store all day Wednesday and Thursday, and at noon on the other work days during the hot summer months. During the busy winter tourist season he would close at noon only on Wednesdays.

As the days, weeks, then months progressed, Alexander found himself completely committed to his growing businesses. Up early each day long before other merchants got to their stores, he remained late at night writing his suppliers seeking new merchandise, new models, sometimes calculating the wisdom of purchasing additional property. Sometimes he would simply rearrange and refresh his inventory displays. Achieving more sales and thus more profits, Alexander believed would result in more independence, more security. And more freedom. During the really slow summer months, Wilbur would stop by the store some mornings with Alexander's new horse in tow. They would then ride out to visit his growing herd of cattle, talking as they rode. Sometimes both would be lost in thought, simply enjoying the ride in the early morning hours.

"Tell me, Wilbur, what brought you to Kissimmee? In the beginning I mean," Alexander said, gesturing with his hand. "Where did your family come from?"

Wilbur responded, "Well, I'm told my family first came from Scotland near the Isle of Wye. My family was poor and, like most, had a small flock of sheep as tenant farmers. The land wasn't rich and fertile and they had short growin' seasons. Times got bad. The English persecuted the Scots who were Presbyterian, and my family was surely Scot *and* Presbyterian." Stopping to think a moment, he continued, "Like a lot of people, my family thought there was freedom and better opportunity in the Colonies. That, my good friend, is when this America was just gettin' started, y'know, back in the mid-1700s. My folks, like most Scots, came to Philadelphia. My family was still poor and couldn't make it in the city, so they went west to the frontier in western Pennsylvania."

"Poor like us?" asked Alexander.

"Yep, just like you and your Dad were," Wilbur replied with a knowing smile. "Just like you."

"You know, it seems like most immigrants who came to America, and they're still coming, are poor, or trying to escape some army, famine or something."

"Seems to me, "Wilbur nodded, "the only difference between you an' me is *when* our families came to America. That's the way I see it anyhow."

"How about T.J. and his family?" asked Alexander. "What about them?"

"I think, Alexander," Wilbur said, rubbing his three-day-old beard with his free hand, "I think they came from England originally, or maybe Germany in the 1700s. I'm not sure. But I do know his family was already in New York when all those Irish started coming here in the 1800s after the Civil War. His people hated immigrants real bad. They killed a bunch of those Irish and called 'em bad names. They thought they owned America and nobody else had the right to be here."

"I think he doesn't like me for the same reason," Alexander shrugged.

"Yep, that's likely, and I'd sure be careful of T.J. He *can* be mean. And don't you wear a gun, Alexander. Best not or he'll come after you and you don't use a gun so good yet."

"I know. He doesn't bother me. I just do my work. But I've got my sling. And I'm not afraid of him."

That was the extent of Alexander's exposure to T.J. for a long time.

After an hour of walking the horses, they reached the gate to the pasture as they pulled the horses up.

"Whoa," called Wilbur to his steed.

"Whoa," followed Alexander as he leaned back, pulled his reins equally, and pushed his feet forward in the leather stirrups, just like Wilbur had taught him.

"Well, Alexander, let's have a look and see what's happenin' with the herd." Wilbur leaned down and unlocked the gate's latch. Then, resuming his position in the saddle, kicked his horse with his heels, leaned forward, squeezed his thighs, and entered the fenced pasture through the gate opening at a gallop. With Wilbur watching, Alexander followed close behind. They would first check the fence line each day, then ride into the herd.

"The grass is growing richer everyday, Alexander, and with this good weather, sun and rain, we got our shares of calves. They're breedin' all the time. Our bulls have been right vigorous," he smiled, "and there's plenty of young heifers here to keep 'em busy."

Looking over his growing herd of cattle roaming the green grasses with the new calves made Alexander lean back, press his stirrups forward, come to a stop, sit squarely in his saddle and ponder. He was more than a little amazed at how far he had come from the humble stone one-room hovel in Douma which was surrounded by rugged, mostly barren mountains.

Quiet for a few minutes, enjoying the morning's dew sparkling on the grass, he recalled the difficult years of his youth during the locust scourge, the four-year famine, the almost total absence of hope that drove his father away to find a new life for them. And the lack of food that, like many others in the village, cost his mother her life. He even recalled his oath: "I'll never be without food again." Confidently, as his eyes swept the herd, he swore it again out loud.

"What's that?" Wilbur asked, turning his head. "What'd ya say?"

He turned to look at his friend. "When I was young in the village back in Lebanon, my family, along with the whole village were totally without food. We were being starved out by the Turks. That's why my father came to America, because he believed he had to. I nearly lost my feet in a snowstorm just trying to get wheat to make bread, Wilbur. My mother died from lack of food, and when I was younger, I swore I would never be hungry again. And as I look at this herd with you, I see the lush green grass, and realize this belongs to me. I am amazed, Wilbur."

"You're doin' right good, Alexander."

"And so are you, Wilbur, because if I do good, you do good." Then, shifting in his saddle with a new thought, he asked his friend, "When do we go to Tampa again?"

"I reckon we're about ready," replied Wilbur, as he pulled a small bag of tobacco from his left breast pocket. Then, as he sat in his saddle, his feet secure in the stirrups, looking over the herd alongside Alexander, he pulled out a packet of thin paper sheets. After removing one sheet, he put the packet back into his shirt pocket. Cupping the sheet in his fingers, then biting the pull strings of the tobacco bag with his teeth, he opened the bag and began thumping it with his index finger, dusting the cupped paper sheet with tobacco shavings. Following his filling of the paper sheet, he rolled his cigarette with both hands, then slowly licked the edge and rolled it tight and slipped the new, primitive cigarette between his lips. "Want a smoke, Alexander?"

"No, I don't think so. My sin is *arak*," he smiled, waving his hand in the air. "Thanks anyway."

It became a daily ritual with the pair to ride out and inspect the herd in the early morning hours. It was also a time of bonding closely in their relationship. Both were grateful for the implicit endorsement by Big John Sommerland to their relationship. That was an added bonus.

"I think," Wilbur paused, looking over the herd, "I think," he repeated typically for emphasis turning his head to the herd, "that we can afford to cut out at least a hundred head and send them to Tampa's yards next week. We don't want to take too many yet; a hundred's about the least we can deliver. And," he added, "prices are gettin' higher all the time. But I think thinning the herd's good. See them yearlings over yonder? Well, next fall they'll be ready and by then the prices'll be even better."

Then, Alexander, anticipating Wilbur's next thought, picked up with, "Maybe we ought to plan on two or three hundred in the fall then?"

"Yep, that's what I'm thinkin.' Let's have a look at some of those calves. See if any are sick or got worms. Can't have any get the others sick now."

After several hours of checking individual cows, yearlings and calves, the two returned to the gate where Alexander rode through and Wilbur remained inside the fence. Waving over his shoulder as he looked back at his employee and friend, and his growing herd, Alexander kicked his heels in his horse, smiling with pride, and headed back at a fast canter to town and his shop.

CHAPTER 23

$\mathcal{L}$ate in the summer of 1924, in the midst of the Florida "Land Boom," Alexander went to Boston with his father to visit relatives. Abigail was now married and living in Tampa. And after four years, he had not received any letters from Madeleine. *Why?* he often asked himself. *Why? Has she totally forgotten? Is she still alive? Doesn't she still remember me? Why doesn't she answer my letters?* Finally, after a great deal of soul searching, listening to his father's continual instructions, admonitions of marriage to a proper Syrian girl, and staying involved in his work and his place in Kissimmee, he reluctantly determined he had to go on with his life in America, marry, and have children. In Boston, his father stayed with Uncle Mike, while Alexander stayed with Salim and his wife Julia. The purposes of his visit were to see the family, to be sure, but more importantly it was to find a wife, a companion, and, in time, the mother of his children. To Alexander, remembering his culture, this was appropriate. He had finally received a letter from Hanna in Marseille saying that Daniella and Madeleine had to go to Paris because of "personal family reasons," and that times were difficult in Marseille. He couldn't truly understand what Hanna was telling him, or more important, what Hanna *wasn't* telling him. But at least, after so long, he now knew that Madeleine was alive…personal reasons? *Did she get married? Does she have children? Is she ill? Is her mother ill?* There were so many questions but still he had received no correspondence from Madeleine. So, Alexander felt he had to stay focused on his own reality and bring his attention to the present and his visit to Boston to find someone. It remained an emotional struggle for him nevertheless.

"Eat your dinner, Iskandar." Julia spoke, still referring to Alexander by his Arabic name. "My sister will be here in a few minutes, and you have been picking at your food. Are you not well?" Alexander looked up and abruptly stopped thinking of Madeleine. Julia and he spoke for a few minutes more until they were interrupted by a knock at the door. Salim went to the door and ushered Helene into the sparse but comfortable dining room.

Alexander stood, and spoke, "Hello, Helene, I'm glad to see you again." In that first moment, he saw a pretty young woman, fully blossomed, no longer the young girl he met when first he came to Boston. His eyebrows rose as his eyes widened, seeing her as a fully developed young woman.

"You have really grown up since we last saw each other. You were only a little girl. Now, you look wonderful." Helene was dressed in the fashion of the day: a clinging chemise that draped over her winsome figure, reaching to just beyond her knees. Her shoes, he noticed, were very fashionable with pointed toes and t-straps across her feet. She wore a pretty ribbon in her hair. He knew she had dressed her best for their meeting, just as had he, to make a strong first impression and get on with the formalities of a proper courtship.

Helene smiled coquettishly, "I was just fifteen, Alexander. Now I am nineteen, a woman." She posed for him, hands on her hips, smiling confidently, turning so he could see her figure. "It's nice to see you too after such a long time. You must like Florida. Uncle Mike says you and your father are very successful. He told me that you have your own store, a cattle ranch, and are buying an automobile. That's exciting."

"Oh," he laughed and replied, pulling his hands as though riding a horse, "I also own a horse and a bicycle!"

Helene laughed with him, impressed by this successful, handsome, determined, yet modest, young suitor with a sense of humor.

Alexander and Helene visited for several hours that evening in the parlor with Julia and Salim, properly chaperoned, as Alexander spoke of his experiences in Florida. "I learned a lot from the Sommerlands," he began as he told Helene of all his cultural advances and of learning English with Abigail as his tutor. He spoke of his cattle ranch, Big John and Mrs. Sommerland, and their daughter, Abigail, carefully avoiding saying anything beyond his platonic friendship with her.

Helene, in turn, described to Alexander her life. She worked in the textile mill in Boston like most young women, had completed high school, and would likely continue working in the mill to help the family's finances, not considering college.

Julia, in an effort to tempt Alexander, exclaimed with a smile, "Two men have come here to meet Helene! They asked her to marry them in the past year. Can you imagine? One was from California; his name was Butrus. He was nice, but Helene didn't think she was meant to live on a farm in California. It's so different and so far away. Another came here from Toledo, Ohio. They were both looking for a wife, for sure. They wanted to find someone our age, of their religion, and Syrian. Helene didn't like them enough, so she said no."

"You said 'no' to two suitors?" he asked, turning to Helene, befuddled. "What would you say to me? That is, if I were to ask?"

"Hmmm," she demurred, smiling, "I'm not sure yet," as she turned her head away coquettishly, with a wink at her sister. "You'll have to ask to find out, Iskandar," she teased.

Her confidence made Alexander want her more. His feelings for this lovely young woman grew stronger each day. After all, he was in Boston for a reason.

❧❦❧

Alexander knew he was on a mission, determined even before leaving Kissimmee that he would find a bride in Boston. He didn't really know even one single girl in Florida. But in Boston, there was a large — in fact, one of the largest — Syrian communities in America. And he knew he had something to offer, including his business success, his tenacity, his resilience and his willingness to accept a challenge. He did find Helene attractive, although she didn't stir his emotions like Madeleine had. But, she was pretty; she was Syrian; she was Orthodox Christian, and her family certainly accepted him and his father. So, he knew all was well, and perhaps Helene would be the means of fulfillment of his destiny. After all, marriage and children were a large part of where his life must go. So, he decided to do whatever it took to sell Helene on the idea of marrying him during his four-week stay. As a result, Alexander spent a lot of time with Helene, Sam, Julia, and the family.

Madeleine's lack of response to his many letters had convinced him to seriously consider another woman.

By the end of the summer visit, Helene had indeed turned down his first proposal, like she had done to her two previous suitors, instinctively knowing how to make sure her man *really* wanted her, but in the end, she finally said yes to Alexander's more convincing second effort, making him very proud and happy.

At the right moment, he had reached into his pocket and pulled out the two-carat blue diamond ring he had bought from his supplier, Syden and Company, when he knew he was going to Boston. On that important evening at Salim and Julia's house, in their living room before dinner, with Salim's encouraging nod and hand motion, Alexander nervously stepped across the room, and stood before Helene. Mustering all his courage, he looked into her eyes as she gazed into his, clearly excited and flattered. He carefully kneeled onto the floor. Then, reaching for her hands folded in her lap holding a rose bud, he whispered so softly she could barely hear his words, "Helene, will you marry me?"

Then, in that pregnant silent moment, as she looked at him without responding quickly, realizing the importance of what all this meant, Alexander got even more flustered. Before she could reply, remembering she had already turned down his clumsy first proposal, and two other suitors, Alexander blurted out, "If you say 'yes,' I will build you a big house! I will buy you a horse and your own saddle! And..."

"Iskandar!" she laughed, "yes!" Then, hearing her own loud laughter, she quickly covered her mouth and giggled silently. "I will marry you because you are too funny to let go! I think you and I can have a good life together, but don't worry about getting me a horse and saddle. I'm a city girl. Remember?"

Still holding her hands, Alexander stood up and pulled her to him very relieved, very happy. "Yes," he said, "yes, Helene, I will be a good and faithful husband to you. So let's get married right away and then let me take you to Kissimmee!"

"Kiss...a...me," she laughed. "What a name! Is that what you do down there? Just kiss...a...me all the time?"

They all laughed together at her joke, dissipating any lingering tension and drawing the entire family into the laughter so that everyone nodded, knowing that this marriage would last a long time.

Alexander and Helene were very soon married at her family church. Marriage was a means to continue his life's destiny, have a family and a lifelong companion.

He recalled his father's admonition. "You can learn to love her later."

Helene liked Alexander very much. She would whisper to Julia, "He is so good-looking, and I think he will be kind to me. I don't think we will ever go hungry; after all he has lots of cows. And," she laughed, "he's very funny!"

These realities were the most important considerations; love and passion would come later.

These were times of family naiveté and joy, so their post wedding days were filled with family gatherings, dancing, dinners and celebrations. Perhaps because of Helene's innocence and shyness, they didn't consummate their marriage for a month, not until after they had arrived back in Kissimmee.

CHAPTER 24

*W*ithin a year, as costs of everything were going up too fast, and realizing that his very attractive bride would not likely want to stay in the upstairs apartment with her father-in-law for long, Alexander decided to invest in a house for the two of them. He quickly proceeded to build a beautiful four-bedroom, frame Victorian new home for Helene in Kissimmee on the west shore of Lake Tohopekaliga, fulfilling his promise that evening in Boston.

He had admired the Sommerland home so much that he used it as a model for Helene's new house. He felt he needed all those bedrooms because he fully intended to have several children, and have a room for his father, if needed.

In the spring of 1925, Helene bore a healthy and beautiful son, Michael. The Thomas's were becoming a family that would become very much a part of the Central Florida landscape. Alexander felt a sense of completeness. His baby son's giggles blocked out any thoughts of Marseille.

"I have a son," he repeated every day. "If a man has a son, he will live forever, it is said. I now have a son who will carry on my name...my legacy. All that I do everyday will be for my son. My life is dedicated to him. He is my life." Alexander began to fully believe he had indeed found his destiny with the birth of Michael.

He spent almost all day, every day, particularly during the busier winter months, at the store, and for several hours into the early evenings on horseback with Wilbur searching for his cattle on the open range. He focused on working to insure his family's life was secure. There was no such thing as "working too hard" to Alexander. He worked long hours with his characteristic sense of responsibility, tenacity, and even stubbornness. "I will do whatever it takes, *Baba*," he would often say to his father, "to provide a better, easier future for my family than you and I had. If it takes working twenty hours a day, I will do it."

But too, he was often home for lunch with Helene, as they grew closer and closer, depending on each other to make their lives full, as warm and happy as possible.

"My son, Helene," he'd say proudly as he played with Michael, fascinated by their incredibly perfect creation.

"Yes, Alexander. We have a beautiful son, thank God," she would always respond lovingly as she watched her husband hold Michael aloft, making him laugh.

They laughed a lot together, especially as they shared the life of their son. Alexander was proud of Michael and was devoted to him and his mother, looking forward to teaching him how to ride a horse. Meanwhile, as Michael's young years passed, Alexander's prosperity kept growing to ensure his family's security.

But fortunes change quickly, often due to conditions beyond anyone's control. The uncertainties of the weather in the subtropics and the wrath of nature had much in store for the residents of South Florida during the 1920s.

The severe hurricanes that swept central and southeastern Florida in the summers of 1926 and 1928 caused havoc, death and economic ruin in the area. They brought great distress among land speculators, citrus owners and cattlemen. Thousands of people were killed when Lake Okeechobee to the south overflowed and broke the lake's southern dike. In an instant, the workers' quarters south of the dike were flooded with waters up to ten feet deep. The devastation to South Florida was catastrophic. It shocked everyone because the 1928 hurricane was so much worse than anyone had ever experienced. Cattle were swept away by wind gusts of over one hundred-fifty miles per hour. And heavy, unprecedented blown rains flooded the Kissimmee River basin, killing thousands of cows and steers, including hundreds of Alexander's herd. It was a terrible time for everyone.

There were other casualties in South Florida. The Henry Flagler Railroad from Miami to Key West was destroyed, eliminating that easy shipping route to and from Cuba. And while that increased the importance of the Tampa-to-Cuba trade routes and the Plant Railroad System that passed through Kissimmee and Orlando to Fort Myers, the horrific hurricanes also were the last straw for the vulnerable "Land Boom."

As a result of the hurricanes and other contributing factors, the skyrocketing "Land Boom" fever burst like a bubble. By 1928, the "irrational exuberance" was over. Land prices plummeted. Fortunes were lost. And prosperity disappeared overnight throughout South Florida. Nearly everyone in the land ownership, development, speculation, and construction business went totally broke. Bankruptcies were endemic. Many had lost everything. Land values plummeted to as little as $1 per acre in just two years. The over-leveraging of just 5% equity caused a collapsing effect no one could have foreseen. While the cattlemen and citrus growers of central Florida still had their lands, their cattle and their citrus trees, the market for beef and citrus completely evaporated, prices fell dramatically every day, and everyone suffered. Hundreds of disenchanted newcomers quickly returned to the northern states looking for jobs and help, leaving Florida in economic ruin. Alexander's fate was no exception. He too was on the financial ropes. There was little or no business at the store; no one had cash, and only with bartering of goods and services did the people survive.

Over in the Palm Beach County town of Boca Raton, on the southeast coast, Addison Mizner's "Greatest Resort in the World," collapsed. In just one week in 1926 at the peak of the "Land Boom," the Mizner brothers, Addison and Wilson, had sold $21,000,000 of land, almost all on credit. Now, only two years later, they were bankrupt. Blue Mountain development in Lake Wales, with its huge, expensive homes, closed down. Many developers, suppliers, and buyers had depended on those who bought from them on debt, expecting they would pay their debts. But they too, like a line of domino chips, fell one after the other.

The "Land Boom" had become the "Land Crash."

As in the Gold Rush days of the Klondike in Alaska in 1899 and in California in 1849, those quiet, patient shopkeepers and makers of tools were the fortunate ones who had survived, but only barely. They sold for "cash only," had little or no debt, and fewer sales just barely sustained them. "In God we trust, all others pay cash" was a familiar sign in most stores. Of course, many shopkeepers had caught the speculation fever too. Fortunately for Alexander, his father had tempered most of his youthful urgings throughout the temptations of the boom. Abraham, with his genetic and nurtured stubbornness in addition to his immigrant's insecurity syndrome, had stood firm. And since Alexander simply could not go against his father, he stayed out of the fever.

It was painful and frustrating for Alexander, but he did invest in one venture.

By 1927, the "Land Boom" had reached its zenith. Abraham had resisted all proposals until someone offered terms he could not refuse. He finally sold each of his two properties. During the "Boom" years of 1925 and 1926, Alexander had built a small hotel, and lost his entire investment when the crash came so suddenly. His builder had left town in the night, leaving Alexander to pay the suppliers and workers in addition to his payments to the builder the day before. As a result, he had paid for his new store and hotel *twice*. Another expensive lesson learned. He was devastated and miserable about it. He was left with little to even pay property taxes. He lost the money, the hotel, and the land, and had to borrow from his father to pay his bills.

In October of 1927, Helene was also in her last month of pregnancy with their second child. Alexander worried how he could afford to feed another child.

"I do hope it's a girl," she would write to her sisters in Boston. "My son has been a wonderful gift from God, and he makes Alexander so proud. But, I'd like a daughter for myself," and, teasingly, she would add, "so she can take care of me when I grow old. A man stands taller when his wife bears a son, for he will soon be able to help him with the ranch. But I wish for a daughter."

Helene had been the second of eight children whose immigrant parents were very spiritual, always gaining strength from their prayers. They steeped their children in the core beliefs of Faith, Faith, Faith and trust in God.

In mid-November 1927, during the worst of times, Helene bore Alexander a beautiful dark-haired daughter they named Helena.

In October 1929, the third blow to Florida occurred with the stock market crash some eighteen months after the Florida "Land Crash." By 1930, after the stock market crash and banks' closings, Alexander and Helene suffered economically along with everyone else though they had become well established in the small community of Kissimmee. Alexander was very proud of his popular wife and mother of his children. He was a happy man in spite of the problems of the business world. Business was much slower, nearly evaporating. But they survived. The reduced demands at work allowed Alexander more time to be on his horse with Wilbur and Michael. Though the area was economically depressed, Helene was pleased with her beautiful Victorian home on the shore of Lake Tohopekaliga, for which Alexander had paid cash. They did not have to face a mortgage debt like so many others. And though she had experienced a great deal of cultural shock leaving thriving Boston to come to this "barren, frontier cattle town," as she called it in her letters home, she became very involved in the church, baked pastries for the church bazaars, helped provide food for the poor, attended the Kissimmee Women's Cultural Association, and tended to Alexander's needs. She always believed her role was to keep their home and raise their children. She assiduously kept them aware of their father's love for them. When they wondered aloud, "Why is Daddy working at the ranch and store so much?" she would remind them, "He works so hard and so many hours to make your lives better than his was. He loves you very much."

"In time this will pass, Helene," Alexander would say optimistically, trying to comfort her. "We must be thankful for what we have. But these are terrible, terrible times," he would remind his loyal wife. "I am doing my best, and we will be fine," he assured her.

She knew conditions were worse in the north from the letters her family wrote to her dutifully, "Almost everybody is laid off. No work anywhere."

He confided with her in their quiet moments, sounding very upset, "Even now, we are experiencing the devil's handwork. There is a fruit bug ruining all the citrus. They call it the Mediterranean fruit fly. We may lose our entire harvest this year and have to destroy much of the groves...it's always something."

Helene could only grip Alexander's hand and remind him, "We must have faith, Alexander. Your family will not be a burden. Just do the best you can."

"All we can do is fight these things and endure. These are bad times, Helene, but the locusts were worse. If I survived them, I can survive anything. And we will."

In 1928, Alexander had followed the advice of his mentor, Big John, and began crossbreeding his growing herd with the newly arrived Brahman bulls that the Stewart family in Bartow and large rancher Bud Parkins had brought to the area from India by way of Texas.

"The Brahman breed can handle the heat better than our cattle. They're larger by far, add more weight faster than our cattle, and are resistant to the Texas Fever Tick," Bud Parkins had told Alexander.

"They sure look strange with that hump on the back."

Will Stewart down in Polk County was also a strong advocate of crossbreeding with the Brahman breed. "I'm convinced, Alexander," Stewart had told him during one of Alexander's visits to Bartow, "that you'd better get your cows to be with my bulls and get ahead of the rest. You ought to get a few cows too. It's a wise decision. Take a few of my bulls and get going, son." He added, almost as a throwaway statement, "I'm gonna build the best darned Brahman herd in the country. That's how strong I feel about this breed."

"You've sure been good to me over the years, Mr. Stewart. I do appreciate your help."

"Yeah, I'll have a couple of trucks sent over with, say, six bulls and a dozen young Brahman heifers. You're doin' the smart thing, son."

Within a few years, Will Stewart, known as one of the finest, most honest ranchers in the region, did indeed build the highest quality closed Brahman herd in America. Alexander knew Stewart's word was gold, that he was a good Christian man and could totally be trusted. The word on him was spreading across America's cattle country. In time, even the Argentines began arriving in Bartow to partake of the excellence of the Stewart farm breeding bulls.

Thanks to his listening to Will Stewart's advice and crossbreeding his herd with Stewart's Brahman, Alexander's herd soon grew in number, size, quality, and value. Each head gained more weight and required less water. Back in 1920, before Alexander owned any cattle, the Texas Fever Tick had struck the area killing thousands of heads of cattle. Those few herds that were at least one-eighth Brahman crossbred were spared.

But, even worse conditions came in the 1930s Great Depression with the plummeting demand for beef in the Northern markets. Alexander and the other ranchers suffered enormously. Many lost everything: their income, most of their herds, and even their land. Conditions got so bad that most owners of large land tracts couldn't even pay the county taxes on the land.

Economic conditions punished the people of America and Europe. Alexander suffered along with the other ranchers and farmers in Florida. Many of the hired cowmen lost their jobs, including T.J. Hatfield. But Alexander did his best to adjust. It was only after several years of pain that the conditions got better in the mid-1930s that he and his father were able to modestly invest in the now severely depressed juice canning businesses in the region after the terrible fruit fly infestation, when citrus and grove prices fell to near nothing. Several years of wise investing enabled them to hold commanding interests in four local juice operations. Some still came close to failing, but some ventures did well enough to carry the others. It was difficult for everyone, but Alexander and his father had been hardened, tempered and tested for years. Conditions everywhere were barren and austere. The country was in an emotional malaise with no confidence in government or even in themselves. It took a lot of adjusting, a lot of luck, and just plain hard work to survive those bleak years. Alexander often was reminded of the harsh years of famine and locusts in Lebanon that drove his father and him into rags and out of the land of their ancestors. Now, he often thought, it looks as if we have to go through theses hardships all over again.

"The past made us stronger," Abraham reminded his son more than once. "But we'll always have enough to eat, if nothing more."

"That's why I always keep our large garden, *Baba*. Thank God for the good land and the weather here where you brought us. Thank you for not staying in the North!"

During those awful years of the early 1930s, when people were practically starving in the North, when unemployment reached the unbelievable level of 26%, and angry men were rioting in the streets of New York and Chicago, demanding work, Alexander sold a minimum of cattle at depressed prices, working instead to save his herd and improve its breeding with Brahman bulls and cows, improving the quality of his holdings. He also did what he could to clear his land of scrub and obtrusive palmetto.

"We're not getting anything for our cattle these days anyway, with beef at almost give-away prices," he would say to other ranchers when they would meet at the Cattlemen's Beef Market. "I'd rather just keep them in the pasture, and improve my breeding with the Brahmans until prices increase. And they will one day. This can't last forever."

"You are always the optimist, Thomas," one of his colleagues would respond.

Day after day, month after month, even year after profitless year, the men tried their best to encourage each other. Some quit and took jobs wherever they could. Some did begin to believe these times could get even worse and maybe last forever. But Alexander, like the Stewarts, the Parkins, and the Sommerlands, never gave up on the cattle business. They found solutions, determined to hang onto their land and precious herds. As terrible as conditions were across the country, Alexander had been through worse conditions in his youth in Douma. Somehow he always found the inner strength to keep on, not to give in to the conditions.

"You know, Big John," he said optimistically, one day as they were all sharing a whiskey at the hotel bar, "It's always darkest before the dawn."

"Yep, Alexander, and don't forget," Big John said, smiling, jabbing his elbow into Alexander's ribs, "it's always darkest before the end too." He laughed sardonically and everyone joined in laughing at this not so funny reminder. There was comfort in being with their friends during these moments when they weren't suffering alone over their dismal books.

Some large landowners did make it through the early darkest days of the Great Depression, but many who were over-extended, lost their lands, tens of thousands of acres, literally hundreds of square miles of pastureland, to the counties and state governments for *ad valorem* taxes. They had no money to pay for *anything*, even property taxes. Few had even the minimal available cash. One rancher lost over 15,000 acres of land for only $200 in taxes. He simply could not put $10 together and the government would only accept cash. He nearly committed suicide. Others, scared and depressed, simply left the region for good.

In 1934, Alexander finally had to borrow to pay taxes on his land. But he was among the few who could find the resources to actually pay on his taxes. No matter what happened, every year the government sent tax statements with the threat that they could take your land. "You don't pay, we take it away." There was so much anger in the region that any collector who dared to show his face was in danger of being shot.

CHAPTER 25

During the slow 1930s, store sales were almost non-existent. In fact, some days there were no sales at all. Often, shopkeepers simply visited one another to pass the time of day, commiserating on the "ineffective" politics in Washington and how "the government should do something." It was so bad that Alexander often invited Wilbur to stay over in his house where Helene would feed him in exchange for his paycheck.

By 1937, economic conditions began to improve. Alexander and his father bought more land at very depressed prices when opportunity arose. During those next several years, they were again able to purchase acres of citrus land with fruit bearing trees and pastureland for as little as fifty cents per acre. Some available land, with better access and less lowland, cost as much as $2.00 per acre. The market for citrus and beef had almost disappeared, but they found their cattle loved the chopped citrus fruit, so they began to feed their herds with the fallen or harvested unsold oranges during the winter season, while the grasses were dry and the citrus was ready for harvest. That year Alexander bought two used trucks for $100 on credit to haul the fruit to the herds. Because the Thomases inherently had long term views, determined to think of their children and their future children, they willingly became "land poor" lacking cash for the short term, forsaking the present and investing for the future. Life at home throughout the 1930s continued to be a frugal, Spartan existence, spending money only when absolutely vital.

By the mid 1930s, Michael was a growing youngster of ten. He helped his mother in the garden...working each day "to make Dad proud of me." He was especially proud when the vegetables ripened and he could bring them into the house. "Do you like my tomatoes, Dad?" or "I'm bringing in lots of beans in a few days. I want to help you, Mom."

"He's just like I was when I was ten, Helene...doing his best to share the burden. I love that boy."

Helena, of course, was a child playfully teasing her parents who doted on her all the time. But she didn't escape her duties. She helped her mother fold the laundry, and assisted her in the kitchen by handing her the utensils as needed, while learning how to prepare the Lebanese foods. Times were very difficult, but, since they always had food, they were better off than many, and they were grateful the family could be together.

During the mid-1930s in Europe, Hitler was advancing; his growing power and armed forces began to threaten the entire continent. Communism also was spreading across Europe from Russia into the Ukraine and the Baltics. Later it was threatening all of Europe, especially France, Italy, the Balkans, and Austria. It was even becoming a growing influence in America. To those in America and on the continent who were out of work, Socialism was a very attractive solution. "Those rich people have everything while we can't even get a job. We need change." Labor union growth was becoming a powerful political force, and the federal government was now more and more involved in everyone's life. The cattlemen of Central Florida were concerned about how to cope with the terribly low price of beef and citrus. They too were becoming concerned about the government taking their land under the guise of "land reform." Shopkeepers were worried about how to keep their stores open for business. Both were at wit's end about how to continue to feed their families and herds. Over time, as Europe became "a front page story," the men began to change their discussions to include the subjects of European politics, government actions, and possible new markets for beef.

"Alexander," some would ask, "what's your opinion on Europe?" or, "Alexander, you know more about Europe than the rest of us, how do you think France, England, and Poland can survive the German threat?"

Each time Alexander heard the news of Europe on the radio, he would think about his family in Lebanon, and Hanna, Daniella, and Madeleine in Marseille, especially Madeleine, wherever she was. He prayed they were safe.

The political conditions and threat of war in Europe were getting more and more serious, and the implications affecting Madeleine, became a harsh reality when Germany invaded Poland, and then, in the summer of 1940, when the German army virtually marched into France, taking over the government and occupying most of the country. Paris and all its treasures were saved because the French surrendered it to the Nazis without a shot fired. But the suddenness of Germany's intrusion in every direction, including southern France, and its' threat to England, became a major diversion of the people and the government of America, in spite of the local problems. "At least *we're* not at war...yet."

Economic conditions got so bad that the state of Florida and its counties were nearing a revenue crisis. Tax receipts were dangerously low. As Hamilton Disston had saved the state of Florida from bankruptcy with his first $200,000 purchase in 1884, so too a new state law was required to save Florida from bankruptcy in 1938. This new law allowed the private purchase of land from the government for only the taxes owed on the land. This enabled cattle ranchers, citrus farmers and any others to buy back much of the land they had lost to their government during the worst of the Depression years. Buyers could purchase just for taxes due all over the state, and while it enabled those with cash to add to their land holdings at very low costs, it also helped the city, county, and state governments to reduce their land-holdings, and provided much needed revenue by putting land back on the tax rolls. It was quite a turn of events for those who could scrape a few hundred dollars together.

Abraham and Alexander saw opportunity in "buying for taxes" and began to carefully invest from their "bank in the field." When the new law came into effect, and as times began to get better, they sat at the same spare table in Abraham's apartment, and scoured page after page of tax sales announcements in the newspapers. The Thomas family was one of the beneficiaries. So were the Parkins and the Stewarts.

Along with a few others, these three families each bought tens of thousands of acres during the improving years of the Great Depression from 1938 for virtually pennies per acre. Many fine properties, including buildings constructed during the "Land Boom," were bought for hardly anything. Sometimes, hundreds of acres were bought for as little as 50 cents per acre.

Trusting the future, and seeing their sales slowly but steadily improve, Alexander and Abraham accumulated numerous improved properties in towns throughout the area, as well as thousands of acres of productive pasture and citrus land. By 1941, they were poised for good times, even though the Depression era was not completely over. But World War II was on the horizon.

By early 1941, Alexander, through cattle crossbreeding with the Brahman and purchasing dirt cheap pasture lands *with* cattle, had accumulated a total of 30,000 acres of pasture, 5,000 head of cattle, and two thousand acres of productive citrus groves. He was now considered among the more successful farmers and ranchers, and was well-respected for his integrity.

His children were growing up; Michael was now a tall and rugged fourteen-year-old, and Helena, at twelve, was a beautiful dark-haired young girl, a tomboy who loved her horse Sheikh, and could ride him as well as her brother rode his horse. Most of the time she wore her long hair in a ponytail like a lot of her girlfriends. "It's cooler this way, Dad," she would explain when her father asked her to wear it down. "Your hair is so pretty when you let it be natural, Helena," was Alexander's response.

Michael, looking much like his father and nearly as tall, rode his horse expertly. He worked the cattle as Wilbur taught him, and was doing well in school. Alexander and Helene were very proud of their son.

The children were happy. They worked the herds with Wilbur and their father, and played at the lake with their friends. Like most first generation Lebanese, they stayed close to home and their parents. The years of the late 1930s were somewhat better for the Thomas family and for most of the ranchers and citrus grove owners as national conditions began to stabilize and improve. Still, they were not yet rehiring their crews they had laid off. Alexander kept his single cowman, Wilbur, on his payroll throughout the entire 1930s. Because he survived and Wilbur was still employed, Alexander's reputation was strong, especially among the cowmen who were searching for any kind of work they could find.

Alexander, now in his twenty-first year in Kissimmee, was considered a shrewd businessman in the region. By 1941, he was asked to serve on several boards of directors: a bank board, a hospital board, and the corporations that owned those juicing plants in which he now held substantial and growing ownership. They found his counsel and advice to be sound, seasoned, and wise.

He was also a good family man.

"Let's go, children," he would say on Saturday. "Which do you want to do today? Hunting or fishing? Michael, you're old enough now to learn how to aim and shoot a gun. And you must learn how to respect it and the land too."

Waving to Helene as they drove away, he would take them in his 1937 Ford pickup truck, ready with his .12 and .410 gauge shotguns, .22 Winchester rifle, and fresh water fishing gear. He had not been interested in fishing until Michael had reached ten years of age. But now, he found Sunday afternoons with Michael to be a wonderful respite. He taught his children, even Helena from the time she was six years old and sat on his lap, how to steer or drive the truck, and to fish and hunt small game like quail and rabbit, and, in the fall, turkey and deer. All were plentiful in the area, especially deer who were overpopulated. Michael proved to be an excellent hunter and impressed his father with his accuracy. Most of what they brought back went to the church for the poor townsfolk. He taught his children to give of themselves, and to help the church. "Help the poor," he would admonish, "and always share your blessings." Alexander had found that during the Great Depression many in the area were without food and other necessities. He and several others who had more of life's rewards gave food to the needy. Deer, small game, turkey, fish, and vegetables were available on Broadway, Kissimmee's main street, throughout the decade on Sunday afternoons.

Like other teenagers in cattle country who helped their families in the summer, Michael and Helena spent their vacation time learning all they could from Uncle Wilbur and their father. Michael was quite the accomplished "cowboy." And even Helena was getting skilled in the saddle. All her friends were "cowgirls," and like them, she wore jeans, work shirts, boots, and had a few calluses on her hands. This certainly was country life, and all youngsters were "country" which was very different than their counterparts in cities like Fort Myers, Miami or Tampa. The Thomas children were excellent in the pasture, working and branding calves from the herd, and cracking their snake-like leather whips as Uncle Wilbur taught them.

"You are a tomboy, Helena," Alexander would say good-naturedly to her as they rode their horses side by side. Her Arabian stallion was a beauty that Helena groomed every day. She loved to ride Sheikh, the fastest horse in their stables. Helena had named her father's black stallion Minuit, French for midnight.

"Yes, Helena, you are quite the horsewoman," her mother would affectionately admonish when she would come home on Saturdays after a ride. "Yet, you must be feminine too. Boys like you to be both."

Alexander, sitting astride Minuit, would laugh out loud as he watched Helena tease Michael in races across the broad-rolling pastures. At these times, even though Helena was only fourteen, he would be reminded of Madeleine and his past.

.

CHAPTER 26

Early in 1941, conditions continued to get somewhat better. Federal government initiatives under President Franklin Roosevelt during the early 1930s were changing the conditions of the country. But times were still not very good. The creation of the Federal Reserve System guarantee on deposits restored faith in the banking system. Federal Work Programs were creating jobs, making more money available for spending, and in the end, increasing the demand for beef and other commodities...finally.

Alexander's efforts at enriching his lands, building his herds through breeding, and improving efficiencies in his citrus operation and juicing plants were beginning to pay off.

Still, times were difficult for most of the world, especially in Europe. In America, prices and profits were still too low to empower companies to hire more help. In 1940, new automobiles could be bought for just $400, bare necessities were very cheap, but most people had to do without. Many Americans were still too poor even to feed themselves despite efforts by the government. War was raging in Europe; France had been invaded by Germany, and England was threatened. But Alexander's world in Florida was still innocent and insulated from the battles overseas. He had his family, and his growing businesses. His son was becoming an adept cattleman, and his cowgirl daughter, Helena, was beautiful, healthy, and popular in her first year in high school. She was tall, slender, and dark-haired, with large brown eyes, a ready smile. Her mother carefully watched over her...as did as the boys in school. Helena, though confident in herself, was also, in a disarming way, modest and feminine. The boys loved being around Helena. So did the girls. She was everyone's friend. And Alexander was proud of both.

"Why don't you have a boyfriend, sis?" Michael asked her.

"I do, Michael. I have lots of friends...most are boys, so I have lots of boyfriends," she would giggle, then smile over her shoulder as she stepped away.

Helena could run as fast as her brother, and could ride her horse now as well as Michael and his friends. She won many impromptu races. "Last one to the lake is a spoiled brat," she would yell to her brother as she kicked her heels into Sheikh's sides. With her long dark hair trailing behind her, she would crouch in the stirrups, laughing and bending forward into the wind, and race to the shoreline. Michael would match her, sometimes beat her, and laugh if she won their race. Sometimes, on Sundays, Alexander and Helene would ride their horses along with their children. When Alexander watched Helena beat Michael, he would remember his friend Abigail racing ahead of him so many years ago, and he would smile. He was happy with Helene. She was a good and devoted wife. He admired Helene. She was his companion, partner, and mother to their children. And, as his father had told him, he had come to love Helene very much. He shared all his life with her, appreciated her, confided in her, kept her informed of his work, and even suggested she keep some of the books. He often let her know how grateful he was for her.

Sometimes, when he watched Helena, he saw Madeleine, remembering his first and lost love running up the hill overlooking the Mediterranean Sea, laughing and calling for him, just like young Helena was doing now. He could not extricate himself from his secret story, and, while torn emotionally with his past, he made himself devote his present to Helene.

Even before the Japanese attacked Pearl Harbor, the demand for beef was increasing as the government that year was buying beef and canned beef products for shipment to its European Allies, especially England. America committed to shipping millions of tons of food, materials, and equipment to England, then to Russia and other countries. Though America was doing its best not to go to war, President Roosevelt was acquiring large quantities of food, materiel, and armaments for the allies in Europe under the Lend-Lease Program.

Alexander, along with his fellow ranchers, including Big John Sommerland, the Parkins family, and the Stewarts, who had in some cases barely survived the economic losses and difficulties of the terrible 1930s, were called on to increase their production of beef, milk, citrus and citrus products. Throughout the dismal 1930s, the cattle ranchers had focused on just managing their herds at minimum production while improving their pastureland. Alexander and Wilbur cleared more trees and palmetto, and underbrush. They planted grass, fertilized the pastures and installed irrigation systems which resulted in a better quality of pastureland and as a result required fewer acres for each head of cattle. While it required ten acres of raw pastureland (including large clumps of palmetto and pine trees) per head of cattle in the 1920s, by the 1940s the improved pastures required only two acres per head. This meant by the time the 1950s arrived, they could raise nearly ten times more cattle on the same grass lands.

Looking out over the rolling open pastures one afternoon, Wilbur said to his friend and employer, "Y'know, Alexander, we've had a lot of tough times, but look at all those rich open pastures...the hills...the clear lakes...we did some good things out here..."

Alexander worked even harder because he was driven, and because, finally, there was a good and growing market. He called on Wilbur to hire more men, increase breeding, move the stock to better pastures, and teach Michael all he could.

"He must learn the business, Wilbur, and I want him to learn it from you, my right arm...my friend. Teach him well. We need all the dedicated help we can get these days. I want Michael to run the businesses one day."

"Sure thing, boss. Hey, T.J. came by lookin' for work. He's been outta work for quite a time."

"You think he'll be okay?"

"Well, I figure it's been more than twenty years since you and him disagreed. He told me awhile back he sure made a bad mistake 'cause you did good since you came to Kissimmee and he'd like another chance. Yeah, boss, I think he's learned the hard way like a lotta people did these past ten years. All of us have. I'd give him a chance. He'll work with me."

Rubbing his chin, thinking on it, Alexander finally responded, "Well, OK, Wilbur. Sure, I think everyone deserves a second chance. Go ahead and hire him. I'll count on you to watch over him."

CHAPTER 27

$\mathcal{T}$imes began getting better for the food and munitions businesses, even though the overall economy was still languishing. And then came "The Day of Infamy," December 7, 1941. *That day, life for all Americans changed dramatically and forever.*

On that memorable date, Helena was fourteen, and Michael sixteen, when America was reluctantly drawn into war. As usual, the family had attended church that morning, and visited with friends during coffee hour after the service.

By one o'clock, they were home, sitting together around the dining room table, sharing their customary Sunday dinner while listening to the background music of Sammy Kaye and his orchestra emanating from their radio, the favorite Sunday afternoon sound for millions of Americans.

Sunday afternoon meals always included *Jiddy* who was there to enjoy his grandchildren, unless on occasion he was in Orlando with his daughter, Leila, and her family. Honoring the Sabbath, the entire community of Kissimmee, as well as most of Central Florida's conservative southern traditional towns, was quiet. All stores were closed, in keeping with the state law. It was a day to rest and be with family. "Blue laws" reigned across much of the country in 1941.

It was about 4 p.m. that day when the music was interrupted by a deep male voice who spoke with a surprisingly serious tone:

"We interrupt your afternoon of listening pleasure to announce that the United States Naval Base at Pearl Harbor on Oahu in the Hawaiian Islands was attacked this morning by the Imperial Japanese Armed Forces. It was a sneak attack that began early in the morning. Casualties are high. Many battleships have been sunk in just a few hours."

Everyone looked at each other, stunned by the news. All day the radio brought announcements by the government with words like "drafting all men over the age of 18." President Roosevelt's speeches and "mobilization" announcements filled the airwaves that day, and the country went into shock, anger, and wonder. The next day, President Roosevelt, before a joint Congressional session, called for a "Declaration of War," and gave his famous

"Day of Infamy" speech. Everyone had believed America was well isolated geographically from Japan and Germany by two great oceans and could stay out of the war.

But that myth was exploded by the attack on Pearl Harbor in Hawaii, a territory of the United States and the main base of the U.S. Navy Pacific Fleet, a place few Americans even knew existed. But the impact on the lives of the people of Kissimmee and the Thomas family was as sudden and as severe as it was across the country. Alexander's mind flashed back to the days of his youth when the Turks occupied his homeland. Would the Japanese be his next oppressor?"

Suddenly, the prospect of Michael going to war engulfed the family.

"*Biyee*, will they come and get Michael?" Helena asked her father fearfully, looking for guidance and reassurance. Her peaceful, happy childhood was suddenly changed, jarred by the reality of war. America was at war.

"Michael is sixteen," Alexander replied. "I think he will be exempted while he is in school. And maybe the war will be over before he becomes eighteen," he said hopefully, but not too convincingly. He, too, was deeply concerned for his beloved only son. Then, turning to his wife, he said "We must look into this and see if it changes his plans for college, Helene."

As the war got worse in early 1942, America totally committed itself to war production by producing tanks, planes, trucks, guns, and even more food for much of the world, as tens of thousands of high school graduates rushed to volunteer to "do my duty" and "defend my country." The closer it came to Michael's eighteenth birthday and his high school graduation, the more the Thomas family realized their world was facing another major personal crisis.

In late June, 1943, Michael, nearly a high school graduate, hesitatingly but proudly announced to his family at the dinner table that night while looking at his father, "Dad, I want to join the Air Force." He paused, waiting for reactions. "I want to help. It's the right thing to do." He paused again, hoping for a response. But none came quickly. "Sure, I could get a deferment by going to college, but would that be right?"

Helena and Michael turned their heads to their father, grandfather, and mother waiting for their guidance, their quiet wisdom. There was a long moment of stunned silence.

Letting his son's profound words sink in, Alexander, at the head of the table with Michael next to him, slowly looked around, in serious thought, hands folded on the table before him. Clearing his throat, he stared at each of them, circling the table with his eyes, acknowledging his own father's focused stare, waiting, not interrupting. Then he reached across the table to Michael's hand and squeezed it, feeling the pain of fear for his family.

He spoke softly, "Michael, you are my firstborn, my son, and while I love you and Helena equally, you were the first. Your life is the fulfillment of my destiny. You are to carry on the family name. You and Helena will receive all that your mother and I have worked so hard to hold onto. I cannot bear the thought of anything happening to you. Neither can your mother." He took a deep breath, gathering his thoughts. "I was eighteen, your very age, when I left all that I knew and came here to a place I knew nothing about. I was driven from my homeland, as was *Jiddy*, by an oppressive, brutal foreign army. Your grandmother and many of our friends in Lebanon died at the hands of the foreign occupiers."

He stopped for a moment, his eyes beginning to moisten from his deep concern for his son. Michael focused on his father's face, listening to every word, wanting to know his wishes.

"All we ever wanted was freedom, the right to come and go, simply the opportunity to work, to have a family...to have a life. That freedom we found in America. This is the greatest country in history. It provides freedom and opportunity to everyone, even immigrants like us." He paused again, thinking with great deliberation as he recalled the terrible agony of his youth, blended with a growing sense of anger at having his son forced to become part of war.

Misreading his father's thoughts, Michael interrupted, "But, Dad..."

Alexander held up his hand, quieting Michael. "And so, my son, as much as we want you to be safe here with us, there is no safe place if angry animals are on the loose. And I believe Germany and Japan are those animals. They must be stopped. As much as it pains me to acknowledge this fact, only America and its people can stop them. You make me very proud that you want to be part of that. *Allah ma'ak*, Michael, Be with God. Trust all that your mother and I, who love you more than life itself, have taught you. Follow your trust and faith in God, pray for guidance, help those who need help, and when your job is done, come back safely to us." He turned to his wife. "God help us, Helene, and God be with Michael. I am deeply saddened but I am very proud of my American son."

Helene extended her hands to touch him, tears beginning to well in her eyes. "Michael, my son, like your father, I want this to be your decision, just as any major decision of your life must ultimately be made only by you. And I too am proud of you and will pray daily for your safe return."

Then Alexander smiled as he turned to his daughter. "And, of course, Helena, we are very proud of you. But we want you to stay here with us, so don't you be thinking about following in Michael's footsteps just yet!"

Helena laughed, "I'm only sixteen, Papa. I'm not nearly ready."

As he completed all he wanted to say, which seemed to be more than his family had ever heard from him at one sitting, Alexander, saddened, turned his head slightly, stood up, and with tears in his eyes, pulled Michael to him, embraced his son with both his strong arms, kissed him twice on his cheeks, and pursed his lips into a small proud smile. Without hesitation, Helena stood, embraced her brother, kissed him, and, honoring her parents, hugged and kissed them both. Then they all stepped to embrace Abraham, the patriarch of the family, still seated at the table, quiet, teary-eyed, representing the link to their culture, their roots, their traditions, and their way of life.

In the late summer of 1943, Michael, like hundreds of thousands of other teenage American boys, enlisted in the U.S. Army Air Corps, and immediately was sent to training camp to become a pilot. After basic training, he was sent to Tampa for flight training and shipped to England by the summer of 1944 to join the 8th Air Force where he would pilot bombers over France and Germany.

The British, under siege for five years, were exhausted. Their air force, weakened by the German attacks, buzz bombs and aggressive bombers and fighters, were assigned the task of nighttime blanket bombing of German cities, seeking to weaken the German citizens' will to fight.

In contrast, the American heavy bombers, mostly B-17s and B-24s, were assigned the much more risky daylight strategic bombing missions to destroy Germany's war-making machinery, including fighter factories, rail yards, manufacturing plants, and submarine bases. Their missions were extremely vulnerable and dangerous, drawing incessant plane-shattering flak attacks from hundreds of German fighters defending their homeland, and by cannon fire. By then, nearly fifty percent of all U.S. Army Air Corps bombers of the 8th Air Force planes had been lost. This is the arena young Michael was sent to. Fellow crews were lost daily, including thousands of airmen lost. Hundreds of the huge bombers, each with ten crew members, were shot down. Until D-Day, when the rules changed, a pilot had to fly twenty-five missions before he could be returned to America. After that date, the missions required was increased to thirty-five.

At home, Alexander and Helene kept a daily vigil, praying for their son to beat the odds and somehow return safely to them.

But it was not to be.

PART TWO

CHAPTER 28

Marseille
1920

"Goodbye, my love. Until we meet again. I will always love you." Madeleine said aloud as she waved for the last time to Iskandar, her departing lover. She still saw him standing at the rail of the stern waving to her and she watched him grow smaller and smaller as the ship sailed out to sea into the bright orange setting sun. As she finally turned to leave the pier, a long painful hour after the ship was out of sight, Madeleine felt slightly light-headed and weak.

During the next several weeks, nausea and discomfort kept her from her work some mornings. At first, she said nothing to her mother, thinking it was nothing. Finally, she decided she must confide in her. They scheduled an appointment with the doctor at the hospital.

"You are going to have a baby," the kindly doctor smiled.

"Oh my goodness, *Maman*, what shall I do?" she asked when they were alone.

"You will have the baby, Madeleine. It is God's will. But we must prepare."

That night, with enormous emotions, Madeleine prayed to God that the baby be healthy, that the baby look like his father, and that soon, Iskandar would come back and take care of her. She missed him so much. The next day, as she did every morning, she caressed her...his...cross in her fingers, sometimes all day. Now, a bit frightened, she thought of Iskandar even more. What am I to do? she asked herself.

Often she went to the hill overlooking the sea, and prayed, "One day, dear Lord, bring Iskandar back to me. I will wait forever. Please, Lord, but please have him hurry," she pleaded.

After a few days, she and her mother spoke about her dilemma.

"Shall I tell Iskandar or not, *Maman*? I have received many letters from him, but they were all from New York. I don't even know where he is I think I should not tell him yet. He must come for me. I don't want him to come back to me because of an obligation, because I am bearing his child. That would not be good. But I cannot lie to him. It would require a month for my letter to get to him even if I knew where he was, another month for him to find passage, and another month for his ship to arrive in Marseille."

"You...no...we must be realistic," Daniella replied firmly, holding up her hands.

"But ..."

"Hush. We must go to Paris to be with our family, to stay for awhile. You are with child, we have no man in our home, and we will have another mouth to feed. We do not have much money. But you are young, very pretty, and you must attract a man to marry."

"But, *Maman*, I love only Iskandar..."

It was in late November of 1920 that Madeleine bore a six-pound, eight-ounce baby, a handsome son who looked exactly like Iskandar. "I am so happy, *Maman*. He has his father's nose, his eyes. He is beautiful. Look at his beautiful hair. I will call him François, after papa. Would that please you, *Maman*?"

Daniella replied, gently touching the baby's head, smiling proudly, "Yes, my love, and I know it pleases your father who I am sure is watching over us today."

Because of the need to conceal a child with no apparent father, Daniella initially told Hanna she and Madeleine were going to visit family in Paris for awhile as Madeleine was not well. But as the weeks progressed, she felt she should be totally honest with Hanna and told him what was happening. But she made him promise not to tell anyone, especially his family members in Lebanon and America.

After two years in Paris with their family, Daniella, Madeleine, and François returned to Marseille. Madeleine's life was almost fulfilled with her love child, "Little François," and yet, there was something missing. She longed to be held by Iskandar, to listen to his voice, to gaze into his eyes. She imagined how proud and happy Iskandar would be to hold his son. Because Iskandar's letters were never forwarded to Paris, she never again saw his letters.

Madeleine took François with her to her shop, keeping him nearby all the time. Most days found her busy in the shop making clothes for those few wealthy ladies of Marseille who still had funds for their custom-made clothes. In the early days, she kept François in a basket by her feet. Evenings alone with François were actually easier for her than before he was born when she was so lonely. Now she had her growing son, a beautiful, dark-haired, handsome child a constant, living personification of her love, Iskandar.

"Run to me, François," Madeleine would laugh, clapping her hands.

"Come to maman, my darling."

On Sundays, she would place him in the carriage and walk to the park, the *Jardin du Pharo*, where she and Iskandar enjoyed their too few days. As François began to walk, they walked hand-in-hand, skipping, laughing, enjoying the days together. She was a young mother, still less than nineteen years old.

In the spring of 1924, when he was nearly three and a half years old, Madeleine began taking François to the hill overlooking the sea. There, she would spread her blanket and place her picnic basket on the very spot of grass where François was conceived in love. When François first asked of his father, Madeleine explained as best she could, with emotion, from her heart, not from knowledge. She would serve them lunch on a blanket as she told François of her undying love for his father, Iskandar, and of his love for her. Her explanation to his inquiries of his father's absence in their lives always included, "Your father loves you, but he cannot be with us here. He is in America looking for a better life for us." She also told him all she knew of his father's heritage, of Lebanon, Douma, and the mountains.

CHAPTER 29

Paris
Spring 1924

"I know they are up to something that will change Europe forever," Philippe Moreau told his superiors in secretive French Intelligence meetings in Paris. "There are hundreds of German undercover agents operating all over Belgium, Austria, and Denmark. This man Adolph Hitler is crazy! He's taken over the German Workers' Party and renamed it the National Socialist German Workers' Party...the Nazi party. He hates France and blames Germany's economic depression and the plight of the German workers on France's Versailles Treaty demands. The Nazis have co-opted many Frenchmen as well. These are difficult times, and I am convinced they are going to get much worse, and very soon." But Philippe's was a lonely voice seeking to alert the indecisive politicians who were too consumed with disputes to respond. His was a lonely, futile effort. If they would just listen. But they didn't. The French government drifted during most of the 1920s, still believing they had defeated Germany forever.

Later, on a visit to his offices in Marseille in the summer of 1924, Philippe called on his good friend, Hanna Chalhoub, in the Lebanese section. The Lebanese were skilled at operating under occupation and during political turmoil with ubiquitous spies and compromises. They would know, especially Hanna, of subversive activities in Marseille as they related to the local media and to shipments in and out of the busy port and the rail station. Because the *Panier* district, with its large Lebanese immigrant community, was strategically positioned between the docks and the rail yards, he knew Hanna was his key man in Marseille.

It was during one of these visits that Philippe met Daniella and Madeleine at a dinner engagement with Hanna. Philippe was immediately struck by Madeleine's vibrancy and beauty.

Later he inquired, "Tell me, dear friend, what is the story about Daniella's daughter, Madeleine. She is the most beautiful creature I've ever met."

"Aah, Madeleine," Hanna replied, she is a magnificent woman. You are correct, *mon ami*. Madeleine is the finest. She is just twenty years old, and yet, she is an exciting, insouciant woman, Philippe. She also has a beautiful son, François, who is nearly four years old."

Hanna felt a strange sense of conflict of loyalty and betrayal while introducing his good friend to the lover of his nephew. While Daniella and Madeleine had finally informed Hanna, they had obtained his promise not to tell Iskandar of his love child. Madeleine was insistent that the child not be the reason for Iskandar to return. She was absolutely convinced he would return to find her when he could, that he loved her as completely as she did him, and that he had had to go to America or he might always regret it and ultimately blame her. Certainly, if this was true, she felt, she did not want him ever to blame her or his own child for ruining his life. "This way is better," she told Hanna. "He will come. I know it. But it must be for the right reasons. Telling him he has a son in France is not the right reason for his return. Trust me, *Maman*. Trust me, Hanna," she pleaded that day before they left for Paris "for family reasons."

"Well, I would like to see Madeleine, my friend. Can you help me? I realize that I am much older than Madeleine, but I am entranced by her, and cannot get her out of my mind. Perhaps in time I can become important to her as well."

Hanna put his arm on his friend's shoulder and spoke candidly to his friend, "Philippe, these are difficult times, and Madeleine is doing her best. She is raising her son by herself as the boy's father left France to go to America in 1920. I'm certain he does not know he has a son. She has worked hard with her mother, and yes, she needs a good man. But I think her heart belongs to, and will always belong to, the father of François. You must know this from the outset, *mon ami*."

Philippe looked directly at his friend and replied, "You say she has not seen him since 1920? If that is the case, perhaps there is a possibility for me then, Hanna."

"Perhaps, Philippe, perhaps."

Madeleine found herself frequently being visited by Hanna's friend, Philippe. He was always kind and charming, and took her to dinners at the finest dining establishments and to cultural events in the city. Over time, she became more willing to accept Philippe in her life.

"I love the bouillabaisse of Marseille, especially at Henri's by the *Vieux Port*," smiled Philippe as they taxied to his favorite seafood restaurant. "His fish are freshly caught each day. Remarkable! Paris doesn't have bouillabaisse like this."

While he spent much of his time in Paris, he returned every available weekend to Marseille. His excuse was to see his family and to meet with his colleagues, including Hanna, in the Marseille offices. His real but unspoken desire for being in Marseille was to see this enchanting twenty-year-old beauty named Madeleine. Within weeks, he knew he was falling in love although he was twenty-five years older than she. But she was a mature, delightful, feminine young woman with a child, making her way with her mother, an excellent and popular *couturière*, graceful, cultured, and fully aware of the fashions of the day. Madeleine, like her mother, made her own dresses that reflected the *au courant*, creating a stir wherever they went together. They emulated the latest designs of Paris so to inspire the ladies of Marseille to visit them and order their wardrobe from these two esteemed fashion models and designers. Strikingly attractive, tall, slender, and finely attired, Daniella and Madeleine personally maintained their shop's reputation.

Philippe felt very proud to have this stunning beauty on his arm even though he knew some looked askance at the "May-October couple." Some were perhaps envious, some judgmental, holding back, with a stifled smile, the query, "Oh, Philippe, is this your niece?"

He could only smile without comment. But he didn't care. He was quite self-assured. His hope and concern was to somehow gain her affection, and in time, her love, by overcoming with his physical presence and charm what her son's father couldn't provide in his absence. This, indeed, was becoming the principal emotional focus of his life. I *will* win her over, he kept telling himself.

Times were difficult for Daniella and Madeleine as with so many others in Europe during the mid-1920s as social and economic conditions seemed to worsen each year.

"Philippe is a handsome man, and yes, he is much older than you, Madeleine, my child. But you must understand the realities of life. Europe is in great difficulty. Our income is not so good anymore. Philippe is wealthy and from a fine family. He has a good job with the government, and will provide for you. All things considered, for your welfare and that of your son, I think you should accept his proposal. François is growing up. He is four years old. He needs a man in his life, Madeleine."

"But, *Maman*, Iskandar is his father, and I still yearn for him. I always will. How can I do this? I do not love Philippe. I have told him so. I know what love is, and I have that with Iskandar."

"You can grow to love him in time, Madeleine, even though he is much older. This has been quite acceptable, and not only in France, although we understand these things better than most," she added with a flourish of French liberal pride.

There were many such discussions between Madeleine and her mother during the months that Philippe called on Madeleine. From time to time,

Daniella would inform Hanna of the situation. Hanna would listen intently, and wisely not offer advice unless requested. Philippe was a close friend to Hanna who felt uncomfortable in this conflicting situation. Still, it *had* been nearly five years since Iskandar sailed off to America.

"I have to refrain from my own opinion on this, Daniella. Iskandar is my family, Philippe is my friend."

"I'm sure he has created a new life in America. And although his letters came every week for a long time, they stopped coming when Madeleine didn't reply during the two years we were in Paris and there have been none since then. Thank you for your understanding in never mentioning Madeleine's pregnancy to Iskandar, dear Hanna. You know we had to leave Marseille for Madeleine's sake. I am so grateful you came to see us so often."

"But of course, my dear, of course."

"And what do you hear from your family in America these days, Hanna?"

"I only know what my cousin Mike tells me from Boston. Iskandar and his father somehow survived the heat and the bad weather storms and have done well in Florida. They tell me Iskandar has a small store of his own in their village." Hanna didn't feel a need to expand on his cattle business and other growing ventures. "And, just last week, I received a letter saying that Iskandar and his father are travelling to Boston for a month. Iskandar will stay with his Uncle Sam, and Abraham will stay with Mike. I think Sam wants Iskandar to meet Helene, the sister of his wife Julia."

Daniella continued to counsel her daughter during these visits from Philippe while Madeleine kept resisting. "Be realistic, Madeleine. We are alone, Iskandar is in America. Even though you still love the memories of Iskandar, Philippe is here...now. He cares for you and is a man of position and wealth. And we are struggling. I have heard you speak with kindness and love to François each time he has asked about his father. I hear your prayers and cries at night. I feel your sadness, *chérie*. And I see you constantly fondle the gold cross he gave you. You're in a difficult position to be sure, having to overcome your conflict of love against reality. It is the eternal struggle. And yours has gone on for more than four years. That is a long time, my child, a very long time. It is time for you to change your thinking...for your son."

"But how can I accept Philippe's proposal to marry him when I still love Iskandar? I will wait forever if I must. How can I betray both of them?"

"Madeleine, listen to me, *chérie*. You are being unrealistic. Don't be foolish. The world is changing very fast. Iskandar is in America and you have not heard from him in years. Be with Philippe. You will come to love him."

Madeleine had never responded to Iskandar's letters because she didn't want to describe François, his son, and make him feel guilty or obligated to return for her. And now it was too late.

François's future was solely dependent on her, and she had to decide how to respond to Philippe's urgings of love.

Ultimately, Madeleine came to realize that she had to be practical. Philippe Moreau was a well-established man of wealth with an excellent social reputation. He had a high position in the government, though she did not know what it was. His family was prominent, and he had many times expressed his love for her. She also knew he would eagerly provide for her and François. And she realized, too, that more and more she was enjoying her times with Philippe. "He makes me laugh, *Maman*, and he's very kind."

In late 1924, Madeleine decided to solve her emotional dilemma by accepting Philippe's entreaties.

"Philippe, you know I find you very attractive, and I truly enjoy your company. I know you understand my love for my son François, and that Iskandar, my first love, remains in my heart. I expect I will always love him even though it has been four years since I last saw him. Yet, I am growing to love you and believe we can be happy together. So, dear Philippe, with that understanding, and, my assurance to you that I will be a good and devoted wife to you, I agree to accept your marriage proposal."

Philippe was ecstatic. "I will make you a good husband, Madeleine, and in spite of these difficult days, I am sure we will be happy together."

They were married in late 1924. They spent two weeks on their honeymoon at Philippe's family estate near the spa in Vichy.

It was the same year that Alexander wed Helene in Boston.

CHAPTER 30

uring their extended honeymoon, and for several months after, Madeleine and Philippe often traveled the one hundred seventy-five miles by train to Vichy, Philippe's family's home, to Paris to enjoy the city. Daniella cared for her grandson, François, during these absences, and all seemed well for everyone.

Within weeks following their marriage, Philippe and Madeleine skied at Chamonix-Mont-Blanc. It was a happy time for both. Madeleine was now enjoying wonderful experiences and visiting different places for the first time in her life. Her youthful responses delighted Philippe beyond his dreams. He adored Madeleine, and she was a good and loving wife. But both knew there was a place in her heart where Philippe could not enter. Still, for several months, both enjoyed each other's company, and Madeleine grew closer to Philippe. Eventually they returned to Marseille where Madeleine could be closer to her young son and mother. Philippe began spending more and more time at government meetings in Paris.

By August 1926, Philippe Moreau was back in Paris alone, more often than not. Political tensions in Europe were growing. Germany was creating major difficulties for the weak and divided French government. Angry, unemployed French were frustrated with government corruption, disarray, internecine political battles, and the depressing economic conditions during the long decade. Philippe's intelligence-seeking teams were becoming stretched thin trying to keep up with the growing subversive activities of the German infiltrators. They had already placed themselves in the press and local political organizations as functionaries in charge of overseeing the utilities infrastructures, including railroads, bridges, tunnels, and the like where they could and would eventually create havoc all over France in coming years.

Each winter, Philippe took Madeleine and François to his chalet in Chamonix-Mont-Blanc for skiing holidays, and then for weekends to Cannes in the late winter and spring. But that was all the time he could afford to leave his job, which was growing in national importance by the month.

As the years passed inexorably into the early 1930s, Germany was becoming chaotic. Adolph Hitler was defeating his domestic enemies one by one and challenging the Communists. He was able to obtain the nation's bankers as supporters who were forced to choose between the lesser of two evils: Hitler and his Socialist Party or their anathema Communists. With their reluctant financial backing committed at a gathering in Munich, Hitler began building his nation into a fascist state with unstoppable determination. By 1935, he became chancellor. German workers became fervent in their renewed sense of destiny only he could inculcate. His mesmerizing speeches enthralled the nation. The demand for more land and resources grew and grew. German outrage over the draconian post-World War I Versailles Treaty, for which they blamed France, created the fiery determination in the German people to make Germany become the most powerful country in Europe once again. More German spies were sent into all its neighboring countries. England, Belgium, Denmark, Poland, the Baltics and, especially, France were politically weak victims just waiting to be conquered, and he intended to exacerbate their political problems.

"I will dance in the streets of Paris!" Hitler boasted. "They wait for us, as weak poultry waiting to be plucked," he declared, laughing, to his legions of followers. "They *want* us. They *need* us."

From 1930 through 1934, France had twelve presidents, reflecting the nation's failures. No one seemed able to deal with the seemingly unsolvable depressed economic conditions, fomenting even more instability and outrage among the populace. The United States, even with so many Roosevelt social programs, could do little to help even if it was concerned with Europe, which it wasn't. Many Americans were also leaning toward Socialism, Communism and neutrality. "Stay out of Europe's business," advocates would declare. Even Charles Lindbergh visited Germany and promoted neutrality. It would take the Pearl Harbor attack on December 7, 1941 to change the world and bring America out of isolation. Very late in the mid-1930s, the French government woke up to Germany's growing threat and finally prioritized it by totally re-organizing its counter-intelligence agency in Paris to track the German "businessmen" who had infiltrated completely and were actually developing intelligence and significant influence within the country's industry, its media, armed forces, and government.

Philippe did not tell Madeleine that as early as 1933 Germany was going through enormous political and economic upheaval and becoming a major, impending threat to its neighbors. The depressing economic conditions in Europe were causing dangerous unrest among unemployed union members. Germany especially was under great stress as it was still paying France what they considered exorbitant reparations for World War I. Millions were unemployed, demanding revenge. The Bolshevik Revolution in Russia in 1917, and the creation of the Soviet Union in 1933 placed enormous pressure on virtually all the governments of Europe, especially of those confrontation states abutting the new Soviet Union now led by the fierce Joseph Stalin. Communist parties were growing everywhere across Europe, feeding on the massive unemployment caused by the Great Depression and little opportunity for labor.

"The rich get richer while the masses starve," declared the Communists. "We must take over society and make it equal for everyone."

Philippe's work in Paris made him acutely aware of the political risks and actions by France's neighbors, partially the result of the huge German reparations bill of one hundred thirty-two billion marks that was still not paid, pursuant to the Versailles Treaty of 1918.

At a presumably secure, crucial meeting in Paris in 1934, Philippe was among many high government officials when President Daladier spoke to them in confidence. "Gentlemen, I believe we should clearly understand that we must now deal with this man, Adolph Hitler. We cannot wait. He intends to take over all of Europe in my opinion, and bodes no good for the French people. His National Socialist German Workers' Party, euphemistically called the Nazis, is ruthless. We must prepare. And we must prepare *now.*"

"Philippe Moreau," the President said in a somber tone, turning toward Philippe and extending his open hand to him, "I call on you to immediately lead a new government agency of counter intelligence services to investigate, monitor, and undermine all German subversives in France. We are under enormous political pressure, as are the other governments of Europe. Because of internal conflicts, we are weak and cannot command the people to take up arms. You must pick your best men and begin surveillance at once. We may already be too late. All areas of France are vulnerable. Our major ports, from Le Havre to Marseille, even Paris itself, and our transportation infrastructure are potential targets, especially the railroad system."

"Of course, sir, I will begin today," responded Philippe, with a respectful nod of his head, in the presence of the group. Others in the meeting showed a variety of concerns. Already, however, there were German sympathizers in the room, perhaps even a few German spies fluent in French, some of whom Philippe knew had now, at this moment, become his adversaries and he theirs. He showed no emotional response, remaining stoic, yet determined to protect his beloved country. He knew he had to completely devote himself to his new organization, the French National Intelligence Agency (FNIA), precursor to the M.U.R., and enlist as quickly as possible former Resistance members who served during the first war. Most were now in their 40s and 50s, and many had served with him. He trusted them and knew of their devotion to France. Around them, he would build his new agency. Yet, he knew he had to gather younger, dedicated French citizens, both men and women, to achieve his important mission.

By 1937, Philippe was spending most of his time either in Paris or traveling about the country establishing teams in every city, building his organization, and bringing in disparate groups who also believed in his mission. He ventured to other countries to coordinate his efforts with his counterparts in London, Oslo, Vienna, Tallin, Warsaw, Zurich, Amsterdam, and Copenhagen. He had very little time to return to Marseille and Madeleine.

"Philippe, I do not want to complain, but must you continue to travel so much? I do understand you have important government work, and yet, you are away from us a great deal," Madeleine finally spoke her feelings.

"Madeleine," he replied, placing both hands on her shoulders, and looking directly into her eyes, "I want to be with you and François all the time, but conditions in Europe are strained and getting worse almost daily with the emerging political turmoil. The communists in Germany, Poland, Italy, Austria, and even here in France appear to be gaining power. The French government is splintered and weak. There is so much happening in Germany. Hitler's influence is growing very fast. I am quite concerned, my dear... quite concerned."

As often as he could, Philippe took François, now a handsome and precocious teenager, with him on his trips. Francois sought the opportunities to accompany Philippe to Paris, where they dined in the finest restaurants, and stayed over in the Maurice, Philippe's favorite hotel in Paris. As a result, François was being groomed with global sophistication.

War was in the air, and Philippe was France's intelligence advisor to the President. The climax of Philippe's efforts came in late August 1938.

"Mr. President, I have just come from Poland. Its army is marshalling along the German border at Lidzbark, near Warsaw. They are quietly preparing against an impending attack by Germany." Philippe was making an urgent report to the nation's leader, the President, keeping him abreast of events.

"My concerns have been growing for some time. It is getting very serious now. I believe the fuse has been lit, and an enormous explosion will soon result. The Germans are poised to invade France to their west, and are building up their forces on their east at the Polish border. Now, just this week on the twenty-third, they signed the German-Soviet Union Non-Agression Pact with Josef Stalin who, as we know, can't be trusted. That makes me believe Poland is first and France is next."

Even sooner than Philippe had speculated, on September 1, 1939, Germany brutally invaded Poland by sea, by air, and by land. Their *blitzkrieg* had begun. Philippe immediately went to Marseille to meet with his agents at Marseille's port and rail yards, and to be with and comfort Madeleine.

On Sunday, September 3, 1939, just two days later, England's Prime Minister Neville Chamberlain declared, "England is at war with Germany." So, too, France declared war against Germany.

"What is this madman doing, Philippe?" pleaded Madeleine, asking what most French citizens wanted to ask.

"Hitler has made his move into Poland, my dear Madeleine. You won't believe this. He actually concocted a ruse by posing a dozen German criminals as part of the Polish army. He dressed them in Polish uniforms and, after injecting them with lethal doses, had them shot *inside* Germany. He then declared Poland was invading Germany! He actually declared war with a trick he called 'Operation Canned Goods.' Can you believe this crazy man? And now, the Soviet Union has invaded Poland also. I believe our beloved France is in their gun sights."

"Philippe, you have been telling me for months that this Adolph Hitler is crazy. But France is in no position to defeat him. What are we to do? Are we safe here in Marseille? What about François? Must I lose him to the army like my father? I am very frightened."

He wrapped both arms around his wife. *"Mon chérie*, I am convinced, although I cannot convince my naïve superiors, that Hitler intends to rule all of Western Europe, if not this month, then soon. Therefore, I must ask you to prepare yourself and François to be ready to leave Marseille with little notice." He paused, thinking. "I have to speak to Hanna to do the same. I don't know what his plans are, but he and your mother should be ready to leave too."

"But where, Philippe?" she pleaded. "Where *can* we go?"

He had no answer yet. Africa was out. So was Sardinia, even Spain. Italy was about to join Germany. *Where can I send them?*

During the following days, life for Madeleine was tenuous at best. While war was declared by France and England, no battles had yet taken place. But times were frightening. News from neighboring Poland was terrible... thousands of lives lost...too many German successes. One day at a time was all they could look forward to. Impending disaster was in the air. The waiting was very difficult for everyone. Hour by hour, day by day, tense and fearful citizens crouched by their radios, frustrated by the waves of static. Or they assembled in the public squares seeking the latest bulletin, frightened and frozen with no ability to resist. The entire nation was tense.

While France's political negotiations were widely described in the press, little was clear about what was happening. Fear began to build into paranoia. Neighbors became frightened of old friends. Many became convinced that no one could be trusted. The French economy was in chaos; the government was torn apart and weak. The communists were hard at work as were the German subversives.

Even so, as always, the spring of 1940 was a time of rebirth, of hope. Madeleine revisited the spot on *Les Calanques* overlooking the sea where she and Iskandar had shared so much. She would sit, think, remember, and pray. "Protect my son, Philippe, and my love, Iskandar, dear Lord, and bring us together. I believe it is Your will. I hope it is soon. Then pausing, she whispered, "Please save us, Lord. Amen." And she would cross herself, believing in this with absolute faith.

Though she had no way of knowing, that beautiful, deceptively peaceful Sunday afternoon in June was the last Madeleine would ever enjoy in Marseille.

CHAPTER 31

Escape from Marseille

y May 1940, the situation in Europe was critical. Poland was nearly completely defeated and occupied by the German army. Between April and June 1940, the German army overran the nations of Belgium, Holland, Norway, Luxembourg, Denmark, and the Baltics. Northern France was completely and quickly occupied. Soon too was central France. In time, even southern France would become occupied and under the military control of Germany even though the citizens under the new French Vichy government, subservient to the Germans, were allowed to come and go. And yet, while knowing much of their freedom was gone, and with it, southern France, the people somehow maintained a sense of *joie de vivre*. Thousands of the wealthy fled Paris, escaping to southern France with their treasures. Chaos began overtaking French society.

On June first, Philippe said good-bye to Madeleine as he boarded the train at the station near the *Panier* and went to Paris where he would likely remain. The situation was now critical. He had urged Madeleine to prepare to leave France immediately. He would make arrangements for her and François.

"But, Philippe, where shall we go?" She sobbed at the thought of leaving France. "What shall I prepare for?"

By the summer of 1940, with Poland and northeastern France invaded, Free French Army Forces were being destroyed in northern France. The British began evacuating from France and disembarking at Dunkirk. It was a terrible disaster. Thousands of lives were lost at Dunkirk at the hands of the German forces. It was a horrendous humiliation. Even so, more than 300,000 troops escaped to England to return and fight Germany another day.

The President declared in a meeting, "It appears all is lost. You were right, Philippe. God help us for our ignorance. We were wrong. We delayed too long. We must rush to organize and unify the scattered Resistance teams with you as the leader."

"Of course. I will do what I can for France. I must go to Marseille and prepare. I promise to return in two days."

"No longer than that, Philippe. There is little time. It appears the German army will conquer our armies at any moment. This information is only for you. We are keeping secret what we know to avoid panic in the streets. Go now, and come back quickly. Already many Parisians are seeking safety on the southern coast."

Philippe returned to Marseille and Madeleine. He described to her that what he had believed would happen was now actually occurring. "The Germans have defeated the Belgians, the English, and the French in the north. They are moving at this very moment toward Paris. I am to lead a new Resistance and cannot return to Marseille for some time. While I do believe you are as safe here as anywhere in France, I think all of France may soon be conquered and occupied by Germany. It is possible the full German army may not come this far south. However, millions of Frenchmen and their families will escape the north, people of Paris and the major cities will come here to the south. It will be very difficult if not impossible for you here. Thousands will descend on Marseille. The S.S., spies, and even German units will come here in droves. They will need lodging, food...everything. They will take what they want. People will be abused. I cannot let that happen to you and to François. Those bastard Nazis! You must leave immediately, my love."

"Philippe," Madeleine replied looking into his eyes as hers filled with tears, "there is no place to go. North Africa is under siege, especially French Algeria. Italy is not possible, nor Sardinia. Spain is dangerous, Egypt is weak and, anyway, the Germans are there already."

Philippe, in his fashion when he became very serious, gripped her shoulders, looked straight into her eyes and declared resolutely, "Palestine is out. Lebanon appears to be the only nearby place that is safe at the moment, while it is protected by the French. But Beirut itself will not be safe for you. I am a marked man, and there are many German spies in Beirut. You share my name which means you may need protection. Go into the mountains in the north. There is a deep valley there that has been a safe haven for centuries. It is near Bsharre, in the Batroun province."

"Northern Lebanon?" asked Madeleine with a sense of irony. "There is one place I have heard of that could be perfect for us. I will take François to his father's village in the mountains. It is very near a place they call 'the Valley of Passion.' I know of it. We will be safe there, Philippe. The village is named Douma."

Philippe nodded and smiled, relieved and confident in her proposal. Suddenly he remembered, "Hanna is from that village. His cousin, Elias, is in Beirut. I will alert him and get you there through him as much as I am able. Please do not hesitate. There is no time. You and François must go now, Madeleine. *Tonight.*"

"Then it is settled, Philippe," she answered, now committed, still very nervous, yet finally knowing where they were going, and struck by the fact that she could possibly be in Iskandar's village, perhaps with his family if not with him. "I will take François to Douma until France is free once again. And, Philippe," she whispered as she embraced him, "I must say to you, you have been a wonderful husband to me, and father to François. I pray you have been as happy with me. You knew from the beginning my heart was full with love of Iskandar. Forgive me, Philippe...I was a young girl...he was my first love. You understood, I pray. Yet, these years with you have been wonderful and I do love you so much, Philippe. Now go, be safe, and as Hanna would say, 'Allah ma'ak.' Be with God. I will pray for your safety each day."

Philippe listened to Madeleine's words, feeling the painful sting of truth, but not surprised at what she was telling him. He sadly understood, and yet was grateful to have been with this magnificent and beautiful woman for fifteen wonderful years. He deeply loved her. Knowing full well he was now a marked man and might not survive the German onslaught, he nevertheless sought to convey his strength, his *noblesse oblige*, and his inherent sense of loyalty to his country. He could not leave France. And there were places he could not accompany Madeleine. Yet he knew too, she was who she was. He had swallowed that bitter pill early on and had, as much as he could, come to accept his destiny with his lovely, nurturing wife.

He had to reply to her honesty with his own honesty, though it was difficult. He sighed deeply and paused before he spoke, holding her hands in his as they faced each other, "Madeleine, while I have loved you so much these years, I must say, it tested me throughout our marriage far more than I have ever confessed. It has been hard for me, Madeleine, very hard. But I also know your special love for me. And you know how much I love you. I will have you with me each day, Madeleine." Philippe whispered in her ear, "Your face will be with me forever...goodbye, my love..." As he caressed her and savored this special moment, he could not help but believe it would be the last time he would see her...hold her...feel her close...

Before they parted at the train station, hands outstretched, fingers touching, she blew him a kiss and, with moistened eyes, whispered, "*Au revoir* and *Allah ma'ak*, Philippe."

When the train was out of sight, she went to Hanna to tell him of the news, and to obtain his assistance in obtaining passage as soon as possible to Beirut.

"You will be safe, very safe, with my family in Douma, Madeleine. But they must never find out that Iskandar is François' father. It would be a disgrace for the family. It would be a terrible mistake. Be *en garde*. Now, my child, you must get ready this minute to leave France. Your mother and I will be safe here in Marseille. We will bury ourselves in the *Panier.* No one can find us here. We'll let you know when it is safe to return. But you must get François out of France or he surely will be taken by someone's army."

After meeting with Hanna and her mother, she went back home, located François in his room, sat with him on the bed to quickly explain and prepare him for their escape. "We must leave France immediately, my son. We will go to Lebanon this very night and find your father's village. Hanna has arranged passage for us. He believes your *mémé* and he can be safe here deep in the *Panier* in Marseille, but we all agreed he cannot protect us. You are at an age that surely you will be taken into someone's army, perhaps even into a German prison. We cannot know, François. I lived through the horror of my father dying during the first war, and I am not going to let that happen to you. We must leave France tonight."

"Tonight, *Maman?*" Suddenly aware of the urgency in her tone of voice, he composed himself and responded, "Alright, *Maman,* then let's get on with it." He wanted to be strong for her too.

And so, at 4 a.m. on June first, Madeleine and François boarded a small nondescript Lebanese steamer at the port near the *Panier.* Customs officers were becoming more prevalent and more enforcing, especially trying to keep young French males in France. Hanna had believed Philippe's predictions months ago and prepared for this event. François, by his father's birth, could have had dual citizenship, however, Hanna obtained a counterfeit Lebanese passport for him. To ensure a smooth escape without a paper trail, he also had gotten a Lebanese passport for Madeleine.

Madeleine and François left France just five days before the German armies were on the outskirts of Paris. With all of France threatened and panic driving millions to the south, France officially surrendered on June seventeenth, only four days after Madeleine and François safely reached Beirut.

Earlier, General Charles de Gaulle had left Algeria for London to set about organizing the Free French Army of the Interior (FFI). Most of those who joined did so in England and Algeria. Gen. De Gaulle organized the Dauxieme, the intelligence section of his staff. They were to coordinate with Philippe Moreau. Philippe was the French intelligence director of all domestic Resistance forces. His biggest challenge was in uniting the various underground splinter factions, principally three power groups which included the communists, also staunchly anti-Nazi. It was difficult at best trying to coordinate their efforts, reduce territorial protectionism, increase their effectiveness, and remind them of their common enemy. It seemed that Philippe had to be everywhere at once, all the time.

CHAPTER 32

$\mathcal{E}$ven before their small Lebanese steamer reached the point where the city could be seen, Madeleine felt tremors within her soul. She had known it would happen. She had known the moment she and François stepped onto the ship that she would emotionally reconnect with her lover and François' father, Iskandar.

"All these years, *chéri*, and now I must come to Lebanon. To your very village," she whispered aloud, as she stood at the bow's railing, eagerly looking for the Pigeon Rocks Iskandar had described to her as they lay on the grass on top of *Les Calanques* where they had loved.

"You will know Beirut by its off shore rocks hollowed out by the sea, and by the Corniche, the promenade high above the shoreline," Iskandar had said.

And now, she thought, here I am approaching this Middle Eastern city known across the Mediterranean Sea. Beirut, capitol of Lebanon, long aligned with her country, France, where most Lebanese Christians speak fluent French. Lebanon was a country where she prayed they would be safe.

At the onset of the war in Europe, during the late 1930s, Beirut was occupied with French forces. It was a safe haven for many who were willing to leave France and escape the onslaught of the German war machine. Others fled to Algeria and embattled Sardinia. Beirut was also a rich haven for thousands who had different, more sinister agendas. Many walked the streets who were ostensibly businessmen from Germany, France, Switzerland, Italy, and the Soviet Union. Most of these, it turned out, were actually spies gathering information much like their counterparts in other fertile cities such as Geneva, Zurich, Basel, and Vienna seeking secret information, following couriers, and stalking runaways. Now, as a result, Beirut was becoming a dangerous and overcrowded city. Most émigrés of late were from France since Lebanon was still a protectorate of France as a result of the terms at the end of World War I in 1918. There were transients in Beirut from America, Germany, Italy, Greece, Austria, Palestine, Iraq, and the Gulf. It had become the epitome of a truly "international city," casually bridging east and west.

Beirut easily became labeled the "Paris of the Middle East," and Lebanon, "Switzerland of the Near East."

When Madeleine and François arrived, it was a very active city, with locals inundated by European informants, Iraqis, Arabs, and escaping Jews.

The last sixty minutes on the steamer passed by agonizingly slow for Madeleine. Anxious to land, she paced the decks. Abruptly, she stopped at the bow, gripping the steel top rail, her pulse racing.

"Oh, François, I hope all is well in Lebanon. I worry so."

"*Maman*, it'll be alright. It's all very exciting, isn't it? I'm going to be stepping on the very soil of my father's homeland. I thought I'd never go to his village. I'm feeling great emotions, *Maman*. As you told me, he was my age when he left Beirut to sail to America. I think his spirit is still here."

"Yes, my son, and I too am sensing his presence...Oh!...Look!" Her heart leaped as she spotted the rocks offshore that Iskandar had described in detail. Unique to Beirut, as *Les Calanques* to Marseille, they stood as proud sentinels. "François, can you see the high rocks there? They call them Pigeon Rocks."

"They're beautiful. You can see right through the large one!"

It was almost noon when the boat finally maneuvered to tie-up at the docks on the north side of the city. Madeleine and François prepared to disembark, gathering their valises, hardly all their worldly goods, but all they could carry with them as they rushed, shrouded, in the night to leave Marseille.

"We'll have to do the best we can, François," she spoke anxiously. "We have so little. We'll both have to purchase new clothes here. We'll just have to take each day as it comes. But first, we must find Hanna's cousin, Elias," she said to François as they both quickly stepped onto the dock, waving goodbye over their shoulders to the friendly captain.

Looking all around her at the city's buildings, the people, and the mountains, she realized that here she was in Iskandar's country, no longer in France, her home. It was a strange, emotional moment for her as she felt Iskandar next to her. She knew she had to go to his village in the mountains. But first she had to find her single contact in Beirut... Iskandar's Uncle Elias, Hanna's cousin. He would help them.

After twelve agonizing, boring and unpleasant days at sea, stopping it seemed at every port between Marseille and Beirut, it was good to finally arrive in Lebanon. Both had gotten seasick more than once on the miserable voyage from a mix of the rough seas, poor food, and their anxiousness to leave Marseille before the Germans arrived.

As they walked down the pier and looked around, they were agape at the bustling activity of all the disparate people in this Middle Eastern trading center and surprised by the abundance of Europeans at the port area. Businessmen carrying leather briefcases seemed to be everywhere seeking deals that would provide them substantial profits as a result of the skyrocketing rents and values of all kinds of commodities. Jews from Germany, Hungary, Poland, the Soviet Union, and even Romania were flooding into Beirut seeking Lebanese passports so they might reach Palestine and safety. Likewise, evacuating Palestinians were seeking shelter in Lebanon and Syria. Most wore Western dress, yet some elderly locals still wore the *dishdasheh*, the flowing robe-like attire.

Products from America and France, including tires, Chrysler trucks, engine parts, even automobiles, were available in Beirut in exchange for goods from other countries, like Syria, Transjordan, Iraq, and Saudi Arabia. International traders were everywhere. Older men, ignoring the turmoil, sat at café tables along the streets, much as in Marseille, playing *towleh* and dominoes, and puffing on their *aguilas*. The pungent fragrance of blended tobacco and fruit wafted through the streets as though the war in Europe was of no concern. Perhaps they were in denial. Perhaps they felt they could do nothing anyway, as conquerors always came and went.

"This city is exciting...like Marseille in many ways. Uncle Hanna would be at home here." François smiled as he spoke to his mother, his eyes dancing across the scenes absorbing everything. While he could not know, he was feeling many of the same exciting emotions his father had felt that day in 1920 when, with his friend Butrus, Iskandar first stepped on the Joliet docks in Marseille.

By luck, after several fruitless inquiries, Madeleine found Elias at his office on the second floor above a ladies dress shop in the chic Hamra District. Elias was seated in a leather chair behind his desk, opposite Madeleine and François who nervously sat down on his matching dark red leather couch. They noticed that his office looked much like Hanna's, but with sketches of the mountains and snow covered cedars unique to Lebanon adorning the otherwise vacant beige painted stucco walls. Fresh air entered through the two open windows.

After sharing customary polite greetings and hot tea, Elias, speaking in polished French, described the unsettled and unsafe conditions for her and François in the city, urging her to get out of the city at once and go to Douma. He cautioned, "Go today to Douma, find Milhelm, and I will contact you later through him. You must leave the city immediately for your own safety and that of your son, my dear, before the Germans here in the city find out who you are. They would like nothing better than to kidnap the wife and son of their dreaded enemy, Philippe Moreau. Let me have your passports. We'll have to get you new ones."

He stood abruptly, and with a sense of urgency, keenly aware of the imminent danger she faced in Beirut during these chaotic times as Philippe Moreau's wife, extended his right hand to Madeleine and then to François. "Go quickly now. Get to Tripoli as fast as you can. *Allah ma'ak.*"

He reached for her, and with a friendly embrace, kissed each of her cheeks, did the same to François, and then motioned them to the door hurriedly in concern for their safety. To Madeleine, it was a good sign that Elias embraced François also, perhaps welcoming them into the family.

"*Merci*, Elias. *Allah ma'ak*," she waved as they left his small, efficient office.

"François, we must now leave the city and find our way to the only place that is safe for us. Philippe has told me that there is a crush of immigrants and German spies in Beirut and few if any places for us to safely stay. And, now with the Germans in Africa, Cairo, and Italy, we must stay in a remote place. We can only hope Iskandar's village will accept us."

Madeleine quickly found a French officer doing his best to maneuver traffic at a busy intersection filled with wagons, pushcarts, trucks and pedestrians. She approached him as he stepped to the curb for a break and inquired in her native French, "Can you tell us how to find Douma? I know it is in the mountains in the north near Tripoli."

"*Oui*, madame," he gestured with a kind salute, tipping his cap, watching the trucks and cars pass by. "I know of Douma. It is in the North, in the *Shimal*," the officer told her in deference, also speaking in French, although with a slight Middle Eastern accent. "You must go to the rail station over there," he pointed, "and take the train along the coast past Jounieh to Tripoli, only one hour north. From there, you will need a ride up into the mountains. Though small, it is well-known in the province of Batroun. If you cannot find a driver, perhaps a horse and wagon will be available in Tripoli. Ask there. Everyone wants a job and money. They will accept your French francs, and they all know where Douma is."

He continued, pleased at the respite she had given him, "These are strange times, madame. People are fleeing from all over Europe. They think Lebanon is safe. And perhaps it is at this moment, but Beirut is flooded with newcomers, with people from France and apparently every other European country. You are better off not staying in the city. There are thieves everywhere. It seems everyone is looking to find someone, steal something, or sell something. *Mon Dieu*, it is crazy!"

It took Madeleine and François all day to reach the tiny village of Douma. In Tripoli, she was able to enlist a man from Farhilde, near Douma, who had delivered his harvest to the markets in Tripoli. He gladly accepted one hundred francs to allow her and François to ride on his horse drawn wagon and eagerly stuffed the money into his pocket.

The winding dirt road up the mountain to the village was steep, curving and dangerous. But the farmer knew the road, as did his heavily burdened horse. They traveled very slowly, stopping at a mountain ridge to rest as the sun began to hover above the horizon.

"We are not far. It is down there. You can see the village, can't you?" gestured the farmer.

"Look at the rocks everywhere. There are hardly any cedar trees," François exclaimed to his mother, pointing in every direction.

"Yes, François," she replied, looking around. "Look. There are so few trees up here. Iskandar told me every conqueror took their giant cedars."

Throughout the ride up the mountain road, Madeleine found herself enthralled with the vistas, the rugged sand-colored, stone-filled mountains, and the cool, dry air. It was as though she had been here before. *You told me all about these mountains, Iskandar. It is a feeling of déjà vu. It is amazing that I know each of these hills and vistas, just as you described them.* Her emotions were ascending in concert with their climb from sea level to the view above the village at a point more than three thousand feet above the sea. Each step of the horse pulling the wagon closer to her destination was felt by Madeleine's soul. She could see her hands begin to tremble slightly.

"This is a very different and ancient place, my son, but it is where your father was born and lived as a child."

"It's much higher too than Marseilles and southern France!" exclaimed François.

Late in the day, they stopped at the lookout point, the curve of the road above the village. Stepping onto the road from the cart, they could not know this was the precise spot where Iskandar paused for his last view of his beloved village and picked up a small stone to take to America. This was the place where his journey to find his destiny began nearly twenty years earlier.

They looked down the mountain to the village far below. "It looks like a scorpion, *Maman,*" François said as his finger traced its shape in the air.

Madeleine shivered as a cool breeze brushed across her face. "Your father said the village was beautiful from the curve in the road above the village. He said the rooftop tiles are red …to remember those who died in the wars, so the legend says. Perhaps this very spot is where he told me he looked back for the last time when he left his home for America. Isn't it remarkable for us, François? He may have stood right here and looked down as a young man just as you are doing now."

She embraced her son as she drew him close, almost as though François was his father, better understanding the stories Iskandar had told her so long ago. She found she actually wanted to cry from her heightened feelings of joy.

"God brought your father into our lives many years ago to provide for us a safe haven from the dangers in Europe. Can you imagine? If I had not met your father when he was exactly the same age as you are now, we might still be in danger for our very lives in France. God works in strange, wonderful ways, my son."

"Time to go, madame," the farmer interrupted "Hold fast to the wagon as we begin our descent to the village. It can be tricky going down this steep mountain. The village is more than one thousand meters higher than where we met in Tripoli, and three hundred meters beneath us at the moment."

It was late in the day when the wagon pulled into the village *souk*. The golden sun was lingering, almost hesitating, over the western mountain tops above the city. There were a few villagers still in the street, shopping and visiting at the last minute. Most shops were closing for the night.

"*Bonne nuit, madame et monsieur, et bon courage.* It's been a pleasure. Do you have a place to stay?" asked the farmer as he helped her off the wagon.

"No, we don't, monsieur," replied Madeleine with a furrow in her brow. "Can you help us?"

"Well," he thought as he stroked his chin, "I have a few cousins here in Douma although I live in Tannourine down in the valley, near Farhilde. Perhaps they know of someone who will take you in for the night."

It didn't take long for the remaining villagers in the small *souk* to note the two strangers arriving in the village, for indeed, it was very small with only a few hundred residents. Most shoppers had gone home for the night.

"*Ahlen wa sahlen,*" said a friendly young girl, smiling as she walked up to the wagon. "Are you visiting Douma? Do you have family here?" the young girl asked in fluent, though accented French.

"We are from Marseille," replied François in French also to the pretty, dark-eyed teenager. "We are hoping to find a place to stay. Can you help us?"

"Perhaps," she replied. "We do not have a hotel, but there are families here who have spare rooms they let out. Everyone is hoping for francs and dollars. You must be hungry after your long journey up from Beirut."

François thought, *If she only knew we've been on a boat for days!*

Madeleine ventured cautiously, "Do you know the Thomé-Chalhoub family?"

"Oh," the girl replied quickly with a smile, "the Chalhoub family makes up much of the village. She continued, "I am a Thomé. And what, may I ask, are your names?

"My name is Madame Madeleine Moreau, and this is my son François."

"Are you Christian?" asked a smiling, hopeful François of the girl, wanting to break the tension.

"Yes, I am Orthodox. We have several churches here. This is a Christian village. And you? Are you Catholic? We have a Catholic Church, a Melkite church, Orthodox, and a Maronite church." She laughed, "It is said we have more than one seat in our churches for each citizen. Thus, we must be a holy and safe village. Everyone attends church at least every Sunday. For us, life is our family, our church, and our education."

She tossed her head with a sense of pride.

"I apologize, but now I must go. I am going to have supper at my sitty's house tonight. If you have no place to go, please come with me. You must meet my father, Milhelm. I am sure he and *Sitty* would be happy to help you."

"Milhelm?" Madeleine asked, almost stunned. "Is *Sitty* your grandmother?"

"No. She is really my great-aunt, but I call her *Sitty* out of respect."

"*Ahlen wa sahlen*, please come in," spoke the silver-haired woman standing in the doorway of the small stone house, wiping her hands on her apron, wearing a welcoming, sincere smile. Sara, sister-in-law of Iskandar's mother Katrina, was elderly now. As a widow, she was taken in by Milhelm and his daughter, Katrina. They all lived in *beit* Thomé Chalhoub on the main road in Douma. It was the family home Abraham had built with his own hands more than fifty years earlier.

As they entered the small, stone house, Madeleine noticed the brightly painted white walls were mostly bare, save for a crucifix over the couch, a painting of a church with mountains in the background, and photographs of family members. The floors were gray cement with Oriental rugs scattered around. They could not help but notice the enticing garlic-laden smells of cooking emanating from the kitchen.

The young girl introduced them, gesturing toward her guests, "*Sitty*, these people are from Marseille. I met them in the *souk*. They need a place to stay so I told them you had space for rent. Is it alright?"

"Please come in," nodded Sara with a slight wave of her hand. "Of course we will be happy for you to stay with us, but you will have to share a room. Ours is a small house." Then, looking over at the woman and young man, she paused and motioned for them to drop their bags on the floor. "All we have is a warm home, food, and beds. We have no money but we have our hospitality." She smiled proudly. As she walked into the center of the immaculately clean main room that was sparsely furnished with a small table and a few chairs, she said, "Please sit and tell us the news. Would you like tea?"

"*Merci, madame, merci beaucoup*," replied Madeleine with a nervous smile. "We have come to Douma for safe haven. My husband, Philippe urged me to leave France soon after Germany invaded Poland. He did not believe it would be very long before Hitler occupied France, so he hurried us out of Marseille...we brought only what we could carry."

Wiping her brow with her handkerchief, apprehensive about being in the home, in the midst of Iskandar's world, she tried to explain her dilemma without upsetting the woman. "Philippe said Hitler hates France because of the penalizing Treaty of Versailles, and will not stop with Poland. He also told me that while Lebanon is the safest place for us, Beirut is filled with immigrants, transients, spies, German sympathizers, and Jews from all over Europe seeking refuge, so he urged us to go north into the mountains of Lebanon. Hanna Chalhoub, my mother's dear friend in Marseille, also urged us to come here. He thought this village would be the best place to stay. Elias, his cousin in Beirut, told me the same thing."

Madeleine, nervously twisting her kerchief in her hands, glanced around the room then brought her eyes back to Sara, hoping for a positive response, asked, "Can you help us?"

She recalled Hanna's admonition that she did not want the family of Iskandar or anyone in the village to even know of his out-of-wedlock son, François. It would mean certain embarrassment and shame. Madeleine knew that in some countries, the child would be killed to protect the family's reputation. She and François had to keep their secret to themselves.

"We won't be a problem for you, madame, I assure you. At the moment we are refugees." She almost broke down hearing her own words. It was horrible for her to admit aloud that she and her son were homeless...without a country...because of Hitler's invasion.

Gathering her composure she continued, carefully choosing her words. "My husband is with the French government as the Director of Counter-Intelligence, the Resistance, based in Paris," she said with pride.

"He sounds very important to me," responded Sara as she leaned forward in her chair, and noticing Madeleine's cup was nearly empty, asked, "Would you like more tea? Katrina, bring a plate of my pastries, please...the ones with the sweet pistachio centers."

Madeleine froze and stared at the young girl. "Did you call her Katrina?" she asked with a look of astonishment, then recoiled at her reaction. She squeezed her hands together anxiously.

"Yes, she was named after my wonderful sister-in-law, mother of Milhelm, Lena and Iskandar. The moment she was born we noted her fair skin and light brown hair. She looked just like my sister-in-law, Katrina...so beautiful. Unfortunately, she died during the famine in 1916. *Allahyurhamek*, may she rest in peace. Her eldest son, Milhelm, still lives here in Douma, but Iskandar is in America with his father and sister. We miss them so much."

"They are in America? Do you know where?" Madeleine asked cautiously, not wanting to pursue the subject too much at this time.

She shrugged her shoulders. "I don't know. I believe they live in Florida somewhere. We have many cousins in Boston, Rhode Island, and then,

Miklos…Mike…in Palm Beach. But I think…I…I'm not sure." Sara bowed her head modestly, not truly understanding the location of the places she had just mentioned. "There are Lebanese people all over America," she laughed.

As Madeleine and François listened intently, nodding at each new bit of family news, they grew more relaxed, feeling the welcoming warmth of this gracious family.

After a simple dinner of *tabouleh*, rice and lamb, Katrina insisted François play a game of cards with her on the table while Madeleine visited with Sara as she resumed knitting a wool comforter lying across her lap.

As they visited, they could hear footsteps outside the door. Then the door opened. Standing in the doorway was a tall, broad-shouldered man. His arms were muscular and his face ruddy in complexion.

"*Ahlen wa sahlen.* Come in," Sara announced as she looked up from her knitting. "We have visitors, Milhelm. Come meet Madame Moreau and her son, François."

Madeleine found herself standing up and staring at the man in the doorway, stunned at his appearance. *Mon Dieu, he looks so much like Iskandar!*

François, picking up on his mother's surprise, and recognizing Milhelm's name from the stories she had told him, almost knocked over the table, disrupting the cards as he stood up abruptly at the sound of the name of his father's brother. This was the man who had saved his father's life on the mountain. He couldn't help but stare at the formidable figure. Milhelm immediately looked twice at François, stunned at his similarity to his brother. But he said nothing.

Madeleine, realizing her astonished behavior could seem strange to the others, signaled to François to remain silent. She turned away slightly, so as not to draw too much attention. She was amazed at how much Milhelm, while older now, still resembled her beloved Iskandar. She almost stammered as she finally spoke, "I…hope…you don't mind that my son and I seek refuge in your home. We're from Marseille, running from the Germans. It appears the mountains of northern Lebanon are the only safe place outside America these days. Perhaps it would be better if we stayed in another family's home?"

"Well," Milhelm replied in French, opening both arms in a welcoming gesture, clearly surprised at the presence of this lovely, cultured lady, "you have arrived here just in time. In Tripoli, everyone is talking about the German invasion of northern France only a few days ago."

Then, nodding to Sara and Katrina, he added, "You are welcome here, madame. Though we are simple people, what we have we will share with you."

Madeleine was now a bit more relaxed in his presence, yet still caught off-guard by the sensations that raced through her as she actually felt Milhelm's large, strong hand grip hers. "You look so much like Is...uh" she caught herself, "uh...like what I imagined a strong man of the Lebanese mountains would look." Embarrassed, she lowered her eyelids in modesty and resumed her seat, placing her hands on her knees and remaining silent.

"These times are not as terrible here as they were before," Sara said, looking into space, remembering. "It has been worse, much worse, but there are many people coming to Lebanon now. They bring all their money and spend it in Beirut. And because the mountains are so beautiful, they come here, but only in the summer. It's too cold and there's too much snow in the winter. The world is in a strange way these days," she added, waxing philosophically, "but we don't feel the political problems here in Douma. Nor do our cousins in the other mountain villages north of here, especially Ehden and Bsharre, where the cedars grow in abundance. They are very popular summer resorts. But in the winter the snow gets very, very deep. Only the French escaping go there."

Madeleine, remembering all that Iskandar had told her about his village, the mountains, his mother, his brother Milhelm, and his Aunt Sara, wrapped her arms around her breasts feeling a shivering sense of relief somehow, feeling very safe and very comfortable. She looked over at François, sensing in the dim light of the kerosene lamp glow, how much he resembled his father. And there he was playing cards with his cousin, sixteen-year-old Katrina. *My, my, how the Lord works in strange ways*, she thought to herself. François and Katrina reminded her of Iskandar and herself. Madeleine carefully reached into her bodice to verify that the gold cross Iskandar had given her was still well concealed. *I must be very careful that no one sees it in Douma*, she reminded herself. *This is no time for a family secret to cause us to have to leave the only safe haven available to us.*

Thinking that they would stay in this house for only a few days before finding another, perhaps larger home, Madeleine could not have known that this would become their home for much longer.

CHAPTER 33

"ᴘARIS OCCUPIED BY GERMANY" blurted the headlines in the Beirut newspapers on June 15th of 1940.

Then, even worse, on June 23rd, the headlines announced "FRANCE SURRENDERS."

"Oh, my God, what are we to do now?" Beirutis asked each other. After all, the French Army had occupied all of Lebanon and Syria as their "Protectorate" since World War I, more than twenty years. Many Syrians and Lebanese believed, and said to one another, that perhaps it was time to consider ending the French occupation of Lebanon. Members declared at Parliament, "We must be free. Perhaps it is time for Lebanon to take control of its own destiny."

It took the Germans little time to exploit the weak, divided French people, at least half of whom did not even support their own government. By June 22, 1940, the new government of France was surprisingly and quickly formed at the spa of Vichy, south of Paris. Henri Philippe Omer Pétain, an eighty-four-year-old former general and father figure, was appointed the new premier by new President Albert LeBrun to lead the new French government in Vichy. He immediately sought a "friendly alliance" with Germany. Soon, his new government became a puppet regime, adopting most of Germany's harsh fascist positions.

The politics of the times caused this new government to reach a painful one-sided armistice, agreeing to four basic terms: (1) the terrible unconscionable turnover to the Germans of all Jews in France, (2) the surrender of the entire French Army except for 100,000 to maintain order, and as a result, 1.5 million regular French soldiers were captured by the Germans and immediately imprisoned, (3) no member of the armed forces was to leave France, and (4) France had to pay for all costs of occupation.

Consequently, Germany occupied the northern 60% of France while the Vichy French, overseen by the German army, monitored the southern 40%. The Vichy government was much too accommodating to the Nazis, adopting many of the Third Reich policies. France quickly became unsafe for nearly everyone. Millions of citizens fled the country, tens of thousands fled to

Marseille, Toulon, and other parts of southern France. And tens of thousands of Jews sought refuge in Palestine and Lebanon.

For four years, Pétain led the new right-wing government, completely allied with Germany. In 1943 a secret police agency loyal to the Nazis called Milice was created under the direction of Philippe Moreau's longtime adversary, Joseph Darnand. It boasted 35,000 members by 1944.

"Cowards," Moreau labeled them.

In Douma, Madeleine fretted about Philippe's safety.

"I do hope Monsieur Moreau is in a safe place," Sara commented to Madeleine when she heard about the German occupation, trying to comfort her new friend, touching her hand as they sat at the breakfast table.

"As do I," whispered Madeleine with sadness in her eyes. "France is filled with Germans once again." She began wringing her hands at the table, twisting her handkerchief, then wiping the tears from her eyes. "I lost my father during the first war when I was just a child. And now I fear for my husband's life. This is awful." She bowed her face into her hands.

"But perhaps," Sara consoled, "he knows exactly what to do and where to stay. His business requires that he maintain his safety. Is it not so? Perhaps all we can do is be optimistic and wait."

Madeleine appreciated Sara's empathy, using "we" instead of "you."

Within weeks, the new French government in Vichy had converted its protectorate government in Syria, including its province of Lebanon, to conform to the Vichy alliance with Germany, making conditions much more difficult in Beirut and the major ports of Jounieh and Sidon.

There was little news in Douma although Milhelm heard that quiet preparations were being made by the English in Syria, Iraq and Palestine, together with the Free French forces to rid the region of the Vichy French army.

"I heard from my cousin that the Resistance is greatly disrupting the Germans in southern France. A Resistance group in Beirut is trying to find out the conditions in Marseille because there are so many Lebanese there."

It wasn't long before Milhelm obtained more information through his channels in Tripoli. He learned that, in fact, Philippe Moreau was safe and in hiding in the *Panier* near the port in Marseille.

"Thank God," Madeleine told Milhelm as he told her the good news. "Thank God he is safe. I believe he is with Hanna and my mother. Can you find out about their welfare too?"

Milhelm's cousin was happy to relate any other information to him. "Of course. We have contacts that can find out about their well-being. The people of Beirut and Marseille have been very close for a very long time and much information is possible through the captains and crews of the boats that go back and forth even during wars. It never seems to stop them. They are clever men, those fishermen. And very independent."

The Vichy government kept troops in Lebanon and Syria, utilizing their strategic location on the eastern shores of the Mediterranean. The English and Free French, fearing German *Luftwaffe* bases being established there, decided to bombard and invade Lebanon and Syria from Palestine and Iraq. By June 17, 1941, the English captured Damascus and signed an armistice with the Syrian Vichy government on July 12th. As a result, pro-British forces controlled Lebanon and Syria until the end of the war. The Druze, a Moslem group and fighters for centuries, especially in the mountains above Beirut, bitterly fought the corrupted Vichy army in Lebanon. Consequently, after mid-year, better information was getting through, although generally weeks late, and for the remainder of the war, Madeleine was kept informed from time to time of Philippe's whereabouts and of Hanna and her mother's safety in Marseille.

"As long as you stay within the *Panier* district, we can protect you," admonished Philippe or his agents to Hanna.

By 1942, Philippe Moreau had achieved remarkable results, having brought together the disorganized underground forces. As a matter of history, in 1941, the Resistance was officially formed to unify a civilian rebellion force against the German occupiers. The Resistance movement emerged as the only possible counterforce opposed to the Nazis. It rapidly became stronger under Philippe's leadership by filling the vacuum and became an instant rallying point for those French loyal to their country and not drawn to Germany-allied Vichy. Thereafter, instead of mere sporadic and isolated annoyances to the German army, the Resistance took on more and more productive means of tying up the German army so it would be less effective against the Allies. Stealthily, and almost at will initially, armed Resistance teams dynamited key bridges and tunnels, German army convoys of trucks, rail yards, and almost any target the French loyalists could daringly attack with hit-and-run tactics. By late 1942, Moreau's strategies and communications systems were becoming highly effective. His teams caused the German army to divert enormous amounts of manpower and materiel from the front to interior Counter-Resistance efforts.

The formerly disparate groups were rapidly becoming a coordinated paramilitary unit working across the country, more in concert with one another. As their impact was growing, so too was Moreau's image and reputation. Awareness of the costs to the Germans' efforts was also reaching upper levels of German officials. "Get Moreau" was the order of the day. As the Resistance became more and more effective across France, Philippe Moreau became a marked man. Rarely did he sleep in the same bed two nights in a row. His drivers were double checked daily. His food was tested at every meal. His schedule was never known. After the autumn of 1942, Philippe Moreau's life was a dichotomy; on the one hand, he was planning multiple and coordinated attacks on the hated Nazis throughout the country, and on the other hand, he was constantly detailing his own safety. An escape route, an "exit strategy," was always preplanned no matter where he was located. He met, dined, and slept only at "safe" houses.

When in Marseille, he stayed in one or another of Hanna Chalhoub's apartments in the Lebanese-friendly section of the *Panier* district near the docks and rail station. He ate only in one of Hanna's restaurants, guarded by loyalists at all times.

Because Beirut and the port city of Jounieh were under siege in 1941 by the Allies' naval forces and the English launched attacks from Palestine to the south seeking to remove the Vichy forces, Beirut was in chaos. Those in Douma and other villages in the remote northern Lebanese mountains remained mostly unaffected and safe. But once again, the villagers had to deal with the shortages of nearly everything, including food and coal. It would be a very cold and bitter winter for the villagers and their new guests, Madeleine and François DuBois.

Madeleine and François found themselves more and more involved with the hospitable and friendly villagers after their confining first winter months, and were asked to help out during the summer months into the autumn season's harvest. There were olives to bring in from the groves along the Farhilde River below the village. Sacks of *zeytoon* were piled on the donkey-drawn wagons, or in bags simply slung over the donkeys' backs. The young men were called on to see that these heavy loads made it to the presses on the eastern most edge of the village. Olives and the coveted Douma virgin olive oil were then delivered to markets in Tripoli. Grapes in the vineyards and fruit in the orchards had to be harvested and delivered.

François was anxious to help, especially when Katrina, not knowing she was his first cousin, cajoled him. "*Yallah*, François, come and join my cousin Marina and me. It's more fun when we do it together." Then, pointing up the mountain, with a devilish smile, added, "Next week we will walk up the trail to the fruit groves above the village to pick the apples and pears in *Figarie*."

Little did François realize, *Figarie* was high atop the mountain reached by a severely curving, steep dirt path at least 3,000 feet higher than the village. Although Katrina and Marina were accustomed to the climb, it would test his physical endurance beyond anything he had experienced before.

"But I lived in a seaport city all my life!" he complained good-naturedly.

That next week, Katrina led François to the torturous path behind the village that led to the fruit orchards. Half way up, François was getting testy and weary.

"How long will it take to get to the top, Katrina? My legs are killing me already!"

She couldn't help but laugh. "Come on, my city-boy Frenchman. We'll make a man of you yet!" As she spoke, she teasingly grabbed his hand and pulled him up the path.

And so the autumn passed, day after day of neighbor helping neighbor bring in the bounty of the groves. After the pressing of the *zeytoon*, Sara would boast each time, "Douma is known for its pure olive oil. It is considered the finest in all Lebanon."

"And our apples!" added Katrina, "Dear, *Allah*! They are the largest, most delicious in the entire Mediterranean."

"And what about our grapes?" added Marina.

Indeed, the apples, about which Iskandar had boasted to Madeline, were larger than most Europeans had seen, and they were so juicy and sweet. After biting into one of the samples Madeleine received from Sara, she exclaimed, "Oh, Sara, these apples are so wonderful! They are just as sweet as Isk…ah.." She stopped herself after almost blurting out what Iskandar had told her with pride. She finished, "…as sweet as can be!"

Katrina and François grew closer and closer.

The autumn season turned into winter in November with the first snowfall and more time was spent inside as the temperature dropped. Madeleine fondly remembered Iskandar's story of being a child at the age of ten, caught in an early snowstorm that nearly cost him his feet. Looking up to the mountains he had climbed, she would often think of him.

Each event in the village reconnected her with Iskandar and bonded them in her heart and mind spiritually and emotionally. And each evening, while alone with François, she would tell him of these emotional bonds. Her heart would swell with pride for Iskandar. She felt great joy at actually being among his family and in his village. Her senses absorbed all that she saw and felt as she realized she was, indeed, growing closer and closer to the Lebanese culture and the people.

François too, felt like he was with his own family, but knew better than to refer to Milhelm as "uncle," although he was in fact his nephew. And he knew that Katrina and Marina were his cousins, but he absolutely could not divulge anything of their connection. This continued to create certain tensions and nervous behavior in François and Madeleine, ever on guard not to err even slightly. They had discussed many times the risks of exposure at length. She had admonished him over and again to be very careful with what he might say or how he might react to a situation.

"We must be quiet about this or we may be told to leave the village. We must not embarrass anyone, especially your father, Milhelm or Philippe. It would be too terrible, I fear, so it is our secret to keep, François."

CHAPTER 34

Beirut
1941

y June of 1941, before the United States entered the war in December 1941, the Vichy government and its forces had been ousted from Lebanon. Lebanon was no longer in the crosshair of the Allies' war machine, and Beirut was safely under control of pro-British forces. Beirut's port activity became slightly improved throughout the war, and the mountains of northern Lebanon became even more attractive to those fleeing the European and African fighting zones. Mountain villagers watched nervously as more and more strangers passed through Douma.

In November 1943, after the siege and complete removal of the occupying Vichy government, Lebanon was actually able to declare its independence. The country was finally free after so many centuries of occupation, beginning with the Turkish invasion in the 1500s and ending now with the French. Lebanon immediately formed a democratic government with a representative Parliament, the first in the Near East. It wasn't until after the war that France once again resumed an official, but only diplomatic, presence in Lebanon, limited to a new embassy in Beirut. Unofficially, the Christian community, particularly the Maronites, resumed their strong cultural, social, and economic ties to France which would have a *facto protectorate* role with Lebanon for many decades to come. As a result, under the new constitution, Lebanon's president would always be a Maronite Catholic Christian even though Christians at the time were only a slight majority. But that would change soon as Palestinians, both Christian and Muslim, escaped the Zionist onslaught in Palestine and entered southern Lebanon by the thousands. Actually, seeds of internecine rivalries germinated at this time of independence would emerge and re-emerge even decades later.

During the war years from June 1941 to 1945, those positioned in trade prospered. The best traders, of course, were the coastal Lebanese. The businessmen and the bankers were near enough to Europe, but far enough away to safely provide excellent and often surreptitious international fund transfers.

Wealthy Europeans, including escaping Jews found difficulty in Switzerland whose politicians in many ways, cooperated with the Germans. As a result, many sought refuge in Lebanon, Syria, Iraq, and Palestine, countries which were still protected by the British and Free French forces. Some European Jewish entrepreneurs even forged strong and trusted business partnerships with prominent Lebanese businessmen.

Europe was experiencing painful difficulties of rebuilding its shattered cities as a result of the war. But, while in America where Alexander and the other cattlemen of Central Florida were flourishing, Lebanese bankers and traders also prospered from the massive, growing regional demands for industrial goods, and commodities required by the burgeoning economies of the oil-producing Arab states. Although their country had no major natural resources, they enjoyed open ports, a convenient location, and a tradition of free trade. The Lebanese survived those war years with their business acumen.

Thousands of immigrants flowed steadily into the eastern Mediterranean ports of Beirut, Jaffa, and Jounieh, often by way of Cyprus and even Sardinia. Those cities burst at their seams with so many new people—some coming to safety, and others to fulfill their own agendas—and still others who would be threatening to the indigenous population, contrary to the terms of the Balfour Declaration, in which England announced its support for a Jewish state in Palestine with the restriction that "the rights of the indigenous population are not to be abrogated."

One day in late 1943, Milhelm, returning from Beirut in a borrowed truck, anxiously drove in less than one hour to Douma. He quickly went to his home and found Madeleine. He was very worried and gave her the urgent news.

"Madeleine, there are people searching for you in Beirut. You must hide. They are French Milice members and German Gestapo who are paying anyone who can be bought to bring you to them. They are saying they intend to kidnap you and your son for ransom. Your husband is wanted by the German government as leader of the Resistance because his organization is causing them so much disruption. They want to make him stop his activities. I am sorry, but you must go farther north from Douma for a while. I think they will trace you here."

"But where will I go, Milhelm?"

"The Valley of Passion is not far away, but we have cousins north of here in Bsharre. The snows there will get very deep soon, so it will be too difficult to go there until the spring thaw. There are a few Europeans there, and many caves for hiding. You must take your son and go now. My cousins will help you. If these men come to Douma, I will see to it that they do not follow you. You must go now...this very minute," he urged. "I will take you."

Nervously, Madeleine and François immediately grabbed their meager possessions, climbed into the borrowed truck, and were driven thirty miles along the winding road atop the crest of the mountain range to the north. They were to stay there until Milhelm sent word that it was safe to return to Douma.

Milhelm returned to Douma and alerted the villagers to be on the watch for suspicious strangers. "They may be two or three or four men. They may be Germans who speak fluent French, or French members of the Milice, the Vichy secret police. Alert me," he admonished, "if you see such people. They are not friends, and they are looking to take Madame Moreau and her son." When the villagers saw a worried look on Milhelm's face, they knew to respond as he asked.

Only one week later, a hired truck drove into the village *souk* bearing two such men who, speaking fluent French, began immediately inquiring if "a Madame Moreau and her son, François Moreau, had been in the village lately. We wish to help them."

When told of their arrival, Milhelm went to work with his plan.

Milhelm met with the two strangers, and, nodding his head stupidly in mock understanding, directed them with great detail to the road out of town toward the east.

"The Moreaus went that way several days ago, there, through the safe passage," he said, pointing to the narrow winding road that traveled along the eastern edge of the 7,000-foot mountain range, the same crest where Milhelm's young brother, Iskandar, was trapped in a freak snowstorm some twenty years earlier.

Amazingly, it was only one day later when word was sent to the Gibran family in Bsharre that Madame Moreau and her son could return safely to Douma. "Regrettably," it stated, "the two blonde-haired German secret police who had come to Douma searching for the Moreaus had left to the east on an old abandoned road and had carelessly driven off the curving mountain roads and had gone over the edge near Douma. Their truck crashed more than 300 feet below and burst into flames. There were no survivors."

Two weeks later, a second group of Germans came to Douma. This time there were four men. Milhelm actually rode with them until they reached the crest where he got out and began walking back to Douma. Then, very soon, he saw their truck careen off the ridge into a deep valley and explode, killing all its passengers. Thereafter, there were no further visits to Douma by the Germans or sympathetic French.

Madeleine returned to Douma and never asked Milhelm how the clever kidnappers had become so careless. It forever remained his secret.

"Madeleine," Milhelm later said to her, his sensitive eyes reminiscent of Iskandar's looking softly into hers as he held her shoulders firmly, "I have watched over my brother, Iskandar, protected him, and revered his life since he was a little boy. For some reasons I cannot fully explain, I find I am compelled to guard over you and your son in the same way. He reminds me so much of my younger brother, Iskandar."

That is all that was ever said. Madeleine began to believe that in his heart, Milhelm felt a connection between her and her son and his brother, but neither he nor she ever explored the very sensitive issue, perhaps fearing what they might not want to hear. He never brought the subject up again, although he couldn't help being puzzled.

Apparently, as the war progressed, the German SS finally determined kidnapping Madeleine and François was not the best solution to their "Resistance problem." And as a result, they instituted more direct plots in several cities of Europe to stop their nemesis, her husband. As it turned out, he was quite elusive. He avoided their snares for many months, causing the *Wehrmacht* great frustration, culminating in the summer of 1944 with his critical coordination of the Allied invasions at Normandy, then Toulon and Marseille.

But Philippe's luck finally ran out. In late August 1944, he was shot and killed in Copenhagen while having dinner in a "safe" restaurant as he met with local agents. As it turned out, members of the French Milice, the Vichy secret police, machine-gunned the group at their table. An agent of Moreau's adversary, Hitler-aligned Joseph Darnand, had finally found his enemy and would be generously rewarded for his efforts. With a promissory note significantly signed by General Joseph Paul Goebbels of 100,000 Deutsche marks in his pocket, he was cut down by Philippe's guards, but too late. The Nazis considered Philippe the most wanted man in France. Now he was eliminated.

When Madeleine later heard the report from Marseille that her husband had been killed by the enemy, and in this case, unbelievable as it seemed, by a fellow Frenchman, a member of the counter-Resistance, the Vichy secret police, she was simultaneously deeply shocked and very angry.

"How could they do this?" she exclaimed to Milhelm. "Philippe's efforts were for France, not himself."

"But that is the problem," Milhelm calmly and thoughtfully responded as they received the news. "Which France? Those brutal idiots think France's future is to be an ally of the scum Adolph Hitler. This is terribly depressing news." He frowned as he lowered his head. "Madeleine, I'm so very sorry this has happened. But, your husband is revered by all loyal French people. He is our hero also and will be remembered for generations, I assure you."

"Thank you, Milhelm," she nodded sadly. "This is just so awful. The first war took my father, now my dear husband, Philippe. Damn those Germans! Damn Adolph Hitler! Damn!" she shouted in anger.

Too many of all those she loved were being taken away from her, including Iskandar. But that loss had to remain a secret in her heart. She began worrying even more about the safety of her mother and Hanna. "Dear God," she prayed every night, "please keep them safe, out of harm's way."

Philippe Moreau had done his work well. Indeed, his accomplishments would long be remembered. His organization of the planning and direction of the Resistance was especially effective in coordination with the Allied invasion of Normandy in June, 1944, and preparing Toulon and Marseille for Operation Anvil, soon after. These efforts were invaluable in significantly reducing German resistance. Through his adept organization skills and exquisite planning, French railroad engineers delayed deliveries by cleverly crisscrossing the country as they carried hundreds of German tanks *away* from the French northern coast where they were supposed to fight the Normandy-invading Allied landing forces. By disrupting German communication lines, their efforts saved tens of thousands of lives of young American, British and Free French soldiers during the Normandy invasion. Even General Dwight Eisenhower properly recognized the brilliant planning and co-ordination of the French Resistance under the leadership of Philippe Moreau, and noted that the Normandy invasion especially *could not have been successful without him.*

His death occurred precisely during the second Allied invasion in the south, the Allied bombardment of Toulon and Marseille in August of 1944 during "Operation Anvil."

It was during that bombardment that Hanna and Daniella were killed.

But Madeleine did not learn of their deaths until after the German surrender a year later.

Somehow, with all the European fighting, thousands of deaths in France, European starvation, prison camps, and brutalities, Madeleine and François were able to safely endure the war years in remote, quiet Douma, the village of Iskandar, ironically for them, the safest place in Europe and the Near East.

It was soon after the Normandy invasion that 19-year-old Michael Chalhoub Thomas of Kissimmee, Florida, François DuBois' half-brother, began his tour of duty as a lieutenant in the United States Army Air Corps, piloting a B-17 bomber over strategic sites in Germany.

After the European war ended, the Lebanese breathed a collective sigh of relief. Many who had fled during the Vichy presence and the devastating Allied bombardment slowly began to return to Lebanon. Beirut began rebuilding into a very prosperous period of post-war exuberance while it was still under control of pro-British forces, and safe. Fears of rampant inflation were unfounded. Commerce and employment flourished. Madeleine marveled at the incredible resilience of the Lebanese people.

Among the leaders of commerce in Beirut with connections throughout the Arab world, was The Kabani Group headed by Marcel Kabani, a most influential industrialist and entrepreneur. Respected for his integrity, loyalty, business acumen, and generosity, he was able to operate easily throughout the region.

Marcel Kabani had remained at his offices in Beirut from where he had so successfully operated during the war years. He also managed to travel to America, Iraq, Brazil, and other lands where trade was possible.

"I go where I must the best way I can," he would explain later. "Thankfully I have extended families all over South America."

But by war's end, his devoted and sophisticated wife, Marina, had become ill and unable to totally take care of herself. She stayed in residence in their fabulous villa in the hills overlooking the city of Beirut near the *Casino du Liban* in Jounieh, one of Marcel's varied and most profitable partnerships.

CHAPTER 35

ne sunny Saturday afternoon in the autumn of 1944, Katrina invited François to join her and her grandmother in the family vineyards on the slopes above the village. She smiled and waved her hand, "Come, François. Let's go harvest the grapes. They are full and ripe," she giggled as she ran ahead. "Come with me!" He was eager to join her, as they had grown close during the war years. She had not yet learned that they were actually cousins. "I packed some olives, *hummus*, bread, and wine. We'll eat under the trees after we collect the grapes this morning."

What a pleasant sight they make, thought Sara, as François, a handsome 24-year old, and pretty, coquettish Katrina, now twenty-years-old, rushed down to the village road past the *souk* carrying their baskets and pulling their wagon together. As soon as they could, they turned left at the vineyard path, parked the wagon, and entered the family vineyards of terraced rows of rich, full bunches of ripe grapes, swollen and ready for harvest. The family's land, worked by the Thomé family for many generations, was tended carefully, and defined by loose stone walls three feet thick and four feet high. Some of the stone walls traced their origin to the Greek occupation nearly 2,500 years earlier.

"You see that old stone box-like building above the village by that large stone outcropping, François?" Milhelm had asked him the day before, as he pointed across the slopes. "Well, that is now a small monastery, but legend tells us it was built by the Greeks three hundred years before Christ as a hospital for their army. Imagine if you can, wounded Greek invaders here in these mountains being treated for everything from arrows to sword wounds. At the same time, my ancestors built the first of those stone walls that separate our land, our vineyards, and our groves of apples, pears, and persimmon. My family has been here a long time, *y'eini*. I am part of this land, and this land is a part of me. That is why I could not leave Douma, even when my brother, whom I loved more than myself, left for America when he was younger than you."

François, visibly impressed with all he heard and saw, had replied, "This place is so incredibly imprinted with history," "How do you remember all these things, Milhelm?"

"It is my heritage, my life. This is where my soul lives, François."

Interrupting his thoughts, Katrina teased, "I'll cut the grapes, François, and you carry the basket. This will be fun, you'll see." As Katrina bounded from vine to vine cutting the lush, deep burgundy bunches and, placing them in the basket, she declared, "Now that the fighting is over in Beirut and the French are gone, there is a good market for our harvest."

After more than three hours of cutting and harvesting the grapes, Katrina pointed to the cluster of trees. "The sun is growing warmer, and I need a drink of water. Let's go down to the olive trees, sit, and rest for awhile. Would you like that?"

He didn't want to let her think he was tired, so he shrugged at her welcomed suggestion of relief. "Sure, if *you* are tired," he emphasized, "we can rest."

Katrina smiled at François' response knowing that although he clearly was tired and was getting too burdened, he would never let her think he needed a rest. *Men!* she laughed to herself. They always want us to think they are made of iron.

Finally they found just the right spot of grass under an ancient, gnarled olive tree. She gestured to him as she bent over to spread the tablecloth. "It's cooler here in the shade. The air is dry but it's very warm today, especially when we're working so hard." She wiped her brow and cheeks. "The sun is especially bright up here high in the mountains."

"Katrina, this is a great day. I love Douma. It has become my home. You must know these past years have been very happy for me. I feel a part of the family, and I'm glad we are close friends."

He liked being with her and looked forward to sharing time with her. "You are my best friend, Katrina."

He smiled, realizing he may have been saying that to his grandmother, Katrina.

Above them, Sara was approaching the two, carefully picking her way down the slope.

"Oh, *Sitty*," Katrina called to her great-aunt, "over here," she waved, "under the tree. We are resting for a few minutes. Look how much we harvested. Isn't it wonderful?"

"Oh, yes, Katrina, "Sara nodded as she reached them. "You and François have done very well today. But of course," she admonished, "more must be harvested before we can send our load to market tomorrow morning."

François, now really tired and wanting to cool off, drank heartily from the jug of water as he tipped it over his shoulder, wiped his forehead, and pulled his tunic over his head. Suddenly aware of what he had done, he abruptly glanced to his chest. *Oh, my God, I forgot to take the cross off after church.* He had found it in a drawer and, without telling his mother, had worn the cross to church that morning to feel closer to his father. Hoping Sara and Katrina would not notice, he reached to quickly hide his father's gold cross he was wearing around his bare neck by covering it with his hand. But he was too late.

"*Shoo?* What? Let me see your pendant, François. Where did you get it?"

Astonished, Sara gingerly stepped over to where François was sitting in the shade leaning against the tree trunk, reached to his chest and gripped the gold cross.

"Where did you get this, François?" she repeated, staring into his eyes as she pulled the cross against the chain. "It looks very familiar to me," Sara exclaimed with furrows growing on her forehead.

"It is my mother's," he replied nervously. "She let me wear it to church."

Sara stood straight, her face now glowering at this young man, who, at her invitation, had lived in her house for all these years. Now, it seemed, he was a stranger. She wondered, *Who is he?*

"Let me see it better," Sara demanded, looking closely at the pendant. "It looks...it looks so very familiar to me. I believe it is very much like a cross I had made many years ago in Beirut. How did your mother get this cross?"

"How can that be, *Sitty?*" interrupted Katrina. "How is that possible?"

"I don't know, Katrina. I don't know but I want to look at the cross more carefully with my glasses." She brushed Katrina aside, very concerned and suddenly suspicious.

François put his tunic back on, covering the treasured gold cross. He was so worried and frightened now that he couldn't talk. *We may be found out. I must speak with my mother about this as soon as possible.*

After Katrina and François had completed their harvest, the three silently walked back down the slope carrying their harvest to the family wagon that they had left at the road. Avoiding each other's eyes, they loaded the wagon and walked along side it to *beit* Thomé, their home. Tension filled the air, and suddenly the group became estranged, no longer bonded. Doubt and fear had breached their relationship.

François pulled the loaded wagon down the road alone. Katrina silently helped him park it by the house.

"I'll tell my mother we are back, Katrina," said François hurriedly, as he ran directly to the house.

He quickly entered the house and located his mother in the bedroom where she sat on the small bed sewing a new dress.

"*Maman,* I am very worried," he whispered hastily, staring out the window. "I think I let you down. *Sitty* saw your cross on my chest and believes she recognizes it. I made a mistake...no two mistakes." His eyes turned to his mother. "I wore the cross to church without asking you, and I forgot to remove it before going with Katrina to cut grapes. I was hot in the vineyards and took off my tunic, exposing the cross. Sara now wants to look at it more closely with her eyeglasses. What shall I say to her, *Maman*?"

Madeleine was stunned, yet resigned. She covered her mouth with her hand, her eyes opened wide. She put her hand on her son's shoulder as she replied softly, "Ohhh...one day, my son, I knew this had to happen. There is only one thing we must do." She quietly let out a deep breath, looked down, and shook her head. "I must immediately be honest with our hosts and tell them the whole truth." She opened her arms and apprehensively shrugged her shoulders. "I don't know how they will react. They are wonderful, caring people, and they have been good to us for nearly four years. But we have kept our secret from them. So, my love, we must finally tell them who we are and pray they understand."

Her soft comforting voice was so familiar to him whenever times were serious.

Madeleine beckoned to him to sit beside her on the bed, placing an arm over his slumped shoulders. "Your father was given this special gold cross by his mother when he was twelve years old. I told you this story when you were a little boy. Do you remember as we sat overlooking the sea in Marseille?"

He shook his head, not remembering.

Madeleine held François' hands in hers as she carefully chose her words, looking lovingly into his eyes.

She continued, very concerned as she held the cross on his chest, "This cross was the most valuable possession your father owned. He gave it to me when we pledged our love to each other. I have treasured it all these years. And now, as we walk the paths of Douma and tend to the vineyards, I feel as though I am walking in his footsteps. And you are beside me also walking where he walked as a boy. And when we walk up the hills and the mountains to the east, I feel the pain he felt as he suffered in that snowstorm. I almost feel I am now Lebanese. I love this cross and one day it will be yours."

François, thinking of his beloved father as a boy, embraced his mother. "I feel the same emotions you feel, *Maman*. I think everyday about how difficult his life must have been. I don't know if I have the courage my father had, to survive the terrible famine, the locusts, loss of his mother, and the Turkish occupation. The story you told me of when he nearly lost his feet in that snowstorm really makes me respect him so much. Can you imagine? The pain, the love of my grandmother to rub his feet every day for two years to save him. If she had not been so devoted to him, you might not have met him and I might never have been born. And to think he left all that he knew to go to America when he was younger than I am now. I can't believe it. One day I *must* see him. Even today, he doesn't even know I am alive." He whispered to her, "It's difficult for me, *Maman*. I want to be with my father, to know him, to embrace him. Someday, I promise, I will join my father and his family."

"Yes," Madeleine whispered, "yes, *chéri*, one day you will know your father. I know he loves me very deeply and I believe deep down he will come to find us. You will know your father. I promise."

"*Inshallah*," he responded in the Arabic manner.

"Now, François, we must go speak with *Sitty* and Milhelm and discuss what we should do." She gripped his hand and stepped to the door.

With a sense of impending disaster, they left their small room.

CHAPTER 36

$\mathcal{OS}$ itting side by side, Madeleine gripped François's hand tightly and as she looked into Sara's squinting, wise eyes. Milhelm, with a quizzical look on his face, sat opposite Madeleine and François near Sara in a chair in the small stone house where Iskandar was born and had lived until he went away to America. The family still lived in the same house built by Iskandar's and Milhelm's father nearly seventy years earlier. Two rooms and a cement floor had been added over the years. But the ceiling still consisted of olive tree limbs tied tightly together holding up the eighteen inches of stone-filled, hard-packed earth that was the rudimentary roof, rolled with the same marble column remnant.

Haltingly, Madeleine spoke. "Milhelm...Sara...I have something to tell you."

Nervously, Madeleine twisted a handkerchief in her hands. She could feel her forehead moisten as her hands began to perspire. She hoped she conveyed sincerity, yet she felt deep concern, almost fear, as her eyes moved from Sara's and then to Milhelm's. She hoped and prayed she would be able to hold onto their love as she carefully and slowly described what she knew would shock them. *Oh, Lord. Help me through this. Do they think we robbed and killed Iskandar?*

"Please, I think you should know the truth about François and me...who we are."

"Yes," Sara interjected brusquely, with a frown. "It is past time, I think." She was quite upset.

Madeleine hesitated, trying to accept Sara's comment. Looking straight into their eyes, clearly embarrassed that she had not been forthright from the start, she began.

"I want to tell you a story of my life that begins in Marseille when I was sixteen years old. It has *everything* to do with your family."

Turning anxiously to her son, and then facing them again, she said, "You deserve to know the complete truth."

Sara nodded silently.

Madeleine slowly and deliberately began her story, recalling the evening she and her mother met Hanna and Iskandar for dinner. Although she knew she was doing the right thing, it was a terribly painful experience, knowing she had betrayed the trust these kind people had granted her.

Choosing her words carefully, pausing often, touching her eyes with her fingers, wiping away her first tears with her handkerchief, she slowly described in detail the exciting events of the incredible six weeks she and Iskandar shared together in Marseille. She paused before coming to the most important part of her story, that portion that forever changed her life so completely, the events that she had carried alone in her heart for more than twenty-four years. She was clear and honest in every detail.

"Iskandar and I loved each other so much. We believed it was God's will that we should consummate our love that day."

Feeling the need to relax for a moment to release tension, Madeleine stood up and stepped away, touching François' shoulder as she passed him. She walked just a few steps before she returned to her place, hoping Sara and Milhelm were prepared for her story, praying they could understand her young love with Iskandar despite the cultural constraints in their village.

"That afternoon on the grassy lawn overlooking the sea, after we gave our love to each other, and promised our eternal love, I gave Iskandar my treasured gold ring given me by my father who died in the first war to symbolize my total love and life-long commitment to him."

"And this treasure," she said as she reached into her bodice retrieving the gold cross made for Iskandar in Beirut so long ago, "this cross, he gave to me for the same reasons. We loved each other so deeply, so completely that nothing would ever still that love. It was magical, I must tell you." She stopped to take a deep breath before continuing. "He was, and remains even today, each day, *this* day, my first and total love, and I was his first. I was a very young girl and he was also an innocent. We shared in our souls a love that only Almighty God can bring to two people who welcomed God into their love. Our love of each other, dear Sara and Milhelm, is truly our life's path."

Then, pausing, hoping to get more than a silent nod, she continued, "Too soon," she murmured, "much too soon he had to go away to America to fulfill his destiny as his mother, Katrina, wished for him, to be with his father. And, as much as my heart ached, I understood. I was in great pain losing him, not being with him." She felt her eyes fill with tears, remembering. "I cried every day for months and months. It was a terrible time for me. I was just a young girl, and I didn't know what to do. It was an impossible situation. We both understood that."

Sara could only nod, wondering where this was going. Milhelm's heart went out to Madeleine, but he was content to simply let her complete her story.

Stopping to muster her strength, Madeleine nervously smoothed her dress on her lap, shifted in her chair, brushed new tears from her cheek and took a deep breath. She knew she had come to the most serious statement—the confirmation of François' heritage. There was no turning back now. She looked to François now, as she knew François, too, was hearing these details for the first time. But he was old enough now to know the complete story.

"It was only after he left that I learned I would give birth to Iskandar's child. I was just sixteen years old. I was scared. But he would be Iskandar's child, our love child, and that strengthened me. Yet it created an enormous problem for me...a conflict of whether to tell Iskandar or not. We were so young. Can you understand?"

Unhesitatingly, reaching her hand to her son, she said, "*François, my handsome boy, is Iskandar's son.* I am blessed with François. But never have I informed Iskandar that he has a son by me. I chose, correctly I believe, not to interfere with his life and cause him difficulty or pain greater than he already felt. I prayed for guidance, hoping I wasn't wrong all those years. So, I did not respond to his many letters, preferring to allow him to be free in America."

Madeleine stood again to stretch her legs, looked at Milhelm, then turning, went to Sara and said, "I hope I have been correct in that decision so that his life would be better, without added complications. I did not want him to come to me out of guilt, but to be free. He sought freedom in America and I was not going to interfere. I believe in my heart that one day, some way, if it be God's will, we will find each other again." She set her jaw firmly as she stood straight and boldly said, "I believe we will." She then sat down and waited for a response. *Any* response. She felt more confident having told her story and, no matter what their response, she was strong again. As she waited, she knew she had said and done all she could. She had now, finally, been totally honest, come what may. And this strengthened her.

Madeleine said softly, "I hope you can forgive me for not wanting to tell you these things when we first arrived."

Sara, listening intently and uncomfortable with what she was hearing, began to shift her position on her cushion, and looked directly at Milhelm, hoping to see in his eyes his reaction, his emotional impact. This kind, loving man who saved Iskandar's life more than once, hesitated several long moments before he cleared his throat. Milhelm, a kind man, filled with sensitivity, could think of no reason to judge or condemn either his brother or his brother's lover. Yet, he knew he had to respond. Remaining expressionless, he eased Madeleine's heart by reaching across for her hand while holding her gaze. With his very large hand, he squeezed it gently, expressing much of the same sensitivity she had felt from Iskandar. She hoped that his message was that she and her son were *partie de la famille*.

He spoke in a low voice. "Madeleine, dear lady, you have lived in Douma with us... Iskandar's family... for nearly five years. We happily invited you both into our home, fed you, protected you, and welcomed you and your son."

Confused by his use of past tense, she began to worry again.

Milhelm continued, now deferring to François, "I have always had a strange bond, a close, warm feeling toward your son. He is about the same age as my brother when I last saw Iskandar." He turned toward the boy. "In so many ways, François, you remind me of him. And finally now I know why that is, and I'm relieved. I didn't know what to think. And yet, I couldn't have suspected this." Milhelm sat back in his chair for a long moment, drawing a deep breath, and then exhaling before continuing, "Thank you for telling us this story. It had to be as difficult for you to tell us as it was for us to hear you. We now must welcome you both into our family. But," he paused, holding up his index finger, "our customs and traditions cannot permit this sensitive situation to become known in the village. It is vital that what you have told Sara and me be kept in this room. Don't you agree, Sara?" he asked as he turned to Sara who was still in a silent state of mixed emotions of sadness, joy, and amazement.

Sara's love for family, for Katrina, Iskandar's mother, was deep and caring. Her thoughts raced back decades. She knew she could not say anything that would offend their memory. She leaned toward Madeleine and said in her soft voice, "My dear, when I first saw the gold cross I myself designed and had made by a cousin in Beirut more than thirty years ago, I thought the worst. I thought for a moment that the cross had been stolen from Iskandar, or even that someone may have beaten and robbed him. That is why now I feel a sense of relief." She sat back. "And, more so, why I am so glad you have shared your love for our dear Iskandar with us. I am grateful." She paused. "You are a kind, caring woman. You have endured much suffering in your silence. Of course, we welcome you. Yet, I believe that for you, for François, for Iskandar's memory in our village and for the entire Thomé family it would be better that you and François leave the village soon, before your secret is found out."

"Ohh," breathed Madeleine, not wanting to hear that thought. "Must we leave Douma?"

Milhelm, in his wisdom, and trying to absorb what he had just heard, broke the tension in the room by asserting control of the situation. He cleared his throat, slapped his thighs and stood up. "I will go to Beirut tomorrow and seek out family there to find accommodations for Madeleine and François. They will have to be told and we must help them as much as we can. The war is over now, and the city is safe."

"Then it is settled," Sara responded quickly, looking to Madeleine. They all stood together, with Sara reaching to embrace Madeleine and kiss her on both cheeks, and then embracing and kissing François likewise. François went to Milhelm who firmly embraced his brother's son before turning to Madeleine, followed suit and did the same. Both smiles and tears enveloped the small group of co-conspirators as they expressed their release of tension. They all sadly agreed that it was best for everyone that Madeleine and her son go to Beirut...and leave Douma.

Milhelm and Sara knew, of course, that Iskandar was now married, and from letters from Boston over the years prior to the war, that he was happy with Helene, a good, Syrian girl, and had two children. Yet, they had come to love Madeleine and her son, so when they discussed all they had heard, they decided it was not their place to tell Madeleine of Iskandar's life in America, nor, God forbid, tell him of Madeleine's life after he left her in Marseille.

"That can bring no good, Sara. We must not interfere with the lives of these two people. We cannot, on our own, involve Iskandar's American family. We'll leave that to God's will."

"Yes, Milhelm, that's what I believe too. Yet, we must do all we can to help her. She needs love and support. And don't forget, François *is* Iskandar's son and your nephew."

"*Khali* Elias, we need your help to solve a dilemma in the family," Milhelm whispered softly to his uncle as they sat at a small table sipping the thick, pungent, hot Turkish coffee from the clear demitasse glasses outside the café on Hamra Street in Beirut amid chatter of the many men sitting at nearby tables and the strolling pedestrians.

"Tell me," he responded kindly with a quizzical look, completely devoted to his family member, "What is your problem, Milhelm? Of course I will do what I can,"

Elias, the elder, smiled warmly, casually asking, not having any idea what was coming next.

Milhelm leaned forward toward his uncle, whispering even lower so not to be heard by ears belonging to those who need not know. "When my brother, Iskandar, left us in 1920, bound for America, he visited your brother, Uncle Hanna, in Marseille where he stayed for six weeks awaiting his ship to America..."

Milhelm took more than an hour carefully explaining to Elias all the details, as he knew them from Madeleine. "She is an excellent, very stylish, smart woman who is an experienced *couturier* and would be perfect as a dressmaker and, maybe, companion to a wealthy Beirut family. Coming to Beirut from Douma now would be especially good for our family. Unfortunately, she cannot stay in Douma; the village is too small."

"Perhaps I can speak with my friend Marcel Kabani. He is now back in

Beirut. He travels all over the world, and Mrs. Kabani is not as well as before the war. Perhaps she would welcome assistance. I will see what I can do. You say he is truly Iskandar's son? You are certain, are you not?" Gesticulating with his hands for emphasis, he added, "My merciful God."

"*Oui*, Elias, and *shookrun*," Milhelm said, shrugging his shoulders and holding up his open palms, silently asking "what can I say?" Mixing his French and Arabic as did many Beiruti, he patted his uncle's hand as it lay on the table. "When you see this boy, François, you will know. He *is* Iskandar. The similarity is remarkable. I will return to Beirut next week in hope that you are successful. Then, I pray, you can tell me to bring Madeleine and her son...your nephew François, to Beirut to meet Monsieur and Madame Kabani."

"Your story explains something to me too, Milhelm. Too often during the war, there were spies in Beirut looking for a Madame Moreau. We did not know she was the same woman. My memory is not so good, but now I believe I did meet her briefly when she arrived in Beirut, but I made no connection. Thank God she went to Douma with her son. Imagine," he murmured, "imagine if they had been found out by the Nazis. Iskandar's son, your nephew, could have been killed. Imagine!" Then with a questioning frown, Elias asked, "Milhelm, what ever happened to those Nazis who were searching for her? Did you see them?"

"Yes, Elias, I did," Milhelm replied succinctly, "Yes, I did."

That was all that was ever said.

Madeleine and François had spent nearly five wartime years in safety and relative obscurity in Iskandar's remote mountain village of Douma. They walked the paths he had walked, visited his school and very classrooms, sat at his desk, and played backgammon on the same mosaic *towleh* board still in the same home. They walked the hills up to the orchards, harvested the apples, olives and plums from the same trees Iskandar had tended as a boy. And now, as they anxiously waited for word from Beirut, they absorbed Iskandar's life into theirs.

On the bright, cloudless summer day following Milhelm's visit with Uncle Elias in Beirut, whereupon he informed Madeleine and François that they would be moving to Beirut, hopefully to live with Mr. and Mrs. Marcel Kabani, the two decided to be alone for a few days with their own thoughts as their time in the village would soon be over.

"*Maman*, before we leave Douma I have to see the place where, as a boy, my father nearly lost his life in the snowstorm. We must go there."

So, they decided to climb the torturous trail up the two mountain ranges to the east.

Madeleine gestured, looking down into the lush Bekaa Valley, "Look at that magnificent valley down there, François. That's where your father swept wheat grains with his little hands. Can you imagine?"

After taking in the dramatic scene and Iskandar's childhood role in it, they walked down the steep, winding footpath to the floor of the Bekaa Valley. The next day they packed a lunch, and followed the same paths Iskandar had climbed back up with his heavy burden of wheat before he was caught in that unexpected snowstorm so long ago. They found the same large protruding stone overhang where Iskandar had been carried to warm his feet during that fateful day.

"I feel so close to my father, *Maman*," François spoke to his mother as they stopped and sat side by side under the stone shelter. "I'm very happy we came to Douma. Except for America, this must be the safest place in the world for us. And it has given me a chance to understand why my father *had* to go to America, why he was unable to stay with us in Marseille. I wish so much I could be with him." Lowering his head, with tears forming, he whispered to her, "I have come to love the people of Lebanon. They have such a desire to live! *And be free*."

"As do I." Madeleine responded to her son. "I have had Iskandar so deeply in my heart that I have been unable to love another man as completely as I love your father. Yet, Philippe was a good husband for me, and a generous loving father for you. We must always feel grateful for him. I was unable to let him know how totally I loved your father. There was little room in my heart for him or any other man. And now, my son, we have been fortunate that the truth has set us free." Embracing her son, she murmured, "I love you so much, François. You have become much like your father in many ways. You are exactly as he was when we were together in Marseille. Exactly. One day, I know that we will be with your father, but now, we must continue to live our lives, do our best and endure his absence. And so, we will move on and begin a new adventure in Beirut. Perhaps we will return to Douma in time. I know you like Katrina very much, and she likes you. You are cousins, and you should remain close friends. After all, she has the same name as your grandmother." Then standing, ready to go, she added, "Let's return to the village, make preparations to go to Beirut, and offer our thanks to God and to our family for the kindnesses we have received from them and from the village."

Before they left the shelter of the stone overhang, they embraced, feeling so close to Iskandar, admiring him, missing him, and more deeply understanding and loving him.

CHAPTER 37

Beirut
1945

$\mathcal{M}$adeleine sat with her hostess and spoke, "*Merci*, Madame Kabani. We are very happy to be welcomed in your home. I will make you the finest dresses in all Beirut, and will enjoy being your companion. My son, François, is a bright, well-mannered young man. I'm sure you will find him a source of joy as I have. He will help you also. Now that Lebanon is a free and unoccupied country, we should all enjoy an easier time."

Madame Marina Kabani responded with a slight wave of her hand, "Madame Moreau, I am pleased you will join us. Elias speaks very well of you and tells me your husband Monsieur Moreau was Director of the Resistance in France. That was a very important position, was it not?" she asked rhetorically.

She continued, looking directly into Madeleine's eyes, "We must all do the best we can under these trying conditions. Monsieur Kabani continues to work very hard, and as more areas become liberated, especially in Africa, his travels have increased. Sadly, I am not able to endure the pace and activities as I once did. There are always obligatory entertaining events at each city, and it has become too much a responsibility for me. I am glad you can help me assist my husband in these cases. This has been a very painful and challenging time for us here in Lebanon. It seems our place as a trading center however, does bring us prosperity, even though the war years were difficult for everyone." She sat quietly for a moment.

"It has been the destiny of the Lebanese to be in the path of history's conquerors. We have been a place of refuge for so many over the ages. Alexander the Great led the Greeks as they conquered Sidon and Tyre in the south, then Egypt. Then came the Romans who took all the cedars they could and used the Bekaa to feed their armies. Our land provided refuge for the Jewish people during the invasion the Europeans call the Crusades. And now, my dear, Lebanon is even a refuge for you and your son, François." She drew a deep breath before adding, "We are a hospitable and proud people; proud of our heritage, proud that our fathers have rebuilt it each time, and grateful to be here for you. My husband, Marcel, is already rebuilding all over Lebanon, Palestine, Iraq, and even Kuwait. He has that amazing resilience and tenacity. But I can tell that you, my dear, have the same characteristics."

Changing thoughts, Madame Kabani continued as her eyes swept the large room, "Ours is a large and beautiful home, and the views from the terraces are beautiful. So are our furnishings, because my husband and I have brought beautiful art treasures from all over the world. We have entertained dignitaries here many times and, I pray now that this awful war is over, we will do so again."

Madeleine's eyes followed her hostess's eyes and marveled at her magnificent home.

"Meanwhile, Madeleine, my dear, you and I must do the best we can to provide a respite for Monsieur Kabani, a happy and beautiful retreat for him." she concluded.

Thus, Madeleine and François found themselves in Beirut in the home of one of the most respected families in the Middle East. Mr. Kabani had been in the trading business since 1926 when he bought his first truck from the American, Mr. Dodge, as a result of his visit to Detroit. He wanted to improve and expand his already successful transport business by means of mechanized travel. A man of vision, he was always looking for ways to bring his region to the same economic levels as the West. He established the first motorized transportation of goods between Beirut and Damascus, then from Damascus to Baghdad, replacing his and others' camel caravans.

As his transportation business thrived, he naturally became a Chrysler dealer for the mercantile-starved Middle East, starting in Beirut, then Sidon, Damascus, and Jaffa before venturing to Baghdad, Amman and the Gulf States. In 1933, when oil exploration development and petrol sales began to dramatically change the region, Mr. Kabani was well positioned to import and market throughout the Near East the needed equipment, cars, trucks, spare parts, and other goods and commodities from America and Europe.

Because of his business ethics and the reputation of keeping his word and his willingness to take on every profitable challenge, his companies became among the most trusted, reliable, and successful in the region, providing a gateway to the rapidly expanding and profitable markets of the "Near East" as it was called in the 1940s.

While the decade of the 1930s was devastating in America and throughout Europe, the Near Eastern countries were just getting started. They were, in many ways, decades, and in some places, centuries behind the developed world. As the world demanded more and more oil and its progeny, lubricants, gasoline, and diesel fuel, the Near East economy grew exponentially, finally able to afford those commodities produced in the West.

When Germany began its military sweep across Europe in 1938, world demand for oil skyrocketed. America and Britain sought alliances with the Saudis, the Al Sabah emirate of Kuwait, and Iraq's king. European and American oil companies which had created Aramco were positioned to provide for the insatiable demand for oil products to feed the Allies' wartime machine. Saudi Arabia, with its almost unlimited and easily accessible oil reserves, became the "golden goose," the treasured ally. King Saud Abdul Aziz, who united the Arabian peninsula tribes, mostly by siring children with the daughters of the various tribes' leaders, created a family dynasty and controlled much of what became the world's known oil reserves.

In time, King Saud became the most important client/friend of Marcel Kabani, channeling his country's needs through Kabani Enterprises. Saud, the world's richest man, personally enjoyed the *laissez-faire* culture of mostly Christian Lebanon. He spent many delightful evenings at the Kabani home enjoying their parties, accompanied by his entourage. Soon, as word spread, Sheikhs of the ruling families, the Al Sabahs in Kuwait, the Al *Khalifa*, of Bahrain, the Emirates, and the Al Thani family of Qatar sought to partake of Monsieur and Madame Kabani's soirees. The Kabanis became the hosts of royals who chose to travel from their native countries with their more constraining social mores and regulations to enjoy the world of the freedom-loving Lebanese in Beirut and their province-wide sense of *joie de vivre*. Kabani Enterprises became one of the principle business beneficiaries of royal largesse, while keeping in close touch with their far-flung network of associates and partners. Mr. Kabani and his family were welcomed everywhere.

Monsieur and Madame Kabani's four sons, all well-educated at Beirut's American University of Beirut (AUB), the Sorbonne in France, or Cairo University in Egypt, and ultimately at the London School of Economics, followed in their father's footsteps. They became his surrogates, representatives and personal delegates, maintaining the Kabani reputation for honesty, integrity, and capability. Their word was their bond. The region's power brokers, royalty, and functionaries welcomed their acumen, integrity and their involvement. It was a very profitable arrangement for everyone.

Marcel Kabani admonished his sons, "Do not become part of the political world; work with it, maintain ties with all factions, but stay out of the fray, and you will survive. We do not seek power. Be friends with those who have the political power, and those who one day *may* have the power. We are traders, careful business people. We are Phoenicians."

By 1945, the four Kabani sons were in their thirties and forties. During the war, one was in New York, another in Cairo, the third operating in Amman,

Jordan, and the fourth in Baghdad. Annually, they visited their parents in Beirut, Marcel's home base, preferring to otherwise remain at their stations with their families. Madame Kabani accompanied her husband to visit their sons, enjoying the respect of her community and her husband's associates.

"My dear," she said, turning to Madeleine, smiling, "we now have homes or apartments in Amman, Baghdad, Athens, Alexandria, and Paris. Of course, we have not been able to visit Paris during the war as it is so difficult there, and it is not so easy for me to travel as before. But one day I wish to return there. It is such a beautiful city. I'm sure you agree. Despite what others may say, I am glad the French surrender meant Paris and its treasures would not be destroyed by that madman, Adolph Hitler. What a pity that would have been. Such beauty would have been lost to future generations. And for what? It would have been a tragedy. So, as for me, I will remain here in Beirut with my friends and visit Paris when I can. It is, after all, a beautiful city as well, but from this room, each day we can watch the magnificent sunsets as the golden glow glistens on the Mediterranean Sea. I always feel God is watching over us as I watch the sunsets."

Madeleine's life during the next two years in Beirut was especially exciting. She and Madame Kabani grew close, always conversing in polished French, and enjoying each day. As Madame Kabani needed new dresses and accessories for social engagements, entertaining and attending palace events following Lebanon's independence, Madeleine designed for her the most elegant attire, shopped in the finest boutiques, and became a most welcome customer. Many times, she would be invited by Madame Kabani to accompany her to events. Other times, Monsieur Kabani insisted she accompany both of them not only to assist Madame Kabani but also to be part of his party. As a result, Madeleine DuBois-Moreau soon became part of the Beirut social scene, enviably associated with the Kabani family and its reputation, and recognized in the upscale Hamra shopping district as such. Others in Beiruti society and in the finer boutiques welcomed her and treated her as though she was actually a member of the Kabani family. Her life was enriching, safe and comfortable. She came to crave the Lebanese way of life.

François also enjoyed similar benefits as a student at the American University of Beirut (AUB). He was popular with his colleagues, and, being quite a handsome, well-mannered young man with the added bonus of being "almost a Kabani," his presence was always welcomed.

By late 1946, Madeleine and François were becoming fixtures of the social scene of Beirut. All was more than wonderful for this forty-ish beautiful, charming associate of Madame Kabani from Marseille and her twenty-six-year-old son, refugees in Beirut who had become a part of Lebanon. They loved Beirut and had come to live beyond their wildest dreams...far in excess of what they imagined that fateful day they arrived on the docks in 1940.

Madeleine always fit in easily. Since she was a little girl, her mother had taught her the importance of social graces. Daniella had taught her, and Madeleine had listened. "Watch the polished ladies of wealth, my clients and learn. Do as they do, behave accordingly. Always be a lady," her mother would admonish. "Stand very straight and tall with hands by your side, smile, be gracious, kind and generous, and by all means, my child, spread your smallest finger. And never point."

"François," Madeleine would in turn, later admonish her son, "I have been teaching you since you were a child those same lessons my mother taught me. It is remarkable that they have served us well so that we are accepted, even welcomed, into the finer homes of Beirut. The people of Beirut are kind and wonderful people, are they not?"

François replied with a smile, "Yes, *Maman*, but after all, I am Lebanese too. I believe we are both Lebanese in our hearts. We speak Arabic fluently and have learned the customs. We have become part of Lebanon, don't you think?"

"Yes, son, that is exactly what I think. We are French, but we are Lebanese also. Your father would be very happy knowing this...and I believe he will, in time."

CHAPTER 38

Beirut
1946

In late 1946, Madeleine decided to visit the French embassy to inquire casually of France and its post-war conditions.

It was less than two months later that Madeleine was curiously invited to meet personally with the French ambassador on "an important subject." She was concerned and quite apprehensive as to why she would receive such a request from the ambassador of her native country.

He welcomed her with a characteristically French flourish and slight bow. "Please sit down, Madame Moreau. I have much to tell you," the French ambassador spoke softly and with great respect as he gestured to the burgundy leather couch handcrafted in the mountains of Lebanon, opposite his matching chair. "May I offer you juice, coffee or tea, madame?"

"*Merci*," Madeleine replied as she properly took her seat on the couch, white kid gloved hands clasped in her lap, head held high. "I am honored that you have invited me to visit with you, Monsieur Ambassador. What can it be that you have to say to me?"

The ambassador continued, smiling, "What I have to say to you, Madame Moreau, may shock you, will surprise you, and, I believe, will make you very proud."

She remained puzzled by his statement, tilting her head slightly in an alluring, yet wondering manner.

The Ambassador poured coffee for them both, then stepped behind his impressive mahogany desk and sat down in his leather chair. He pulled a large, flat envelope sealed with red wax from a drawer and placed it in front of him.

Folding his hands together and resting them on the envelope, he hesitated for maximum impact, then leaning toward her for emphasis, he began, "As you may know, your husband Philippe was unfortunately killed while performing most important work for the French people during the terrible German occupation of our beloved country.

"His work was incredibly vital to the successful liberation of France and he is at this moment being recognized with enormous gratitude by a private French foundation, yet not by the government. This is, I hasten to explain, because we, the official body of France, cannot be officially involved. But, please let me assure you, the French people and its government are most grateful to your husband, madame. This particular foundation, with government approval, is dedicated to the welfare of families of the brave deceased members of the Resistance during the war.

"The recognition of your husband's extraordinary leadership is shared by all those in positions of influence and authority, including leaders of the Allied forces and by General Dwight Eisenhower himself, Prime Minister Winston Churchill, President Charles de Gaulle, and even President Harry Truman. They know that without his leadership in organizing the Resistance into an effective coordinated force, the Allied invasion at Normandy would not have been successful and all of Europe could have been lost. Forces of the Resistance, organized under your husband's leadership, prevented the Germans from being able to deliver their vaunted panzer divisions to the northern front. The Resistance delayed all German efforts to stop the invasion! Your husband's leadership, organization and instructions were incredibly successful. Trains carrying those tanks were deliberately delayed with planned accidents by the train engineers, and tunnel explosions. It was fantastic and so vital. Actually, many believe we won the war *because* of your husband, Monsieur Philippe Moreau, my dear madame." He paused, allowing his last comment to take effect.

"His work required that after Normandy he immediately go to Marseille to prepare the Resistance in southern France. His new headquarters were secretly based within the *Panier* district in that city. It was very dangerous there with 15,000 Germans garrisoned in the city. Under great pressure and personal danger, Monsieur Moreau created an effective program of sabotage by the Free French Army in preparation for, and in co-ordination with the United States and the Allied invasion which freed the entire southern region in August of 1944. That invasion at Toulon and Marseille was also quite successful due to Monsieur Moreau's planning and leadership."

"Ironically, while he was in Marseille, he stayed in the home of your mother and Hanna Chalhoub. Hanna was Philippe's principal contact there, providing offices, safe apartments, information, coordination, and assistance in every way to drive the Germans from the south of France. He and your mother were indispensable to efforts in preparation for the Allied bombardment of Toulon and Marseille, and the Allied invasion called Operation Anvil. After completing his plans prior to the invasion, monsieur Moreau had to leave Marseille to meet with colleagues in Denmark. Sadly, it was during the siege of Marseille that your mother and Hanna were killed. John Giordano of Toulon, their friend and a respected Free French compatriot, was meeting with them at the time. He was fatally wounded as well. They were among the thousands who suffered so much during those days when the battleships and Allied bombers were trying to rid the area of German forces. German artillery and errant Allied bombs bombarded the *Canebière* while they were there dining, German shells hit the restaurant directly." He lowered his head in a show of respect. "I am told that, gratefully, they did not suffer."

As the ambassador paused, looking up from his papers, he focused on Madeleine's eyes. "I am profoundly saddened to have to tell you these events concerning your mother and your husband, my dear Madame Moreau. Philippe left Marseille in early August, leaving your mother and Hanna, his dear friends, to travel to Copenhagen to co-ordinate with the Danish Resistance leadership. It was there that he was found by the Nazis and assassinated. This was a tragic turn of events for all of us."

"Without his extraordinary leadership, it is believed by his grateful countrymen, as well as the English and the Americans, that France would still be occupied by the hated Germans and controlled by the terrible Vichy government."

As he finished reading his papers and commenting, the Ambassador looked at Madeleine with an empathetic expression and continued.

"Madame Moreau, it has been my privilege and my sad duty to tell you these details, as dreadful as they are. Tragically, millions of French people died during 'this nasty business,' as Winston Churchill described the war. But it is certain even more French and, indeed, American and British would have suffered and died had it not been for your husband, Philippe Moreau."

Concluding, he spoke with authority as he rose from his chair and stood quite straight. "It is my great honor to inform you that a grateful nation wishes to extend to you its thanks by permitting and endorsing this private foundation's actions to honor your husband's name with monuments in Paris and Marseille. In addition, they wish to give you a token of our appreciation in the amount of one million French francs, to be used by you in any way you wish. I regret that there is only our gratitude and enormous thanks to give you for the incredibly brave and loyal activities carried out by Monsieur Hanna Chalhoub and your magnificent mother."

Unclasping his hands, the ambassador picked up the envelope, stepped around his desk toward his visitor. Perplexed, Madeleine, with a look of sadness, took his cue and rose from her chair. The ambassador came to her, stood stiffly, and with great respect, leaned toward her and, with French elegance, formally kissed her on both cheeks. He then bowed in respect, stepped back, extended his hand to her and gave her the envelope containing a letter signed by the president of the unnamed foundation containing the official cheque in the amount of one million francs, and an invitation to come to Paris and Marseille for the presentation and unveiling of the monuments.

Madeleine, caught completely off guard by this presentation, felt suddenly weak and gratefully sank down in her chair. She remained motionless for several moments while she read the official document shaking in her hands. She reached into her leather handbag, retrieved a lace handkerchief and lightly touched her moistened cheeks.

"Please forgive me, your Excellency. I am very sad, although very proud. I have lost a wonderful husband, my mother, and her dear friend and mine, Monsieur Hanna Chalhoub. I have lost so much, but I am also honored and proud." Then, with a nod of her head and the beginnings of a slight smile, said, "Of course I will go to Paris."

She again sat quietly thinking, and then asked. "You say none of them suffered? Is that true?"

"Yes, madame, that is what I am told. While they agonized along with all of France during the war, they did not suffer at the end."

"One question, monsieur," she whispered, leaning forward and raising her hand. "Was Marseille totally destroyed by the bombardments? I mean, were the holy places destroyed?"

The ambassador carefully flipped through his papers, scanned the appropriate pages, and looked back at Madeleine.

"It appears most of the churches were left intact. Though, of course, there was severe damage everywhere. However, since Marseille is the city of my youth, I am pleased to say the most prominent church, Marseille's pride, although it was temporarily the German headquarters, was left virtually untouched. Of this I have official confirmation. It remains as beautiful as it was before the war. The German commander wisely surrendered to the French commander only a few minutes before the church was to be bombarded by the Allies and destroyed. It was so imminent that it is almost a miracle it still stands. Do you know the cathedral Notre-Dame-de-la-Garde?"

Madeleine, watching the ambassador's face carefully, suddenly gasped, brought her hand to her opened mouth and cried aloud, "Oh, my God, thank you God." She wept quietly, both hands covering her face, remembering. In seconds, her mind recalled the hours she and Iskandar had spent there together. She remembered the love they shared as they held each other so close, gazing on the church from their place on *Les Calanques* with a stunning view of Notre-Dame-de-la-Garde, hearing the bells chime.

"Is that place important to you, madame?"

Nodding, she replied between her silent sobs, her shoulders shaking slightly, "More than I could ever describe to you, monsieur. So much more."

Collecting her thoughts and remembering her proper etiquette, she continued, "I am so sorry for my outburst, Monsieur Ambassador. I must be alone now, *s'il vous plait*. This has been a most difficult moment of remembrance and, yet, gratitude for me. I do hope you understand. Would you kindly have someone locate a taxi for me?"

"Of course, madame."

Safely settled in the taxi, she leaned back against the backseat cushion, closed her eyes and sighed, *"Mon Dieu!* What shall I do now?" She felt emotionally drained and alone with her thoughts as she returned to *Beit* Residence Kabani tightly holding onto the envelope containing the pronouncement and the cheque.

Madeleine couldn't help but think of Marseille, her mother, Hanna, and her loving moments with Iskandar. She knew she needed to be alone with her memories for she knew that her life was now going to be so very different. For too long she had been torn by the conflict of being Madame Moreau and yet loving Iskandar. The war and its casualties had now created a new world for her. Philippe was gone; her mother was gone. And as a result of this news, she was drawn to Marseille by a new powerful tug. She knew she had to revisit the city of her youth, and she felt, quite naturally, the yearning to go back to *their* place atop *Les Calanques* where she left her childhood and became a woman with her first love. She knew she had to take whatever time it required seeking the truth within her, to clarify her feelings and determine her life's new course. Now, as a result of Philippe's heroism, she found herself actually made very wealthy by virtue of her marriage to a national hero. She felt a sting of guilt for not being able to totally commit her heart to her husband, while subconsciously finding herself longing for the embrace of Iskandar.

As she rode in the taxi to the Kabani residence for respite, she knew she must be with her hostess, and now her mentor, who was anxiously awaiting her return. But Madeline held back, not ready to share the entire message from the Ambassador.

Madame Kabani, receiving Madeleine, did not know what had happened, but she could easily tell that her friend was distraught. Sensing her sadness, Madame Kabani, in her nurturing manner, listened quietly, and then spoke as she reached for Madeleine. "You should be alone for awhile, my child. You must find your desires, clear your head. Be only with God. Let Him guide you." Then, patting her hand affectionately, added, "Take your time, *y'slemli.*"

Madeleine couldn't get rid of her nagging contradictory thoughts, the emotional conflict that tore at her heart. In time, she decided to open her mind to the needs of others as a way of getting away from her own personal concerns and agony. These moments of introspection brought both pain and solace to Madeleine as she tried to determine what to do with her life.

After several days of strolling alone in the gardens in thought and meditation, she had Madame Kabani's driver take her to downtown Beirut where she walked in solitude for more than an hour on the Corniche high above the sea. She sought out a café there where she could sit quietly among strangers, many of whom had suffered—so much more than she and François—during the Allied bombardment to rid Lebanon of the Vichy presence in 1941 and 1942. She wanted to be an anonymous observer, to think alone, not to converse with them. As she sat at the table by the railing, high above the placid sea, she sipped tea, leaned back, calmer now, and closed her eyes to the world around her. Memories of her mother, her youth, and her life in Marseille as a young girl in simpler times flooded her consciousness. She was grateful Daniella was with Hanna at the end, and that the end came swiftly and without suffering. Then her thoughts turned to Iskandar. "The cliffs were our place," she whispered aloud, gazing at the sea, thinking of his touch, his smile, their love. She recalled Marseille and the serene beauty of the sea from the hill overlooking the magnificent cerulean waters, much the same as Beirut. Every detail of her moments with Iskandar seemed to fill her mind. She was again overwhelmed by feelings of sadness mixed with loss and guilt. *Should I have stayed in Marseille to be with Hanna and Maman? No,* she quickly decided. *If we had stayed, surely François would have been forced to join the army or imprisoned, and would perhaps have been killed or wounded like so many young men.* "When older men fight, young men die," she said aloud angrily, making a fist and staring at the sea. *It is so tragic. So sad. Those of us left behind must accept these terrible losses of life, of war. I lost my father. I lost Iskandar. I might have lost my son. And now, I have lost Philippe...my mother...Hanna. Four I have loved, although in different ways, are all gone. Yet Philippe, even in death, carries on providing for me. How wonderful a father he was to François. Such a loving husband to me. Now, he is gone. And all I have left are my memories.*

She watched as a mother in worn clothing walked toward her table with two small children. Her remembrances quickly dissipated as she was struck by the appearance of this woman who had lost an arm, probably in the bombardment that destroyed the lives of so many in Beirut. The woman's eyes made contact with Madeleine's as she held out her open palm asking for money.

"*Madame, s'il vous plaît?*"

Madeleine looked closely at the woman and her two sad-looking little girls in ragged clothes and unkempt hair tugging on their mother's skirt, their eyes beseeching Madeleine to help. The oldest girl was walking with crude crutches as one foot dragged; the other had a bandage over one eye. Madeleine instantly felt great empathy for this woman and her children. "Of course," she nodded with a loving smile, handing the mother a more than generous amount of money.

The mother stared at the sum of money given her and almost wept. Looking into Madeleine's eyes with deep gratitude, she bowed in respect and whispered, *"Shookrun,* madame, thank you so much."

The more Madeleine looked around her, watching the people at the café and along the broad Corniche, the more she realized that many people, so many children, more than she had imagined, were injured from the bombardments. *They are innocents,* she thought, as she began to realize how fortunate she was, and very grateful for her son's health and safety.

Her thoughts went to François. *He is there, across the boulevard at the university. Safe, not wounded, like these poor souls. Merci, mon Dieu.* Compelled to do more, she reached into her purse and beckoned to the woman. "Come back here, madame. I have something more to give to you and your children. They are so beautiful...with such big brown eyes." She offered the woman another generous amount, holding the woman's hand and closing it around the money. Then, on impulse, she stood, reached out and embraced the woman. After a moment, she crouched down to hug the children. "They are darling."

She stood again and, placing her arm around the woman's shoulder, asked, "Do you come here each day?"

"Oui, madame, *merci, merci beaucoup,"* the woman replied with a sad but grateful smile. "It is so terrible. I am so proud and I hate doing this but I must beg to feed my children. We have no food, no home. We do the best we can. Thanks to God, many people are kind and generous."

As the woman turned to leave Madeleine's table, she spoke, "Be with God. *Allah ma'ak."*

"Allah ma'ak. I shall see you again," Madeleine promised.

After she finished her tea, Madeleine paid the *garçon* and walked out of the café perched high above the Mediterranean overlooking Pigeon Rocks. She suddenly had a wholly different, less self-oriented view of the world and of Lebanon. Into her life had come unpredictable events of monumental impact. First, her father's death in the World War I, then Iskandar completely fulfilling her need for passion and love; her son, François, Philippe, the war, then her escape to Douma...ah, lovely Douma, and now, enormous wealth and, incredibly, the epiphany-like awakening to the plight of others, a more realistic awareness of the suffering that surrounded her; the wounded, the poverty, the misery of the poor. She was experiencing a revelation, a change of her spirit. She gazed out at the sea, thinking, for a long time. Then, she turned away from the sea. Her eyes swept the city landscape, including the ruins remaining since the siege. For the first time, she truly witnessed the heavily damaged apartment buildings, the pushcarts bearing goods, the young boys trying to sell anything, some begging. Most were in torn clothing, some without shoes. All looked hungry. She thought about Iskandar when he was very young. He too was very poor. She saw children everywhere. Some were playing in the streets, others, unable to play, sat and watched.

Feeling a sudden sense of urgency, she walked to the curb and signaled the oncoming car. "Taxi!" As she climbed into the backseat, Madeleine instructed the driver to take her to the Kabani home.

With a sense of enlightened determination, she entered the luxurious residence and sought out Madame Kabani.

"She's in her room," said the maid in her perfectly starched white blouse and black skirt.

Madeleine climbed the staircase energetically and knocked at the bedroom door.

"*Entrez!*" said the voice of Madame Kabani from behind the door.

Excitedly, Madeleine quickly turned the polished brass lever handle and entered the room. Breathlessly, she declared, "Oh, madame, I must speak with you! After a most difficult week, I have now had a most incredible day." She was excited to share her experiences.

Madeleine sat in the chair opposite Madame Kabani with their knees almost touching and began speaking in a low voice, affected by her emotions as she spoke. She recalled in detail her meeting with the French ambassador, leaving out nothing.

"Oh, my dear, it must have been terrible for you to hear of these events. I am so sorry for you. War is so painful, for those who fight and as well for those who must mourn. I am sad for you, dear Madeleine. As Homer wrote, '*Even those who must stand and wait, they also serve.*'"

And then, with a positive smile, her voice at a higher pitch, Madeleine told of her visit with the woman and her children. "I have seen for the first time what I must do with my life, how I can help others." Pausing for a breath, she continued. "I have decided to use the money from France and do something for these poor children of Lebanon. This is my country now, in my heart, and I cannot bear witnessing the suffering without doing something." Madeleine was passionate as she described her thoughts, her vision to make life better for the orphaned and under-privileged children of Lebanon.

"You are right, my dear. What a wonderful decision! I'm sure M. Kabani will assist you in your efforts. He will be home soon. Let's discuss your intentions with him this very evening. Perhaps he will have some suggestions. And I am sure our friends can be convinced to participate."

With François and Monsieur and Madame Kabani at the dinner table, Madeleine enthusiastically repeated the day's events. She carefully and deliberately explained her vision, her plans to do all she could to provide medical help, rehabilitation, and housing for those whose lives were so terribly affected by the war. Her passion was obvious and contagious. "I am very excited about this, Monsieur Kabani. Will you help me?"

Stunned by this turn of events, he replied, "Of course, my dear. This is an excellent proposal. We can do this together. There is so much to do. So many

Lebanese suffered during the war. I will speak with my friends. I am sure they will support your efforts as well."

"Monsieur," she asked with her head lowered modestly, "Another favor…I also need your counsel and guidance. Will you please help me protect my funds? You are so much wiser than I about these issues."

"If you ask, certainly I will be happy to watch over your new-found funds. You have been given a great deal of money. I think it is a good time for you to invest. The world is rebuilding everywhere. I myself have recently invested heavily in the United States. There is much opportunity at this time in Europe as well. Your funds must, at first, be secure. And if we invest them well, you can accomplish your desires to help the poor of Lebanon and still not substantially reduce your largesse. *Inshallah*, God be willing."

CHAPTER 39

Paris
1948

$\mathcal{U}$sing their Lebanese passports, François accompanied his mother to Paris to participate in the French foundation's honor to Philippe. During their stay, he enrolled at the *Université du Paris*, the Sorbonne.

"Paris is so beautiful, François, truly one of the most beautiful cities in the world. It's good that the Germans didn't destroy it. At the time, surrendering the city without a fight didn't seem to be so brave. Many French were opposed and wanted to fight the Germans instead. But now, it is seen as a most wise decision. You'll enjoy your stay in this loveliest of cities here as you attend the Sorbonne."

Madeleine, who had come to Paris with her mother in late 1920 to give birth to François, and then later returned with Philippe, was now introducing her son to his new home so that he could continue his education at what she considered one of the finest schools in France.

"You will meet so many fascinating people from all over the world now that the war is concluded."

"*Oui, Maman*, I'm going to enjoy Paris very much. They say that even the American tourists are beginning to come here these days...after all, it is 1948," François responded with a smile.

Within a few days, ceremonies were held in the city honoring the heroes of the war, especially Philippe Moreau, with appropriate monuments standing in the prominent parks. Afterward, Madeleine went to the Sorbonne to say goodbye to François. She hugged her son and smiled with pride at his handsome face. "You look so much like your father, François. Perhaps one day you will meet him. I pray so."

Later that day, as she sat in her compartment on the train to Marseille, listening to the clickety-clack of the wheels on the tracks, she watched the countryside pass by, almost in a blur, with feelings of nostalgia, of emotions that swept her, as she considered her return to Marseille, the city of her youth, the city of her first love, Iskandar. She watched the forests and gently rolling hillsides transform to vineyards, broad expanses of open land, farms and lakes as central France passed by and the terrain of Aix-en-Provence in southern France began to enter her consciousness.

She recalled François's parting remarks, "Remember, *Maman*, the love of so many who have come into your life. You have given love and you have been given love by those who care for you." François had learned well from his mother and grandmother about love. For theirs was a total willingness to give completely. Daniella loved Hanna, and Hanna was totally and absolutely devoted to Daniella and Madeleine. Iskandar, although obligated to continue to America, had been completely in love with Madeleine, and Madeleine, now a beautiful woman in her forties, some twenty-eight years later, was still in love with and committed to Iskandar. And François's love for his mother was exceeded only by hers for her son. *Love indeed begets love*, she thought as she hugged herself with a sense of calm.

"So, while you are in Marseille with so many memories, remind yourself that you have been surrounded by love there, be grateful, and don't be too sad. I love you, *Maman. Je t'aime...au revoir.*" He felt a bit strange advising his mother, and yet, all his life she had confided in him on matters of the heart. Perhaps now it was his turn.

As the train drew closer to the city, Madeleine felt it begin to slow down. Now by herself for the first time in her life, she felt a strange sense of *déjà vu*, yet as a visitor, not as a resident. She felt an almost detached sense of remembrance, as though it was not she but someone else, as she watched the city's buildings come close. She thought about that special first evening when she, a sixteen-year-old girl, and her mother had walked from their apartment above the *Canebière* down to the *Panier* several blocks away to meet dear Hanna Chalhoub and his handsome nephew, Iskandar, newly arrived from Lebanon.

Madeleine's thoughts were about a trip of memories of love, of excitement. She was uplifted by her new purpose, and, in a very positive way, was seeking reconciliation in a search for completeness in her incomplete life. By coming to Marseille, she was hoping to find a ratification of her newly chosen life, to find out if she still felt enough love for Iskandar to continue her life with him in her heart and keep open the promise that one day she would see him again. Or, should she put the past behind her and be willing to meet someone new? She would have to confront her memories, pray, meditate, and seek her answers.

"Taxi! Please take me to a hotel on the *Canebière*."

The driver, noting her chic clothing and expensive luggage, delivered her from the rail station to the elegant Charles V Hotel, as she requested.

After she checked in and her luggage was placed in her suite, an anxious Madeleine DuBois-Moreau stepped out of the hotel, stood on the walkway, took a deep breath, and looked around. She smiled with a new sense of peace.

There were many familiar sights, but, sadly, many buildings were run-down, others still showing damage from the invasion. Perhaps the *Canebière* had indeed seen its better days too. She reminded herself that, after all, there had been twenty-eight years of depression, turmoil, social battles, political unrest, and even war, to say nothing of the Germans' cruel occupation. All in all, she decided, Marseille had survived, even though a bit worse from wear.

She knew the restaurant where her mother and Hanna had been hit by the German artillery and avoided looking in that direction. She preferred not to think of their last moments. Rather, she simply stood at the curb for a few minutes. Even though her striking beauty attracted stares from the passersby and nods with tipped hats from the gentlemen, she was not distracted from her mission. She knew exactly what she wanted to do, where she wanted to go, what she wanted to see. She couldn't wait another day. It must be now. She stepped to the left to find her way to *Vieux Port* and then walked to the *Panier.* She had no time schedule. She was now, for the first time, independently wealthy, had no obligations to anyone or anything. Her son...all that remained of her family...was safely ensconced where he should be, in Paris.

And so, she would do as Madame Kabani had admonished with true wisdom: "Take as much time as you need, my dear. You must savor this time in your life. You have earned it and you deserve to find and feel your true inner emotions. You are never alone, as God is with you. Have faith, my dear. Remember the beauty of your loved ones, the passion of your youth. If you do, you will find the truth. Listen to an older woman, Madeleine. Go and find the enrichment of your spirit. Nourish your soul and be not afraid. And when you do, let it be a magnificent moment."

Madeleine knew Madame Kabani was correct. Her sagacity convinced her of what she must do no matter how long it took. Suddenly, walking on the cobblestone sidewalk along the port, she was aware of an older, well-dressed man who stepped directly in front of her as though he was a close friend. His face was filled with surprise as he thought he was gazing on Madeleine's mother, Daniella.

"*Bon soir!* Madame DuBois, is it really you? *Mon Dieu!* How can this be?" He looked very closely at Madeleine's face. "Oh, *pardon,* I am so sorry. You startled me because you look exactly like the woman my Uncle Hanna loved during *le guerre.*" Sensing her hesitation, he quickly asked sincerely, "Are you her sister? Do you know of whom I speak?"

Madeleine looked at the swarthy Lebanese man staring at her quizzically, and then turned her head and saw that she was, in fact, at *Place de Liban*, the Lebanese label of *Place de Lenche.*

"She was my mother," Madeleine nervously responded in a loud whisper, stunned at his statement but pleased to have her mother remembered in this way.

"Well, I knew your mother and Hanna Chalhoub. They were most popular here in the *Panier,* especially during the war. Everyone believed your mother to be the most gracious and beautiful woman in the south of France." Then, hopefully, he asked, "May I join you, madame?"

"Some other time perhaps, monsieur," she demurred. "Today I wish to be alone with my thoughts. You have been most gracious."

She barely noticed as he bowed in respect and stepped toward the restaurant entrance.

She looked at the familiar tables and chairs scattered across the plaza and, feeling slightly dizzy, almost as though she was floating, realized that she had somehow found herself at the *Café Liban,* Hanna's restaurant, not in the summer of 1920, but rather, in the summer of 1948.

Her eyes searched the plaza. She gingerly sat down at a remote table, deliberately avoiding the table where she first met Iskandar. Automatically searching her purse for her compact, she carefully powdered her nose, then hand-signaled the *garçon.* "A glass of wine, *blanc, s'il vous plait.*"

She thanked the waiter, and sipped delicately from the wineglass, lost in her own thoughts while looking at the familiar buildings on three sides of the plaza. She couldn't help but remember every detail of that evening so long ago when she, just a sixteen-year-old with great feelings of anticipation, had come to this same place with her mother to meet Iskandar. It was as if she somehow had stepped back not only in time, but had also instantly morphed into the happiest moment of her life, which was when she had stumbled on the cobblestones, then tripped and stumbled into Iskandar's arms. She smiled as her thoughts went back to the moment when she was walking down the gentle slope of the cobble-stoned walkway and saw dear Hanna, his hair carefully combed as always, and his young, so handsome nephew that she was about to meet. How very foolish she had felt stumbling, yet happy at how it had prompted Iskandar to leap spontaneously from his chair to come to her assistance. Such a gentleman he was, she remembered lovingly, exhibiting his thoughtfulness and concern for her at that awkward moment. She had wanted to impress him, but her awkward spill, while embarrassing, had turned out to be a beautifully innocent, yet intimate, moment of their first meeting. She almost burst into laughter as she remembered her bizarre beginning with Iskandar! How wonderfully they fell in love!

She did not know what to expect from this visit to the place where she met Iskandar, but she was beginning to realize that the painful dilemma she feared would envelop her was not to happen. Rather, at least at this point, it was bringing a new perspective, a sense of reality, truth and acceptance.

She felt the time she would spend alone in Marseille would allow her dreams of the future to build on the memories of her past and she would remain focused, young and hopeful. She also began eagerly to see the present, and look to the future with hope and confidence. She now knew what she must do to provide others with assistance. She would remember the past, but do her best to put it behind her and focus on her new life with its efforts to help others. It was a natural segue for her as she had always been a giver, but now she had a new direction.

She became aware that more and more people were walking by. Then, glancing at her wristwatch, saw it was becoming late in the day. Spontaneously, her eyes looked to the east to gaze on the familiar Notre-Dame-de-la-Garde, the symbol of Marseille, the place she had taken Iskandar, the place on the hill where he had, in his joy with her, kissed her for the first time. Her body trembled as she heard the distant bells of the cathedral, recalling how they rang the moment he had kissed her that day, and again after they had loved on *Les Calanques*. It was magical. Two young people in love for the first time. She was sixteen, he eighteen. It was as though they felt at the time that God Himself was blessing their union. Now as she heard the first bells strike, her tears began to flow. "Six o'clock, exactly six o'clock. Oh," she softly asked out loud, "Iskandar, where are you today?"

She placed money on the table for the waiter, stood tall, and began to walk down the steps at the edge of the plaza. She waved to the Peugeot. "Taxi!" she hailed with her arm outstretched. She looked at her watch. She still had time.

"May I help you, madame?" A tall, well-dressed gentleman asked as he walked toward her.

The man was clearly interested in her, but at the moment, she was consumed in her thoughts. "*Merci*, monsieur, but not at the moment." Madeleine was quite aware of her striking beauty and height—fashionably and richly attired with exquisite jewelry, scarf, and dress. She was always quite the fashion statement, self-assured, and seasoned in dealing with men who found her polished *savoir faire* alluring. But she knew she had to be somewhere special in a very few minutes.

The taxi pulled up to her place at the curb. "*Où allez-vous?*"

"Notre-Dame-de-la-Garde," she replied as she quickly climbed into the rear seat.

The taxi driver smiled as he looked at this lovely face in his rear view mirror. "Do you want to make the last service of the day, madame?"

"Well, in a manner of speaking," she replied. "I would like to reach the church before the sun sets."

"*Oui*, madame, we can be there very shortly."

In minutes, the taxi reached the slope leading to the cathedral. Madeleine signaled the driver. "Stop here, driver. I would like to walk the rest of the way."

Madeleine paid the driver and exited the Peugeot, collecting herself as she tentatively stepped up to the walk. Still not quite sure she was doing the right thing, she looked up the hill at the stone structure, the familiar bell tower, the glistening gold of the statue of Saint Mary at the pinnacle of the dome, and the surrounding pine trees that canopied the rugged stone of the hills. Her legs felt weak as she took her first steps up the steep ascending stone walkway. Almost instinctively, her right hand went to her head as she crossed herself.

The memories of this place were almost overpowering. She looked over her shoulder and gratefully saw that she was alone, isolated with her memories. The afternoon visitors had departed. She smiled as she vividly recalled running up the steps with Iskandar, giggling, holding his hand, and loving every second of that day so many years ago. Her mind began playing on her emotions with visions of Iskandar's face, his smile, his touch weighing in her thoughts. Thinking now as an observer, she remembered herself as the coquettish sixteen-year-old with her lover-to-be, and smiled. *I was so very happy. This is too much*, she thought as she felt a tingling and sensual sensation spread through her body, warming her flesh from the memories.

Madeleine turned and crossed to the steps, counting them until she reached the quiet place where she and Iskandar had sat together that late afternoon. She looked at her watch. *Mon Dieu*, she thought, I am almost there at exactly the same time. Her eyes scanned the grassy knoll, the magnificent trees posing as sentinels...I remember everything, she whispered to herself.

Gingerly, now without hesitation, she stepped eagerly to the place overlooking the city and the sea where she had been with Iskandar, and sat on the bench at that very spot. After a long respite of gazing at the sea, she looked around the promontory with her chin propped in the palms of her hands, her knees supporting her elbows. She was a picture of a woman content in her deep personal thoughts. Assured that she was alone with her fondest, happiest remembrances for what seemed only minutes but was actually more than an hour, Madeleine relished the sensuality of her first kiss from Iskandar in this very place. She was in heaven remembering every detail of that late afternoon with her first lover. Her eyes closed languidly as she thought of the way she felt when Iskandar later reached to her and kissed her deeply, how she trembled when she allowed his searching tongue to reach past her lips, caressing her waiting tongue. Her thoughts leaped anxiously to the moment when they first embraced, arms eagerly wrapped around each other.

She whispered to herself, almost in a prayer, "Oh, Iskandar. I want you, I need you, I love you. When am I going to be with you again? Come to me...please."

Madeleine partially opened her eyes with a serenely wistful expression on her face, then closed them again. She knew now she had done the right thing in coming back here, the very spot they had shared so long ago. She was absolutely certain that she and her young lover would meet again, that God would make certain it would happen.

"One day, Iskandar, one day, you and I will return here together. This is our place, the home of our love. Soon, my love, *mon amour.* Soon."

As she turned her head, Madeleine watched the sun begin to set into the sea as it had so many times before when she visited this place with her son, remembering…watching.

Finally, satisfied, she stood up, smiled to herself as she straightened her dress, looked at her watch and moved toward the steps that would lead her down the hill. She was a happy woman once again, but also a woman who knew she was loved and now, a mature woman who had found a purpose beyond herself and her past.

Every afternoon during the following two weeks, Madeleine happily returned to the cathedral and to the promontory to be alone with her thoughts. She dined either on the *Canebière* or at the Lebanese cafés at the *Place de Liban*, savoring the memories, enjoying the food of the Levant.

She decided not to allow stress to enter her life any more. She was convinced that she had found her place in the world by now devoting herself to others. She concluded that this would be her best and most fulfilling course. God would help her, she deeply believed. "I will do my best to solve those things I can, and simply accept those things I cannot. But I will keep my faith in Him and in Iskandar." She was determined to accept her fate. She loved Psalm 46:10 which says: *Be still, and know that I am God!* Reminded, she believed she must simply be…do what she thinks she should in service to others, and let God do the rest. *I cannot make it happen. It is in His hands.*

After many days that turned into weeks of her sabbatical, her quest, she found her truth. And she was content.

She decided, with a peaceful sense of purpose, to return to her new home, Beirut, and to devote herself to her honorable cause: to come to the aid of the poor children of Lebanon.

By 1950, Madeleine had built several private homes for the poor, orphanages, health clinics, and small schools. She became involved in the welfare of the children with the city's various religious groups and their fund-raising efforts. She also became active in the restoration of heavily damaged apartment buildings, particularly in West Beirut near AUB, to provide even more lodging for the poor. And as she progressed, visiting the orphanages each week, speaking to groups, even enlisting students at the university to volunteer for her cause, she attracted others who enthusiastically became part of her philanthropic campaign. Within a few years, Madeleine's efforts were making a substantial and visible impact on the social and cultural life of the city.

Meanwhile, sound investing was paying great rewards for her too. Marcel Kabani watched over her investments, carefully soliciting advice from his network of financial institutions in Beirut, London, and New York. Indeed, her wealth was growing even as she invested so much in the foundation she had created.

François, learning from his mother, became eager to participate in her causes. They decided that upon completion of his courses at the Sorbonne, he should spend a year at the London School of Economics, and afterwards return to Beirut.

As Madeleine involved herself in her charities, she became admired for her generosity and passionate dedication to the welfare of the underprivileged. She also carefully followed her son's progress at the Sorbonne. After giving considerable thought to what she should give François upon his graduation, she decided to have a Beiruti goldsmith make a ring identical to the ring given to her by her father in 1917. It would replace the one she had given to Iskandar.

"It must have the exact same design," she told the goldsmith. "Include a French cross with the initials F.D. on either side, for François DuBois."

CHAPTER 40

Paris
Summer 1948

"This is the most exciting city in the world," André mused to his friends, feeling very positive about their lives, and Paris itself. "You must explore it, celebrate it, partake of all that it offers," he smiled with a twinkle in his eye, "even its cultural facilities. Most of all, enjoy each day, *mon amis.*"

François was listening intently to his younger, passionate new friend and classmate, André Chacôn, a free-spirited student of French history, at the Café Mediterranean. They were sitting on black metal chairs with curved backs at a small round four-legged metal table on the sidewalk overlooking the River Seine watching the people, especially the pretty coed students, stroll by.

This was François's favorite place to spend sunny, breezy afternoons after classes, often joining his collegiate friends, writers and artists, on what was known as the Left Bank, a meeting place of liberal-thinking students who, as a group felt they actually learned more from their conversations with each other than they learned in their classrooms. Their communal discussions, virtually an extension of their classes, were encouraged by the professors at the Sorbonne.

The serenity of the river, just across the street, with its endless flow, reminded the students of the *Université du Paris* that life was not just a moment in the passage of time, but rather, was a process that should be explored to its fullest, and that thoughtful philosophical discussions were a vital part of the human experience. The professors encouraged their students to look far beyond the destruction of the horrendous battles and chaos of World War II where, except for the city of Paris, most of the major cities of Europe were almost totally destroyed. They were ravaged by the invading, arrogant Germans who were determined to conquer all of Europe, or by bombardment by the Allies who were equally determined to destroy the German war machine and obtain an unconditional surrender.

Gratefully, Paris was spared the blanket bombardment of the Allies since the weak French government chose instead to surrender the city to Hitler so that its jewel, the locale of so much historical and cultural treasure, would not be destroyed. Even so, the German occupation was a terrible time of tension and abuse which impacted the French psyche for years.

"They were all crazy," André continued, "war is stupid. Young men must die so that older men can fulfill the dreams of their egos. It has always been and always will be, I suppose." He paused, leaned back, lifted his glass of chilled white wine, and sighed, "I prefer the ways of the poet."

"Ah, André, of course you do. You were spared, being a Parisian, the terrible onslaught of fighting. But, if you are being attacked, I believe you too will fight."

"François, you say these things, but, I think you too are a lover, not a fighter," he laughed.

François, now twenty-eight, and a few years older than André and his other classmates, had a slightly different and more mature view of the war. He smiled, "Well, it is true that I never actually was part of the fighting. But I have seen the destruction of war, though mostly in Beirut and Marseille. And I can tell you, when someone is attacking your homeland, you will fight back, even to death. Yet, André, I think there is more at issue than ego. There is a sense of survival of one's freedom, family, and one's way of life and culture. It depends on one's point of view."

And so their daily conversations continued. Much discussion focused on the growing influence and threat of communism, not only in the Soviet sphere of Eastern Europe, but also because of the increasing instability that the communist threat presented in Italy, Austria, and in France itself. Its presence was self-evident, and the Sorbonne, like Paris itself, was a fertile garden of liberal, leftist thought.

The almost daily gatherings at a favorite outdoor bistro were very much a part of François' life experiences at the Sorbonne, influencing his own thinking. Classroom lessons focused on his chosen curriculum of economics, accounting, and history, but much of his collegiate life was spent commiserating, debating, exploring, and discussing geo-political issues over glasses of wine with his fellow students at the sidewalk cafés of the Left Bank.

The war was over, but the political repercussions continued for years. Paris, like Marseille and many other major cities of Europe, was a beneficiary. The city was the destination sought by refugees from other countries too destroyed to provide in the near future a quality of life comparable to anything known prior to the German onslaught. And while there was enormous reconstruction throughout Europe, there remained deep-rooted anger toward Germany and Germans, especially by the French people. Paris was a refuge of guarded optimism, civility, cultural treasures, and fine hotels. The Sorbonne was its own oasis of freedom, intellectual discourse and learning.

Students from all over Europe sought admission, not only because a degree from the university was a cherished symbol of an excellent education that, except for schools in England, was the finest a European student could hope for, but also for the personal relationships that would be beneficial in later years. Often, students inquired of their fellow students about their hopes, their dreams, and their aspirations. Most of these discussions would likewise take place at the café tables or during walks on campus or along the Seine river bank, known as the Left Bank, a haven for artists, writers, students, and anti-establishment liberals.

One late afternoon, François was enjoying his second glass of wine with his friends, feeling a sense of euphoria, and a slight light-headedness. Cool breezes were blowing over them. The leaves of the sycamore trees that lined the avenue rustled lightly, a testament to new life. Small puffy clouds drifted above in the celestial blue skies. Their party of six was spending the late spring afternoon watching people—shoppers browsing among the small specialty booths in the open-air market for their favorite fresh vegetables and freshly killed chickens.

"The women have to shop everyday," commented one at the table. "They don't own refrigerators. Only the rich can afford luxuries like that. The cost is too dear for electricity, so they shop each day, only for the day."

"France will rise again," said another, with a shrug. "One day we will live like the Americans. They have so much there."

As André turned his head to look at the pedestrians, he directed François' attention to the tall, striking young woman walking toward them. François, not wanting to miss an opportunity, boldly stood up and moved toward the sensual, dark-haired beauty. His confident, nonchalant swagger impressed the young woman.

"*Bonjour,* mademoiselle," he smiled as he slightly bowed in respect, clearly seeking her favor. "Would you care to join us? I believe I have seen you on the campus. My name is François DuBois. We are discussing matters of great importance, solving the troubles of the world." He gestured with a wave of his arm toward his table of friends. "We invite you for a glass of wine."

"*Merci, monsieur,*" she replied with a lovely smile. *Hmm,* she thought, *he is even more handsome close than from a distance.* "Monsieur DuBois, you say?"

"*Oui,* please sit with us." He smiled as he pulled out a chair for her. "And, I assume correctly, I hope, that you are indeed a student at the *Université,* are you not?"

"I am indeed."

"I can tell you are not French. Although you speak the language well, you have an Eastern accent. Where are you from, mademoiselle?"

"No, I am not French, but I have lived in Europe, and one must speak French, *n'est-ce pas*? I am from Poland, although I have lived in France since 1937 when my family and I came to Paris. So I perfected speaking French although, as you say, I still have a slight accent."

"Well," smiled François, "you are a pleasant sight for a man, wherever you are from, and I am delighted to meet you. And now, let me introduce you to my friends. Tell me your name, please."

"My name is Leah," she said softly, deliberately refraining from divulging her last name. She was still defensive and reticent, she knew, but felt justified as the war had caused her to be very careful with people she didn't know.

After all had exchanged courtesies, François delved further into his new friend's life while describing his own, his body language speaking volumes.

"Yes, I love Paris," she exclaimed with a friendly, easy smile as she surveyed the faces in the group. "Everyone has been so nice to me. The weather is lovely now, the flowers have bloomed, the rains have ended, the birds are in love, God is in his heaven, the war is over, and all is well in the world. At least here."

"Well, I think we are the fortunate ones," André interjected, keeping the conversation light, as most students he knew did, recognizing others had too many awful remembrances of the atrocities that had ended only a few years ago. The memories of loved ones who had been lost were now comfortably internalized, and most did not want to resurrect them, especially with strangers.

"We are all finding ourselves at new crossroads in our lives," François said, boldly moving to find out what he could about this lovely young woman who had now entered his life. "For example, I am part French and part Lebanese. I am studying economics. I hope to go to the London School of Economics for my advanced degree, and live in Beirut where there are excellent opportunities." Then pausing for effect, he added, "My mother is very involved in charitable causes there. I believe now that the war is over there will be an increase in international finance. The needs for capital investments and job-creating industries are enormous. Don't you agree?"

"Oh my," responded Leah, lowering her eyes from his face, "I have no opinion on that issue. My interests are more in the area of art history and world politics. You see, I hope to complete my studies and some day teach school. I speak five languages as well."

François, listening intently, reached to touch her hand that was resting on the table by her wineglass.

She watched as François touched her hand and, rejecting an initial response to withdraw hers, smiled demurely instead, willing to see where this conversation would go. François observantly noticed the almost quizzical expression on Leah's face turn friendly in a most brief moment, belying her internalized fear his forward touch triggered.

"Please do not fear me, Leah. We are all good-natured fellow students here."

"I am sorry, François. Forgive me. The war has made many of us reluctant to trust. I have had a difficult time trusting, for you see, I am Jewish, and Jews have had a most terrible time in Europe, especially the last ten years, even in France when Pétain's dreadful Vichy government took on the anti-Semitism of the Third Reich. So, I have a bit of difficulty relaxing with someone I don't know well...with almost all people, actually."

"I understand, Leah," he nodded, "but be assured that I am in Paris for only one reason, and that is to learn as much as I can while obtaining my degree."

"To be sure, Leah," interjected André, "there is a second, although subordinate occupation of my wealthy friend he has not yet admitted. He is a man who enjoys as much of his life in Paris as is possible. He is the perfect example of *joie de vivre*." Continuing, he laughed, "Oh, how he could play the innocent while hoping you will like him enough to have dinner with him later. Is that not so, *mon ami?*"

Leah looked from François to André, then back to François, as François replied quickly, feigning outrage at the pain of insult, yet smiling, "Oh, André, how could you? I am simply trying to be friendly. Certainly *carpe diem* is what I live by, but dinner hadn't even crossed my mind." Then, glancing at his wristwatch, continued, "But, as a matter of fact, it is getting late; it is nearly eight o'clock. Time has flown by. But isn't that always the way. So, it is either continue our discussion or go home to study, I suppose. On the other hand, my new friend," François said, now looking into Leah's demure eyes, "would you be interested in joining me for dinner?"

"Aha!" laughed André, both arms outstretched. "Thank you, *mon ami*, for proving me a psychic. I knew it! You are so predictable, François."

"But, André," he shrugged, still smiling, "how could I not invite our new friend to join us for dinner, eh, *mon ami?*"

"Us?" André exclaimed with a look of surprise on his face. "When did it become us, you rascal!"

"Just now," François laughed, "when you pressed the issue. What was I to do? She is, after all, a lovely, intelligent student who looks like she would enjoy more conversation with us while sharing the delicacies of a fine Parisian restaurant. Wouldn't you, Leah?"

She was amused at his audacity. "I can't help laughing at you two. And how could I resist your generous offer? You both are too silly for words."

"Well, André, you nearly got me into trouble, but it looks like we must be off for an early and perhaps intellectual dinner so that we all can retreat to our rooms for our studies which we all eagerly live for." François winked at André, "After all," he said with a thin smile of devilishness, "we are here for our collegial education, *n'est-ce pas?*" He silently wondered if Leah actually believed him as he unsuccessfully tried to portray himself as an innocent... clearly not an accurate description of one who appeared to be among the oldest and most sophisticated of the group.

Leah remarked, "By all means, shall we have an early dinner so there will be time for our studies?" She smiled at André as if he were a co-conspirator.

"Yes," André quickly responded, "and maybe afterwards, we will escort our friend, François, to his flat to ensure he is home safely with his books." He paused and, with a wink, added, "Ahem."

They all laughed together at their joke on François.

"Enough," François laughed. "Let's just go have a bite to eat, shall we?" he said, recognizing it would be a better start with this new, tantalizing creature to go along with the joke, not press the issue, and come across as a good spirit. There will be another opportunity, of that I am sure, he thought to himself. Then he smiled, stood, and reached out his hand to Leah as she rose...and rose...and rose, until he noticed she was as tall as he. *How gorgeous, what a shapely figure, long legs, an incredibly beautiful face with full, sensuous lips, and long dark, black hair that drapes to her shoulders.*

"*Mon Dieu,*" François said to André too softly for her to hear, "she is magnificent." He thought to himself, *I must wait and be patient with this woman. I wonder how old she is. After all, most students at the Université are in their mid to late twenties because of the war. I am twenty-eight myself, but with her life experiences, I cannot let age be an issue. None of us are young and innocent anymore.*

That first evening went very well for everyone in the group, especially for Leah, François, and André. The others enjoyed their own separate conversations throughout dinner. They laughed, drank more wine, relaxed, and forgot about their studies that night. François, in full pursuit, invited Leah for a walk along the Seine before walking her to her flat. Kissing her hand at the door, he invited her to join him the next afternoon at Café Mediterranean.

"Do you think you would like to eat foods of the 'Med'?" he asked.

She smiled, "I don't know. I really haven't tasted those foods...perhaps."

"Well then, let's just find out," he responded with a tantalizing smile.

"Tomorrow then," Leah whispered as she bent toward him, lightly kissing his cheek.

"Goodnight, *mon ami.* Thank you for a lovely evening and dinner," she said, closing the door as he turned to leave.

Once inside, Leah leaned her back against the door, thinking; he's very nice, funny, and handsome. Tonight was very nice. But...we shall see what we shall see. She stepped into the kitchenette, which was actually central to her one-room studio apartment.

"Here, kitty," she beckoned to her stray cat she had nursed back to good health, "I know it's late, but come here and get dinner." She poured milk into the bowl and watched, bent over, hands on her knees as her kitten lapped it up.

After their second evening together, François and Leah found they both wanted very much to be together often. To Leah, at twenty-two, François was mature, considerate, sensitive, intelligent, and always with available money...more than the other students. She didn't question him on any personal issue. He was a pleasure to be with. He had not tried to pursue sex, at least not yet, which she found to be not only a surprise, but a pleasant and different experience, a welcomed behavior that drew her to him, leaving her wariness and reluctance behind. As a result, Leah was becoming friendlier, happier with François, and more vulnerable, allowing herself to let her true personality emerge. This was exactly what François was hoping would happen. He was sure she was still very cautious, so he responded accordingly. In time, she found herself opening up more and more to the group, sometimes expressing her opinion on Europe's experiences, describing the fear the European Jewish community shared across the continent, and soon beginning to appreciate the friendly banter of the group, even as they laughed at their own jokes.

François was a charmer. He knew exactly how to behave properly with this lovely Polish-Jewish refugee who had every good reason to be defensive, to be reluctant, sometimes petulant, sometimes shy. He felt that if he did not cause her fear or give her reasons to raise her protective defenses, her behavior would be more honest and her guarded natural insouciance would become apparent. In a word, he extended to her great respect.

After a few weeks of newfound camaraderie, she began to laugh easier, and even found a refreshing new bounce in her step. Life could be truly good she was surprised to find. The two became almost daily companions, both having no expectations, placing no demands on the other, but, in all honesty, hoping...

Still, they joined André and the others friends almost daily. Over time, Leah began to forget the horrors of the war, living more and more in the present, while François too became more engrossed in his life in Paris, inexorably expanding his own sense of self, and independence from his past. Leah became so comfortable with François that she would even reach out her hand for him to hold as they walked together.

"I am so happy here, François. You have helped me rid myself of the demons of the war. It was so awful, but now I feel a sense of freedom that I have never felt before."

"It's the same for me, Leah. You somehow bring out the best in me. I can even tell that my priorities have changed somewhat. *Merci, mon amie, merci.*"

Their days, then weeks together exploring the city and its principal attractions were as valuable as their more intimate evenings. Both continued focusing on their studies, but there was no doubt about their growing attraction to each other. Although the idea of a long-term relationship was never discussed, perhaps because intermarriage of their very different religions and cultures might not acceptable to either family, or simply because each had life goals that came first, they both felt comfort in each other's presence. They too began to realize that they were slowly but surely falling in love. They never talked about it. They never feared it. It just seemed to be so natural, and so welcomed. It would be just a matter of time.

CHAPTER 41

$\mathcal{A}$nd so it was that wonderful summer...

As they held hands walking along the Seine one Saturday night following a special birthday dinner for Leah of pressed duck at the spectacular restaurant *Tour d'Argent*, one of Paris' finest restaurants which overlooked the Seine and the lighted, magnificent Notre Dame, they simultaneously felt a romantic culmination of their weeks of friendship and affection.

It was a beautiful evening with a clear sky full of stars. The cool night air, with only a hint of a soft breeze off the river induced them to walk closer together. Leah, reaching a spot in their walk exactly opposite the cathedral, stopped, and, with an overwhelming feeling of sensuality, turned to François, pulling his hand to turn toward her. She felt a warmth in her breasts that she could not resist. She knew her feelings for François were growing, almost overwhelming her. She knew she was ready to offer herself to him. And she knew she was safe feeling this way because she felt his sincere love for her.

"You see that young couple over there, François?" Leah whispered to him, lowering her eyelids, reflecting her growing sensations of sensuality.

"There, by the river, Leah?" he responded in feigned innocence.

"*Oui*, François. You see what they are doing?"

Smiling, he grasped both her hands and pulled her close to him. "They are in love, Leah."

"And so am I, François," she whispered, resting her head on his shoulder. "Oh, please hold me."

"Of course!" François said, feeling her body against his. His eyes closed as his emotions increased. "I want you Leah. You make me warm all over."

They embraced closely, eagerly wrapping their arms around each other, pressing their bodies against each other. It was so natural after weeks of companionship. Leah's firm, full breasts pressed against François's hard chest muscles, exciting both even more.

Leah, feeling François's swelling muscle, leaned against him even more, and murmured, "Ohhh, François, you feel so good. You excite me so. I can hardly breathe. This is so wonderful. I never thought I would feel this way." She could feel her palms grow moist and felt droplets form on her upper lip.

"You know, don't you, that I have never been with a man before." She lowered her chin in innocence. "I realize that may sound strange, but it's true. I just couldn't trust anyone to come close to me...until you."

Together they relaxed their tight embrace and pulled back slightly so that they were face to face, staring directly into each other's eyes, hoping to be assured their growing feelings and hopes were the same.

"Kiss me now, François," she offered.

"Oh, Leah," he whispered as he moved his lips to touch hers. *Her full lips, so soft, so succulent*, he thought as his tongue lightly traced them. Her mouth opened slightly inviting him. He kissed her eagerly and deeply as he held Leah close to him, sensing her hips moving even closer against his, making him grow even harder.

After a moment, she pulled away slightly, whispering, "Oh, François, you feel so good. Perhaps...perhaps, the feelings are *too* good." She turned her head, wanting more, but not sure she should stay. "Perhaps I had better go home now, darling."

François sensed her hesitation, yet felt her desire for him. "Leah, I'm not sure how long I can stand this. I want you so much and am getting close to losing control. Let's go to my apartment. It's just over there. Either that, *mon amour*, or we must go over to that park over there...behind the hedges."

Convinced it was indeed their time, pulling his hand and leading him, she whispered, "Come, François, come with me. I cannot leave you. I must be with you tonight, my darling."

Together, they crossed the grassy area of the park, stepping without hesitation, through a narrow opening in the six-foot hedge and emerging through the green, thick bushes on the other side. They didn't know whether to laugh at the destruction of the path in the hedge they had created in their unstoppable haste or to sigh at their mutual nearness to sexual culmination. Without doing either, they fell to the grass, Leah hastily pulling up her skirt while François fumbled with his buttons.

Perched above Leah, on his hands and knees, François looked down into her moist eyes, filled with the sensual emotions of love, of copulation.

"Please take me, François, please," she moaned softly with her eyelids lowering as she pulled him to her, "I want you now."

"Oh, Leah, you are so beautiful, so lovely. I have wanted you since the moment I first saw you that afternoon at the café. You are so magnificent. *Je t'aime, mon amour.*"

He gently moved on top of her as he tenderly fulfilled her wishes and his desires.

Afterward, they lay together, side by side, caressing each other, fondling, savoring the moment, smiling at each other, sharing.

She murmured, "I am so happy you are with me here tonight."

"You are more wonderful than I ever dreamed, Leah."

She touched his lips with her fingers. "François, thank you for being so gentle and patient with me. I am not experienced in these matters, and this was so beautiful.

"Waiting was difficult for me, Leah, because I wanted you so much. I don't know how much longer I could have waited! But I'm glad we became close companions first."

After a few minutes of enjoying each other, with Leah stroking his chest and François fondling her breasts, Leah began inching closer to François, getting more excited. Her hand began to move down his chest to his hard stomach, then to his upper thighs. As she caressed him, he began to grow hard again. She touched him lightly, tantalizing him even more, and as she did, she became moist.

"Oh, François, make love to me again. Please, François."

"Leah, you are incredible," he whispered as once again he moved on top of her, then with a strong move, he thrust himself inside her, feeling the height of ecstasy. She groaned as her pelvis began a rhythmic movement back and forth in concert with his hip movements, causing him to enter her deeper and deeper. She wanted to devour him.

"Go gently, but please don't stop. It is so incredible." She looked up into his eyes, ecstatic in their intimacy, almost screaming with joy as they climaxed together.

"My God, Leah, no one can surpass you. You have made me so happy."

The post-war years of Paris were an exhilarating relief from the awful dangers before, and with their new total freedom, these years would become a time of social change, of exploration by young people. With the massive rebuilding across Europe, fueled by America's Marshall Plan, money was flowing and political thought thriving, especially at freethinking institutions like the Sorbonne. There was a similar urging to be free and in love with life. Couples openly expressed their affections as France led the way worldwide in the sexual revolution and in fashion, while, in America, there remained a puritanic constrained behavior and strict social governance of the late 1940s and 1950s.

François and Leah enjoyed the following months free of constraint, happy to regularly share their time together in intimacy as they both pursued their studies, supporting each other.

But, in time, their life together received an unexpected and significant turn of events.

Leah broke the news to him one afternoon as they walked along the Seine watching the clouds drift, the passersby, and the river with its inexorable flow.

She stopped to turn and face him. "I've been thinking a lot lately, my dear François, and there is something I must tell you now that the school term has ended." She hesitated for a moment. "I must leave Paris."

"What?" he gasped, stunned.

"Because I love you so much, this is the most difficult decision I have ever had to make. I must go to Palestine immediately to be with my own people, to help build a homeland."

François couldn't believe his ears. This news was such a shock to him. He clearly did not comprehend the deep-rooted emotions Leah felt. Yet, he cared for her so deeply and thought they would never become separated. He reached out to her.

"Leah, I love you too much to let you go. And I know you love me the same way!" Turning away, staring at the river, he sadly realized she had a much different agenda than he. Lowering his head, he turned back to hold her, saying softly, "I know I can't stop you, but I hope I can convince you to stay. You're breaking my heart, my love." He sighed sadly and looked to the heavens for help, then turned back to her. "Of course, you must do what is in your heart. I can only hope one day I will be able to understand."

She lowered her head against his chest, also feeling great sadness, and whispered, "You know you are the only man I have ever loved. And you will always be the only one. I hope...no, I *believe* in my heart, my love, that in time we will be together again. Please, you must understand and forgive me, François."

"I believe we *must* find each other once again. I can never forget you, my love, my dear Leah." He tried without success to smile and accept this tragic turn in his life.

They embraced tightly, holding each other for a long and emotional time as tears overflowed onto their saddened cheeks.

After what seemed like hours of agony, they murmured "*Au revoir, mon chérie*" to each other as they stepped apart, arms extended, not wanting to let go.

François found that after Leah left and he was truly alone, he really didn't find life at the Sorbonne as fulfilling, as enjoyable, or as enriching as before. He didn't laugh as before. His friends also noticed a lingering sadness. He thought of Leah much of the time, but he forced himself to focus even harder on his studies, deciding reluctantly that he had to move on and come to his own self-actualization.

As he wrote his weekly letters to his mother, he remembered her descriptions of his own father's determination to fulfill his destiny, and was convinced he could and *should* do the same. He believed that he too would find his own way to go "beyond the cedars." He also felt his lost love with Leah was so similar to his mother's with Iskandar and understood what she must have felt. *What can I do? What is to happen to us?*

It was at François's graduation from the Sorbonne in the spring of 1949 that Madeleine proudly placed the treasured likeness of her father's ring on her son's little finger.

"You make me so proud, François. I want you to have this ring which is identical to the one your grandfather gave to me before he went off to war. It is that ring I gave to your father as a symbol of my eternal love for him. And this ring, my son, is a symbol of my deep love for you. I believe if your father were here today, he would be so proud of you too, and express his love and pride as I do."

"Thank you, *Maman*." He smiled as his eyes moistened from her poignant gesture. "I will wear it proudly all my life. Wouldn't it be something if my father, even after all these years, still wears the ring you gave him?"

"*Oui*, François. Let us believe that he does treasure my ring as I do his cross."

François decided it was time to broaden his knowledge, expand his horizons, and focus more on his career. He had had wonderful years in Paris. He had grown philosophically while living the good life in an intellectual atmosphere and experiencing the best life he could. He felt very good about himself. He had a continuing generous allowance from his mother, accessing him to the finest restaurants and cultural events. Also, as much as possible, he had painfully put his rich memories of Leah behind him. Because he had to.

He began to want even more career-fulfilling experiences. François was maturing. As he had discussed with his mother at the time of his graduation, he enrolled at the London School of Economics, recognizing it was the finest school of its kind in Europe, one that would introduce him to American and British scholars and leaders in global economics. He could also sharpen his English.

While he concentrated on his graduate studies, he still found time to enjoy London and its sophistication, and time to expand his relationships with several lovely women, some students, and some simply attractive and wealthy. But nothing and no one could fill the void left by Leah's departure.

While he was still at the Sorbonne, he received short notes from Leah from time to time. But they were too brief for him to know fully what she was doing and where she was now living. What she always wrote did remind him of her love, signing her letters with "I will always love you, François."

After he left Paris for London, her letters could not find him and he had no way of finding her. He was bound to simply wait for her to somehow contact him.

PART THREE

CHAPTER 42

$\mathcal{T}$ he years of World War II were life-changing for everyone worldwide. Those in Europe suffered invasion, occupation, loss of life, loss of human rights, rape, slave labor, atrocities, and, in many cases, total destruction. France, except for Paris due to its early surrender, suffered greatly at the hands of the Germans. Hardly a European community was spared.

In the Pacific arena, it was much the same. Civilians everywhere suffered indescribable tragedies: looting, fire, bombings, loss of limbs, all kinds of horrors. Even those prisoners of war on all sides were not spared the terrible damage. Some were burned or maimed so badly, they were unidentifiable. Even German POWs shipped to camps in America arrived severely injured, burned, and mutilated, many without at least one limb.

"This war has been a terrible thing for everyone," Alexander commented to Helene and his father one Sunday afternoon as they listened to the news on the radio describing the latest battles. Like parents across America, their greatest fear was for their sons and daughters who were in harm's way. And while everyone across the country felt relatively safe from the destruction taking place in other countries, they worried constantly about the welfare of their children across the sea. Parents knew so little since all mail was censored for security reasons.

Michael, son of Alexander and Helene Thomas and grandson of Abraham Thomas was stationed in England, flying in the Eighth Air Corps. He was a pilot of a B-17 bomber who, with thousands of young airmen, daily bombed the factories, submarine bases, and rail yards in Germany. The assignment of the U.S. Eighth was daylight strategic bombing which made them terribly vulnerable to German fighter attacks, flak, and artillery. Losses were consistently very high, often as much as fifty-percent. And, like many of his compatriots, both American and English, he was, during these worst of times, just nineteen years old. By the time he had ten missions behind him, he had experienced a frightening loss of friends and emergencies—dangerous experiences a man of sixty in normal times would not have encountered. And yet, amazingly, he had not yet reached his twentieth birthday when he had completed his twenty-fourth bombing mission.

Like every other American serviceman in Europe, he was not allowed to write home telling his parents where he was, what he was doing, where he was flying, and even what he did on weekend furloughs in London. Parents and families kept innocent vigil with a lighted candle in the window next to a small flag, and lived each day in ignorance except for news reports on the radio and in the afternoon newspapers. As a result, letters from home were filled with newsy dialogue including reports of who recently got married, who had a social at their home, the weather, and the like. Some simply said, "We miss you...take care of yourself...we love you and hope we see you real soon." Other not so pleasant letters the soldier, air cadet, marine, or sailor would receive might be from his girlfriend or "three-day wife." When a letter came informing the combatant that his girlfriend back home had found someone new who was nearby, a "dear John" letter, this terrible news in some cases drove the already depressed serviceman even deeper into depression or worse.

Because of the mail restrictions, most families were not aware of the condition of their sons and daughters except for the War Department sending representatives to tell families of the young man's status, either serious injury, lost in action, or death.

Helene and Alexander lived from day to day with concern for their son Michael. They were filled with anxiety, uncertainty...and no idea where Michael was...or if he was safe.

Helene did her best to keep herself busy at the church, helping in collection drives for the war effort, and keeping her home a place of respite for her husband and daughter. Her happiest times were in her kitchen when she prepared Alexander's favorite meals.

One afternoon in late 1944, she and Alexander would find their world changed forever.

◦◦◦◦◦◦

Taking a moment to pause from chopping the lush parsley for the evening's *tabouleh* salad, Helene looked out the window overlooking the lake and fondly recalled watching Michael and Helena as young children racing to the shore and splashing into the dark waters of the lake. With a lingering smile, she returned to her dinner preparation.

Unknown to her, two uniformed U.S. Air Corps servicemen drove into her driveway in an army green-colored Ford sedan. Stepping out of the car, they straightened their jackets and pulled on their caps. They carried leather satchels as they briskly walked to the front door of the Thomas home and knocked firmly on the door.

"Who is it?" called Helene cheerily from the kitchen.

"Mrs. Thomas? Mrs. Alexander Thomas?"

"Yes, yes, just a minute," she replied as she placed her knife on the counter, wiped her hands on her apron, and walked down the hallway to the front door.

"I'm coming!" she smiled with a welcoming expression for her visitors before she could make out the two figures standing at the door. Then, recognizing the uniforms, she thought, *Oh..oh...why are they here?*

As she neared the door, she could see the green-colored automobile with stenciled lettering "U.S. Air Corps" in white paint.

"Hello. I'm Helene Thomas. What can I do for you?" Nervously, she opened the screen door. "Won't you come in please?"

Removing their caps, they stepped into the foyer. The taller of the two spoke first. "Mrs. Thomas, I'm Air Force Captain John Reynolds and this is Captain Ray Jones. Is your son Captain Michael Thomas of the U.S. Army Air Corps?"

"Yes, he is. Why do you ask? What is it? Tell me...is he hurt?"

"May we come in?"

"Of course, do come in."

"Yes, ma'am," he replied as they followed Helene to the living room. "It's about Captain Thomas. We have been instructed to inform you personally that your son, Captain Michael Thomas, was killed in action over Germany."

"Oh, my God, not Michael!" she screamed. "Oh, my God...Michael..." Suddenly she felt very weak as she pressed one hand to her mouth, the other to her heart. Hyperventilating, she began to faint.

The two reached for her as she collapsed to the floor, sobbing, both hands over her face. The two airmen lifted her and took her to the nearby couch in the living room. Her shoulders shook as she struggled to sit up, thankfully with their help.

"Please, dear God, let it not be so..."

"Ma'am, we know this is a terrible thing for you to hear, and believe me, we wish we didn't have to be the ones to carry this message. We are so sorry, ma'am, so very sorry."

"How...how...did it happen? Do you know?"

"Yes, ma'am, we do know," replied the other serviceman. "We have a full report for you along with a citation of his bravery in action, and several medals he earned. From what the report says, he was quite a brave man, Mrs. Thomas. You can be very proud."

"Proud you say?" She lifted her head to look up at them and clearly replied, "I've been proud of my son all his life. He was such a good boy. Now I must find his father. Can you help me to the telephone? My God, this will kill Alexander. His whole life is for his son. Maybe I better tell him later, when he comes home..."

"Whatever you want Mrs. Thomas. We do have this citation for you, with much more detailed information. I can assure you that Captain Thomas surely earned the respect of his fellow airmen."

He pulled the citation from his case and began reading:

"Captain Michael Thomas's B-17 was one of two hundred and sixty flying over Germany that day. His was the lead bomber, the one whose navigator and bombardier guided the rest of the planes to the target. Observations of pilots of other planes nearby testify to his leadership and bravery. Despite attack by numerous German Messerschmitts and a sky filled with black clouds of flak, that is, thousands of pieces of steel exploding that could have virtually shred his plane, Captain Thomas steadfastly, and at great risk to himself and his crew, flew directly to his primary target. Just after his plane flawlessly released its load of bombs, flak artillery hit his plane. The observing pilots believe it struck the plane's nose, ultimately fatally injuring Captain Thomas, the co-pilot and bombardier. The plane went into a steep dive. Captain Thomas held the plane as steady as he could, thereby allowing able members of his crew to parachute out. That bombing mission is believed to have resulted directly in saving thousands of GIs, hastening the war's end, and giving a solid boost of morale throughout the Eighth Air Force."

After reading the citation, the designated informant continued, "Mrs. Thomas, your son earned the Distinguished Flying Cross and A Purple Heart for bravery beyond all call of duty."

Helene sniffed and cleared her throat as she wiped her eyes as she tried to respond to these fine young men.

"I really don't know what to say...I just can't believe my wonderful only son is gone. But I do know thousands of boys have been killed, yet it is so very painful. I'm not sure I'll ever get over this news...I do thank you both for coming here today...still, I'm not sure how I'm going to tell his father. He loves Michael so much. A son is everything to a father. But..." she paused as she thought a moment. *I must tell him today.*

After an hour, Helene felt she wanted to be alone with her memories of Michael. She stood to end the meeting she wished had never happened. Responding to her, the two messengers also arose respectfully and moved toward the front door.

"Well, Mrs. Thomas, if there is anything the Air Force can do for you, please feel free to call the number on the card. We're based nearby in Tampa. And here is the box with Captain Thomas' citations, battle ribbons, and honored medals for your safe keeping."

Respectfully saluting her as she stood at the doorway, they stepped to their automobile, got in and slowly drove away with a goodbye wave as they departed.

Helene, taking a deep breath, decided to wait until Alexander arrived home after his workday. She felt she needed time and went to bed with her sadness.

Oh, Michael, Michael...what are we to do now?

After dinner, while Helene was not animated as usual, and Alexander, feeling something had happened, watched her. Rather than press her, he waited in silence. When she had finished eating only a portion of her dinner, she rose and looked at her husband while reaching out to him with her hands. "Alexander, come with me, for I have something to tell you." They walked side by side out to the porch overlooking the lake.

After a few moments they began talking in hushed voices. Helena, still clearing the dinner table, was carrying several dishes to the kitchen when she heard first the raised, angry tone of her father's voice. "What? Oh no, Helene, not Michael...not my son...oh God!"

Helene's voice followed, "Oh, Alexander, I so wish I didn't have to tell you. This has been the most horrible day of my life. I love you, Alexander, and now we must accept this. It's happening all over America. Hold me, my love, hold me. I need your strength."

"Oh, Helene...my God...Michael...my son...my only son. I'm lost...I don't know what to say. We have always feared that this day might come. Now there is no hope...only the truth...oh God..." he stammered as he stepped to his favorite rocking chair, sat and silently gazed out at the lake as the setting sun behind him slowly allowed darkness to overcome the Thomas' home.

Helena, having overheard part of the conversation, rushed outside to embrace her sobbing mother. "Oh, Mom, not Michael!" she cried. "What are we going to do without him?" she begged rhetorically. "What are we going to do without my big brother?" Helena, now crying too, then went to embrace her father as he sat staring, dumbfounded, with years flowing down his cheeks. They remained together for several hours, long after the sun had set, in sadness and despair, each with his or her own memories.

The next day, Alexander awoke, skipped breakfast, and, wanting to be alone with his lost dreams for his son, wandered to the backyard, walking through his beloved fruit trees, under the oaks, and out to the boat dock. He spent the entire day alone feeling lost, abandoned, cheated. He could hardly keep his breath...tears flowed down his cheeks as his throat choked up throughout the day, causing him to breathe with difficulty.

Helene spent the day in her house, her refuge, only venturing out to the porch in the afternoon to sit and watch her husband in his mourning, emotionally reaching out to him, being visible as he would glance over at her from time to time...

...in denial, she thought. *Maybe it isn't so...maybe the Air Force made a mistake...maybe he just bailed out and he's now a prisoner...maybe...?*

Alexander and Helene, in their own ways, close to each other and dedicated to their children, spent the next several days aimlessly existing in their pain, sorrow, and emptiness. They felt a gaping void in their hearts that only a parent who has lost a child could understand. Helena silently took over the household chores, allowing her mother to be free to do nothing but reminisce and wonder what might have been.

Alexander, feeling pain as never before, recalled the hurt when his mother died...and the terrible emptiness in his stomach and the pain in his heart when he had to leave Madeleine behind. But this was even worse, as though nothing before had prepared him for this day...nothing. "Dear God," he prayed, "what did I do to deserve this? Why? Oh, why did Michael have to suffer and then leave us? He was so young...so good. He was my heart, my eyes, my life. All I have endured, all I have done was for Michael and Helena... not for me. Please don't let anything happen to Helena, nor to Helene. Let us have peace. Help us...guide us." Then, gazing at the clouds overhead with his arms stretched out to the side, he exclaimed aloud, "Michael, where are you, my son? *Where are you?*"

Day after day he sat on the dock, his glazed eyes staring into space, alone with his memories, thinking, lamenting, and mourning his greatest loss. Alexander ached inside. Only when Wilbur came by after several days to check on his friend did he feel able to go to Helene and Helena, exhausted, drained, cried out.

"I have no more tears, Helene," he said as he embraced his wife. "I'm lost, but Michael has been with me all these days. Now I want *us* to be together, Helene." Looking around, he asked, "Where is Helena?"

"She was visited by her girlfriends who learned the news about Michael. I believe that after the Air Force messengers left me that day, they informed the mayor too. Then word spread quickly. I thought it would be better if she spent some time with her friends. You remember when the McLaughlin boy was killed in the Normandy invasion? Well, the town found out the same way. Alexander," she said softly, "sit with me. We need to talk." Looking at him, she reached for his hand. "We must honor Michael. We must remember our son, and we must live on. We have to somehow be strong for our daughter. Helena needs to see us strong, don't you agree? Yes, my husband, we are sick with pain. Our loss is great and we will never get over...this." She stopped to breathe, stammering now, "...get over...I don't think I can even say the word..."

"Get over losing our only son, Helene?" Alexander interrupted. "I don't believe a father can ever get over the loss of his only son...not me, anyhow. But you're right, Helene. As always, you are right. Yes, we must honor Michael and we will. And, I believe that he would want us to continue living our lives, as difficult, as almost impossible as it will be. Yes, Helene, together we will honor Michael's courage and bravery. But it will be hard, Helene, it will be hard. He was my life." Then he added as he lowered his head, "No, Helene, I don't think I'll ever get over losing my only son."

After weeks of near sleepless nights, Alexander awoke one morning and went for a walk toward the lake, simply to think and be alone. He thought for a long time on all that had happened and what his life would be like without his son. Finally, his sadness gave way to acceptance. And he began to look at life in a different way.

"Meaningless!" he exclaimed aloud. "My life would be meaningless without Helene and Helena. Yet I haven't spent enough time with them, working all the time. That is wrong...and I must change my ways."

Until now he had worked diligently, more than anyone, more than anyone should expect, seeking financial security to be able to provide all he could for his family. But now, Michael's death had shown him how fragile life could be. He made a resolution that his future would become very different by focusing on the emotional needs of his family and the needs of others less fortunate.

Alexander, experiencing a veritable spiritual epiphany, began to develop interest in local charities. He knew from his impoverished youth the misery and pain of lack of food and medical attention. He became more aware of those who had so little as he inquired into the needs of others in his post-war community and learned of veterans going through painful rehabilitation.

He became acutely aware of the enormous needs of so many wounded. Each day he visited hospitals in Tampa or Orlando. He witnessed many unable to take care of themselves. These wounded veterans required profound assistance and were really only teenagers or in their early twenties. "They're so young," he would tell Helene. He was overwhelmed by the sacrifices these young people had endured for him, his family and the nation to preserve their freedom.

He even began to visit the children's health center in Tampa, then the one in Orlando. Each time he saw poor, hungry children, he remembered his own youth, recalling his difficult days with an empty stomach, watching his friends in the village begging for food. As he and Helene visited with these poor children, his throat would choke. His eyes would well up with tears; he felt their pain in his heart. Almost immediately, he would kneel beside them, embracing each child one at a time. He knew deep down how they felt. And he knew he had to find ways to help.

During World War II, Alexander and other successful businessmen had formed the Florida Cattlemen's Association, a strong financial and political force in Florida. Their influence at the capitol in Tallahassee was becoming as powerful as any group in the state. Now, Alexander, keenly aware of the health care needs of others, especially injured young people, met with his friends and proposed that they form a foundation to take the lead in providing health care and rehabilitation throughout the Central Florida region.

They started small, first focusing on the veterans' needs at the Tampa VA rehabilitation clinic, then creating new health centers in Sanford, Bartow, and Kissimmee as they sought more support from political leaders in Tallahassee and Washington. Alexander met with his cousins, the Chalhoubs, in Palm Beach, and friends in Miami to use their influence to obtain state involvement and financing that would improve the lives of poor families, handicapped children, and impaired veterans. He was turning his talents and focus in a new direction, helping those outside his family for the first time, becoming very involved in their health care needs. He tapped deeply into his personal resources to finance the Boys and Girls Club in Kissimmee. He generously supported similar efforts for rehabilitation clinics in Tampa and Orlando.

He enjoyed having Helene and Helena accompany him on his visits to the hospitals, and clinics and welcomed their support of his endeavors.

"We have the means to do God's work," Alexander would say.

"I'm grateful," Helene would proudly answer.

That is how, in the early 1950s, he met a fellow Lebanese immigrant in Miami, Anthony Abraham, who would become one of his dearest friends.

CHAPTER 43

In 1948, three years after World War II changed the world and her family forever, Helena Thomas enrolled in Vassar College, the same year François began his two years at the Sorbonne. Despite her father's "traditional" thinking and his wish that she stay nearby, Helena finally won him over. Alexander relented as he came to realize that his daughter was determined, independent and stubborn—a mirror image of himself.

"What can I do?" he shrugged as he rhetorically asked his wife, Helene.

"Dad, I'm not ready to get married, and I want to see more of the world. Times are changing and I want to be part of it. I know that it may be hard for you to understand, but since the war, lives of women will never be the same. Many of us are not in a hurry to get married, have children, and ignore what we feel inside. Sure, I want children someday, but only if I find the right man, and after I have tried my own wings for awhile. During the war, Dad, women flew airplanes; they worked in factories; they were in the Pacific and in Europe. I think I am feeling what you felt when you left Lebanon for America to find your destiny. I'm so much like you, Dad, and just because I'm a girl doesn't mean I can't try, does it?"

Alexander, listening intently to his daughter, now a woman, and looking into her pleading eyes, couldn't decide if he was sad from lamenting the passage of his "little girl" into a young woman, or feeling pride and reluctant understanding. Somehow, his daughter profoundly reminded him of her mother when he first met Helene. She too was a "free spirit." And for an instant, she reminded him of his lost love, sixteen-year-old Madeleine when they met and he became so enchanted by her lust for life, her youthful exuberance and optimistic sense of adventure. *They are the same.* After some thoughtful moments, he smiled and reached to Helena with both arms, with the love a father has for his daughter. As she stepped toward him to be received into his beckoning arms, they embraced and both felt loved...and trusted. Smiling, Alexander held her close and tightly drew her to him. "I love you, my little girl, my dear Helena. You bring me joy. I hope you can understand too what I am feeling. It seems the lives of men are going to change because the lives of women are changing so much." He shrugged, "Perhaps that is the way our lives will be. *C'est la vie.*"

It wasn't easy for Helene and Alexander to say goodbye as she boarded the train at the Kissimmee station, bearing all sorts of luggage, hugs, kisses, farewells, and best wishes from all her high school friends that September day.

"*Allah ma'ak, y'slemlie,*" Alexander and Helene whispered into her ears as they hugged her and kissed both her cheeks. Write often."

While embracing, Helena whispered to her father, "Dad, you are going to be proud of me, I promise, but I think I want to be like you. I don't think I'm cut out to be a housewife. Times are different. It'll be fine, you'll see." Then she squeezed her father and kissed both his cheeks.

"I'm always proud of you, Helena!" he exclaimed.

"I love you, Mom and Dad," Helena yelled from the rail car steps. "I love you too," she yelled as she waved to her buddies and friends from school. "See you at Christmas, y'all."

As Alexander watched his beautiful daughter leave, he felt the same emotional pangs of emptiness and loss in his stomach that he felt watching Madeleine standing on the Marseille dock, so long ago, and he found himself rubbing her ring as he waved to Helena. "We will miss her terribly," he said to Helene as he wrapped his arm around his wife. They both felt their bodies slump with sadness, yet with pride and a sense that their "baby" was becoming a woman, stretching out her wings and leaving the nest.

"The house will seem very empty now with her gone," sighed Helene sadly as she closed her eyes, tears running down her cheeks.

Helena, meanwhile, put her bags away, settled in her seat, leaned back, closed her eyes, and with a silent smile of pride and feeling a sense of wonder, whispered, "Here we go! I wonder what it's going to be like at Vassar."

Helena's initial year at Vassar College was an adventure she would never forget. Everything and everyone were so different. Her classmates were mostly from the Northeastern states, although many came from major cities of Ohio, Michigan, and Illinois. She reckoned she was the only freshman from Florida. All were from upper income families, as this was, indeed, one of the finest, and most expensive, women's colleges in the country.

After World War II, women were becoming more independent, but yet not universally so. Lots of Helena's college friends clearly were sent there by their parents to become "perfect mates" for up-and-coming young men from wealthy families attending Harvard, Dartmouth, Brown, Yale, and the other nearby top Ivy League schools.

So, attending Vassar was a special introduction for Helena into an entirely different social world. The people were different. Their speeches, their interests, their social ways were all different. Almost all were from multi-generational wealthy, "old money," families. Some were down to earth, and others were, frankly, spoiled brats or "princesses."

She found the mountains of upstate New York exciting, especially during her first autumn with the colors everywhere. "I love the maples, especially when the sun is bright on them," she exclaimed. It was certainly different from the flat, open pastures and citrus groves of Central Florida. To some girls, she seemed like a backward "hick," but in time her confidence and Southern charm won over most of her classmates once they got past their initial elitist prejudices, though there were a few who let Helena know that she was "different," meaning less, and expected her to prove herself to them.

She was keen on getting good grades, especially in economics, accounting, and French: her favorite subjects. She also found time in the winter to learn to snow ski, especially after seeing her first snowfall that November of her freshman year.

In the spring, she learned to play lacrosse, wearing knee socks and skirts to play organized sports for the first time in her life. Already athletic, once she figured out the rules of this new physical game, she played well. But she wasn't that interested in team sports, especially when she was faced with the tricks a few of the girls played on her. Some seemed unable to accept a "cowboy" in their midst, her nickname to a few.

Some rode horses to be sure, but jumpers or dressage on English saddles, always formally attired, and quite strange to her. Helena kept slipping off the saddle. "Where's the horn, anyway?" she asked more than once.

Helena was really dedicated to her studies in her junior year. After two good years of excelling in Accounting, Micro- and Macroeconomics, and corporate finance, she was called in by her adviser.

"Thank you, Miss Thomas, for coming." Her career adviser, Frances Biddle, standing in welcome, nodded with a practiced firm business-like handshake and slight smile. "Do sit down, my dear." She was dressed in a tailored dark suit and crisp white linen blouse.

"Good morning, Miss Biddle. Have I done something wrong?" She perched on the edge of a chair and pulled her long, flowing dark brown, almost black, hair behind her ears and shoulders. She knew her hair was part of her identity at this campus occupied by mostly blonde or light-brown haired women.

"Oh no, my dear. On the contrary," Miss Biddle responded quickly as she sat down in her leather chair behind an antique, grand, oversized desk, selected precisely for its imposing size and shape in an effort to intimidate anyone who ventured into Miss Biddle's "lair of wisdom," as it was known among the dormitories. Helena registered Miss Biddle's formal, dark, pin-striped, mannish suit.

"It is my responsibility as your career advisor to be ever mindful of your progress here at the college. You know, although I am from Philadelphia, I attended Vassar, not Bryn Mawr, and though it may seem decades ago, it really wasn't *that* far in the past," she smiled as she spoke. "I graduated in Administration Studies with a minor in Sociology. Of course, that was before the war and, since then, there have been enormous changes in curricula as well as an explosion in career opportunities for women. It's about time I'd say."

Pausing, Miss Biddle carefully watched Helena's eyes for her silent response and seeing none, continued, "I think, strange as it may seem, the women of the world, certainly in America, must look to the events of World War II as the watershed of opportunities for women. It unleashed women as a group, proving to the men that we can indeed perform and even excel in many of the careers heretofore not available. I mean, it's obvious to anyone with half a brain, and that definition, I suppose, sadly, would clearly include most men," she laughed out loud at her joke, "that if women could successfully weld war planes together, fly them across the country as did the WASPs at only eighteen to twenty years of age, then women can, should, and *must* be accepted in the halls of corporate America."

Helena smiled at the sexist comments but made no reply.

"And that, Miss Thomas, brings me to your career discussion."

Helena stifled a smile as she observed Miss Biddle, heiress to a centuries' old Philadelphia blue blood family, go through her programmed presentation. The students referred to her as "Biddle." Her close friends in Philadelphia nicknamed her "Frankie." Every young girl in Philadelphia society had cute nicknames it seemed to Helena. Like "Marts" for Martha, "Middie" for Mildred, or "Boots" for Barbara.

Watching Miss Biddle, nearly a campus legend for her presumptive snobbery, pedantic speech, and yet, "right-on-the-money" information, advice and counsel, was something Helena had actually looked forward to. Each of the girls who had already gone through this junior year series of private meetings at the dorm laughed about the performance, the bashing of the "men's world," and championing the rise of women in business and the preservation of Anglo-Saxon cultural excellence.

After flipping through several stacks of files on her desk, glancing up and down with a frown, first at Helena's face, then back down to her papers, Miss Biddle found the file she was looking for. She lifted her head, exposing a prim tortoise headband keeping her hair pulled away from her face in the conservative pageboy style, and assumed an expression of superiority. Miss Biddle thrived on control and intimidation in keeping with Machiavelli's *The Prince* which sat prominently displayed on the dark mahogany end table by the couch.

Helena shifted in her chair, hoping the preliminaries would soon give way to substance. Furrows appeared on her forehead reflecting her growing impatience and concern. *Where is this going?* she asked herself as she looked around the tastefully decorated room with several exquisitely framed Currier and Ives prints hanging on the walls.

"As I was about to say," began Miss Biddle, smiling slightly at Helena to get her attention, "it is time we at Vassar present the best we have to offer to the best in our corporate community, Miss Thomas. Your excellent grades, your research projects, and comments from your professors indicate, in my opinion, that you could have an excellent future in banking. Perhaps even in international banking which is opening up nicely since the war. You are studying French and you speak fluent Arabic. I believe you have outstanding opportunities you must be aware of and should prepare for. It won't be easy, my dear. And you might get disappointed by America's corporate reception. But I think it's worth your while to seek such a career."

"The Rockefeller family is quite enlightened, and so that might make an international career possible for a woman at Chase Bank in New York. It is a fine institution as are J.P. Morgan, and New York City Bank. But I'd prefer you consider becoming part of Chase. You may even want to consider obtaining a Masters Degree in Economics or Finance.

"In sum," Miss Biddle concluded after twenty minutes of discussion, indicating she had reached her decision and singular advice, "if you agree, I will do what I can to help you become the first Vassar graduate to be placed in Chase Bank's International Department. My dear Helena, you are in exactly the right place at the right time. With your dedication, you should succeed very well, and, in doing so, pave the way for young women who will follow you. You will meet some of the finest and smartest people in the world. And with your Middle Eastern heritage, who knows where this could lead?"

Helena was stunned by this presentation, believing she would simply complete her years at Vassar, graduate, enjoy a few weekends in New York or skiing in the Adirondacks, then return to Kissimmee and get a job at one of the banks in Tampa, Osceola or in Polk County. Now, however, this conversation presented a whole new world she would never have dreamed existed. And she liked the feeling of adventure it brought her. She was encouraged, and began to change her opinion of this austere woman.

"Miss Biddle, what if I *were* interested in locating in New York and possibly joining Chase Bank. What is your advice to me? And do you really think a woman, especially a cattle rancher's daughter from Central Florida could obtain a job offer from Chase Bank that isn't just a glorified secretary's job, or someone's assistant with no real career possibility?"

"It's true my dear that you would probably find returning to Central Florida more comfortable, not nearly as stressful, and monumentally simpler and easier, but without much of a future. And I believe that while New York City can be a frightening challenge to most anyone, to a person as adventurous and intelligent as you, it could be that you would find the experience extraordinarily rewarding, difficult as it might be. It's not as civilized as my hometown of Philadelphia to be sure, but it *is* the banking center of the world. You would be in a new environment that surpasses almost anywhere else in the world. The men may find in you a competition they will try to undermine, and maybe even try to do you in. So, if you decide not to consider this option, my dear, I certainly understand. At the same time, I have already spoken to Carole Whitaker, your classmate, about the same possibilities. You know 'Car' don't you? She's from the Whitaker family of Haverford outside of Philadelphia. She is considering the same option I'm presenting to you."

"Oh sure, Mrs. Biddle. 'Car' and I are close friends. She's one of the nicer girls I've met from Philadelphia. Some of the others are such snobs, you know. But not 'Car.'"

"Snobs? From Philadelphia?" snorted Miss Biddle in mock insult, thrown aback by this charge as she brought her hand to her breast, clearly chagrined at the label by this "cowboy" from Florida. "What do you know about snobs, Miss Thomas? I can tell you a few things, and Philadelphia is, contrary to popular opinion, hardly a place that condones snobbery, my young impetuous friend. Justifiable pride to be sure, but not snobbery. Please rethink your opinion, my dear."

"If you say so, Miss Biddle, if you say so." Helena smiled as she contritely lowered her head, looking up from the tops of her eyes, knowing she had made a *faux pas*.

"So, do I understand you would be open to pursuing this course of action?"

"Miss Biddle, I really appreciate what you have told me. I believe that yes, I would like to pursue what you've described. But I think I should speak to my parents. Maybe tonight." Shaking Miss Biddle's hand in a formal good-bye, she rose and left her office with a constrained excitement she had never felt before.

"Today is the greatest!" she whispered to herself as she nearly ran out of the Administration Building.

CHAPTER 44

Kissimmee
1949

One summer Sunday afternoon Abraham visited with his son at Alexander's lakefront home. Sitting side by side in rocking chairs on the porch, looking out over the expansive grassy lawn with scattered fruit trees and beyond to the breeze-blown, choppy waters of enormous Lake Tohopekaliga, they spoke with a strange foreboding sense of nostalgia.

"You have done very well, my son," he murmured with a sweep of his arm, "and I am proud of you. You have made a good life. Your wife Helene is wonderful and happy. That is a good sign. If a wife is happy, it is because her husband takes care of her needs...all of her needs. She adores you, and like you, has been devoted to your children. And now you are involved with many others' needs. I have watched you now these past, my goodness, nearly thirty years, and I am grateful to have you as my son."

Abraham paused, his forehead slightly furrowed between his eyebrows, eyes squinted, still gazing across the lake wistfully, searching his mind for the right words. Alexander couldn't help but wonder where his father was going with this because he had never begun a conversation in quite the same.

"I have decided, Iskandar, to return to Lebanon." He hesitated briefly, looking into Alexander's eyes for a visceral response. "I am in my late seventies, Milhelm is now a grandfather, and I miss Douma. I want to see my other son again. And I want to hold his children while I can. It is time, *Baba*. You are secure; you have fulfilled your destiny... your mother's wishes. Shortly, I will make arrangements."

Pondering his true issue, he tried to play down the potential danger in his next question of his son. "But, there is something I wish to discuss with you, *Baba*," (Abraham used his Arabic pronoun in referring to his son as he always did in personal discussions) "something I have wanted to discuss with you since the day I saw you arrive in New York from Marseille. I felt it best to wait for you to tell me, but you never have. So, now, I must ask you. Of course," he shrugged, "you don't have to tell me if you do not wish to."

"*Biyee*, what is it?" Alexander felt there was a deep concern in his father's carefully chosen words but had no idea where this conversation was leading. "You tell me you are leaving America now after so many years. My God, how wonderful it has been for me to work beside you all this time." Alexander laughed, "There have been terrible days and wonderful days, and there were days I was so angry with you; sometimes you are so stubborn. Sometimes. But there were so many good days; so many wonderful experiences. We have had a joyful life together."

"I am stubborn, Iskandar?" Abraham waved his arms in the air as he shifted in his chair, his voice increasing in pitch several notes. "You think it is I who am stubborn? How can you believe that? It is you who has been the stubborn one!"

Abraham laughed and slapped his son's thigh. They laughed together, enjoying a not so frequent happening. But, as both knew, they were secure with each other and they had done their best under very trying conditions: carving out a life as immigrants in a strange but free country, in the South Florida sub-tropical frontier with its swamps, droughts, floods, freezes and hurricanes. They came from not even being able to speak the language, too embarrassed to try lest it be too obvious that they were different from others. Now after nearly four decades since Abraham arrived, they were a significant and prosperous part of the regional community—well respected, and considered equals among their peers, influential in the politics of the agricultural community and at the state capitol in Tallahassee. They had done extraordinarily well.

"Even now, Iskandar, it is said that if a man seeks to become governor of Florida, he must first visit the Stewart brothers in Bartow, the Parkins in St. Cloud, and Alexander Thomas in Kissimmee. That is *something*, because this could not have happened in Lebanon. We were not of the right families, but here in America anything is possible. How I wish Milhelm had come with you." He paused to reflect. "It is too late now, so I must go to Douma and help the family, perhaps build them a home large enough for the entire family. It is still a very poor village."

"And, as for those houses I built for the poor workers here in Kissimmee during the years before the war, I will give them to our tenants. You don't need them. There are thirty-four now, and they have been good tenants. Before I leave, their homes will belong to them. Even after I leave, you must continue to send goods to our village."

"And your question, *Baba*. What is your question to me?" Alexander asked with a quizzical look.

Abraham shifted again in his rocking chair, faced his son and cleared his throat before he spoke.

"Your ring," he pointed to his son's hand. "What is the meaning of the gold ring you have worn on your finger since you first arrived in America?

You and I are not people of jewelry. You have not even worn a watch on your wrist, yet you have never removed that ring. Why is that?"

He was caught off guard. "It is nothing," he shrugged and turned his eyes away, not wanting to discuss the ring's meaning. He simply didn't want there to be any conversation about Madeleine because his sense of honor would cause him to feel betrayal to Helene and his family. It really was still on his finger out of habit more than anything else.

"It is something, Iskandar." Abraham raised his eyebrow. "It is important to you. You may not want to tell me, but it is not nothing, my son," he emphasized, as he focused on Alexander's eyes,

"Not now, *Baba*." Alexander smiled at the father he had always adored, always respected, and stood up. He slowly stepped down from the porch to the grass at the last step, knowing he must be honest with his father. He could not shrug this question away. *His father deserved better.*

"Walk with me, *Baba*," he said as he turned to look back at his father.

The two men, both with a slight thinning of hair, and nearly the same size now, a bit overweight, their belts slightly lower on their stomachs, strolled together on the broad green grass expanse toward the lake. Alexander led the way to the fruit trees and reached to his favorite tree where he picked a mature, burgundy-colored pomegranate so native to the Lebanese mountains.

"Ah, *remáhnet*," smiled Abraham.

"You see this fruit, Father? Like the fig trees and this pomegranate in my yard I have planted, I preserve my heritage so I will never forget the important times of my early life. I often walk here alone, tasting, when I can, the wonderful fruit of home. They remind me of mama and the village. It makes me happy."

Abraham could see his son's eyes moisten as they always did when Alexander was feeling something dear deep inside.

He handed the *remáhni* to his father who rolled the round, firm ball of fruit in his hands, feeling the hard, brittle skin, remembering the pomegranates that grew on the terraces of Douma before the locusts and the famine.

"Yes, Iskandar, I understand, holding this beautiful *remáhni* in my hands. It does bring me warmth and good memories."

"And this," Alexander said to his father as he reached into his pocket, "this is a stone from the mountain I brought with me so long ago. It was the last thing that I touched from the path above the village before I began my walk to Beirut. I have carried this stone with me since my last day in the village. It is always with me to remind me of where we come from. I will never forget my roots, *Baba*."

"But what does a mountain stone and a pomegranate have to do with your ring?"

"It is very much the same." Alexander, smiling slightly, whispered as he lowered his head in careful thought while fondling the ring with the fingers of his left hand, "This ring reminds me of my wonderful visit in Marseille. It was given to me by a dear friend, a friend of Hanna's as well.

Abraham touched his son's arm and said, "A good friend gave you that ring and you've worn it everyday most of your life? That is a good friend, son, a very good friend. I am happy for you."

He put his arm around his son's shoulder. "Was she very beautiful?" Abraham asked with a loving sort of mischievousness, delving.

Alexander nodded yes silently and smiled. *My father is so wise.*

Abraham could see from the look on Alexander's face that he had said all he was going to say about the ring. Noticing Alexander's slightly embarrassed responsive smile while listening to him, he also knew that the "friend" whose ring his son wore had to be very beautiful and very important. He didn't press the issue, realizing that Alexander had withdrawn, concentrating on his memories of Marseille. He could see his son growing pensive as his son's fingers gently fondled the ring. He felt Alexander's inner conflict, shrugged his shoulders and began walking ahead alone.

Alexander lifted his head and spoke to his father in a low and melancholy voice, "That was many years ago, *Baba.*" He tried to explain but was unable to remove the memories.

"Another time, Iskandar. Tell me another time, if you wish." He turned and reached for his son, wrapped his arms around his shoulders, received the same from his son, and felt a special warmth of a father-son embrace as they stood beside the beautiful lake, soft breezes on their faces, drifting clouds, and the sound of silence broken only by the lapping of the waves on the shore. It was an important moment of love, of mutual respect and bonding.

As he held his father, Alexander whispered to him, saying, "Yes, *Baba,* I remember her with great love. If you hadn't been waiting for me here, I would have stayed in France to remain with her. She was that important to me. But I have not permitted those memories to be part of my life with Helene. Helene is a magnificent, wonderful woman and fine mother of my children. She and my children have been the most important people in my life. As are you."

He did not speak of the cross his mother gave to him, now with Madeleine, as a symbol of his commitment to her, his first true love. *It is better that my cross remain my concern alone.*

Helene stood with her daughter on the porch looking at the lake, happy with her life, watching her husband with his father, turned to Helena and with a knowing smile said, "I'd better start dinner while those two men talk about life."

Except for their tragic loss of Michael, life had indeed become very good for Alexander and his family.

As they talked together, remembering, Abraham spoke. "My son, as I taught you when you were a boy in Douma, you have been a good teacher to your children about life. May Michael rest in peace," he whispered as he made the sign of the cross. "I have watched you with them...here in this very place...instructing them how to respect the land, to grow living things, to graft fruit trees...when and how to prune them, to respect the earth, to remember your heritage. Michael became a fine young man because of your closeness to him, Iskandar. We are a people who treasure the bonds of family and hold God close within the family. It is only because we have been so close that we have survived."

They were indeed very close as a family, and all who knew them recognized that as a strength. Yet, still dealing with the loss of Michael, they had overcome many challenges and difficulties, and had faced conditions that had brought down many of their neighbors, especially during the Great Depression when no one had *any* money. Everything was hard, sparse and trying. But they had survived the worst of times and, when conditions improved, together they enjoyed the best of times. They thrived through devotion to family, hard work, dedication, determination, faith, and to be sure, a stubbornness that would not let them quit under any circumstances. Quitting or giving up simply was not part of their beings, their heritage. They counted on each other throughout those years. Faith and enduring, resilience and tenacity were their strengths.

All of these characteristics were to be tested as 1949 came to a close. Helena, becoming more independent and more grown up each year, was in her junior year at Vassar. Wilbur was very much involved in running the businesses. Alexander found himself more and more involved in his continually expanding business enterprises of cattle, banking, citrus production, and juicing plants. Even so, he was very much focused on his growing philanthropic endeavors in health care.

His charities had become very important to him. He found himself increasingly networking with "the boys in Tallahassee" seeking state grants and support for establishing new hospitals and rehab clinics. Other times he represented the Florida Cattlemen's Association, and helped form the Florida Citrus Federation of growers, producers and transporters. Although Central Florida was still very rural, sparsely populated with small towns and few cities, it was becoming very important as a producing region.

Alexander was a very busy man in the prime of his life, dedicated to his daughter and wife.

Smiling, Helene proudly announced at the country club the night they happily celebrated their 25th wedding anniversary, "Alexander's life is his family, his businesses, and his charities. Our home is my domain. He is my husband, and I am his wife. We are and will always be partners. I pray we will be together forever." She laughed, "For at least another twenty-five years!"

The gathering of friends stood and applauded their beloved neighbors after her brief statement.

They belonged here, she knew, and the love of her friends and family showed on her happy, radiant face, especially when Alexander stood, walked over to her with a proud smile and embraced her.

But it was not to be.

CHAPTER 45

Vassar
May 1951

$\mathcal{H}$aving just completed her final exams at the end of her junior year, Helena felt really good about her grades and her college career. Gazing out the window, she thought about entering her senior year in the fall and how amazing it all was. She smiled at her roommate and said, "Next year should be a blast, Lucy!"

The phone rang loudly in the hall interrupting Helena's thoughts.

"Hello?" answered a sorority sister walking by, "Pi Phi house." Then she shouted, automatically, "Helena, it's for you. It sounds like it could be your Dad!"

Helena ran down the hall, grabbed the telephone and eagerly said, "Hello?"

"Helena, this is your father."

Your father? She knew instantly something was wrong. He never spoke like that unless he was very serious, very concerned. His voice was unusually nervous and sounded urgent.

She asked quickly, "What is it, Dad?"

"You must come home immediately. Your mother needs you by her side. She is very ill. It's serious. I need you here. And I need you now."

"Oh, my God," she stammered, "What? What is it?" Her heart was racing, not understanding how her mother could become so ill so quickly, with no warning.

"We are not sure, but we believe it is cancer. Come tomorrow, Helena. Call us as soon as you make your travel arrangements."

"Oh, my God, mama has cancer?" Helena uttered again as she put her hand to her head in disbelief at this frightening picture in her mind of her seriously ill mother as she hung up the phone. Tears welled up in her eyes and overflowed down her cheeks. Lucy and her other sorority sisters joined her in her room as she fell on the bed sobbing. She knew cancer was a certain death sentence.

Early the next morning they helped her get to the station where she caught a train for New York City. Her heart was filled with dread the entire seemingly endless trip home on the train, from New York to Philadelphia to Atlanta, Jacksonville, and finally Kissimmee, where she was met at the station with warm embraces from her father. While happy and grateful to see her, he could not disguise the ache he felt in his heart. This impending, frightening unknown thing called cancer had crippled his beloved Helene. By now, she was so weak that she was in bed almost all of the time.

Quickly they climbed into the car and drove to the house where Helene had had her nurse help her dress and brush her hair so that she would look her best for her daughter's arrival.

"Take me to the porch facing the lake," she had requested of her nurse. "I want to be there when Helena arrives. Not in the bedroom."

And that was where she sat in her rocking chair looking out over the lake, relishing her view she loved so much, her favorite place that gave her peace and serenity, when Helena leaped from the car and ran up the steps to the front door.

"Mama? Where are you, mama?" she cried out, running through the house.

"Out here, Helena," she called out weakly. "I'm on the porch. Come to me, my darling. Give me a hug. Oh, Helena, I'm so glad you are here."

She rushed to her mother. "Mama, what is it? You were so vibrant and happy at Christmas. What could have happened?" Helena's eyes began smarting, so she turned her face away so her mother would not see her sadness and fear. She could easily see her mother had already lost a lot of weight. Her cheeks were hollow, her eyes deeper.

"It's cancer, darling. It happened so fast. We didn't have any warning. At first, I just felt sick, like the flu or something. I thought maybe I was just tired after the busy holidays. The doctor didn't think it was serious either, so I took his advice and went to bed, took some pain killers, and simply waited to get better. Then, a few weeks ago, the pain began. It has gotten worse, darling, and no one knows for sure what to do. The doctor is hopeful, but so little is known about this disease. But now, at least, I am happy because I have my family with me. Even my parents, my sister Julia and Sam are here too. Everyone seems so worried. Your father has been wonderful, God bless him. Your father hasn't left the house since this all began. He refuses to leave me alone. He has grown so much more sensitive since we lost Michael in the war. I'm afraid for him, Helena."

Each day, Helena tended to her mother as she watched her grow weaker and weaker. On Sundays, she drove her into town to church and to see her friends. Alexander and Helena brought friends from the hospital auxiliary, the church, and Helene's social club as often as they could. Each day Helena and Helene sat side by side on the porch talking "girl talk," looking out over the lake as long as Helene could tolerate sitting, a blanket over her shoulders.

Actually, Helena began to find these hours, extending into days and weeks, a mixed blessing. While her mother's health deteriorated at an accelerating rate, she treasured their hours together.

"I love these quiet times with you, Helena. I'm sorry you had to rush home from school." She constantly held, patted or simply touched her daughter's hand as she spoke to her, not wanting to let go.

"Don't even think about that, mama. I am so glad we have this time together. It's bringing us even closer." She turned her head as her tears began again, not wanting her mother to see.

She listened intently as her mother recalled in whispers her youth in Boston, growing up with her sisters, describing what it was like during the "Roaring Twenties," Prohibition, then coming to this frontier town of Kissimmee, becoming part of "cattle country," and what it was like being married to Alexander.

"He's a good man, Helena. Your father had nothing. Your grandfather started here as a railroad notions peddler, as they called them back in those days. And, with all their hard work, long hours, dedication and determination, they provided you and me with a home...a beautiful home...food on the table, and, most important, he gave me you and your brother Michael. I will be forever grateful to him for my so many blessings."

She stopped for a moment and gazed out over the familiar waters of Lake Tohopekaliga, then turned to her daughter. "Helena, there is something I think you should one day speak to your father about after I'm gone. He has always shared everything with me. We always spoke of his boyhood days, his life before we married. He has always been faithful to me. But there is one thing he has never talked to me about. When we first married, I asked him to tell me about the ring on his small finger. He has never removed it. It's the one with the French cross in the middle with the letter "D" on the other side of the cross. All I know is a dear friend gave it to him in Marseille where he stopped over on his way to America. He was eighteen years old. He told me that it was a reminder of where he came from so that he would never forget his humble beginnings. He had so little when he arrived. That ring was his most valuable possession. He was penniless. He had only that and the clothes on his back, a small valise, and that silly stone he carries in his pocket. I believe it reminds him that he was so poor as a boy that he could not stay in France, but had to continue to America. Your father never wanted to forget that no matter how successful he became, he came to America to be free, to find his destiny and fulfill the wishes of his mother before she died. That's all. He has told me over and over how much he loves us and that he believes his mother knows in heaven that, indeed, he did fulfill his destiny with me, with you, and with Michael. It nearly killed him when Michael died." She paused, then added with a slight smile, "And now with his success here in America..."

"He always said he only wanted freedom and opportunity."

"So, Helena, that is all I know of his mysterious gold ring. Perhaps there is more. Perhaps not. Perhaps it reminds him of a young love. I don't know, and I never pursued the issue. It didn't matter. What came before me has not hurt me, and I accepted it. One day, you might ask your father to share the story of the ring with you after I'm gone. But I want him to know that if it belonged to his love before me, he should not feel any guilt. He should know I never thought anything of it. Tell him that, Helena...for me. Do you understand?" She yawned, "I'm tired now, Helena. Please take me to my bedroom. I feel sleepy."

It was only three months after Helena had received the call at college to immediately come home when her mother went to sleep for the last time.

That afternoon, after visiting on the porch overlooking the lake, Helena helped her frail mother into the wheelchair and pushed her inside to her bed in the master bedroom on the first floor. After helping her onto the bed as Helene winced with pain, though never complaining, Helena lovingly reached for the light blanket and pulled it over her mother's shoulders.

"Glass of milk, Mother?" she asked.

"Actually, Helena," she replied with a wan smile, "I think I'd like a glass of your father's orange juice."

"I'll squeeze some right now, Mom," Helena laughed as she stood and stepped toward the kitchen.

She grabbed the best Temple oranges from the refrigerator and squeezed them for her mother, then added the sweetest juice from the Honeybells. Calling out to her father sitting in the den to come join them, Helena poured three glasses of juice, put them on a tray, added a small vase of flowers, and carried it to the bedroom.

They toasted together as a family. Helena carefully lifted the glass to her mother's lips for a sip, and then placed it on the nightstand. Fluffing the pillows, she gently helped her mother lie back down. Helene softly rested her head on them and gratefully closed her eyes, smiling peacefully.

They all held hands as Alexander kissed his wife on the lips, whispering, "Helene, I love you so much. Always know that."

"Iskandar," she replied in a weak voice, "I am a lucky woman to have had your love and shared so much with you. Don't be sad, my husband." Then, after a breath, "Helena will need you now more than ever. And, Iskandar," she smiled as she used his native name deliberately, "please be good to yourself. Life is too precious. Don't be alone too much."

Helena, standing near her parents as they tenderly expressed their love to each other, felt tears welling in her eyes. She stepped to the bed, pressed her cheek to her mother's, kissed her on her lips and told her how much she loved her.

Alexander and Helena continued to sit on the edge of the bed holding Helene's hands, sensing that the end was near. Helena was stroking her mother's hair when she felt her head turn.

Helene's eyes closed and she quietly, peacefully exhaled for the last time. Suddenly she was gone from their lives.

Alexander, experiencing a *déjà vu*, recalled the last moments he had shared with his own mother when he endured the same tapestry of sadness, deep love, and the almost unbearable sense of losing one's mother. Just like what Helena was going through now. He recalled the sharp pangs of loss, the sense of despair of a mother, and now a devoted wife leaving him forever. And he began to cry.

"Don't do that, Daddy. If you cry now, I'll never get through this," Helena whispered, putting her arms over her father's shoulders as she felt her own tears begin to flow. "I don't think I'll ever forget her last minutes. I'm so glad we were here with her. I think that made it easier for her," she said as they hugged.

Alexander thought to himself, Helena is calling me "Daddy" again instead of "Dad" which she has used since she turned sixteen. She's my little girl again. He reached for her again.

After they hugged, Helena looked into her father's eyes and whispered, "I love you, Daddy."

CHAPTER 46

*H*elene's death was a major blow to Alexander and Helena, and, to the entire community. Like most families of the Mediterranean, the wife-mother is the glue of dedication and love that holds families together. She had carried the emotional burden of the family, smoothed over all frustrations, disappointments and conflicts within each member's life. "Momma" then "Mom" could and did solve everything. Every childhood sibling argument, scratch, bruise, or wound physically or emotionally got better and its pain seemed to mysteriously disappear when she gently touched or kissed the "*wa-wa*." She was an angel, doctor, psychologist, arbitrator, healer, sounding board, and storehouse of love and loyalty. She raised the children, she defended them when necessary. She taught them all she knew, arranged all birthday parties and social events and maintained relationships. She had helped Alexander with his English writing and speech, then sat beside Michael and Helena as they did their schoolwork.

And while the Thomas family was close and appreciative, they never knew what hit them when Helene passed from the scene. There became an absence that left her home so empty, a vacuum that seemed to virtually remove the air from the house. For Alexander, who had relied upon Helene for so long, there was an enormous loss of companionship. She was his partner in all things, his companion. She had nurtured him, provided food on his table, supported and understood him, constantly reassuring him of his importance in her life, in the life of the community, and in the lives of their children. She had a unique way of making sure he knew he was appreciated. She knew that "if Daddy, *Biyee*, is happy, everyone is happy." When as a child, helping set the table, Helena might ask, "Where is the head of the table, Momma?" Helene would reply with a smile, "Wherever your daddy sits is the head of the table." Alexander never felt the slightest competition from his wife, his helpmate. She was never a burden. He ran the businesses, working long hours at the store sometimes six and seven days a week, whether at the store, on the ranch or in the groves. Helene was mistress of their home. What she said in the home was the rule, as her husband never expressed disagreement in front of the children.

In their early years together, he had tried but never really could fully appreciate her loneliness in her new home away from her family because he was too busy, too focused on survival in his long days at work to be very involved with her emotional needs. He was on a mission then, anxious to make a good living to provide them basic needs like a home, food, a better future for them and the children. He was so frugal, resisting buying anything, never forgetting his humble beginnings when money was almost non-existent and nothing could be wasted. His clothes were always the same: dark wool slacks, white long-sleeved dress shirts that he wore open-necked with his sleeves rolled up two folds. He was content to wear his clothes until they wore out, and would have but for Helene taking care of that problem too. He always wore the same pair of laced, black, smooth-toed shoes, which he shined daily himself. He had one pair of boots for when he was on his horse or working in the pastures.

Now, only days after her funeral, he was suddenly aware of how lonely he was, how he missed Helene. The house was empty. Its heart and soul were gone.

What now? This house is too big now, he said to himself as he walked from room to room, subconsciously looking for his wife.

Helena had returned to Vassar College to complete her senior year. Alexander's father, Abraham, had returned to his beloved mountains in North Lebanon more than a year before Helene had grown ill. Michael was gone. And Alexander was alone…again.

And now, in 1952, at the age of fifty, Alexander was by himself in his beautiful but silent five-bedroom Victorian house situated on the shore of Lake Tohopekaliga overlooking the expansive rolling lawns to the lake shore, the boat dock, his garden, and his favorite giant oak trees. He still loved admiring and picking the fruit from his pomegranate and fig trees, and grapes from his small vineyard, all reminders of his youth in Douma. For years, Helene and the children harvested the young *wada-areesh*, the grape leaves, in the spring, while the new leaves were soft and pliant, so they would always have the leaves available for rolled grape leaves served with lemon juice or *laban* just as Alexander had eaten in his homeland as a boy. Helene always cooked his favorite meals for him: *kibbee, tabouleh, yabrah, imjadara ma' roz,* and *kafta.* He loved her *baba ghanoush,* and *hummus.*

And now, she was gone. Their home, her palace, was without its mistress. He was alone and quiet much of the time. He recalled Helene's infectious smile, her laughter, her humming as she prepared meals in her kitchen. It was so comfortable with her all those years. During the warm, breezy summer afternoons when business was slow and he didn't have to work until dark, they had walked together under the huge moss-draped oak trees they had preserved. He remembered fondly when they bought the land for their new home soon after their wedding. Helene had come with him to this hot, unfamiliar new frontier of Central Florida, away from everyone she loved and everything she enjoyed. But now, as he walked alone among the oak trees, almost every day that first year after the funeral, pondering his new life, seeking solace from his grieving, he found that he better understood her feeling of emptiness and loss as he himself now felt this gut-wrenching loneliness.

"Helene..." he cried out as he looked back from the trees to the Victorian railings of the porch, fully expecting her to be standing there where she always stood at the top of the steps by the post of the porch at the white railing. She would watch him with a loving smile, cherishing his presence, the father of her two beautiful children. She had always let him know that their companionship and marriage had completely fulfilled her. He felt rewarded by her.

But this day, like every day since her illness, he looked but didn't see Helene standing there. "I miss you, Helene," he spoke aloud as tears welled up. Then, he would turn and continue his stroll, alone with his thoughts, feeling the grass crunch under his feet, the familiar breeze on his face, watching the thunderclouds form in the summer sky. This became his daily ritual every afternoon since Helene's passing.

Even after taking the advice of his friend Abigail, and hiring a housekeeper and cook, Alexander still felt alone. So much was irreplaceable. He kept himself busy each day going into his office after sitting alone, eating the breakfast his housekeeper had prepared for him. He would read the morning paper on the leather couch, sipping coffee, with not quite the same familiar taste as Helene would prepare for him, then sitting at his desk answering correspondence, making his daily telephone calls to friends and business colleagues. Then, he would eat a light lunch consisting of soup and a sandwich, which soon became a very boring and uninteresting ritual. It wasn't like being with Helene when they often shared a *mezza* of olives, cheese, *hummus*, grilled lamb and salad, all eaten with *khobaz*, pita bread. As with Helene in those days, after his daily lunch he would drive to the ranch, saddle his horse, and ride, now alone most of the time, among his cattle, viewing his land, and thinking.

Many days, he found his solace on Sheikh as he would saddle up in the mornings, meet Wilbur, his closest friend, and ride through the herds in the pastures. They had been riding together, almost as brothers, for nearly thirty years, Wilbur in his sweat-stained, well-worn Stetson, and Alexander in his. They knew each other's mannerisms and priorities. Sometimes Wilbur would answer Alexander's questions before being asked. They were very close. Both understood the goals of the Thomas ranch, a major part of the growing, prosperous Thomas Enterprises, a conglomerate respected throughout

Central Florida, one of the largest beef production areas in the United States. The brand ATA was respected by everyone in the business from the feed providers to the railroads, from the trucking lines to the buyers, and from the major meat wholesalers across the country. Although people now rarely saw the master of the ranching family, they knew and respected his name.

Gratefully, Alexander was still an integral part of the leadership of The Florida Cattlemen's Association, wielding quiet but powerful influence in the office of the Governor, the halls of the State of Florida Senate and the House of Representatives in Tallahassee. He was a significant part of the financial strength of the important Central Florida counties, and was often consulted for his opinion on many issues confronting the enterprise and quality of life in Florida.

It was during the early 1950s when the U.S. Senate Reform Committee was investigating gambling in Florida, that Alexander and his Polk, Osceola, and Orange County colleagues were asked, "How far do you want this investigation to go? It could embarrass some powerful Florida leaders, especially in Miami and Jacksonville."

Remembering his son Michael's sacrifice, Alexander took the lead and became spokesman for the group, reflecting the conservative nature of Central Florida and recalling the returning veterans he tried to help. He responded forcefully, "My son, and the sons and daughters of many Floridians, rich and poor, white and black, fought in World War II to preserve freedom for all of us at great cost. Young lives were lost, limbs ripped from their bodies; they suffered much pain and destruction. Dammit! I don't want to see all those sacrifices wasted so that the poor souls in our state can lose everything they have at the gambling tables and casinos. No sir, we'd just as soon gambling in Florida be stopped, at least as much as it can be. So, go as far as you need to to get the head of that monster. Don't worry about who you find. Let the chips fall where they may."

The Kefauver Commission did just that, and many said they could not have gone so far had the determined but politically savvy Senator Estes Kefauver from Tennessee not gotten the green flag from the powerful cattlemen of Kissimmee, Bartow, Tampa, and Sanford.

With all of Alexander's charities and activities, he still maintained his original shop on Broadway even though he had sold his father's store when Abraham returned to Lebanon in 1949. He significantly expanded beef production to help meet the growing, almost insatiable demand for more and more beef products during the years following World War II. He often remembered swearing years ago, "I promise I'll always have plenty of food for my family."

The nation and Europe were faced with enormous pent-up demands for almost anything that could be produced. By the late-1950s, Americans were awash in money, demand, and a newfound ability to produce almost anything the world needed at breakneck speed, an enormous departure from the moribund isolationism of the 1930s. The "Sleeping Giant," as described by the Japanese Admiral after the attack at Pearl Harbor, had indeed awakened. Parents, mostly those who grew up with very little during the 1930s and 1940s, became determined to have and to provide for their children all that they didn't have while growing up. As more and more families acquired more and more pets as never before, all sorts of beef products were called on to provide food for this new phenomenon.

As a result, Thomas Enterprises was thriving beyond Alexander's wildest dreams. Earnings skyrocketed, each year far exceeding those the year before. Americans were traveling more on vacation, and many began leaving the cold winters of the North for the South. Visionaries declared there would be a major population shift from the northern "Rust Belt" states to the "Sun Belt" states, and Florida, with its disproportionate enormous coastline, pristine beaches, more than adequate supply of water and other resources, and temperate year-round winters, was sure to benefit. Land values began to escalate during the 1950s. Pastureland for which Alexander had paid only $2 or even $16 per acre was now worth over $100 per acre. His 30,000 acres were now of enormous value, more than three million dollars.

Even with all this happening around him, Alexander, a widower, found the days, weeks and months after Helene died to be empty and depressing. He missed Helene so much that staying alone in the house without her familiar voice was almost unbearable.

Some days he would sit on a porch chair and think about his youth in the mountains playing with his brother and his cousins, climbing the olive trees and the larger ancient cedars. Nostalgia had become his pastime, it seemed.

Other times he would recall his early years in Kissimmee, the embarrassment he shared with his father at not speaking English well, of being "different" for the first time in his life, being with his first American friend, Abigail, learning from her, and admiring her all those first days in America. He vividly remembered learning English from this young, exciting woman who might have been the mother of his children, but for her mother's prejudice and his father's insistence. He remembered Abigail's father, Big John, and the store he opened at eighteen. *Eighteen? Could I really have opened a store when I was just eighteen years old? My God, I was in a big hurry!*

And then he would recall sitting under the oak tree behind his store during the long, slow summer days, with his back leaning against the trunk, whittling a piece of wood with the penknife that he always carried with him, or practicing with his sling.

He smiled as he remembered the day he first met Helene in Boston. How cute she was at fifteen. And how lovely a woman she became by the time he went back to marry her. And how loving and loyal she had been as his wife, a dedicated mother of his children, and a caring daughter-in-law of his father. *All those years, even during the difficult times, she was by my side...all those years she never complained. How lucky I have been,* he thought. *How very lucky. And now, Helene, you are gone.*

"All I have are the memories," he confided in Wilbur on more than one occasion. "Michael is gone, and now Helene."

Once, he paused as he gazed across the pasture and said, "Wilbur, with all that we have built, I am still so empty. I'm not the sort to be alone."

One Sunday afternoon, with no work that had to be done, he took a walk across the lawn down by the lake. His thoughts deepened as he reached down, pulled up a long leaf of grass and stuck it in his mouth. His thoughts turned to the three women he had loved. *I had to watch my mother die too young. I had to leave my first true love, Madeleine, in Marseille. Now I must face life without Helene. Even my father has gone away. And my only son is gone.*

It was while riding across the pastures that he began to catch himself subconsciously fondling the worn gold ring on his small finger he had received from Madeleine.

He often found another haunting thought in his mind: *Helena will someday be married, raise her own children, and find her own destiny. That is how it should be, for it is written, "where you go, your children cannot follow...and though they came through you, they are not from you. You cannot be with your children forever."* He found himself reflecting on that as he reread the thought-provoking book *The Prophet*, written by Khalil Gibran, his countryman. This book of philosophy became his companion and made him proud. He had nearly memorized the book, he loved it so. It also provoked him into finding acceptance, healing, and a sense of the realities of life.

And so, on that particular day, reflecting on all these thoughts, he decided, *I must find what God wants me to do with my life now that it has changed so very much once again. I will pray on this. There is so much to do outside of myself. Many things. I can do more for the handicapped, for the poor children. I can prepare for the changes that are sure to come to Florida very soon.*

His life was a continuing metamorphosis from focus on survival, work and success to a more spiritual, giving response toward his human side and a growing passion for helping others.

CHAPTER 47

$\mathcal{A}$lexander rarely attended social events during the first few years following Helene's death even though others invited him to dinners, parties, soirees, and to political rallies in Orlando, Tampa, Miami and Tallahassee. Events he reluctantly agreed to attend were only those to which he would not have taken Helene. He just couldn't bear visiting people who would ask him so many questions and express their sympathy.

While he guarded his privacy and stayed in the Kissimmee area most of the time, he began to make time to visit his good friend Anthony Abraham and the Elias family in Miami, his cousin Elias Chalhoub in West Palm Beach, and the Barakat family in Jacksonville. Sometimes, when he didn't attend his own Episcopal church in Kissimmee, he would drive over to Orlando to visit his sister and attend her small Antioch Orthodox church.

Meanwhile, the recognition of Thomas Enterprises as one of the more successful businesses in Central Florida allowed Alexander to delegate more and more time and money as he was becoming a sought-after contributor to local health organizations providing health-care therapy, aid to the poor, and especially to underprivileged children's causes. His wisdom was sought even by boards of civic and business organizations of which he was not a member.

In Miami, Anthony Abraham, a treasured friend of Alexander, was building his automobile dealerships into a very successful operation. Alexander made it a point to buy all his vehicles from Anthony.

Anthony convinced Alexander to invest jointly in beachfront properties and vacant lands near the growing Miami International Airport. During the 1950s, they even ventured into investing in South Palm Beach County by purchasing farming tracts there. Sometimes they bought quarter sections of one hundred-sixty acres at a time for the going rate of $50-$70 per acre. During the 1950s and 1960s they occasionally bought property in Delray Beach and Boca Raton for $10,000 per oceanfront lot.

During Alexander's visits, they would spend a lot of their time together at Anthony's house just talking about life and sharing memories as they played their favorite table game, *towleh.*

"You can't beat oceanfront land, Iskandar," Anthony would say, addressing his good friend in his native language as they visited in his Miami home, "especially if you can live with the bugs! Water is like gold, you'll see."

"I don't know. They're asking a lot of money, Anthony. In Kissimmee, lakefront lots go for $500." Alexander's mind wasn't focusing on business as much as before, and Anthony could sense he had lost a lot of enthusiasm for work and was much more inclined to speak of life since he lost Michael and Helene.

Anthony, more familiar with land prices along the southeastern coast, and with a different perspective because he was from the North, would only smile and reply, "Iskandar, trust me. It will be like gold in time. You'll be pleased with these purchases in a few years. We have to be patient, my friend, and we can afford to be since taxes are so low."

Anthony and Alexander had much in common, the foundation of their long friendship. They both had come from poor beginnings and were almost the same age, Alexander being two years older. They arrived at almost the same time from Lebanon; Anthony in 1924 and Alexander in 1920. They both were young during the "Roaring Twenties" and fought the good fight during the rock-poor '30s. And both were anxious to succeed, were somewhat impetuous, but learned their lessons well from the land and stock market crashes.

Anthony began his career in Chicago in the industrial north, and had experienced the terrible stock market crash more than Alexander. But both were convinced from that experience that they would be better off owning land, not participating in the stock market or trusting banks. They looked to their basic businesses and land ownership for their success.

"I like land, Anthony. I can touch it, walk on it, look at it, and to me, land is the best you can leave your children."

They both had a common vision of Florida's future and were convinced long-term investing in Florida real estate was a wise decision.

"I did well in Chicago, Iskandar, but I got tired of the snow, the cold, and the difficulties of living in the north. That's why I moved to Miami. And I think lots and lots of people will continue to do the same. They will need new houses and places to shop. Yes, Florida's future looks good to me"

They spoke often of how wonderful it was to be in America, and how grateful they were that their fathers came to America. Both felt very fortunate to have prospered beyond their wildest dreams.

"We have received so many blessings, Iskandar. Just look at us. We have food to eat, clothes that fill the closets, financial security. We must find a proper way to give some of it back to America."

"I agree, Anthony," Alexander nodded in assent as he raised his small glass filled with *arak*, now milky-white from the melting ice, "and that is why I've gotten so involved in the health clinics for veterans in Tampa and Orlando. And as for you, I know how you have been helping the children of Lebanon by helping a new group finance new hospitals there, and even here in Miami."

Anthony smiled. "But we can do more, Iskandar. I've been looking for something that all of us from Lebanon could do together, even as we would still continue to help our own individual communities."

"We could pool our resources and bring in the Barakat family from Jacksonville, too," responded Alexander enthusiastically.

"And the Haddads and Mansours in Orlando and the Maloofs in Tampa," added Anthony. "Okay, let's have some fun. How about a game of *towleh*? We've had two glasses of *arak*, so we should both be bold in a game."

"Right you are, Anthony," he laughed in response, "and we both should be easy to beat too."

One day, the following month when Alexander was back in Kissimmee, the phone rang while he was at his desk reviewing the monthly figures from his various enterprises.

"Hello, Alexander Thomas speaking."

"Mr. Thomas, this is the operator calling. I have a person-to-person call for you from Archbishop Antony Bashir."

Alexander's mind raced, remembering his favorite cousin and childhood neighbor in Douma. They were playmates as boys. Antony was now an archbishop, he remembered, the Metropolitan of North America, the largest church of Syrians and Lebanese in North America. Then he heard the deep, familiar voice over the phone.

"Hello, Iskandar. How are you today?"

"*Sayedna* Bashir, it's good to hear from you. Your voice is so clear. Are you in Florida?"

"No, I'm in Los Angeles on an important mission and I need your help. Something wonderful is happening and you need to be part of it."

"You know, Your Eminence, the only time I remember ever saying 'no' to you was when we were boys in Douma and you warned me not to climb to the top of that tall cedar. You were right. That was the day I fell and broke my arm!"

Archbishop Antony laughed, "Yes, I remember." He chuckled again, "You were so sure of yourself. But you have always been sure of yourself. I remember you once told me, 'I want to be sure of myself ninety-five percent of the time and correct at least fifty percent of the time.' I never forgot that, Iskandar."

"Thank you. What can I do for you?"

"There is something you should know, and that's why I'm calling. Danny Thomas has begun a crusade. He is fulfilling a pledge he made to St. Jude years ago to build a shrine, and that shrine, he has finally determined, will be a hospital for sick children. It is to be called St. Jude Children's Research Hospital. Fundraising has begun by his friends in Los Angeles, New York City, and Detroit. Christians, Jews, and Muslims are joining together to make this dream of Danny's come true. It is a labor of love, of faith."

"Now," he continued with his sales pitch, "all Lebanese and Syrians in America are being called on to join this crusade. This hospital can be the single best way for all of us to thank America for the freedom, opportunity and prosperity that we and our families have received in this great country. Danny has formed a fundraising organization named ALSAC, which stands for *American Lebanese Syrian Associated Charities*, and *Aiding Leukemia Stricken American Children*."

"That sounds pretty impressive," Alexander interjected as the Archbishop took a breath.

"It is! This hospital will be located in Memphis."

"Memphis, Tennessee?" Alexander asked, surprised.

"Yes, Iskandar, Memphis. There are very good reasons that I'll explain later. I believe so much in this cause that I'm urging all Antiochan Orthodox churches in America to join in this crusade to find a cure for leukemia that kills more than 90% of the children with this cancer."

"*Cancer! I hate that word*," Alexander thought as he remembered Helene's pain.

"Iskandar, it's one of God's challenges to us. He's calling on us as human beings to find a solution. You must help us, cousin. Danny has taken on this mission and I can tell you, he has dedicated his life to it. He has already brought the Lebanese together with his success in Hollywood, and makes us proud of our heritage by making us laugh with his weekly television program."

Alexander smiled remembering the last episode of "Make Room for Daddy." Listening patiently, he waited for his passionate cousin to pause so he could respond. He also remembered that terrible illness robbing him of his beloved Helene.

"Now you've caught my attention. I've watched Danny's show every week for a long time. It's obvious he's proud to be Lebanese. And I really laugh at his 'Uncle Tanoos.' I think we all can identify with him since we all have our own version of 'Uncle Tanoos.'"

Archbishop Antony picked up on his cousin's interest and, being an experienced at fund-raiser, knew exactly what to say next.

"Danny is having fund-raisers in most major cities, including Miami.

Mike Tamer is committed to this cause, Iskandar. He is a one-man campaign, and running this massive effort. He's from Indianapolis, the president of the Midwest Federation. Can you believe it? He took a year off from his business to devote himself to raising funds for St. Jude! Mike is the driving force with Danny."

Enthusiastically, he continued, "Danny is looking to his people, and I'm asking you, to help be responsible for funding the operating costs of St. Jude." He paused just a second to catch his breath. "Most of the money needed to build the hospital has already been raised, Thank God. But we need more. You've been without Helene for some time and hardly anyone in our community has seen you lately. Now it's time for you to get involved in this wonderful cause. Be a leader. I am aware of your generosity in Florida. Anthony Abraham down in Miami keeps me informed. It is good you donate so generously, Iskandar, and now I am asking you to give even more. Your cousin Elias Chalhoub is already on the Board of Governors. I want you to join him."

Alexander could always count on his cousin to find a painless way to get in his pocket. He smiled, knowing the Metropolitan was wearing a slight smile as he went to his favorite closing.

"I am counting on you to match Anthony, Iskandar."

How many times he had heard the Archbishop utter those very words when he stopped by to visit on those occasions while he was in Florida. The scenario was always the same. After a fine dinner served by Helene, they and the children would sit around the table for hours listening to *Sayedna* Bashir, one of the most revered Lebanese religious leaders in the world. He was beloved by all, no matter what church they belonged to. His sincerity, humility, and dedication to God's works were renowned. His quick sense of humor was always part of his persona that endeared so many to him. "Even the Pope is my good friend, Iskandar," he would say with a proud smile.

The Metropolitan paused and Alexander heard him whispering, "Here, Danny," as he handed the telephone to Danny Thomas, "speak with your brother."

Listening to Danny himself and feeling his enthusiasm, Alexander was quickly convinced that his decision now was not if, but how much. After Danny made his pitch, Alexander knew he was committed.

"I'm with you, Danny, and I have friends I will speak with."

Danny then moved on and asked, "Can you come to Miami and meet with Mike Tamer and me? There will be a fine dinner. It's being sponsored by Anthony Abraham. Do you know him?"

"Know him? I sure do," Alexander replied, smiling, thinking how much more he was going to have to donate to keep Anthony at bay! At the same time, he felt a little upset with Anthony for not calling him first.

"How long has Anthony been involved? When did he agree to sponsor a fund-raiser?"

Alexander was just like the others in his community. Now he was in friendly competition with his friend, exactly what the Archbishop and Danny were hoping for.

Danny knew his brethren. "Nobody wants to be first and nobody wants to be last." He laughed, understanding what Alexander was thinking. "I just now spoke with Anthony and asked him. *Sayedna* Bashir and I have been on the phone for hours setting up dinners around the country. Why do you ask?"

"Well, Anthony and I are very close and he'll brag to me about underwriting the Miami dinner without me. And now it's too late. So why don't I organize another dinner in Tampa? Then you could make both cities on the same trip! As a matter of fact, I'll even match Anthony's contribution!" Alexander laughed.

"Okay, Iskandar, I'll call Anthony and tell him. But be prepared, you know Anthony, if he finds out what you are doing, he might even increase his contribution."

"Well, let me know if he does. I wouldn't be surprised," Alexander chuckled, thinking. "God, I love being part of this family. Let me know your schedule, Danny."

"I'll have my office contact you later today, Iskandar. The Archbishop sends his warmest regards. *Shookrun. Allah ma'ak.*"

With a smile, Danny placed the phone on the cradle and shook hands with Archbishop Bashir as he jammed one of his legendary Macanudo Churchill cigars into his mouth.

Alexander felt uplifted from this conversation as he hung up the phone and swiveled his chair around to look out the window of his office at the lake he loved so much. Pulled out of his doldrums, he now knew he would be among people of his homeland on an important mission...together. He felt included now, no longer alone.

He leaned back, chuckled to himself and murmured, "I wonder how much *that* phone call is going to cost."

CHAPTER 48

Nearly two years after Helene's death, Alexander knew he would have to stop living in the past and find a way to begin a new life. He felt a deep sense of emptiness without a woman's love. Alexander never liked being alone, although in truth one couldn't tell by watching him. He always seemed so focused on his work.

Sitting still in his saddle each day looking over the herd, often crossing one leg across the horse's withers, leaning back in the saddle and feeling the breezes on his face, a Stetson hat protecting his eyes from the bright sun, Alexander, not as content as he looked, would proudly survey part of the thousands of acres of his holdings and meditate on his life, thinking of where God would take him now that he had no companion.

He found himself thinking more and more of Madeleine, unable to escape the gnawing feeling in his stomach, the increasingly aching affection he still felt for her that he had been able to put aside in respect for Helene for so long. He began to realize that his thoughts of Madeleine were becoming a larger part of his consciousness after relegating those memories of his first love and the weeks they shared in Marseille to his subconscious years ago, where they had remained undisturbed for nearly thirty years.

Even though he could keep very busy most days, his afternoons and evenings were very lonely. More and more he found himself thinking of his lonely life, of Madeleine, recalling the loveliness of her face, her smile, her touch, her laughter…the ring…Notre-Dame-de-la-Garde…*Les Calanques*.

He was very much aware that he had to respect Helene's memory, yet he was inching day by day toward a new confrontation with his destiny.

On Christmas of 1958, Helena flew in from New York where she had gone to work for Chase Bank after obtaining her Master's degree. She did indeed find the culture at Chase to be friendly toward the few women who worked in the International Corporate Finance Department. Her year of graduate school at Radcliffe, the only quality graduate school where women could obtain such a degree, helped her career possibilities enormously. Coupled with her fluency in four languages, Helena's skills were in great demand. She was often asked her views on the opportunities to do business in Europe and in the Arab countries of the Middle East. Since her father had often explained to her the culture of Beirut, the international banking of that key city and profit center, she was well versed, and becoming an important resource of insight. It also helped her career that she had spent the months following Radcliffe working in Paris and Geneva in an exchange program with Credit Suisse. When she could, she would travel to other cities and spend "familiarization periods," as the bank called them, in their offices in Beirut, Athens, Amman, Baghdad, and Dubai. She had become one of the few true internationalists in the bank, called on to make sure those who would travel to those countries representing the bank were well versed in the local cultural protocols. In a word, she had become an important asset to the international post-war vision of the bank's global interests, to say nothing of her polished and graceful beauty that often belied her sharp mind and perspicacity. She was determined to succeed in her career, and, like her father, was resilient, and tenacious. She conscientiously watched and learned from everyone around her, chose her mentors carefully, was sensitive to interoffice politics…not participating…which only added to her mystique…and aligned herself with her mentor and the bank's leaders.

"Daddy," she told her father during one of their bi-weekly telephone conversations, "I really love travel to the Near East. I always get chills when I'm asked to visit our offices in Beirut, thinking of you as a young man there."

"Did you ever get to Douma?"

"Gee, Daddy, it's always so rushed…in and out. Most of our meetings are at the golf club near the airport south of Beirut. I even met Mr. Marcel Kabani who owns the club. He's so nice."

The bank involved Helena in much of their Near East growth so that by the end of her first year at the New York offices, Helena was considered a "rising star." But of course, the possibility of joining the upper ranks of any major bank in America was still exclusively for men, and she knew it.

She knew, therefore, she might not stay with Chase under those circumstances more than five years. After that? Who knew? Maybe the tugging in her heart to return to Florida would be too much to overcome. Yet, she was determined to learn all she could, advance within the bank, make friends and business contacts of those she would see again, making sure she left favorable impressions everywhere. What Helena, this striking, tall, olive complexioned beauty, found was that men wanted to be around her. Her ebullience, founded on solid self-esteem and confidence soared when she stepped into a meeting, smiling and upbeat. She was not at all intimidated, and became more and more comfortable as her involvement grew. Her loyalty, love of life, and ready smile made her all the more attractive. Her laugh was infectious and disarming.

She was very smart in banking and had learned and believed in the bank's purpose: "We lend money to help good companies, we want it back, and we charge interest for using it. What's so complicated about that?"

She had indeed made her father proud as she had promised, and when she came home for Christmas, she announced her holiday plans.

"I can only stay a week, Dad. I promised to go on a bank conference trip to Garmisch, near Munich, for New Year's. We'll all go skiing too. I hope you don't mind, *Biyee?*"

"You're skiing in West Germany? Why not Switzerland?" asked Alexander.

"Actually," smiled Helena, "we have found that the West German companies have come back strong during the ten years since the end of the war, and several leaders of European industries will be there. France too has grown, but their political situation, like Italy's, is still a problem; too many Communists and banks hate Communists. Now, with the success of the Marshall Plan, the European countries have really rebounded. So, after our holiday in Garmisch, a team of us is going to be calling on companies in Munich, Frankfurt, Stuttgart, and Marseille, France. I think I'll be in Marseille for more than a week."

"Marseille? Why Marseille?" Alexander quickly asked in a pronounced tone of voice that surprised his daughter. *Madeleine...I see her smile.* The sound of the city's name stirred Alexander as he subconsciously twisted the ring.

"Our research indicates there is a terrific potential in Western Europe, particularly in France, West Germany, Spain, and even Switzerland. But Credit Suisse has a virtual monopoly in Switzerland for now. Spain and even Portugal have some strange laws that are so different from English Common Law that we are familiar with. So, we think we can do just fine by focusing on England, France, and West Germany, and staying out of Spain and Portugal for the time being."

She continued enthusiastically, "Marseille has always been a vital port of call and departure for shipping and trading companies. It has quite a history too."

This last remark got Alexander's attention. "Yes, it certainly has quite a history, Helena," he replied as he thought of his own history there while he rubbed the ring with his left hand.

"I may spend a lot of time in Marseille as well as Paris, Dad."

"Hmmm," said Alexander. "So, you will be in Marseille after New Year's. Do you know that I lived in Marseille for nearly six weeks, Helena?"

He looked at his hands and saw his finger fondling the ring. When he looked back at his daughter, he saw she too was watching him rub the ring. He also saw her move her eyes from the ring to his eyes, tacitly asking him to say something. He put his hand away.

"Of course, I was just a boy then, in 1920, after the first war."

During those times alone or when Alexander visited his sister and her family in Orlando, his emotions would do battle in their ambivalence. Leila had her husband, her home and her family, including three grandchildren, and he was happy for her. But his visits reminded him too of what was missing in his life. Without Helene in his life, he really had no sense of belonging to someone. His desire to change that caused him to think more and more of Madeleine, and their love and intimacy in Marseille. He realized that those characteristics he loved in Helene were so similarly lovable in Madeleine. Both loved life, both were nurturing, and he had loved both. While his love for Helene had culminated in marriage, *his deep affection for Madeleine had never truly been resolved.* There was a growing sense of urgency in him that he had to bring that relationship to a resolution or he would never be at peace with himself. It was time to do something!

And so it was that one summer Sunday afternoon, upon his drive home from Orlando, his thoughts turned completely to Madeleine. He resolutely parked the car in the gravel driveway near the door, and with a newfound attitude of determination walked briskly from the house to the lake's shore. There, under a darkening thunder-cloud filled sky heavy with moisture roiling above him, he stepped onto the dock, walked to its end two hundred feet out into the lake. With a firm jaw, he placed his hands on his hips and stared out into the distance—just as he did on the ranch or in the groves when he had faced a major decision he had been pondering for some time. While looking across the lake, then up at the power of the dark, roiling clouds, he felt a sudden sense of energy that seemed to pull him from his two years of malaise.

He knew he needed to make a decision. This could not go on. It was getting too painful. Indecision was something that was always difficult for him to live with. Creases in his brow brought by serious thought gave way to a thin smile that began to form at the corner of his lips as he looked across the large lake whose surface was broken by choppy, steady wind-driven waves lapping at the dock's pillars. He looked up at the dark gray thunderclouds, building and churning as they threatened to bring a powerful, seasonal storm. A single osprey sailed with the wind across the lake. The quickening wind, brought by the rain clouds, suddenly increased in strength and seemed to be sending him a signal. He brushed his thick gray-speckled, dark brown hair to the side as he felt it respond to the wind. His deep brown eyes opened larger as though he was looking east across a vast ocean. He thought deeply for a long time and became transformed, teeth clenched as his hands formed two fists down by his side. He felt enriched and empowered by finally coming to a decision. The first lightning flashes struck offshore brightening the lake's surface...then a sharp thunderclap...and another bright flash.

Alexander shouted into the wind as if to reinforce his solution. "I don't want to be alone anymore...Why should I? It is time...I *will* find her. I will go to Marseille and find Madeleine, no matter how long it takes. I will find her!" He shook his fist at the sky. "*It is time. I will go now! There...it is done...I have decided!*" He stood tall and rigid and stretched his arms to the sky, beseeching the powers.

He was convinced that he *would* find her no matter what it took or how long. He now *knew* it! At this moment of decision, of his commitment, he absolutely *believed* God's universe would conspire to assist him in his quest. Another major flash of lightning seemed to make his point. Then seconds later, another even louder thunderclap.

That evening he excitedly called his daughter in New York to tell her he was going away for awhile and was anxious to get started.

"Helena, when I finally decide, I cannot delay taking action any longer. That's who I am."

At first, Helena assumed that he was probably returning to Lebanon to revisit his childhood village of Douma. But then, remembering her mother's words, she paused on the phone and swallowed thickly before asking what she knew was a very personal intrusion. She simply couldn't stop herself.

"*Biyee*, does this new upbeat sound in your voice and your decision to travel have anything at all to do with the ring you always wear on your finger? Are you going to Marseille?"

Alexander's forehead furrowed quizzically as he listened to Helena's question, surprised at her query. He then realized he would have to be absolutely honest with his daughter and try to explain that this trip would in no way reflect any lessening of his devotion to his family. He knew it would not be easy, but he had to be totally forthright with her to spare her any pain or confusion.

"Yes, Helena," he said with a mixture of compassion and forthrightness, "I am going to Marseille. I need to find my new life. I must try to locate a dear friend from long ago. I'm sure you will understand, *y'slemley*. Tomorrow, after I see Wilbur and deal with business, I'll fly from Tampa to New York. Please arrange a room for me in the city. We'll have dinner the next evening and discuss my trip. I'll explain everything to you and we can discuss whatever you wish."

"Thank you, Daddy. I would like that."

Helena felt relieved and a bit apprehensive, sure his explanation would be difficult for both of them. She felt a strange sensation while listening to her father—initially like a co-conspirator with him, then experiencing a brief sense of betrayal to her mother.

But she remembered her mother's admonition when they spoke those last days, "Life is for the living, my darling. You have a full life ahead of you. Live it. And don't let your father be lonely. I know he loves me, but he must move on. He is still young. And if you ever hear the story about the ring as I asked of you, remember, I *know* he has always loved me, and anything that happened before our life together was not important to me or to our marriage. Never forget what I tell you now."

Helena, comforted, looked forward to her father's visit all the more.

CHAPTER 49

New York
1959

*T*wo days later they met at the Waldorf-Astoria Hotel. Helena squeezed her father's hand across the table and lovingly smiled at him as they sat in the hotel's elegantly decorated dining room. Their booth was in a quiet corner. Fitting, she thought, for they needed time without distractions.

"This is nice, Daddy. I'm glad you came here so we could have this time together."

Deciding that the Waldorf was an appropriate choice for her father's visit, she had made a reservation for him there. She knew that he would never have selected the city's most expensive hotel, staying true to his frugal nature and lack of self-indulgence. But, she felt that he had worked very hard all his life, had reached a respectable level of wealth and prominence, and deserved the very best. So, at the last minute, she had booked him a suite.

Now here they were, father and daughter, to discuss this new adventure of his, totally out of keeping from all she knew of her father's rural life in Kissimmee. She was quite surprised at her father's behavior and certainly had mixed emotions about his sudden decision to go to Marseille, France.

Helena felt a slight disappointment, or perhaps a semblance of pain. She had a fear that possibly her parents' relationship had not been all it had seemed to be, that maybe a secret life, somehow, had been kept from the light of day, so to speak. Did my father truly love my mother, she asked herself, or was it just a surface relationship? No, she thought, it *was* real. *But who or what is it my father is seeking to find? How much does that person mean to him? And where does that leave me? Should I remember and hold inside what my mother asked of me and not be concerned about the past or the future?*

During their dinner, Alexander deliberately delayed presenting the real reason for their meeting and tried to start the evening with light conversation in a fatherly way by asking about his daughter's career and other aspects of her personal life.

Helena, curious, yet keeping her professional demeanor in order to control her inner turmoil and eagerness to hear her father's words, enjoyed telling her father about her life in New York. Finally, anxiously waiting to hear about his intentions, she brought up the true subject of his visit.

"Please, *Biyee*, tell me what is on your mind, what you are feeling. Daddy, I want to know. Look at me and tell me what this is all about, what it means. Please," she repeated, looking deep into his eyes.

Alexander felt his daughter's hand squeeze his as he looked with love and concern into her eyes. As he did, he could see her eyes moisten, belying her vulnerability. It was a poignant moment for both of them. He could not hurt his daughter…his only child. He had to be honest in a way that she could understand without condemning him. Alexander knew he had to present to his daughter his entire story to assuage her concerns as best he could, not completely sure she would understand, recognizing her closeness to her mother, especially in the final weeks of Helene's illness. For an instant he mentally connected her pain to his when his own mother died while her husband, his own father, was away. Uneasily, he began…"Helena, my lovely daughter, you embody all the dreams of your father and your mother. I love you, and I loved your mother. I revere her memory and am grateful to God for our many years together, for the gifts of you and your brother, and our sharing of our lives together for so many years. But, it is hard for me now, and has been since your mother passed away." He paused to gather his thoughts though his eyes never left hers, then continued speaking almost in a whisper, carefully and gently, "I cannot live alone. I have too much love to give. I am aching inside, *Biyee*. I believe your mother would feel the same way. After having a happy marriage for so long, it is too difficult. The emptiness, the loneliness. It makes me sad all the time."

He reminded himself to be very sensitive to Helena's concerns. Although she was now a mature, educated and bright woman, she was still her mother's only daughter, and that bond they had always shared would very naturally cause her to be protective of her mother's memory even though she respected and loved her father.

Softly, deliberately, he told her, "Helena, after my mother died, may she rest in peace, *Allia hummah*," he wiped his eyes and continued, "when I was very young, at her urging, I decided I had to leave the mountains of Lebanon. I left all that I knew and everyone who was dear to me, except my father and sister who were already in America. I had to leave my brother, my home, my cousins, my beloved village, my mountains, and my ancient cedars of our homeland. I was an innocent eighteen-year-old boy.

As he recalled his youth, Helena knew he was terribly saddened. She watched with emotion as his eyes moistened while he spoke of his memories.

"You know some of my history, but I am now going to tell you about a part of my life no one else knows. I am going to entrust with you a part of my life I have never shared with anyone. You must trust me, and you must accept with love what I tell you because it is the truth. Your mother, *Allia hummah*, may God rest her soul," he whispered, hoping Helena understood, "your mother did not ask about my past and it was never an issue between us. I gave my whole life to her and to my children. I don't believe I have to tell you that I have been totally committed to my family. You know I have been, Helena."

Helena nodded, her eyes heavy, as she listened, not yet sure where he was going, nor was she totally comfortable with this conversation. Nervously shifting slightly in her chair, she reached to her purse for a tissue and dabbed her eyes. She knew they were getting close to something that could cause her to lose control.

A bit wistfully, he looked across the table at his beautiful daughter, seeing her for the first time in a stylish business suit. *She's grown up now and looks so sophisticated.* He sat back, sipped from his glass of water, placed the corner of a napkin with his free hand to his lips, and took a moment to think while gathering his thoughts, their eyes locked into each other's. He spoke in a low soft voice as he leaned toward his daughter, both arms folded on the table, carefully choosing his words. Helena's eyebrows pursed, causing a crease between them as she wondered how his words were going to impact her feelings.

"I bunked in steerage on an old World War I converted Turkish steamer ship from Beirut to Marseille to board another ship to New York. I hoped to get to New York quickly and meet my father, but I had to stay over in Marseille six weeks before I could leave for New York.

"Was the trip difficult, *Biyee?*" interrupted Helena, prodding him, trying to ease her father's concern for her sensitivities.

"I can tell you it was awful...the worst experience I have ever had. I got sick almost all the time just like everyone else and spent most of my days bending over the railings. I was fresh from the mountains and had never been on a boat. I have never sailed on another ship like that again, and likely never will. My friend Butrus and I leaped, literally leaped, onto the pier when we reached Marseille, we were so grateful." He smiled, breaking the tension he felt in his muscles. As the words he spoke struck him, he laughed. "We were very happy to be on land, in France, and off that old boat!"

For the next hour, Alexander softly described the six weeks of his stay in Marseille, leaving out no detail. She could tell from his voice he was recalling truly happy times in his life. His face brightened and his demeanor seemed uplifted and cheery. And she was pleased. He told her of Uncle Hanna and Daniella. He described his adventures and his growing feelings toward Madeleine, his first love, this sixteen-year-old vivacious beauty. He told of the days in the parks, *Les Calanques*, the day on the cliff, and the moment she gave him the ring and he gave her his treasured cross.

Helena asked to hold the ring. Alexander slowly twisted the ring from his finger as he watched Helena's face. Then slowly, he handed it over to his daughter. It was the first time he had ever let anyone touch Madeleine's gold ring.

"So that's how you got this," she exclaimed with a look of wonder on her face.

"She was the most beautiful, most charming creature I ever saw, Helena. She swept me off my feet. She was sixteen years old, two years younger than me. Can you understand? For a long time I couldn't think of anything or anyone but her. Yet ever since your mother and I married I have always focused on the present each day. Although I have never removed this ring, I have always been devoted to your mother and you children. However, I must confess to you that since your mother's death the memory of Madeleine has re-entered my thoughts during my loneliness."

He took in a deep breath, then let it out slowly, trying to ease his tensions. "This is an unresolved part of my life. It lingers with me and haunts me. There is a void, an emotional emptiness. Can you understand what I'm telling you? I must somehow find a resolution. I owe it to myself. Actually, Helena, as I think about this situation, I believe I owe its resolution to you as well as to myself."

Then relaxing back into his chair, he lowered his eyelids as his hands twisted his cloth napkin. Wanting to connect with his daughter, he reached for Helena's hand. "As you know, I am a passionate man. I do not love for a moment or a day. When I love, it is totally and forever. I will always love your mother. Yet, I must admit to you that I still feel love toward Madeleine."

He stared into her eyes looking for a sign, hoping she understood.

"Helena, I was surrounded by love when I was young. I lost that love when I lost my mother, when I was only twelve years old. I loved and still love my brother, Milhelm. And now, I have lost my life, and I have lost my wife...your mother...my dear companion. Before that, I lost my only son...your brother Michael. Now, however, I cannot continue without doing everything in my power to resolve the feelings I have for Madeleine. She is the only one left for me, Helena."

Then he hastened to add, "This in no way takes from my love for you, nor for your mother's memory. It is separate. It is vital. It is my destiny that I must follow that path until I find her. I promised long ago to return for Madeleine, but we lost touch before I met your mother. Now, I will search for her until I find her, or find out what happened to her. You'll simply have to understand, and know that I need your support." He was now almost pleading with her.

Helena listened intently and, surprising even herself, began to recognize how proud she was of her father. She had inherited her father's intense warmth and passion. She could do nothing but listen with a sense of love, compassion, of even a feeling of vicarious excitement for her father. She leaned back, having let go of her father's hand, and lowered her eyelids while the beginning of a small smile crept onto her face as she accepted her father's plight. She searched for the words to let her father know she understood, surprising even herself, and that she did not find what he felt and told her to be offensive to her or her mother's memory. She, in her young, yet independent and worldly way, understood that he had to do what he had to do.

Her very thoughts caused her to smile and nod her head to him. She did not feel threatened, but felt instead empathy, a compassionate, stronger emotional bonding with her father. She also knew it would be impossible to change her father's mind. That, she knew, would be unfair, casting a sense of guilt on him, causing him great conflict. It would be an exercise in futility... an exercise she was not about to initiate.

In a way, she identified with his dilemma, his devotion to his heart's yearnings. It reminded her of what she had read in Khalil Gibran's *The Prophet*. It was that book her father had given each of his children on their sixteenth Christmas, explaining that *The Prophet* was written by a close friend of Uncle Salim in Boston, now deceased, and that Gibran was from Bsharre, a village north of and very close to Douma, his own village. "Read the chapters on friendship and love, especially the chapter on children, and you, our gift from God, will better understand what life is truly about," he had said when he gave her her own copy.

The Prophet was very popular at Vassar, she remembered. Much of it was used in her philosophy classes as well as by the girls in the dormitories and sororities as they talked in groups at night, discovering and exploring their philosophies of life, relationships, friendships, and, of course, love.

"*When Love beckons to you, follow him*," Helena spoke aloud, remembering Gibran's words as she looked at her father.

"Oh, Daddy," she exclaimed, reaching for his hands, "I love you so much. Please, go find her. Find Madeleine, follow your heart, Daddy. It would be selfish to ask you not to. And Momma was not a selfish person. I know she would understand. She always told me her life was totally devoted to your happiness, Daddy." Helena felt her eyes well up. Wiping her cheeks she continued, "I *know* you were always devoted to her. She would want you to be happy and as fulfilled as possible."

"Thank you, Helena. Your mother was the most wonderful, most giving woman a man could ever hope to find. She was selfless. She nurtured. She gave. She understood. I know that I tried to be the same way with her. That is why I do not feel a sense of betrayal or guilt. Believe me, since your mother died, I have prayed a lot for guidance, for acceptance, for strength, and for understanding. Now I am at peace with God and the memory of your mother.

But it was most important that you listened to me tell you what was in my heart." He paused, looking at her. "I can't tell you how much I appreciate your understanding and your encouragement to resolve these haunting emotions I must deal with." He smiled and held out his hands to her. *"Allah ma'ak."*

She squeezed his hands as she whispered to him, looking into his deep brown fluid-filled eyes, *"Allah ma'ak,* Daddy."

CHAPTER 50

1960

$\mathcal{QS}$itting in his seat by the window on the flight from New York's Idlewild Airport the next afternoon, Alexander felt relaxed, optimistic yet anxious, like a great burden had been taken from him following his painful but positive visit with Helena. He had been torn by the compelling need to be honest with his daughter, though very much aware that there was a risk she might possibly resent his desire or, his *need* to search for his first love. He sought a message of forgiveness from Helene through Helena's response, indicative of a daughter's bond with her mother. *What if Helena became resentful toward me?* He had asked himself that question a hundred times before reaching New York. Thank God she understood.

He was grateful that his only daughter was as empathetic toward him as she was protective of her mother's memory. And it made all the difference to Alexander as he turned his thoughts from their conversation to the searching journey he must now make. Helena's office had arranged his itinerary from New York to Marseille. He would fly from New York to London, then to Paris. From Paris, he would ride the train to Marseille where he would begin his quest to find Madeleine and recapture the memories of his youth.

Throughout his transatlantic flight, he realized that he was, as was his nature since boyhood, optimistic that he would indeed find Madeleine. As he gazed out the window of the airplane, he also felt the growing sense of reality that it had been nearly forty years.

"*Forty* years!" he whispered to himself. "*Who am I kidding?*" It was the question he had not yet allowed himself to think about. Instead, as was his nature, he kept all negative thoughts pushed back, not allowing them to deter him from his goals. "Be sure 95% of the time," he said to the window.

His cupped his right hand under his chin as he rested his elbow on the seat's armrest. Helena had convinced him to travel first class, contrary to his frugal habit of not frivolously spending money on himself.

"You deserve it, Daddy," she had smiled at the hotel. "Let me take care of your travel arrangements. We have a travel department at the bank that will make all the preparations, including drivers in every city. You should travel like the bank's executives. They often make very successful and important business contacts in first class too." She had arranged window seats for him on each flight, giving him the option of visiting with his neighbor or not, enabling him to courteously avoid conversation if he chose. He was, after all, on a mission, not a pleasure trip.

Reluctantly, he had accepted her advice. Now comfortable in his over-sized seat, he was glad he did.

Helena had arranged for a connecting flight to Paris after Alexander had insisted that he did not want to take the time to be transported into London for a few days layover. "I want to get to France as soon as possible," he had told her. "London can wait until later. Get me to Paris," he had insisted. He had to wait three hours anyway because he still had to go through customs and London's Passport Control before being permitted to leave the main terminal to be transported to the separate Air France terminal for his continuing flight. By the time he had verified his luggage transfer in the early morning light, passed through the second passport control booth, stepped down to the concrete pad where the connecting plane rested, and climbed the steps to the door of the Air France propeller-driven DC-6, he was aware he was nearly exhausted. It wasn't until he finally boarded the plane, walked the few steps down the narrow aisle, found his seat and settled in, that he could relax. His body was tired and drowsiness quickly overcame him. He fell asleep thinking of Madeleine as the wheels left the runway and the flight was en route... to Paris, France.

The man standing in the terminal was holding a sign reading: "M. A. Thomas."

"I am Monsieur Thomas," Alexander said, recalling his French.

"Monsieur Alexander Thomas?" inquired the man.

"Yes, that is I."

"Come with me, monsieur. The car is waiting for you at the curb. I am to take you to The Maurice Hotel. I will go now and collect your luggage. Please wait here for me."

He marveled at his daughter's attention to detail. *That Helena is something.*

The driver flagged a porter, handed him the luggage coupons and instructed him to bring the suitcases to the black Peugeot at the curb. With a nod, the porter followed his instructions. Within minutes, the driver had placed Alexander's four suitcases in the trunk of the taxi, settled in, and began the forty-five minute drive into the city.

The sedan pulled up to the curb at the Maurice Hotel in the middle of the city. Immediately, the formally attired doorman opened the rear passenger door allowing Alexander to step out. Alexander barely noticed the tall, stunningly lovely brunette woman stepping into the taxicab in front of his after she left the hotel with two suitcases.

"Welcome to the Maurice Hotel, monsieur. Your name, *s'il vous plait?*"

"Alexander Thomas. I'll be staying one night, perhaps two, sir."

Early the next morning, as the sun's brightness entered his room through a crack in the drapes, Alexander awoke with a start. He looked at his watch to check the time. As accustomed as he was in Florida to always get started at 7 a.m., waking in response to a wake-up call in Paris now at that hour was just two in the morning in Kissimmee. Still, he was anxious to begin his first full day in France. He remembered he had made an appointment at the U.S. Embassy to make the staff aware of his mission in France, to gain advice in accomplishing his task and insight as to how best to proceed. He picked up the ornate French-styled phone from its cradle, waited for the operator's voice, then ordered breakfast. He enjoyed his Continental foods, especially the croissants with local cheeses and jellies, boiled eggs, coffee, and juice. "*Hmm,*" he thought with a smile, "*this juice is really good!*" He couldn't help but smile at himself as he compared it to his own orange juice. As he sat at the table on the terrace balcony of his luxurious suite, he couldn't help but peer over the ornate wrought iron railing and look around the city, marveling at its broad expanse of dense buildings anchored by the famous Eiffel Tower, Paris' tallest structure. *It's not as tall as I imagined.*

When he stepped back inside the suite with his cup of coffee, he surveyed its elegant interior. He was in one of the most desirable hotels in the world, he reminded himself as he selected a period Louis XIV chair, sat down, slid back, and felt the smooth, taut fabric and, for a moment, while admiring the exquisite furnishings, couldn't help but remember the bare furnishings in Uncle Hanna's apartment in Marseille that he had shared with Butrus so long ago. He smiled at the incredible contrast.

Remembering his father's admonitions, he told himself aloud, "Never forget your beginnings. Remember your roots, *Biyee,* and you will stay humbled and happy. Enjoy the fruits of your labors, yes, but never forget."

After his morning shower, he shaved and dressed, remembering to check outside the door for his shoes. The porter had told him to leave his shoes at his door so they would be shined for him before morning. Alexander had, for his entire life in America, shined his own shoes. In Douma, and even in Kissimmee, shining shoes was a luxury few, if any, could afford. Certainly, as a boy, his well-worn shoes and sandals were more for protection than for dress. But in Europe, he followed their custom even though, out of habit, he had made sure he had brought his own shoe polish and brush.

After his meetings at the Embassy where he was instructed to call on the Consul General in Marseille, he ate lunch, and undertook a preliminary meeting, as he was advised, at the government Hall of Records in Paris. There he received a perfunctory lesson in records search, but no information of value. After a fruitless, frustrating morning, he returned to the hotel.

Anxiously hoping to find some answers in Marseille, he caught a taxi to the central rail station to board his train to the south of France. He would arrive in that port city before nightfall, where he knew he would spend his first of many evenings at a certain café on *Place de Liban*. He could hardly contain his emotions as he boarded the train, checked his luggage, and took his window seat. His thoughts immediately turned to Madeleine. "I'm coming for you, Madeleine. I'm coming back to Marseille, finally, my love," he whispered to himself as he looked out the window, his heart filled with anticipation. *I hope I didn't wait too long like my father.* As he watched the countryside pass by, his mind began playing with his imagination. Then, he thought seriously, *how can you expect that she will be in Marseille after all this time? Are you acting like a foolish old man? You are, after all, fifty-eight years old acting like an infatuated teenager. Do you really expect she will look the same? Do I? Will she care anymore? Does she have a husband? Does she have children? Is she even alive? What am I doing? Am I really being fair to Helena?* A frown formed on his face for a moment as he thought about the wisdom of returning home. After all, he reminded himself, she had never written to him in response to his many letters.

But he knew he was doing what he had to do to fulfill his heart's desire and find resolution, or he would never get on with his life. He had fallen deeply, completely in love with Madeleine. She was his passion, his soul mate. She would always be so. His mind couldn't stop focusing on the total bonding they both had felt toward each other and the belief that God had blessed their union. He remembered…how they had become essential to each other… the electric sensations he had felt just seeing her each of those days in Marseille…the powerful and exciting emotions that were beyond anything he had ever felt before or since…the spontaneous outbursts of joy, of love, of mutual attraction, of their laughter…almost giddiness…as they explored each day together, enjoying every moment. She had become a vital part of his life so quickly. "Your soul is entwined with mine," he murmured aloud to no one, staring out the window watching the vineyards of southern France whiz by, almost as a blur, reminding him it would not be long now.

You are and will always be my life's love, dear Madeleine. Wherever you are, I will find you. I swear it.

"Marseille...Marseille, *s'il vous plait.* It is time," the conductor announced as he approached Alexander's row of seats, interrupting his thoughts.

Alexander felt the train slow down as the conductor stopped at his seat, bracing his feet as the train slowed, responding to the steel brakes being forcefully applied to the wheels.

"We are here. And thank you Monsieur Thomas for telling me your beautiful love story. It is wonderful that after all these years you did not forget, that you are seeking to complete your destiny. You are a determined romantic, are you not? Perhaps your heart is, in truth, French," the conductor chuckled.

"*Merci,*" Alexander smiled to the conductor. "I'm grateful that you were not too busy to listen to a man who has lived a full life, who was too poor when young to remain with the first love of his life, but had to wait forty years...*forty long years* to determine it was time, time to find his lost love, time to follow his heart." His voice grew firm, "We have but one life to live, only one, and none of it should be wasted. Indeed, I did not waste those forty years. I had a wonderful marriage. I worked very hard and did well. I was loyal to my dear wife and we raised two lovely children. But after she was taken from me, I found the only way I could be fulfilled was to leave everything and find my lost love, Madeleine." He loved saying her name aloud. "And now, here I am, returning to where we first met, to trace our steps, to recover the love of my heart, my very soul I left behind so very long ago. I am here once again. And I thank you, sir." He shook the friendly conductor's outstretched hand.

"*Bonne chance, mon ami.*"

Moments later, Alexander departed the train with a small wave to his new friend. Outside the terminal, he signaled for a taxicab, instructing the driver, "Drive me to the *Panier* by the Joliette pier, *s'il vous plait.* I am late, very late for a reunion," he smiled with new energy.

"You wish to go to the docks, monsieur? Would you not prefer your hotel or a restaurant on the *Canebière?*"

"Later, driver, later, but first, if it is still there, please take me to the *Place de Lenche,* or as it was called, the *Place de Liban.*"

Alexander first wanted to go to the familiar *Panier* to revisit the spot where they first met. Then, he would have the driver deliver him to the Charles V Hotel on the *Canebière,* not far from Madeleine's mother's shop he had visited so many times long ago when he was young.

CHAPTER 51

Alexander carefully watched the mostly five-story stucco buildings pass by as he settled in the backseat of the taxi, remembering, but noting so much had changed, increasing his apprehension. There were new buildings everywhere, especially along the *Vieux Port* and the *Panier* waterfront.

"Everything seems different here by the port, driver," he remarked aloud. "I can't believe those rows and rows of new buildings along the *Quai du Port.*"

"*Oui, monsieur.*" With a scowl he reminisced and continued, "This part of the *Panier* was destroyed by Hitler and the Vichy government because they are so close to the rail yards and the port. They knew the *Panier* was a breeding area for anti-Nazi sentiment. Then it was heavily bombarded during the 1944 invasion to rid the city of the Germans near the end of the war. After the war, the rubble was removed and the government rebuilt these more modern apartment and office buildings. They are handsome, don't you think?"

"Yes. And so new looking. The *Panier* is known for its older buildings, a place for poor immigrants, is it not?" Then, noticing a cluster of flowering bushes, he exclaimed, "Ah, I remember this park although the flowering trees, benches and shrubs seem new."

"Well, much of that park was replanted after the bombardment. There were many *jardins* built in tribute to the French who lost their lives during the war. That park, dedicated to those of the Resistance who lost their lives, is lovely, don't you agree?"

Acknowledging the beauty of this new garden, Alexander's emotions on this quest began alternating between angst and excitement. His eyes scanned the old commercial port, now filled with small sailboats, mostly pleasure crafts, and fishing boats.

"Do the fishermen still sell their catch each day along the docks on the *Panier* side of the quay?" he asked the driver as he pointed in that direction.

"No, actually the fish market was relocated to the north end of the *Vieux Port*, closer to the *Canebière* where it is more convenient. It's not as large as before, but still daily offers the best fresh fish, escargots, and other goods like wine, handmade candles and soaps, flowers and perfumes. The fresh seafood is the draw for shoppers even today."

"Well, it's still beautiful, but so different. Now please take me to *Place de Lenche* for a few minutes. I wish to see if a certain café remains today."

Alexander felt a little dizzy as he sensed being an observer of Madeleine and himself at eighteen years, a sort of "out of body" experience.

A few minutes later the driver waved his left arm. "There is the *Café Liban*. Perhaps that is the restaurant you wish to visit," he said, pointing out the window. "Would you like to stop here now or go to your hotel? Do you recognize what you are looking for?"

Alexander sat up in the seat, looking up at the plaza with its familiar tall sycamore trees and their paper-thin, multi-colored trunks' skin and large green leaves shading the tables and chairs beneath.

"I've seen what I want to see, driver," Alexander responded, settling back into his seat behind the driver. "Yes, please take me to the hotel."

Thinking he might earn a good fee if he attached himself to this American tourist, the driver said to Alexander over his shoulder, "Monsieur, pardon moi, would you like me to be your driver during your stay in Marseille? I have lived here all of my life. I was born here in 1910, before the first Great War. Perhaps I will be familiar with all that you need to find, or to ask about. And I have many friends in the Lebanese community as well."

Lost in his thoughts for a moment, Alexander replied, "I am looking for an old friend since before the second war. Do you think you can help me?"

"Well, *je ne sais pas,* it will be difficult but I'll try. I know many people, and the police are my friends. We shall see. Try me. Oh, monsieur, my name is Jacques du Chavelle."

Alexander nodded, "Let me think about this. My name is Alexander Thomas. I'll check into the hotel, rest, and take a shower. I'd like you to return in two hours to pick me up. I particularly wish to be taken to the Notre-Dame-de-la-Garde before the sun sets.

"*Merci*, Monsieur Thomas. I will return in two hours."

"Thank you, Jacques. Six o'clock then."

Minutes later, Alexander exited the taxicab as the doorman opened his door to welcome him.

"Welcome to the Charles V Hotel, monsieur. Your luggage?"

"*Merci*," Alexander smiled as he nodded and stepped to the heavy glass double doors. The lobby was elegant, with period furnishings. His feet felt the change from the polished marble floor to the plush carpet as he stepped to the registry desk.

"Passport, monsieur? Kindly fill out this card. And how long will you be staying with us? Ah, Monsieur Thomas," he exclaimed with a smile, "we have been expecting you. Everything is in order. The bank confirmed your arrival just this morning. I will have your luggage taken to your suite immediately. Welcome to the Charles V Hotel."

Alexander couldn't keep a small smile form on his lips as he noted the incredible contrast when compared to his arrival at Uncle Hanna's office so many years ago.

As he stepped into his luxurious suite, Alexander, turning his head to view the entire space, smiled broadly, and said aloud as he opened his arms and surveyed the room, "Well, Butrus, Marseille is certainly different than it was for us in 1920, thanks to Helena's cosmopolitan tastes and my good fortune." Then he whispered to himself, "Now, if I can find Madeleine, everything will be perfect."

After unpacking and showering, Alexander lay down to rest. *It's been a long, emotional day and may get even more so*, he thought as he placed his head on the finely textured white cotton down pillows with their crocheted fringes and fell fast asleep.

Promptly at six o'clock, the taxicab pulled up to the curb. Alexander was waiting.

"Very good, Jacques. Let's go to the cathedral now. I would like to visit awhile and look at the sea at this special time of day."

After a brief but poignant visit to the cathedral, he had the driver take him to the Corniche, passing by the *Jardin du Pharo*, and farther east to *Les Calanques*.

"Stop here, Jacques," he instructed, tapping the driver's shoulder.

"Here?"

"*Oui*. I want to look at the cliffs here and the small cove below," he gestured. "These are important places for me."

For the next fifteen minutes, while his driver stood beside the Peugeot and waited patiently as he kept an eye on his passenger, Alexander retraced the familiar places he had walked hand in hand with Madeleine, looking and thinking.

Over there is where we were. He smiled, remembering, as he looked toward the grassy spot where he and Madeleine had shared their love and whispered, *Here you are, my beautiful Madeleine. And here am I. I remember every detail, every wonderful moment. I remember your smile, your soft voice, your touch. I remember everything about you, your hair, your embrace, your love. Everything.*

He sat down on a stone ledge and, facing the sea, gazed at the same panorama they had shared so long ago. The sun was nearing the horizon. He looked to his right and focused on the sea, his thoughts totally on Madeleine, their closeness, their sharing, her face. He could never, ever forget.

After the sun had begun to set and before darkness began to envelop the sea, Alexander looked around one last time, then walked hesitatingly to the waiting taxi. Suddenly, he stopped for just a moment, looked back over his shoulder and whispered, "I will be back. I will return to this place with my beloved Madeleine. I promise."

"To the restaurant, Monsieur Thomas?"

"*Oui*, Jacques. *Place de Lenche* and the café."

Alexander watched the vaguely familiar streets pass by the taxi's windows. He focused on the older buildings, small parks, new hotels and office buildings, eager to spot a particularly significant sight.

"Here we are," spoke the driver, over his shoulder. "Here is the *Place de Lenche*, or *Place de Liban* as the Lebanese call it. Go up those steps and you'll see the *Café Liban*, on your left."

"Hmm..." replied Alexander, "it's amazing. The park and the apartments really look so much the same. The café's sign is newer, but the restaurant is still there! The front of the buildings have improved, some of the shutters look the same, some look freshly painted, but the tables are placed almost exactly as before, and I see the backgammon games on the tables. Isn't that something? It is said that 'the more things change, the more they remain the same.' It is true, *n'est-ce pas?*"

"Yes, it is true," replied the attentive driver. "Would you like me to return to take you to back to your hotel, monsieur?"

"No, *merci*. I'll find my way back. I'll enjoy the walk."

The minute Alexander stepped from the taxi onto the stone street and walked up the stone steps to the restaurant's front door, carefully stepping between the tables and chairs so not to disturb the customers, or bump into the hustling waiters in their familiar outfits, he felt a powerful poignancy sweep his consciousness, much like what he felt at the cathedral and on the Corniche. Everything was familiar to him, causing delicious memories to flood his consciousness.

"My God," he said aloud, "the memories are so strong. I had no idea I would feel this way." His eyes seemed to glaze over as his mind went back, and yet they saw so many things that made him seem miles away.

The waiter, noticing how distant his customer appeared, interrupted Alexander's thoughts, asking, "May I help you, monsieur." Like the other waiters, he was dressed in black pants and white shirt, a small white towel apron tucked in his waist. He had a thick moustache, typical of Middle Eastern men. As customary, all the waiters serving the clientele of *Café Liban* were men. And just as customary, the person at the cash registry by the front door was the co-owner, a serious-looking, dreary woman, perhaps in her sixties, dressed in a dark burgundy dress with a black hand-crocheted shawl draped over her shoulders, her long graying hair twisted into a bun in the back. Her expression and facial lines belied her destiny. She had worked hard most of her life, much of it tending the cash register in the restaurant she and her husband owned. At the instant Alexander stepped in, the lady smiled with a friendly welcome that relaxed him. By the look on her face and her demeanor, Alexander quickly formed a more favorable impression of her, hoping she would know something of Hanna, Daniella, and Madeleine.

"*Ahlen wa sahlen*," she greeted him, immediately recognizing Alexander as being of Lebanese or Syrian heritage. "*Ibn* Arab? Are you the son of an Arab?"

"*Oui*, I am Lebanese."

"Ahhh...welcome. Please come in and make yourself comfortable, monsieur. But you are American, aren't you?"

"Yes, but I was born in Lebanon," he proudly responded. "Let me guess. Are you, with your husband, the owner of *Café Liban*?"

"We bought it from the estate of the owner at that time, Hanna Chalhoub."

"Oh, my God," replied Alexander, "Hanna was my uncle. Can you help me? I am seeking to find a dear friend who was close to my uncle, *Khali* Hanna, many years ago. Did you know him and his friend Daniella DuBois?"

Her face lit up, her eyes widened as she smiled. "Yes, of course, we knew Hanna and Daniella very well. We were terribly sad, *and* angry, when they were lost during the invasion."

"*Mon Dieu*! How did it happen?" he exclaimed, shocked, never having heard anything about the war's impact on his uncle or Daniella. From 1939, neither he nor any relatives in Boston received any word, mail or otherwise, from Marseille or Douma. Most didn't write letters as news was never good, and government restrictions made writing to America almost impossible. Alexander was totally ignorant of any events in France or Lebanon for more than fifteen years, difficult as it may seem. He too had his life struggles in America during the Great Depression, and while he often thought of his brother Milhelm or Uncle Hanna, there really was little reason compelling enough for him to actually correspond.

His mind raced as did his questions, making the woman smile. "Please tell me as much as you can. When was it? Was Daniella's daughter, Madeleine, with them at the time? Would you sit with me and tell me all you know? Uncle Hanna and Daniella were very good to me when I was here years ago." He didn't want to go into detail regarding Madeleine just yet, but grew hopeful at this possible opportunity to pursue his inquiry.

Looking around the restaurant, he noticed the growing number of diners entering the café as the evening began in earnest. Empathizing with the owner, he quickly added, "Madame, I realize your evening is just beginning and you are busy, but if I could have just a few minutes with you, I would very much appreciate your kindness. I have just flown in from America on an important personal search, and I need your help." Now energized, and six hours ahead of Florida's time, he was not tired although he had had a full day.

"Perhaps I will have more time to spend with you tomorrow, but come sit a moment now with me," she replied tentatively, looking him over, satisfied this man would not be a problem. "I'm always happy to visit. Here, we will talk at this table."

Alexander could tell by the table's location and lack of settings that this table was her choice as she could see the entrance and the kitchen door from the same chair.

In unison, they sat down on the wooden chairs at the table, and, after a moment, were served glasses of wine.

"My name is Wedad. Now, tell me your name, where you have come from, and who you are." She folded her hands, placed them on the table and looked straight into his eyes.

He returned her direct gaze and started, "I am from America. My name is Alexander Thomas. My Arabic name, before Ellis Island," he smiled, "is Iskandar...Iskandar Chalhoub Thomé." For a brief moment, he recalled Madeleine whispering, "Iskandar." His eyes began to moisten as he began telling the proprietor of his past. He instantly felt a rapport with this woman and, perhaps, with a willingness to be naively candid and hopeful because the possibility existed that she and her husband could help him. He became very relaxed and forthcoming, gesturing over the table as he described his stay in Marseille.

"I first came to Marseille from Beirut in 1920 when I was on my way to America," he began. "I stayed here, in this very building, for six weeks as a guest of my Uncle Hanna. How did you know him?"

"Well, Iskandar, this is a large but in many ways a small community of Lebanese immigrants here in Marseille. We know almost all of our brothers and sisters here, especially those of the *Panier,* and for decades, most of us have attended the same churches, St. Mary's Antiochan Orthodox and the Catholic Church on the hill. Although, I must say, since the Middle East war, many new people have settled here, mostly from the south of Lebanon and from Palestine. But until 1947, most of us were very close, almost like one extended family, as they say. Now, it is much larger and more diverse." She lifted her glass as a demonstration of friendship, then sipped from her glass. "Excuse me," she smiled as she turned and beckoned to the man moving towards her, "here comes my husband, George. He knew Hanna very well."

George, slightly shorter than Alexander, had a handlebar mustache, dark olive complexion, a balding head, and wore a cream-colored, long-sleeved silk shirt and black trousers.

"George, meet Iskandar," she said as George extended a thick, calloused hand to Alexander. "He is seeking information about an old friend of yours, Hanna Chalhoub."

"*Mahrharbahr. Ahlen wa Sahlen*," George smiled, returning Alexander's. "Of course. How can I help you, Iskandar?" he asked as he pulled out one of the four wooden chairs at the table and joined his wife and her visitor. "Hanna was a very popular man in Marseille, especially the *Panier*. And after it was found out what he had secretly done to assist the Resistance during the dangerous Nazi occupation, the city of Marseille almost built a shrine to him. The entire local Lebanese community wanted to honor him. Yes, he was a good man and a good friend, Iskandar. Now, what can I do to help you? Tell me. I can take a break right now. You have come at a good moment. One hour later and I would have had to ask you to come back tomorrow."

Alexander sat back, sipped from his glass, and ordered a *mezza* platter of *hummus, baba ghanoush, zeytoon, tabouleh, jibneh*, and pita. "This will hold me for the evening," he smiled. "I love this food so much." Then after a bite or two, he paused and, looking directly into the owner's eyes, said, "George, I'll get right to the point. I am on a mission. I have come a long way to find someone and must start here. This is where my story begins. I hope you can help me find Madeleine DuBois, daughter of Daniella DuBois, close companion of Hanna Chalhoub." Alexander paused to take a long breath, trying to determine how much he needed to share with this man. He decided not to go into the details of his relationship with Madeleine, at least not at the moment.

"Iskandar, I will help you all that I can, but I must tell you, Hanna and Daniella were killed during the American invasion of Marseille in September of 1944. They were together and, *Allia hummah*, may they rest in peace, they died practically in each other's arms. They were on the *Canebière* in a restaurant dining when an errant Allied bomb hit that restaurant directly. There were many innocents killed those days from so many poorly aimed cannon fire and bombs. I do not know what happened beyond their being killed at that time. I do know that Daniella's daughter, I believe her name was Madeleine, was not with them. By then, she was a grown woman and married." He caught himself and added, "I believe she had a child. Yes, she had a son."

"Married? A son? Ohh..." Alexander frowned, disappointed, then asked with a note of sadness in his voice, "Did she still live in Marseille at that time?"

"Well, no," he responded, "she left Marseille just before the war actually began. No one knew where she went. Her husband was a leader in the Resistance, and a marked man. The Nazis were after him all the time. He and she simply disappeared one day.

"She disappeared?" asked Alexander, opening his arms in wonder. "Does anyone know where she went?"

"*La'a*," replied George, "no one heard from her again, even her mother. And Hanna didn't speak of that either. Her husband was gone much of the time, meeting with groups all over France, never sleeping in the same place two nights in a row. Perhaps he sent her to a safe place. Maybe Switzerland or America?" George's forehead furrowed as he looked to his wife, then questioned himself and Iskandar. "I do not know, my friend," he shrugged, holding both palms up. "I do not know anything more, I am sorry to say."

"Yes," Marie nodded, "her husband was deeply involved in the Underground, and Hanna was close to him. He provided "safe" houses here in the Lebanese sector of the *Panier* throughout the occupation. Monsieur Moreau traveled a great deal. Daniella's daughter was here before the invasion. We never saw her or heard of here during or after the war. Never."

George agreed. "Yes, that is so. I do not believe she was in Marseille during the Occupation. Of course, we assumed she was safe, did we not? But perhaps she died during the war as well?"

"*Oui*, you are correct. Madeleine left Marseille before the Germans came, but I do not know where she went. No one, to my knowledge, knows where she went, or how, or why, really. Maybe she went to Sardinia. Or maybe she was killed."

Alexander joined the conversation, looking to Marie, "So, you say she was married to a man named Moreau, and lived in Marseille until before the Germans arrived. Is that as you understand it? And then she left and never returned, *n'est-ce pas?*"

"Well, Iskandar, that is my understanding. We were close to Hanna, but not to Daniella's daughter. I am not sure if anyone I know has more knowledge than this. It has been nearly twenty years. Let's see, no, it has been even longer. Most people here now arrived after the war. Perhaps the authorities will have more information, but, of course, many records were destroyed during the Occupation." Lowering his eyes, he added, "I am very sorry." George looked toward the door and stood as he saw a couple enter the café.

"*Merci*, George, for all of your help. I very much appreciate your time. I can see you are busy, and that this is going to take more investigation, but I have time. Now I must go, but not before I congratulate you on your fine foods and your superb *arak*. And most of all, I am very grateful you have kept the *Café Liban* intact and similar to what I recall. It holds many wonderful memories for me." He bowed his head to George and Marie as he stood to leave. "*Shookrun*."

"*Afwan*, you are welcome."

As he walked to the door, he stopped and turned back to his new friends,

"Thank you again. I will return to visit you."

"*Inshallah*, Iskandar." Maria added, "When exactly did you last visit with Hanna and Daniella here at the café?"

"It was the summer of 1920, a long time ago."

"1920?" she exclaimed. "Indeed, yes. So much has happened since then, don't you agree?"

"Beyond your wildest dreams, madame," Alexander replied quickly with a dubious smile, "beyond your wildest dreams."

"And tell us, Iskandar, where are you staying in Marseille?"

"I am at the Charles V Hotel," he said, standing in the doorway entrance to the café.

"And for how long?" Maria asked.

"For as long as it takes, madame. For as long as it takes," he answered, the second time in a whisper to himself as he stepped through the doorway into the cool, balmy night.

CHAPTER 52

⟨⟩

$\mathcal{T}$ he following day, at the end of his meeting with the U.S. Consul General, Alexander, having listened intently to every word and deciding there really wasn't much the Americans could do to help, determined that he would need to follow the only sound suggestion he heard: "Try the local police department. Perhaps they can help you."

And so he did. But the Marseille police station was of little or no help, being preoccupied with current local crimes, including predominantly, the importation of illegal drugs. They had no time to assign personnel to missing persons, especially those missing during the war.

"Monsieur Thomas," the officer gesticulated with his arms, "you must understand three things. First, the person for whom you are looking may be dead. Second, there are no records of any sort to which we have access...so many were destroyed by the Nazis during the Occupation and the Allied invasion. Third, we have no information of any one by that name. I'm sorry, but we're not able to help you."

Alexander felt frustrated that there seemed to be no one who knew of Madeleine's whereabouts or when she was last seen or heard from. Yes, Hanna was well known, but even he, after such a long absence, was becoming only a vague memory to many, and nonexistent to most, especially the postwar generation. Most of his closest friends were also killed during the war, and most of those who weren't left Marseille very soon after the war as life became almost unbearably difficult in the cities. Food was so very scarce, transportation systems and streets were wrecked, buildings shattered, water often unavailable, and electricity sporadic at best. Many escaped to the countryside where they could farm to feed themselves. It was only after the U.S. aid, as part of the Marshall Plan, the enormously generous gift to Europe from the U.S. under President Truman, and spearheaded by America's outstanding Secretary of State George C. Marshall, that cities in France, as well as the other European countries began to rebuild themselves into livable communities. And that took several years. By 1950, the demographics of Marseille had changed dramatically, impacting on the culture of the citizenry. As a result, the Lebanese community changed almost completely.

Many had left for other places, to their extended families in Lebanon, Syria, Canada, and the Americas. So, Alexander faced a near vacuum of people who might have even known Hanna or Daniella, but certainly not Madeleine.

Day after frustrating day, extending into endless weeks, Alexander called on everyone he could think of who might be helpful, no matter how remote the possibility. Everyday he was at the *Place de Liban* and the *Canebière* asking shopkeepers, clientele, *gendarmes*, and taxi drivers, who seemed to know about everything and everybody except the whereabouts of Madeleine DuBois. Some older residents on the *Canebière* knew of "Daniella DuBois and her adorable daughter," but they had less than precise memories, or knew of nothing after the German invasion.

Each day was a frustrating experience for Alexander. He was not accustomed to this kind of fruitless endeavor. He always felt like he could make things happen. But here, every day was empty for him.

At least four times each week, Alexander visited the *Café Liban* where he would lunch or visit in the late afternoons, make acquaintances, renew his backgammon, sip *arak*, dine on a simple *mezza*, and ask questions of those diners who looked old enough to possibly know something. He spent many hours at the café sipping the pungent thick Turkish coffee from a demitasse cup, one of the many lingering traditions of the Ottomans that most Lebanese continued to cling to. He, Maria and, most often, George would talk of many things. Sometimes the subject would become Lebanon. He became a familiar habitué, sometimes drawing sympathetic glances from those who noticed him so often.

"What do you think of the U.S. Marines in Beirut? Do you agree your President Eisenhower did the right thing, Iskandar?"

"I think so, George. It seemed to me the political difficulties in Beirut with the infighting of the powerful political families will need U.S. involvement for a long time. I'm glad Lebanon stays close to France and the West and doesn't align with the Soviet Union. This whole "Cold War" thing has me concerned. I don't like politics that much anyway, and maybe it's because I am Orthodox, since we have no aspirations concerning the presidency in Lebanon. As you know, only the Maronites can ascend to the presidency... it's in the Constitution. They send their children to school in France ensuring that close bond, counting on the power of France to keep them in place. So yes, George, I supported Ike in that decision. I hope they can keep Beirut and Lebanon at peace."

"*Inshallah*," replied George with a smile. "More coffee, Iskandar?"

And so it went...the weeks now extending into many months...as he sought information in cities outside of Marseille, including Paris, Aix-en-Provence, Le Havre, Lyon, and Toulon...most of France. Still nothing. Alexander's time in Marseille was pleasant enough being around his countrymen, but being unsure what to do next, where else to look or with whom to inquire. He wondered to himself many days, *What am I doing? Maybe I should go home.* "No," he would whisper in response to his own words, "no, I cannot. Not now. Something is sure to turn up. Yes, it's frustrating. Everything is beyond my control. All I can do is continue my search...and wait."

His inherent tenacity that would not let him quit his mission was sorely being tested, and he knew that.

"Day after day...nothing!" he muttered, shaking his head.

✷

It was in Alexander's twelfth month of residence in Marseille when someone who had heard of his search came to his hotel one late afternoon. He didn't realize how long he had been here and was about to fly home to reassess his actions when one evening he received the phone call.

Rarely did his hotel phone ring, so Alexander anxiously reached for it. *"Allo?"*

"Monsieur Thomas, there is a visitor here in the lobby asking for you," said the concierge. "He says he has information you may find interesting. Would you prefer to meet with him your suite or in the lobby?"

"Neither," replied Alexander rather eagerly. "Ask him to meet me in the lounge. I'll be right down."

"As you wish," replied the concierge efficiently, wanting to serve his hotel's continuing guest.

Alexander, encouraged, yet not quite ready to be too optimistic, reached for his tweed jacket, brushed his hair back, grabbed his wallet and keys, and stepped to the door, hoping for some news beyond what he had been hearing repeatedly for so long: "I'm sorry, Mr. Thomas, but we cannot help you in your search as much as we would like to."

Alexander strode quickly to the elevator. As he stepped out of the elevator onto the marble lobby floor, he expected to see someone approach him. He looked to the concierge at his small desk. The concierge made eye contact, smiled slightly and nodded his head toward the lobby lounge.

Alexander received the signal and stepped across the lobby to the lounge where a man stood waiting.

"Monsieur Thomas, the American?" the man asked. "I think I can help you."

Alexander, after an endless time of a seemingly dead-end of information, looked at the man suspiciously, surveying him closely with concern. He was a few inches shorter than Alexander, about the same age, and was dressed in a modest French dark blue suit that a mid-level bureaucrat would wear. Lebanese in appearance, he was olive-skinned, with silver hair at his temples and wispy strands of hair atop his balding head. He seemed a bit shy and had a worried expression on his face.

"I am someone who worked for many years as assistant to Monsieur Hanna Chalhoub. I have heard of your investigation. Can we sit and talk?"

"Of course," Alexander answered as he led this man, who appeared to be sincerely eager to help him, to a booth in the corner of the bar.

"Let's sit here," spoke Alexander, gesturing toward the booth. "What is your name, monsieur?"

"I am Amjad Hamra. My family is from Tyre on the southern coast of Lebanon, but I, myself, have been here in Marseille since the end of the first war in 1919. My only job was working for Hanna Chalhoub, your uncle. I was his assistant, bookkeeper, and collected his rents for more than twenty-four years until his unfortunate death in the late summer of 1944. We were very close, monsieur, very close. He trusted me with his business many times when he traveled, and I trusted him in his fairness and appreciation for my efforts. He was a very generous man, Monsieur Thomas. I respected him very much."

Alexander, watching, listening to every word, nodded as the man spoke, keenly interested in what he might know.

"We were close for many years even though he was a Christian and I am Sunni Moslem. We trusted each other completely. But now he is gone and I miss him. I miss my friend so much. He had no family, you know. No wife, no children. Only his work, his buildings, and Daniella. He intended to leave everything to Daniella. Did you know that?"

Alexander couldn't believe his ears. Mr. Hamra seemed to know so much and sounded so sincere, so honest. He was surprised at the revelations of this stranger.

"Why do you come to me at this time?" asked Alexander. "And, if I may ask, what do you wish from me? Or do you have new information for me?"

"Oh, Monsieur Thomas, I do not ask anything of you. Monsieur Chalhoub told me of you many times, wishing you were his son. He told me except for life's twists and turns, you might indeed have been his son. And," Amjad continued, "since I thought of Monsieur Chalhoub as my uncle, you would be my family too. When I first heard of your questions in the Lebanese section of the *Panier*, I wasn't certain what you were doing or who you were. But, after so many months following your path, I decided I should try to help you. After all, Hanna left most of his buildings to me. Did you know that? He had written in his will that all he owned would be given to Daniella DuBois. But, if she was not alive, it would be given to me. Of course, I did not know that, to be sure. And now I am a wealthy man because of him. Perhaps, sir," he paused, looking at Alexander, studying his face, "perhaps I can help you. That is my desire, so in some ways I can help further Monsieur Chalhoub's hopes and dreams for his 'almost son.'"

He paused again. "I do not want to mislead you, sir," the man continued, looking directly into Alexander's eyes, "I do not know where your friend Madeleine DuBois is today. But I do know some things that may lead you to that information. Would you like me to continue, sir?"

"Yes, of course" Alexander interjected without hesitation, filled with renewed hope, "please continue. I am here in Marseille on a mission of my heart, and if you can help me, I am most interested in what you have to say."

"Mademoiselle DuBois was a lovely young woman, Monsieur Thomas, whose heart was broken when you left her. Yet, she did the best she could. She was just a young girl, you see. Several years later she met Monsieur Philippe Moreau, who was a close friend of Monsieur Chalhoub's. He was much older than Madeleine DuBois and quite wealthy. Life was difficult in those days and she found it necessary to marry this well-respected man who could take care of her."

Alexander, listening intently, suddenly began to feel great regret and sadness. He felt a sickening sense of having abandoned Madeleine and leaving her to the fates. He had to hold back his emotions as Amjad Hamra shared his detailed information. He had not known anything of Madeleine's life after he sailed on to America. He had had no way of knowing...eighteen years old, very poor, totally dependent on his father, no responses to his many letters to her. Yet, he felt somehow responsible for Madeleine's fate. *Should I have stayed? Should I not have left her? Should I have returned much sooner? Did I repeat my father's actions? Will I have to live with that? Oh, God help me if I failed the one person who lives so deeply in my heart.* Alexander's stomach tightened. He began to ache from his actions.

"Monsieur Hamra," whispered Alexander, "this is so difficult. I am appreciative of all you are telling me. I have loved this woman since I arrived in Marseille in 1920, some forty years ago, and now, you tell me she had to marry because times were too difficult for her. And now, I feel that I abandoned her and must do something." Alexander wiped his face with his handkerchief in silence.

His heart heavy, he continued, "I promised her I would return for her. But, I didn't until now. I let her down. Perhaps, perhaps," he repeated, "she is even now married. And perhaps she has several children. I have no way of knowing. But, my heart tells me she waits for me as I long for her to return into my life." Taking a deep breath, Alexander continued more humbled, "Hamra, I am reminded of the words of our countryman, Khalil Gibran, as he wrote in his book, *The Prophet*, when Almitra spoke of Love. Those words are so true to me. They haunt me every day. Do you remember? I think they are burned in my mind. I remember these words:

When Love beckons to you, follow him,

Though His ways are hard and steep.

Though the sword hidden among his pinions may wound you.

And when he speaks to you, believe in him."

"And so, my dear man," Alexander said as he waved the waiter to the table to refresh their glasses of wine, "I ask you to tell me all you know that I may find Madeleine, my first love."

Amjad smiled. "Well, Monsieur Thomas, I will do all that I can, and with pleasure. There is a man who lived in Marseille for many years, Jean Pierre Armand, who now lives in Paris. Perhaps he can help you. He was a close friend of Monsieur Chalhoub's and was in the Resistance throughout the war. You are aware, are you not, that Monsieur Chalhoub was extraordinarily helpful to the French underground, the citizen's army against the Germans?"

Alexander shook his head, and with his hand beckoned the man to continue without delay. "Please continue, Monsieur Hamra."

"Yes, sir, happily, but I wish to keep my facts straight, as I am not the young man that I was, so bear with me."

"Of course, please continue at your pleasure. I have time, as much as you need," Alexander replied with a grateful smile.

"Jean Pierre Armand was very much involved, as I said, in the Resistance during the war as a high-level agent based in Marseille, and, on occasion, in other cities nearby, like Toulon. He worked very closely with Philippe Moreau, who was at that time Director General of the Resistance, a very important man, and Madeleine's husband. Monsieur Moreau was a brave man, very intelligent, and somehow successfully brought the various Resistance groups together. At the beginning, there were three major groups across France. Very dedicated to France to be sure, but they would not or could not coordinate their efforts. Politics, sir...always politics." He paused as he shook his head. "Even so, the Germans came. But Philippe will long be remembered as a French hero. And, I believe that Jean Pierre Armand, a dedicated man to the Resistance who was very close to him, may have the information you need. I recommend you find him. There remains a small separate office in the French Defense Department in Paris for those who fought in this way. They may have the information for you. It's almost a secret agency, Monsieur Thomas, with its documents not for common knowledge, so you must be cautious. They jealously guard their information for, as they say, 'security reasons.' I am sure you understand. It would be like trying to obtain information from your CIA or FBI, *n'est-ce pas?"*

"I understand, Monsieur Hamra. And I thank you for this information. I will leave for Paris in the morning. *Merci, merci beaucoup."*

They both stood and acknowledged each other with a slight bow before Hamra departed the hotel.

Alexander had followed too many false leads during the past months, resulting in nothing but more frustration. So he cautiously restrained himself, not yet willing to believe he had begun to find an avenue to some answers. In fact, he had not. Still, Amjad Hamra seemed knowledgeable and sincere.

"George," he asked his friend at the *Café Liban* later that evening, "tell me what you know of Amjad Hamra."

"Of course, *mon ami*," he nodded as his eyebrows raised up, "Amjad was Hanna Chalhoub's protégé for many years, and one of the luckiest men I have known. Do you know that Hanna gave him these very buildings after his death in 1945? He is now my landlord and a good man. Why do you ask? Are you interested in Marseille real estate?"

"No." He laughed at the thought. "I think I have all the real estate I need at this time. I met Amjad and he told me of a man who might have helpful information in my search. Have you ever heard of Jean Pierre Armand?"

"Yes, of course, but many years ago. He was here in Marseille during the Occupation. I believe he was involved somehow in the French underground. But, I must tell you, I was not involved in those things at that time. Only a few Lebanese in Marseille dared to become involved in the Resistance. It was too easy for the Germans to kill us and suffer no retribution. If they killed the French, the French fighters could and would retaliate, you see. As for us, we were too vulnerable." He paused before continuing, "But I do know he was a close associate of Hanna's. I should have told you before, Mr. Thomas. I simply didn't think of him. Forgive me, please."

"Please do not feel badly, George," he smiled. "I leave for Paris in the morning. Perhaps I will return with the information I am seeking. It depends on how cooperative Monsieur Armand is and what information he has at his disposal. Until then, *mon ami, au revoir,* and thank you for your encouragement."

I pray Monsieur Armand will share his information with me.

CHAPTER 53

ʿ hroughout the train ride to Paris the next morning, as he watched the vineyards, pastures, farms, and rivers of southern France pass by, Alexander's thoughts were about Madeleine's life after they parted. He was consumed with questions. *Does she live in the south of France? Perhaps in one of those houses? Is she even in France? Did I wait too long for the woman I loved, just like my father?* Only a few shared weeks in their youth were reality. But in his mind they had grown into a lifetime of enormously important emotional fantasies, thus realities of the mind, giving him a sort of roller coaster of agony then ecstasy, sadness, then joy, emptiness, happiness, anger at himself. *Well, at least I finally have a good solid lead to pursue with diligence.* He thought about the questions he would ask of Jean Pierre Armand, and what he would say someday to Madeleine.

"Driver, take me to the National Defense Department office building," Alexander instructed the taxicab driver at the central Paris railway station.

In deep thought, he hardly noticed the Paris skyline and all the people on the sidewalks as his taxi drove slowly, inching its way through the crowded streets. Finally, the cab stopped at a large downtown government building. "We are here, monsieur," the driver announced over his shoulder.

"*Merci,*" Alexander said as he handed him a generous fifty francs.

"*Merci,*" replied the driver, seeing his tip.

Filled with optimism, Alexander strode briskly to the entrance of the building and went directly to the security officer sitting solemnly at his desk in the outer office to get directions to the French Resistance Division.

"Oh my," the officer replied to Alexander's query, "I am so sorry to tell you, monsieur. That division has been eliminated as of the first of the year," the guard announced sternly, shocking Alexander from his optimistic mood.

"Eliminated? What do you mean eliminated?" Shocked, Alexander raised his voice to the guard. "Goddamnit! How could they just *eliminate* an entire department? How can this be? Is there anyone left I can speak with? I am seeking a meeting with Jean Pierre Armand. Do you know of him?"

The guard raised his eyebrows at Alexander's outburst and, maintaining his composure, responded, shrugging at the impatient American, "Of course

I know of Monsieur Armand! He came here every day. He was a kind old man, very friendly with many stories about the war, you know. I myself don't know much of the war. I was a small boy, you see, but it was most difficult, I remember, monsieur. But M. Armand told me many exciting stories of the Resistance. He was a high level official, a wanted man, you know. It is so sad," the guard's voice trailed off.

"What is so sad?" asked Alexander, now almost pleading, exasperated.

"Well, perhaps you don't know, monsieur. You are an American, after all, aren't you?"

Alexander sensed a bit of cynicism in the guard's voice and questioned gently, "What happened? What is so sad?"

"Well, when the offices were eliminated, closed down, Monsieur Armand, who was Director General of the division, was devastated. He became very depressed from the date he was informed of the closure. Of course, he was not a young man, and it seems," the guard continued, speaking a bit more sensitively, "that his sole purpose in life was taken from him. His wife and children were killed by the Nazis during the war, and all he had left was his work, looking after veterans of the Resistance. When that was taken from him, we believe he died because he had no further purpose. No one needed him. He died of a lonely heart."

"He died? Good God!" exclaimed Alexander, now a bit embarrassed, increasing the pitch of his voice. "Jean Pierre Armand is dead?"

My God, will I never run out of obstacles and disappointments? Alexander thought for a moment, then asked the security guard, "When did Monsieur Armand die?"

The guard looked at his calendar, "Hmm, let me see. Yes, it was three months ago. Three months ago next week, monsieur." He looked up from his desk, and wearing his most official expression of importance, said impatiently, "Will there be anything else?"

Dejected, he stomped his foot on the marble floor. *Damn! Only three months! Why did I wait so long?* "No, I don't believe so, monsieur," he answered the guard. Then, turning to the exit, he stopped. "Forgive me, but he was my last hope. Are there any other veterans of the war who also served in the Resistance that you can refer me to?"

The guard, sensing Alexander's desperation, answered, "Perhaps, if you explained the purpose of your inquiry. I can direct you to someone who can help you." He lowered his voice, "For example, if you are seeking a person who was in the Resistance...?"

"Well, yes...I am. If you could direct me to someone, anyone who may have such information, particularly with regard to Marseille, I would be most grateful, sir."

"In that case, may I suggest that you see André Duval? He is familiar with the Veterans Administration Department and may be able to help you."

"*Merci, merci*," responded Alexander with renewed hope.

"Go to the second level, Room 206."

After waiting for Monsieur Duval for more than an hour to no avail, and growing in frustration, Alexander decided to leave and return the following day. He had left most of his belongings in Marseille, so he carried only an overnight valise as he walked to his hotel, expecting to remain in Paris for just one or two nights as he had hoped.

━━⟨♦⟩━━

The next morning, Alexander returned to the same rudimentary offices at the Defense Department building, and waited again, this time successfully, for André Duval.

"Please tell me how I can help you, Monsieur Thomas," the well-dressed official said coolly to Alexander as he ushered him into his small, austere, but functional office that lacked any décor whatsoever.

Alexander found a chair opposite him, separated by a small wooden desk, and casually looked around before addressing this obviously low-level, low-pay government bureaucrat, whose sole incentive was to stay safely in his position until his pension arrived, some ten years into the future.

"Well, monsieur, I am on a mission to find someone, and I have reason to believe if I can locate Philippe Moreau, then I will be able to locate the person I am seeking."

The official responded, "Did you say Philippe Moreau? The same Moreau who was so instrumental in the Resistance during the war?"

"*Oui*, monsieur, the same man," replied Alexander with a nod. "Do you know how I can find him?"

"Well, Monsieur Thomas, if you are seeking the same Philippe Moreau who was the director of the Resistance during World War II, I am afraid I have bad news for you. Unfortunately, he was killed in 1944. Moreau was high on the list for assassination by the Nazis, and was shot dead."

"Oh, that is very sad. I am sorry to hear this news...sorrier than I could ever explain." Alexander shook his head, subconsciously realizing that could mean Madeleine was now a widow. "Did Moreau have a family? Would they be in Paris?"

"Sir, please...understand, sir...it has been more than fifteen years since his death, and while we do our best to maintain contact with French veterans and their heirs, that is only true if the heirs are receiving any pension benefits from the government. Let me see if we can locate the necessary files and determine the current status of Monsieur Moreau's survivors."

"Thank you. I appreciate anything you can do."

"Certainly, but it will take some time. I will have to delegate the file search to a member of our staff, and, unfortunately, we are always understaffed. You understand, don't you? Also, I must tell you, there will also be a slight fee for our services."

"*Mais oui*, I expected that. I will certainly pay whatever you charge."

"Very good. Will you be staying in Paris?"

"Yes," Alexander replied, "I am staying at the Maurice."

"Ah, the Maurice. That is one of the finest, most expensive hotels in all of Europe. Excellent choice. I am sure you will be quite comfortable while you are here." The official smiled warmly, and sensing a good personal opportunity by obtaining several fees from this wealthy American, Duval smiled again and continued, "Perhaps you should enjoy your stay in Paris while we find out what we can. I will contact you at your hotel. It could take a few days though."

"A few days?" Alexander asked incredulously.

"Yes, sir. We will do the best we can."

"Well," Alexander replied, "I will count on you. Perhaps it will help if I paid you double the fee in advance in case you must ask several people to assist you." Alexander thought it would make his case a priority and speed up the effort if he opened the gratuity door for Duval without offending him, recognizing that this official, like most, felt underpaid and unappreciated while struggling to make ends meet...so, why not offer more funding?

"Ah, thank you, monsieur. I believe that suggestion could enable me to hasten the process of mobilizing my staff assistance. Let us say, day after tomorrow. Can you return to my office at eleven in the morning? I will know at that time if there will be any additional costs."

"Until day after tomorrow." Alexander stood, and with a cynical smile shook hands with the official before leaving. "It's nice to meet you. Thank you, Monsieur Duval." He was being overly pleasant, knowing this man could choose whether to find the information, or simply declare it lost!

He stepped from the office, closing the door behind him. *Well, maybe I'm making some progress here...maybe Madeleine is living right here in Paris....maybe I'm getting close...maybe she didn't remarry and is living alone...maybe she's till waiting for me...maybe...*

At exactly 11 a.m. two days later, Alexander knocked on the door of Room 206.

"*Entrez, s'il vous plait*," the familiar voice called out.

Alexander turned the knob, opened the door and entered.

"Ah, Monsieur Thomas, I have some news for you. Please sit down."

"*Merci*, Monsieur Duval. Please don't hesitate. Tell me of your findings."

"Fortunately, after a great deal of searching, we have located the file section for Philippe Moreau. It was difficult even though he was a hero in the war. However, our news is both good and not so good, monsieur." He shook his lowered head.

Alexander's optimism and upbeat emotions took another nosedive. "What is the news, Monsieur Duval?"

"Well, Monsieur Thomas, as I told you, our work and our files are relevant to those Free French Army veterans and their families who are still alive and receiving government pensions."

Alexander looked quizzically at him. "I don't understand."

"It seems that although Monsieur Moreau was part of the French underground, or Resistance as they were also known, he was not officially part of the French government's armed forces. Members of the army were, of course. But those members of the Resistance never became eligible for pensions. Alas, they were never officially qualified. As a result, there are no records of any pension payments whatsoever to Moreau's heirs. I am afraid that as far as the Veterans' Administration Office is concerned, we are without any information whatsoever that could help you." He shook his head sadly, "I am very sorry, Monsieur Thomas."

"Damn!" Alexander's face fell as he slammed his open hand on the desk, accurately reflecting his disappointment and prompting the official to speak again.

"Perhaps there is another way, monsieur. I have a suggestion for you. I urge you to enlist the assistance of a very good private investigative agency. They are freer to search records and make inquiries than are we government employees...privacy laws and all that. You understand, I'm sure. So many resources and contacts have been utilized by these independent agencies since the war. It's possible that one of them could be helpful to you. I have cards here from two such firms. I suggest you consider this approach because I believe you would be wise to obtain quality private assistance in your search rather than seek answers exclusively on your own. There are so many possibilities for discouragement if you are not aware of the necessary sources, and, of course, you are not familiar with the French rules and regulations for obtaining government information. We must get many approvals to search files. We are still finding ourselves with incomplete files and information. All our work is still done by hand with so much time required to process all the files. It is a laborious, time-consuming task, monsieur. You need specialized help. I am sure you agree?"

"You are right, Monsieur Duval. I would appreciate the cards of your contacts."

After two quick phone calls from Duval's desk, Alexander had appointments to meet with representatives of "the best in Paris," as Duval described the two firms with which he had previously arranged for a fee when any prospective client made his initial deposit payment.

"So," he mused, looking at the business cards, "I will meet these gentlemen at the Maurice Hotel today at 4 p.m. Thank you, Monsieur Duval. We will see where this path leads. I will make my choice by this time in two days. And if they are successful, I will return and reward you handsomely."

"Until then, Monsieur Thomas, good luck. I am certain that whichever agency you select, you will be pleased. Both are considered very trustworthy and effective."

Alexander took the official's advice and, after interviewing representatives of both firms, selected the one he felt most comfortable with, paid a generous retainer fee, and scheduled a meeting two weeks hence. He felt relief at his decision and felt more confident with others assisting him in his search.

Two anxious weeks later, Alexander and the detective from the agency met for lunch at a quiet sidewalk café near the hotel.

"Good afternoon, Monsieur Thomas. It's nice to see you today." The man stood at Alexander's able. He was tall, good-looking, wore a trim dark suit and was impressive in his manner.

Alexander looked up and, with a welcoming smile, said, "Sit down, please, Monsieur Trudeau. Do you have information for me?"

After sitting down at the table, the detective deliberately opened his leather briefcase and pulled out a thin file, hoping to impress his new client. "Monsieur Thomas, we have been researching every government agency that could conceivably have information, yet we continue to find nothing. It is very frustrating. But we will continue looking. I will contact you as soon as we locate anything that will lead us to resolving this situation. Do not despair, Monsieur Thomas. If Madame Moreau is in France, we will find her. I asked you to meet me here today because I do have something to show you. We found this in a private archive, a museum of sorts, in a small village on the outskirts of Paris that was devoted to information on the Resistance, the French Underground as we called it, and its activities and individuals. A daughter of one of the Resistance members lives there and is the self-appointed 'Keeper of the Legacy.'"

Alexander looked at him quizzically and said, "Yours is the first bit of news I've had that is not negative. Tell me what you have."

Jean Luis Trudeau looked directly at Alexander and, handing his client a copy of a newspaper clipping, said, "We found this newspaper article that we believe has merit. It is the first indication that Madame Moreau actually exists or even existed. At least this indicates she was alive in Paris in 1948. But that, of course, was fourteen years ago. Where she is today is unknown to us at this time." He added, "It also states in the article that her son accompanied her."

Alexander clenched his hands to this unexpected news. "She had a son?" *What does that mean? Will that impact her feelings toward me?* Alexander wondered aloud, "I think that this is a profound bit of news, monsieur. That means she wasn't killed during the war, doesn't it? And it means she was in Paris after the war!"

Alexander studied the article that included two small, somewhat blurry photographs. One was of Moreau. The caption and story told of a private foundation committed to honoring the members of the Resistance, and the dedication of a memorial to Philippe Moreau. It began, "In gratitude of the heroic leadership of Philippe Moreau..."

Alexander's eyes moved almost instantly to the second small photograph. The caption identified the two individuals in the picture as: "Monsieur Rene Chounard, Director of the Chounard Family Foundation, presents a certificate to Madame Madeleine Moreau at the site of the new memorial..."

Alexander's hands began to tremble as he looked at the photograph. He was clearly shaken, seeing for the first time any evidence that Madeleine was still alive, at least after the war. His eyes were dancing at the sight of Madeleine's face. Without any hesitation, he burst out loud with shock, "My God, it's her! I cannot believe it, but it must be her. The photograph is so small. Oh, my God, Monsieur Trudeau, you cannot imagine what I am feeling. If this is truly her, we must now find her!"

"Yes, that is our goal, and if she is still alive, we will do everything we can to locate her."

Alexander, excited at the news, yet afraid to become too optimistic, tried to restrain his emotions once again. "*Merci*, Monsieur Trudeau. Thank you for this news. As you locate any new information, I can be reached through my hotel concierge." Relieved, he stood and reached out his hand to conclude the meeting. "Until then, *au revoir.*"

Alexander returned to his hotel room and decided to call Helena with the good, albeit incomplete, news. He checked his wristwatch as he sat at the small desk in his room.

"Let's see, there's a six-hour difference between Paris and New York this time of year. So, it's just after nine in the morning in New York."

"*Allo*, how can I help you, Monsieur Thomas?" the hotel's operator responded.

"Person-to-person, please," he instructed, "to Mademoiselle Helena Thomas at the following number in New York City, America."

Momentslaterthephonerang.AlexanderanxiouslyreachedfortheFlorentine-looking telephone and brought it to his ear. "Fancy phone,"he mumbled.

"Monsieur Thomas, I have Mademoiselle Helena Thomas on the telephone for you."

"*Merci*, operator. Hello...Hello...Helena?"

"Yes, Daddy, I'm here. It's so good to hear from you. You must have some news. I haven't heard from you for so long. What's happening, Daddy?"

Alexander spoke eagerly to his daughter. "The investigation firm I hired has finally come up with something."

"What is it, Daddy? Tell me," she responded to his excitement without a second's hesitation.

Alexander described his meeting with Jean Louis Trudeau—the clipping, the photographs. "Based on this clipping, we believe that Madeleine was in Paris at least in 1948. We cannot be sure she is still here, or even that she is still in Europe, much less France, so we still have much to do. But it's the first evidence we have found..."

"That's wonderful, Daddy," she interrupted, "I'm happy for you. I must tell you though that Uncle Anthony in Miami has been trying to reach you. He says it is important. Danny Thomas and Archbishop Bashir want you to join him and other members of the Board of Governors of St. Jude in Memphis. Can you call him or should I tell him you are out of the country?"

"No," Alexander replied, "I'll speak with him. I'm feeling good right now. I must admit, *Biyee*, I've been very discouraged for a long time. Call Anthony back and tell him I'll try to reach him today."

"Oh, Daddy, I'll do that. Good luck."

"Bye, Helena. I'll be back in touch."

Alexander waited for his daughter to replace the telephone in its cradle before replacing his. "God, I love that girl," he whispered to himself, grateful for her understanding, as he sat back in his chair.

"Iskandar," the familiar voice said, "I'm glad you called. We've been worried about you. The family, all your friends at ALSAC and St. Jude. We've missed you. You've been gone so long. Are you alright, *khai-yi*?"

"Yes, Anthony," Alexander spoke into the telephone, "I am better today. At last I have some news."

"Good," responded Anthony, "I hope the weather is cooler in Paris than it is here in South Florida."

Alexander asked, a bit nervously, "What's on your mind, Anthony. What is so urgent?"

"Iskandar, you need to come back, and very soon. We have been working on the new St. Jude Children's Research Hospital for several years now. The time has come for all of us to witness the fruit of our labors. Danny Thomas wants us all to be in Memphis for the official grand opening of St. Jude's Hospital. *Sayedna* Bashir made me promise I'd get you there, *khai-yi*, and now you need to come. We broke ground in 1958 about this time, if you recall. That was the same year President Eisenhower sent the Marines to Beirut...God, what a mess that was. You know, Iskandar, the opening will be our proudest moment. And, for Danny and his family, it is the fulfillment of his promise so long ago to St. Jude. Imagine, Iskandar, it was only five years ago that you and I got involved in this dream of Danny's when Mike Tamer, George Simon, Archbishop Bashir, Danny, and Fred Gattas convinced us to join in, at a time when all they had were drawings and a dream."

"Yes, Anthony, I remember. You can tell Danny and the boys that I'll be there."

Anthony replied, "Good, Iskandar." Anthony told Alexander the dates, schedule and function highlights. "I'll have a telegram sent to you. The events are in two weeks. I'll count on you to be with us."

Alexander replied, "That's fine, Anthony, I'll be there. Meanwhile, I'll keep my people on with my search, but I have no way of knowing when or if they'll get new information here." *Where are you, Madeleine?*

The weeks passed slowly with no new information as Alexander planned his trip to Memphis. Almost daily, he called Jean Louis Trudeau inquiring, "Any news today?"

The response each time was always the same disappointing, "I am very sorry, Monsieur Thomas, but we do not have any new developments. There have been so many futile efforts...so many dead-ends...but we believe that eventually we'll find something."

En route to the airport before departing, Alexander stopped by the offices of Trudeau Investigations, Ltd., and left a packet of information explaining how he could be reached while away. In addition, as his parting comment, Alexander said to Jean Louis as they shook hands, "Contact me as soon as you have any news. And if you cannot reach me, call my daughter, Helena. Her information is here in this envelope."

Trudeau responded with a reassuring smile, "We will be in contact immediately when we have something to report, Monsieur Thomas."

Trudeau had grown personally involved in the romantic search of this American. He believed this man deserved results, and felt as if he were drawn into this effort beyond a simple business transaction. He was determined to see this through to resolution no matter where it led. Alexander had proven he would bear whatever the cost. But he was no longer as optimistic as before.

They embraced and the investigator kissed Alexander on both cheeks in the French tradition. *"Bon voyage."*

CHAPTER 54

$\mathcal{A}$ lexander arrived in Memphis the day before the grand opening of St. Jude Children's Research Hospital and, as always, checked into the Peabody Hotel, the "home away from home" for all members of the Board of Governors when in town to attend board meetings, committee meetings, or other gatherings of the hospital or of ALSAC. This was the funding organization of volunteers, most of whom were of Lebanese heritage, with some of the Jewish faith, and some of the Muslim faith.

It was late in the afternoon when he arrived.

The clerk at the front desk asked, "Shall we have the bill sent directly to your offices as always, Mr. Thomas?"

Alexander nodded, finished filling out the registration form, looked up and, with a smile, acknowledging the soft lilting Southern accent, replied, "Thank you, yes, as always." He noticed the clock on the wall behind the clerk as it approached six o'clock.

"Pardon me, Mr. Thomas, but I would like to say to you and all other members of St. Jude's Board of Governors how much all of us here at the Peabody admire you for giving of your valuable time and paying all your own expenses. We find it remarkable that St. Jude pays for all expenses of the children, their parents' visits, food, room, and medical expenses. It's unheard of anywhere. That's very unusual, you know. For all of us here at the Peabody and, I think for all citizens of Memphis, we thank you for being here. St. Jude is a wonderful contribution to Memphis and to Tennessee."

Alexander smiled proudly and replied, "Thank you, young man. It's our way of thanking America, and helping Danny Thomas. It's for the children. Give Danny all the credit." With a feeling of warm pride in his heritage, in his friends, and in his fellow board members, Alexander stepped into the elegant lobby full of families with children. He then watched with amusement the march of the mallard ducks as they left the fountain waters where they had been swimming all day to step down the wooden steps to the red carpet and waddle to "their" elevator that would take them to the rooftop to complete the trademark march which concluded each day at six o'clock sharp. The ducks would not reappear until the next morning when they would step from "their" elevator onto the red carpet and parade back to the fountain. Giggles of joy from the children and parents, crowding closer to get better views, accompanied the procession as onlookers thrilled to this daily ritual.

Alexander watched, enjoying the parade, relaxing, and feeling good upon his return to Memphis, the Peabody, and to his dear friends at St. Jude.

He was pleased to be back in America after months and months of fruitless searching, agonizing over what appeared to be a futile, exhausting search for an impossible dream. He had been away from his family, his businesses, and his friends for too long. And, as a result, he felt a sense of being strangely disconnected from his previous life.

While his friends on the Board of Governors of ALSAC and St. Jude let him know by their words and behavior that he was respected and missed, he knew he had been separated for what seemed an eternity. The worst part to him was that as a result of having put his whole heart into his search for Madeleine his emotions were indeed frayed. He needed a break with friends. His colleagues in America had reached out to him, but it was clear his agenda had taken him on a different path from them for too many months. He knew he had to dedicate himself to his search. It was very important for him. And while he understood there was no guarantee of success, his tenacious determination made him really believe there was a strong possibility he would locate Madeleine even though he had waited more than forty years. *Forty years!*

Because he had waited so long, and so much of his life had transpired, he blamed himself for his lack of success. Yet, he also reminded himself he could not have sought to find Madeleine sooner. After all, he insisted in his mental debate, he simply could not have returned to Marseille to find Madeleine from the date he married Helene. And never did he receive even one letter from her. So, he began to understand that questioning himself was an exercise in futility.

Move on. Get back into your life. But what now? he asked himself over and over. He was considering these thoughts in silence in his room at the Peabody Hotel when the phone rang.

Fred Gattas's voice was on the line, "Iskandar, join us in the ALSAC hospitality room. All your friends are there. Danny is 'holding court' and wants all of us to join him in Suite 777. Your cousin Elias and your buddy Joe Ayoub haven't seen you yet. You're family, Iskandar. I'll come get you in fifteen minutes. Be ready."

Shaken from his thoughts, Alexander smiled, thinking they weren't going to let him be alone too much.

"You are my brother, my friend. We are worried about you. No one knows what's bothering you, and we're not going to ask. But, we want you with us. See you in a few minutes, Iskandar."

"I'll be ready. Thanks, Fred."

Alexander listened for the "click" signalling Anthony had placed the telephone on the cradle slowly, not sure if he was actually ready for a mixer, he softly hung up the phone.

As he was finishing dressing after a quick shower, he heard a knock at his door.

"Be right there, Fred."

Alexander opened the door and found Elias, Anthony, and Joe waiting for him. All jovial, they grabbed Alexander and ushered him down the hall to Suite 777. At the door, Marlo and Terre, Danny's daughters, were waiting. "Come on in," they said in their young voices. "Daddy's waiting for all of you."

The suite was filled with members of the Board, wives, and friends. The mood was quite jovial. Almost everyone was standing, most with a drink in one hand, the other free hand gesticulating as one on one conversations loudly filled the air.

Danny stood up from the sofa where he had been sitting with his son, Tony, and several other board members. Raising both hands for attention, he spoke aloud the second he saw Marlo and Terre signal that everyone was in the suite. "*Ahlen wa sahlen*, come in and gather around me. I have some very interesting news for all of you."

The bartender asked of those just arriving, "What'd you like to drink fellas?"

"Scotch on the rocks," they answered with grins.

"You've got it."

After a few minutes of congenial exchanges, Danny asked for quiet and their attention. "Gentlemen, we did it," he announced with his familiar wide grin. "As you know, I made a promise to St. Jude Thaddeus when I was at the lowest point in my life, and together, we made the dream come true. I'm grateful you're here to share this exciting news!"

He continued, "Mike Tamer carried most of the load these past years. He's my hero. And so are you men, your families, your wives, your children. We have also fulfilled a promise to our heritage." Pausing to look at the many familiar faces around him, he continued, fumbling his ever-present Macanudo Churchill cigar in his fingers, "And, as you know I've said, as I believe, if a man isn't proud of his heritage, he has no heritage. We, together, share a wonderful heritage as Lebanese, Syrians, and as Americans. Now, together, we have unified in thanking America as never before. And I am so very proud to be among you. You honor me.'"

They all applauded their leader as some yelled out, "No, Danny. You honor us!"

After a moment, smiling and very happy, he looked around the room and continued, "And now, I have some exciting news for us all. The President of Lebanon has invited us to come to Beirut and be his guests for a gala celebration. He and our countrymen are aware of what we here at St. Jude have done, and he thinks it appropriate that we come to the palace in Baabda to receive a grateful thanks from Lebanon for continuing the tradition of our Phoenician ancestors in traveling the world, being successful in our trade, doing so in peace, honoring our heritage, and exemplifying all that is good in our history." Then he stopped for emphasis, looking around at the faces watching him, anticipating. "Of course," Danny said smiling to his friends, "you are those about whom he is speaking. I'm just a saloon entertainer who did good."

That self-deprecating remark brought forth loud laughter, and comments like one who yelled out, "That's true, Danny...Sure, Danny, you're just a saloon entertainer, movie star, friend of Doris Day, dreamer of honorable dreams, uniter of our people, most famous, most beloved Lebanese-American in the land...Yes, Danny, just a saloon entertainer!" They all laughed at the joke.

Danny, feeling proud of what he and his countrymen had done, spoke loudly above the crowd, "The most beautiful part of all of this is that it is for the children! We must always remember what ALSAC stands for and never forget it: Aiding Leukemia Stricken American Children. Never forget!"

"Now," he continued firmly, "we must not stop here. We must do all we can to support our doctors, nurses, and researchers. We must give them all they need to rid the world of this terrible disease."

"I'm proud," he said in all seriousness, his voice lowering, reflecting his mood change. "I am proud to be a beggar for the children. And that's what I want all our people to be, *beggars for the children*. Even though we dedicate our beautiful hospital tomorrow, with nearly ten thousand people expected there...can you believe it?...ten thousand people will come to watch the doors of St. Jude open for the first time," he was on a roll now, "...even though we dedicate the hospital, we truly have only just begun. We must find the cure. We must treat every child at no cost to their families. We must provide the very best care. Never forget this. Our job has only just started. And we will succeed."

"*Inshallah!*" echoed several in the crowd in unison.

Danny took a deep breath and, with tears of gratitude moistening his eyes, he spoke again, "*Shookrun*, my friends, my brothers." Then with a bow from the waist, "I thank you for all you are doing. Thank you."

After a moment of respectful silence, some of the proud, extraordinarily successful men of the Board of Governors from throughout America shifted noticeably on their feet. They all felt a sense of goodness, of enrichment and human fulfillment in pursuing such an honorable goal. These feelings would remain with them for years and bring energy to their lives.

Danny spoke again, "Mike Tamer will fill you in on the invitation to go to Beirut. The President wants it to be in mid-June, a time of rebirth, a time when those of us from the mountains will be able to travel to the villages of our birth without being blocked by deep snow. Those from the Bekaa or the south can go anytime," he grinned again.

Mike thanked Danny and began describing the proposed gala in Beirut and travel arrangements.

"The President asked us to select those Americans of Lebanese heritage who have exemplified the finest characteristics of success, philanthropy, ethics, and character that Lebanon can honor. Actually, we created a committee to do this. It was comprised of the most respected individuals we could find in America. Archbishop Antony Bashir was the chairman. There were a dozen on the committee. No one in this room, excluding the Archbishop, was on the committee, not even myself or Danny. The ambassador from Lebanon selected many of the committee members. He also asked President Eisenhower to select members. Members came from each religion—Orthodox, Melkite, Maronite, and Islam.

He stopped for a few moments to let all of this sink in, then concluded by saying, "Of the fifty members of the Board of Governors of St. Jude and ALSAC, thirty were selected. Another twenty outside the Board were also selected. They were chosen not only because of their support of St. Jude, but also in recognition of their many years of active, dedicated philanthropy, humanitarianism, career success, reputation of honor, ethics, and always their remembering and honoring their heritage: Lebanon. Those selected will be formally contacted. We ask that you be prepared to go to Beirut and stay in Lebanon for seven days during June." He flipped through his papers making sure he hadn't forgotten anything, then continued, "Please coordinate your travel plans with my office; all airline and hotel reservations can be arranged with us to make it easier for you. And," he laughed, "as usual, you'll be sent a bill. You know, St. Jude pays only for direct hospital costs, research, and patient care."

Everybody joined in the laughter. Albert Harris called out, "Mike, after seeing those sick children today, none of us minds that at all. It's the least we can do."

"Alright then," Mike finished, "after this week here in Memphis, the next time we'll all meet again will be in London where we'll get on the Middle East Airlines flight to Beirut. May God bless you all."

At breakfast, on that dedication weekend in Memphis, Alexander visited with several of his friends on the Board and, sitting next to Danny, he found himself listening to Danny's lovely and supportive wife, Rose Marie, talk about their children's hopes and dreams, and Danny's vision into what he wanted St. Jude Hospital to become. And yet, as he listened, he found himself thinking of far away places...Marseille, Paris, and now, Beirut and his village of Douma.

"Imagine, Danny, in a couple of months we'll be in Beirut. I haven't been back. God, I wonder if I'll recognize anything."

Danny turned in his seat and, lighting his ubiquitous, enormous cigar, replied, "It's going to be wonderful, Iskandar. Y'know, I wanted to take the family several times, but something always came up. Four years ago it was the politics in Beirut, and Ike had to send in the Marines. Then, it seemed there was a movie or series commitment, just when things were calm in Beirut. But I'm really looking forward to getting up to Bsharre. I love that place. It's beautiful, Iskandar."

"Yes it is, Danny," Alexander replied with a smile, "it is so beautiful with the cedar forest and that six thousand year old cedar by itself. And Gibran's birthplace. It's magnificent. But right now, Danny, in February, the snow is so deep, I don't think you could get there."

Alexander laughed, "That's true, Danny. Lebanon is a most incredible, tiny country. They even grow bananas all along the southern coast. Bananas! Can you imagine? And the largest apples you ever saw. Remember, its mountains hold more water than any place in the Middle East, and in the Bekaa Valley, there are ponds and streams where you can hunt birds, ducks, and fish to your heart's content."

"I'm really glad we are going together," said Danny with a smile of pride. "We've all done some good things here in America, Iskandar, but I have to tell you, St. Jude Hospital is really the pinnacle of my life, my dear friend. And it brought so many of us together. That's one of the things I'm most proud of, along with my children." Danny reached to the ceramic bowl-like ashtray and flicked his growing cigar ash. "I mean, look over there—there's George Simon and his family from Detroit, the Shakers from Chicago, the Thomas family from Wilkes-Barre, Elias Chalhoub from your neck of the woods, and on and on. Young Dick Shadyac is new here, and I can already tell that he will be extremely dedicated to us and be a significant presence. He's a good one."

"And soon," Danny continued, "soon, the sons of all these guys will pick up where their fathers left off. I tell you, Iskandar, I am damned proud of what we've done here. We are going to save a lot of children. And while we're doing it, we're thanking America for our opportunities and our blessings. And now we'll be going to Beirut together. Man, I feel good."

Alexander smiled, put his arm on Danny's shoulder and said with complete sincerity, "Danny, like most of these guys, I've done well in America. I've had two beautiful children. My daughter, Helena, is going to be thirty-two this year. As you know, I lost my son in the World War II. And then Helene died too. But I have to tell you, being a part of ALSAC and St. Jude has been really important to me. You and the hospital pulled me from a sad time. I'm grateful I could be part of this hospital and part of your dream. Thank you, Danny."

He paused, then continued, "Still, I'm involved with something personal. I have to go back to France soon. I'll meet you and the others in London. If that's not possible, I'll fly to Beirut from either Paris or Marseille. I've got some important business to conclude there, one way or another."

"Till Beirut then, Iskandar," Danny replied, patting Alexander's shoulder. "Good luck."

As Alexander got up to leave Danny to his family and others who wanted to visit with him, Danny also rose, and, with pride showing in his eyes, embraced Alexander. While hugging, these two friends kissed each other on their cheeks, pulled apart, smiled and, almost in unison spoke, saying, *"Allah ma'ak.* Beirut in June."

CHAPTER 55

arly one morning at home, Alexander placed a call to Paris. "And what news do you have for me, Monsieur Duval? Anything new?"

"I am so sorry to tell you, Monsieur Thomas, but..."

"Nothing?" he interrupted.

"No, sir. We cannot find Madeleine Moreau anywhere. We know she's not in France. We have covered all of Europe. Still, nothing. She seems to have completely disappeared. We've been in close communication with Interpol, and with our associates in Switzerland, Britain, Sardinia, and Spain. But nothing has come of our efforts. We do know she was briefly in Paris in 1948 when Philippe Moreau was honored, but that is all, except that she stayed in the Maurice Hotel for a few days that year. Apparently, from their records, she has not stayed there since. I am sorry, but one never knows what will come up in these matters. Don't be too discouraged. Perhaps in time...We'll keep the file open, but cannot at this time encourage you."

"Time? Where the hell could she be? She must be somewhere! Find her, damnit!" he angrily demanded in frustration as he banged the desk with his hand.

He leaned back in his chair behind his desk and pondered, *What am I doing? Maybe I should stay here and focus on Helena and my businesses.* Then he realized that the memories would not go away and the aching need to find Madeleine would grow even stronger. He was lonely and needed the presence of his first love if at all possible. *Or is she dead?*

During the following days, Alexander busied his life in Kissimmee, trying to set aside his emotional battle. Occasionally, he visited his sister in Orlando. He visited the clinics he supported; and he met with his friends, the Stewarts in Bartow.

Still, as much as Alexander got more involved locally, evenings at home were the loneliest times for him.

Over the next several weeks at home, Alexander began more and more to re-involve himself in his enterprises, not accepting the fact that he might never find Madeleine, but thinking that at this time, it was better for his daughter and himself that he not be so deeply engrossed in a disappointing and stressful effort that might not result in a successful conclusion. Weekly calls to Paris were all he could do anyway. He realized that being in France didn't really improve results. It was an unfamiliar sense of impotence, of not contributing to his mission...having no influence to resolve his problem. He hated having to rely totally on others in this situation. His inability to make things happen was driving him crazy. It was at these times he would remember Psalm 46:11, *"Be still and know that I am the Lord."* He had to face the fact that there may not be anything more he could do and that, as agonizing as it was, he would simply have to let God take over and resolve it for him.

As his business life got more active, he began to feel somewhat better, becoming reminded of the many blessings in his life. He telephoned his beautiful daughter each week. Sometimes he would drive to Tampa to visit Abigail, now widowed, in her bayfront home. And Wilbur, who managed the ranch so well.

"Well, dear friend, how are you feeling today?" Abigail asked the moment she saw him at her door. "Any news? Come in and let me give you a hug."

"Hi, Abigail, it's good to see you."

"As I see you these days with such sensitivity and warmth, I'm so grateful we've stayed close all these years. Isn't life strange, Alexander? My mother kept us apart. Although I have to bear the responsibility because I was not courageous enough to defy her when I cared for you so much. She would say, 'He's not for you, Abigail...a nice man, but of a different world. You can be friends, but that's all.' I'm sorry, but I was too young and naïve, I guess."

"That's history, Abigail," Alexander replied in a soft voice as they embraced, "that's behind us. Let's speak of today...of the future."

"Alexander, I want to tell you something I've been thinking about for some time. Sit down." Looking at him, she said, "My husband, Bill, was a good man, but he couldn't stop his drinking. In truth, I am convinced he was always jealous of you. You came here as an immigrant with no money. He had every privilege: social prominence, family, wealth, good looks, but he never felt adequate. He never felt he had earned anything. I think he was in great pain. It was awful watching him even long before he took his own life that day...and very bad afterward for me too, but now he is finally at peace. And I am finally at peace. And, dear friend, I hope soon you will be at peace. But you aren't now, you know." Her eyes focused on his as she drew her breath. "I'm going to tell you something." She pointed her finger at him and spoke firmly. "You must either fully devote yourself to your search for Madeleine, or you must find a way spiritually to completely put her and your past with her behind you. If you don't do this," she admonished, watching his face with all seriousness, now sitting beside him on the couch in the living room, putting his hand in both her hands, "then, your emptiness and your sadness will rule your life. You will lose your passion for life. And that, Alexander, would not be fair to Helena nor to your friends. This has lingered too long. It's time, Alexander, for you to decide."

She paused, thought for a moment and continued, looking into his sensitive eyes, "You were there when Bill died. You embraced me, and spoke strongly to me. And now, that is what I'm doing for you." Then, sitting straight up, and changing the tone of her voice from one of sympathy to firmness, said, "Alexander, make your plans now. Go back to Marseille. Find her or not, but end this search one way or another. It's been long enough. If you find her, bring her to me. She and I have much to talk about. If you don't find her soon, then as you told me, it will be time for you to get over it and get on with your life. You need to know. *And so do I.* Now go, and may God be with you."

Alexander listened to what he knew had to be said to him. He had to come to a decision. "Thank you, Abigail. I guess I needed to hear those words from you. I think you are right." He slapped his thighs and stood up. "It's time to bring this search to an end one way or another. I'll always be grateful for your support and your love. I have to be in Beirut in June and I've decided to go to Douma to visit what family I still have there. I haven't been back since I left so many years ago. I'll simply leave it in the hands of God and the detectives in France."

As he stood at the couch, she reached out her hand so he could assist her as she arose. "I've been thinking," he said, "I'll leave next week, spend a few days in France, see if there is any news, and then meet with my friends in Beirut. I'll be sure to see you before I leave."

Nodding her head, she smiled and said, "I'll come get you and take you to the airport."

He stepped to her so that they could embrace as very dear, very special friends.

⚜

In early June, as they had planned, Abigail picked up Alexander and took him to the Tampa airport for his flight to New York that would connect with his flight to Paris.

Alexander's flight that day took him to Idlewild International Airport in New York. After an early dinner with Helena in the city the night before, he got a cab to the airport and boarded Air France flight 202 bound for Paris.

Alexander spent the six hours on the plane thinking about his life, about his children, about Abigail, about his charity efforts, but mostly he thought about Madeleine.

As he perfunctorily responded to the inquiries and deliveries of food from the attractive stewardess, he also realized how quiet it was in the new jet's cabin. Then he noticed the middle-aged woman sitting next to him put down her magazine as she sighed.

"Life is so unpredictable," he said softly to her. "Here I am, nearly sixty years old, searching for my first love, when she was sixteen and I was eighteen. We spent an incredibly beautiful six weeks together in Marseille forty-two years ago. How do you explain such a phenomenon?" he asked her rhetorically. "How do you deal with such a thing?"

Then, not able to stop himself, he told this listener his story of Madeleine and how she has remained in his heart for so long, so endearingly.

She nodded from time to time and replied, "Sir, there is no way you can rationally explain such matters of the heart. It is like faith; either you have it or you don't, you either feel it or you don't, and, in all candor, you either deal with it or you don't. If you want my opinion, since you told me about your story and you asked me, I'd say to you, you have to see it through. You have to exhaust yourself seeking a conclusion or you'll never be at peace. Find her. Either she's still hoping for you to find her, which, as a woman, I believe is true, or she has a full life, a husband, a family, and has no room for you. In either case, you must find out. You have to continue your search or put it behind you."

She paused, looked to the attendant, waving her hand to get her attention, and asked for refills of her glass of wine and his iced tumbler of Scotch. When that was done, she turned, looked into Alexander's eyes, reached for his hand, and said, "I can only speak as a person who just met you tonight, heard your story, and sensed your emotions, but I do believe you will find this lucky woman." With a smile, she added, "I wish I had a handsome, sensitive man like you looking for me."

She leaned toward Alexander to look out the window. "I think we have crossed the coast of France. The weather seems fine." Sitting back, she turned and whispered to him, "Yes, I do believe you will find your Madeleine. But, if you don't..."

After landing at the bustling Orly airport, Alexander was once again driven to the Maurice Hotel. *You were here in 1948, Madeleine. Where are you now?*

He showered, had a leisurely breakfast, and arranged to meet with

Monsieur Duval at the hotel.

Duval sat beside him in the lounge. "*Allo*, Monsieur Thomas, and welcome again to Paris. I really am sorry to say to you, sir, that, still, we have no new information to offer you. Nothing. Madame Moreau is nowhere to be found. There is no record of her marriage, death, pension, hotel reservations... nothing. She must be outside of Europe. We simply don't know."

"Well, you say you searched everywhere? England? Sardinia? Switzerland?" responded Alexander with a sigh of exasperation. "I expected this would be your report. It is so frustrating to me. Still, if you find anything, *anything at all*, please contact me through the Charles V Hotel in Marseille, or contact my daughter in New York. You have both numbers. After a few days in Marseille I'll be flying directly to Beirut and staying at the Phoenicia Hotel."

"Yes, Monsieur Thomas, to all of your questions. I can honestly tell you that we have done our best and have come to the conclusion that we are not able and will not likely be able to locate Madame Moreau. In all likelihood, I am sorry to tell you, we believe she has passed away. We are not convinced that she is still alive...good luck to you, sir. Good luck," he repeated because he truly wanted this man to succeed in his search.

"You may be correct, Monsieur Duval...you may indeed be correct. However, if she is still alive, I will find her. But I must be successful, or I must assume that is no longer possible. And that decision I must make soon, I am very sad to say."

Alexander spent three days in Marseille before leaving for Beirut, often visiting his friends at *Café Liban*, the *Canebière*, paying homage at Notre-Dame-de-la-Garde, and sometimes preferring to sit alone quietly on the promontory he shared so long ago with Madeleine, anticipating that it may indeed be the last time he would visit the site. He had great difficulty finally accepting the possibility that Madeleine would not be found, that she may indeed have passed away, and that he had waited too long. He was sad and felt a sense of deep futility. He was coming to the point of accepting that he would never find her.

On June 11, 1962, Alexander boarded the Mideast Airlines flight to Beirut.

CHAPTER 56

Beirut
April 1962

rançois leaned back in his luxuriant chair as he pulled away slightly from his large mahogany desk. Each morning he arrived at his office at 8 a.m. to examine and analyze financial reports before the telephone began ringing with its incessant demands. After a couple hours of concentration, he liked to turn his chair toward the large windows of his corner office on the thirtieth floor of the Credit Suisse building in West Beirut overlooking the usually sparkling Mediterranean Sea and enjoy his coveted view.

He loved his work as an investment banker with Credit Suisse, one of Europe's most highly respected banks. His years at the London School of Economics had served him well. In only a few years, his education, his personal style, his relationship with the Kabani family, and his fluency in three languages enabled him to become a friend and financial advisor to Arabic speaking rulers of Kuwait, the Gulf States of Bahrain, Qatar, the Emirates, and Saudi Arabia. Many were now fluent in French as was he, but few could speak English as he did. His talents were highly regarded, especially as his clients from Europe and America visited Beirut. He was often called on to host visitors, taking them to the finest restaurants and to the elegant *Casino du Liban* which rivaled the best in the world, including Paris' Crazy Horse Saloon, and the casinos of Monte Carlo and Las Vegas. He was also popular among his mother's growing circle of commercial and philanthropic leaders.

Life was very good for François who was frequently asked to speak on global economics to students at the American University of Beirut, the finest university in the Near East.

Yet there was something missing.

François' heart belonged to the most beautiful, sensual woman he had ever met...his lover in Paris...Leah. *Where was she? Was she still alive?* All he ever knew was what she had written him when she abruptly left Paris to go to Palestine in 1948...so long ago. He never received further information of her whereabouts or activities...just her words that she would always love him.

He had never forgotten her, even as he had progressed in his work.

During his late morning respites, François loved to clear his mind as he gazed in the distance, sometimes watching ships sailing the sea to and from the ports of Beirut and Jounieh.

Looks like a storm brewing, he thought as he noticed the scattered rain drops begin striking against the large glass panes...pinging... a staccato sound that he enjoyed. *Maybe, just maybe, it will help cool off the political battles going on in Lebanon and in Palestine, and now Israel, to the south.*

It was spring of 1962, and while there was turmoil among the powerful political families, it was much calmer in the city after President Eisenhower sent the Marines into Lebanon. Beiruti businessmen and bankers, who always seemed to stay above the fray, remained as apolitical as possible, the wisest course for economic survival, a posture the Lebanese traders had perfected over centuries of invasions and internecine battles.

And to the south, God knows if the Palestinians and Israelis will ever find a way of occupying the same land. So far, since 1947, the Israelis were in control.

Such were the thoughts of François Moreau, Vice-President of Investment Banking in the Near East offices of Credit Suisse during those difficult years that Lebanese had to survive. But this particular morning would be different for him.

As he enjoyed quiet concentration during his brief reverie, the telephone beckoned with its familiar "buzz-buzz." As he reached for the telephone, he went through his typical decision: French or Arabic?

"*Allo*," he answered in French. "François speaking."

"François?" the soft feminine voice responded breathlessly in French. He instantly recognized the lilting familiar voice from his past that had resided in the recesses of the most private places in his memory cells.

Unnerved, his throat suddenly tightened and his hand began to shake. "Leah! Is it you?"

"*Oui, mon chéri.* I am in Beirut, at the airport."

"At the airport? But why? Are you coming or going?"

"I just flew in from Paris, François. *Our* Paris. Do you remember?"

He couldn't help but smile, almost breaking into a happy, nervous laugh, at the sound of her voice...all it took for his emotions to become charged with sensuality and joy.

"Do I remember? Oh, Leah, yes. Of course! I have never forgotten you."

"Nor I you, my love...nor I you."

"But, Leah, you left with just a note. And now it's been...what...nearly fourteen years? *Mon Dieu!* Can I see you? Will you stay in Beirut? For dinner at least?"

"*Non, mon chéri,* I must be here only to go south to Israel. You remember, don't you, that I had to leave Paris to help my people. I knew then as I know now if I saw you instead of leaving you the note, I might never leave you... ever...I still love you so much, François. Are you married now?"

"Married? To another? How can you ask such a thing? You still fill my heart, Leah. And while I have lived and continue to live a wonderful life, I have something missing in my soul. You are that something, Leah."

"Perhaps, François, when times are better and I have done all I can do, then perhaps, I pray, I can be with you. It is so difficult."

"What is it you are doing, Leah?"

"Don't you remember, François? I told you in Paris, and I cannot speak of my mission at this time. But, please know that you are always in my thoughts and that I will always love you. And soon, I hope we can be together. This insanity has to end, God knows. As for now, I must go on and yet keep you in my heart."

His emotions bounced from excitement to disappointment to joy to anger. "This is terrible, Leah! How can we love each other so deeply and not be together? *What kind of destiny is ours?*"

"One day, François, I promise we *will* be together...forever." She nodded and waved to the airline agent who signaled it was time to board the plane to Amman. Her voice lowered. "For now I must say *au revoir,* my love...until later."

"*Au revoir,* my love. Be safe."

He stared at the telephone in his hand as he heard the taunting, disconnect tone. Frustrated, yet grateful to hear her voice once again, his mind raced back to Paris and his days at the Sorbonne. Especially his evenings with Leah in romantic Paris.

"She is magnificent," he whispered aloud to the room, to no one. "And like it or not, I still love her so much. Just the sound of her lilting voice, her laughter, makes me excited. My lover, my friend!" Then he laughed, "My elusive ghost!" But he knew that he had no choice but to accept his destiny, so resignedly he thought, "One day, *inshallah.*"

He set the telephone back on its cradle and turned to the darkening clouds in the west, over the sea, to better understand that Leah and the sea were alike...in the case of both, he seemed to have no influence to change the path of either.

Mon Dieu. I think I now have a better appreciation for my father and mother's life, he thought wistfully. *Am I destined to repeat their love affair?*

CHAPTER 57

Alexander, in a window seat as usual, watched the blue waters of the Mediterranean slip beneath the plane's wings as he anxiously awaited his return to Lebanon.

"Forty-two years...it's been forty-two years," he said softly to the lovely Lebanese attendant moments after she announced to him, "We'll be descending shortly, monsieur. Our arrival in Beirut is on time. Welcome home."

"Forty-two years," he whispered again to himself as he continued looking out the window at the cloud-flecked sky as it met the high, rugged snow-capped mountains beyond the city. He had deliberately sat on the left side of the plane so he could look to the north of Beirut as they began their southern descent west of the meandering shoreline of Lebanon. He watched the mosaic pattern of the majestic mountain ranges, while feeling a surge of strong, poignant emotions in his body. His skin tingled at the thought of returning to his homeland.

Home. I'm coming back home. He almost started shaking at the thought. Instantly, memories of his childhood in Douma flashed through his mind. He was feeling his deep love for Lebanon.

"Miss," he spoke to the attendant as he pointed out the window, "those are the mountains where I was born. Look! You can still see the snow on the high mountains. Even in June the snows will be there."

"It's so magnificent, monsieur. I can see why some call Lebanon the 'Switzerland of the Middle East.' No wonder the Lebanese always come back. My friends and I snow-ski in the mountains of Lebanon, and within less than an hour we are water-skiing in the sea. Amazing!"

"That is true..." he smiled proudly, with a twinkle in his eye.

His gaze on the shoreline of Beirut jutting out into the sea cast an excitement in his heart. Looking to his left, to the north, he could see the coastal town of Tripoli, then Byblos, then Jounieh with its large port, and beyond was Beirut. Up the mountains to the east of Tripoli he focused his eyes on the terrain hoping to recognize where his tiny village of Douma was located. Its unique shape would be recognizable, but it was a bit too hazy to clearly see it. He could see the patches of cedar forests, snow on the taller mountains, and the greening valleys of olive groves as they responded to the warming of spring.

Ah, there is the mountain range where I was born. My God, how different it looks. I've never seen those mountains and my village from the air. And there are the groves of giant cedars. They look so small from here. I used to climb them as a boy, and they seemed enormous.

As the Mideast Airline's Flight 109 descended, it banked gently to the west, then back to the east to begin its approach to the Beirut airport just a few miles south of the city.

As the stewardess returned to her jump seat toward the front of the plane, Alexander braced himself for the landing. Shortly, the tires squealed as they safely struck the tarmac runway.

His emotions were high. *Home. This is almost too much*, he smiled to himself.

"*Ahlen wa Sahlen! Yallah*," shouted the airline representative impatiently waving to the disembarking passengers as they left the plane, "please follow me to the terminal gate marked shaish. There you will find the immigration and custom officers."

Alexander climbed down the steps of the airplane ahead of most of the passengers who were eagerly seeking the gate. When his foot touched the tarmac, he carefully looked all around him. "Beirut," he whispered in amazement. He had never even pictured what it would be like if he ever returned, so, the sensations were simultaneously exciting, unfamiliar, and unexpected. He breathed in the familiar smells of the nearby sea blending with the odors of the airport.

"I left by ship...an old, slow ship...and I return by jet airplane," he laughed and said aloud. "Amazing!"

After he concluded passing through customs, Alexander emerged to the large, noisy baggage area where several planeloads of passengers were waiting for their baggage to arrive. All bags were being hand placed on a stationary, sloped stainless steel bank, crowded by anxious travelers hoping to find their suitcases, boxes and bags filled with everything from clothing to gifts for relatives.

The ubiquitous porters moved through the crowd with their hand wagons. "Do you need help?" they asked everyone.

Alexander watched, not feeling a sense of urgency, but preferring to "people watch" as he noticed everything. In the jostling crowd there were people from all regions of the Middle East and several countries of Africa.

There were black-draped Muslim women from the more Islamic and fundamentalist nations, including Yemen, Sudan and Oman wearing their different styles of abeyehs; Saudi or Kuwaiti sheikhs in their fabulous woolen cloaks, and *keiffeyehs*; Egyptians, Jordanians, Syrians, and Iraqis in western dress emulating the attire of Europe.

Europe's influence is still very strong, thought Alexander as he observed the crowd. The faces were a mixture of all shades ranging from the white-faced Syrian and Europeans to the tanned Lebanese to the brown Egyptians and visitors from the Gulf States. *Fascinating*, Alexander thought, *and so different, the whole world is here, it seems. People from everywhere, coming to the laissez-faire Lebanese society. The balance of Christians and Muslims seems to work here, at least for now.*

Of course, the difficulties of the late 1950s, and need for U.S. forces to quell the street battles in 1958 were the manifestation of the seemingly endless internecine political jousting. Even so, Alexander was confident that the resilience and tenacity of the Lebanese culture were so strong that they would come back very well indeed.

We always come back, he remembered.

"Taxi!" he shouted at the curb. As a cab pulled along side, he ordered, "Take me to the Phoenicia Hotel."

The taxi pulled up to the curb at the hotel, where Alexander paid the driver in Lebanese pounds he had acquired at the bank exchange branch in the airport.

"*Shookrun*," responded the driver, smiling, as he opened the rear door while accepting his fare.

"Thank you, driver," Turning, he went into the hotel where he was met by a uniformed doorman.

"Your bags, sir?" he asked in French.

"In the car please, and yes, I'm checking in for several days," Alexander responded as he handed the doorman a gratuity.

He entered the ornately decorated lobby featuring a mixture of European-design furniture, area oriental rugs spread on polished Lebanese marbled floors, and Middle Eastern wall hangings. Crystal and gold light fixtures sparked above. Alexander admired the fabulous décor of the renowned Phoenicia Hotel, one of the finest in the world.

Alexander's eyes fixed on a woman in an *abayeh* who was kneeling on a small oriental rug in a remote corner of the lobby, kneading dough on a flour-dusted tray. As he walked toward her, along with several others, she threw the flattened dough into the air until it widened to a round sheet eighteen inches across, like a large pizza pie with a very thin crust. When she had achieved just the right thinness and size of the dough, the woman looked up at the crowd and smiled proudly. With the dough in both hands, she gingerly spread the piecrust-shaped dough across the bottom of an inverted stainless steel bowl that was already becoming hot from a small charcoal fire on a bed of stones in front of her. The woman looked up at the crowd and smiled again. Quickly the very thin dough began to bubble from the yeast as the thinner parts and edges began turning brown. In just a few minutes, the thin dough was baked into bread.

"Her presence is a way of reminding ourselves and our visitors of our heritage and culture," spoke the hotel concierge to no one in particular, but loud enough for Alexander and several observers to hear.

"*Attinee khobaz*," spoke a man standing next to Alexander.

"Ten pounds, sir," responded the woman modestly, then, gingerly lifting the bread from the convex bowl, she exchanged it for the fee, handing the man the full sheet. He folded it in half, tore it, and offered the other half to Alexander.

"Would you like part of this *khobaz*?" asked the man as he turned his head toward him wearing a proud smile.

"*Shookrun*," nodded Alexander, accepting the generous portion the man had torn from his bread as though he was tearing a newspaper.

"Ahhh, it tastes so good," smiled Alexander.

"It always does, especially when it is just baked. It's the best bread in the world," he said smiling, waving his arm around his head.

He savored the warm soft bread, inhaling the fragrance of his youth.

"Iskandar," shouted Anthony Abraham from a few feet away. Alexander recognized his familiar voice, calling him by his Arabic name. "I'm glad you are here. We were concerned about you since you were the only one of our group that didn't meet us at Heathrow. You're just in time. The gala and awards ceremony are day after tomorrow."

"*Mahrharbahr*, Anthony," smiled Alexander, putting his arm over his friend's shoulder. Alexander was about three inches taller than his friend, yet they were otherwise equal in so many ways, respecting each other as brothers.

Everyone, including Anthony and his wife, were planning to visit their family villages the next day.

"Marie and I are going to Zahle tomorrow to visit her family. Are you going to Douma, Iskandar? It's an open day with nothing scheduled, although we are all warned to be back in the hotel by noon Saturday for the big event that night."

"Well, Anthony, I think I'm going to take a taxi up to the village. I haven't seen my brother in so many years. It's time. But since my father died in 1956, and my brother has never written…I'll never understand that…I really want to go there." Then, he thought a minute before continuing, "Quite frankly, Anthony; I'm not sure what I'll find. When I left, conditions were so terrible.

My memories are not happy ones. When my mother died, part of me died. But I love the mountains and the cedars. I'll go see who's still there."

"Of course, you must. After all, it's been more than forty years, and how many times do we come back to Lebanon anyway?"

"You're right, Anthony. It seems you always are. I think I'm sad that I'm alone here. Helena's not with me, and I have been totally unsuccessful in France. It's so strange. Madeleine is nowhere to be found anywhere in Europe. I don't know how much longer I'll continue looking for her. But right now I'm not feeling so good."

"Maybe you should have brought Helena, Iskandar. She would have loved to see Beirut with you, I'm sure."

"Helena couldn't leave her work. I would have loved to show her where we came from. Maybe another time soon. Still, it's exciting to be here, Anthony, and I'm looking forward to the drive north. I might go up to Bsharre with Danny. It's beautiful up there in the mountains. That's where both our families are from, you know."

"Khalil Gibran too," responded Anthony quickly. "That's right, Gibran lived up there."

Then, changing the subject, "Have you ever seen the Jeita Grotto just north of Beirut? The stalactites and stalagmites are fabulous...among the most incredible in the world."

"Good idea, Iskandar. We'll go see it. A bunch of us are going to the casino tonight. Why don't you join us? It'll do you good. Come on, we'll have some fun. They say it's as good as Las Vegas, and a lot like in Paris! We're meeting right here in the lobby at 8 o'clock. In fact, why don't you join Marie and me earlier for dinner in the hotel restaurant?"

"Maybe I'll do that, Anthony. Thanks. But first I'm going to my room, take a shower, and telephone Helena."

Later, they enjoyed a delicious dinner of local fish, *hashweh*, *kibbee*, and eggplant soufflé. Later, part of the larger group assembled in the lobby to go to the *Casino du Liban* up in the hills above Jounieh in two vans. The drive at night was spectacular looking down at the city lights.

"Not all of us are here tonight. The others are getting an early start in the morning," announced Danny to the group in the van. "As for the rest of us, we're going to have a good time, so let's go. Everyone be ready to have some fun! Look at that view! What a city!" he exclaimed, pointing.

They gathered on the casino balcony on the western hillside overlooking the shoreline and the sea. It was a startling vantage point. They could look down on Beirut with the flickering lights from the homes, apartments, tall office buildings, and shops...a city of over one million people during the best of the halcyon days of the early 1960s when indeed it was the "Paris of the Middle East." The view was magnificent.

"Beautiful isn't it, Iskandar?"

"I'm glad I came, Anthony. I do feel a lot better. And looking down on Beirut tonight is a sight I've never seen. It's incredible!"

"It's great to be here for all of us, Iskandar. They treat us like visiting royalty; everyone is warm and welcoming, friendly to a fault. I love our culture. It's too bad more Americans don't visit here to see for themselves."

"It's a real eye-opener for me. I've been so involved in my businesses. But now, I am reminded of my heritage, where I came from. It's really something isn't it, Anthony?"

Marie turned from gazing down on the city, and, looking at her friend, said to him in a soft voice, "Maybe you should consider bringing Helena back here next year, Iskandar. It would do her good to see where her father and his father came from."

"Good idea, Marie," responded Alexander. *Make the best of your situation. You are in Beirut for the first time in forty-two years. Have some fun!*

"Maybe your life will find a new direction now that you have returned to your village," spoke Anthony pensively as they stood side by side at the railing of the balcony, looking down on the city a thousand feet below. "Maybe something good will come out of our visit, my friend. We all were peasants, went to America, became peddlers, and, thanks to God, we succeeded. And we helped others. So, Iskandar, rest easy and feel good about yourself, and your life. You are still young. Put yourself and your life in the hands of God, my friend. You may be surprised at what He has in store for you. Maybe you'll even find a beautiful Lebanese woman here in Beirut," he chuckled, only half kidding.

Alexander patted him on the back. "You're right, Anthony. Thank you."

"Hello, fellas," spoke Fred Gattas as he sauntered up to them "Are y'all enjoyin' yourselves here?" Fred's southern drawl made them smile.

"Fred," Alexander replied, "I've lived in Central Florida for forty years and I don't think I've ever heard as thick a southern accent as yours or Albert Harris'."

Anthony joined with Alexander as they both laughed.

"Waal," Fred responded, accentuating his West Tennessee drawl even more, joining in the humor, "ah know y'all make fun of ma accent, but I'll tell ya, if I didn't talk like this in Memphis, my business would surely go away. They'd think I was a Yankee or sumpthin' else."

"No, sir," George Maloof stepped in and spoke, "Fred, nobody would ever call you a Yankee, at least not in Cleveland. Your drawl is so thick, I can hardly understand you sometimes. Even when you speak in Arabic, you have a drawl. It's really funny to listen to you talk 'Suthin'," he added, mimicking his friend.

"You boys having a good time?" It was Danny Thomas. "I'm having a terrific time here myself. We're going to drive up to Bsharre in the morning and we might be going to Damascus on Sunday after church. Anyone want to join us?"

Everyone was feeling a sense of renewal, of camaraderie. After they all enjoyed a couple of hours in the casino, they assembled at the front glass doors where they would meet the limos that would take them back to the hotel. The evening was a pleasure for everyone that night. Yet, all of them anxiously wanted to make a pilgrimage to their home villages the next day. Some even planned to make a second visit to their relatives' homes after the awards ceremony two days hence.

"Okay then, we'll see you at the Saturday night events," Danny announced in the hotel lobby as he and his family turned to leave.

"Heck," Fred said to the few remaining in the group, "none of us did what we did at St. Jude's for an award. Don't get me wrong, fellas, ah'm right proud to be here and ah'm surely honored to be among such a crowd of you successful guys. It's excitin' just to be part of this."

"Don't give us that 'I'm jus' an ol' suthern farmboy tryin' tuh make a livin' and y'all are so rich compared to me' stuff, Fred," laughed Emile Hajar, from Boston. "We all know you're the wealthiest guy in Memphis. You've got a beautiful family, and without you there might not have even been a St. Jude Hospital. So, brother, just let us stand in your shadow and we'll be grateful."

Fred laughed at the friendly teasing and they all enjoyed their exhilaration, buoyed by the visceral sensations of actually returning to their homeland, most, if not all, for the first time.

CHAPTER 58

$\mathcal{T}$he next morning, Alexander gazed out the window at the sea as his taxi drove north along the coast to the center of the port city of Tripoli. The taxi then turned sharply right at the key intersection downtown. He felt his weight shift in the back seat.

Kassem, his driver, turned his head, looking at his passenger sitting next to him. "We will be going up the mountain now. We should be in your village soon, *inshallah*," spoke the driver to Alexander in his native Arabic, Alexander fully comprehending.

"*Shookrun*," he replied, looking at his watch. "We should be in Douma by eleven o'clock then. Stay with me; depending on what we find, we may drive north from there."

"*Na'am*," the driver replied, nodding his head. "Do you like my car, sir? It's a five-year-old Mercedes. I take very good care of it. My brother's son is an excellent mechanic. He takes care of the motor and brakes for me. I shine it each day. Of course, if I didn't the dust from these mountain roads would be as thick as bread!"

During the forty-minute drive up the winding mountain road, Alexander noticed most of the pavement was only wide enough for one car, with occasional spots where a car could pull over to allow another car or truck to pass by heading in the opposite direction. It was a well-worn passage that in some places in centuries past was just wide enough for single file soldiers to march across the mountains down to the sea, adequate for the invading Greeks before Christ. It was first widened by the Romans to provide room for their war wagons, then later by the Islamic movement followed by the Crusaders. Over the centuries, this very road served as a trade route and connected the region to the port. It was only in the mid-twentieth century after World War II that the government was able to widen and pave part of the trail with asphalt, still barely wide enough room for two cars to pass.

All the way up the curving, winding mountain road, the car careened along the edge of the precipice, too close for Alexander's taste. He guessed that the driver, in his mid-forties, was trying to impress his customer with the capabilities of his prestigious car. They were now high in the mountains overlooking the lush olive groves a thousand feet below.

"Take it easy, Kassem," Alexander finally shouted over the din of the noise of the wheels on the road. "We've got plenty of time. I know this road from my youth. But when I travelled here, it was a dirt path. I did it on a donkey or wagon. I've come too long a way to end it on this road, no matter how pretty this car would look down that ravine!"

"Yessir," shouted the driver over his shoulder, "whatever you wish."

"Kassem," Alexander spoke after the car slowed down and the sounds softened, "How long have you lived in Beirut? Tell me of your family."

"My family came from Jerusalem in the late 1890's. At that time, Palestine was the commercial center of the eastern Mediterranean, Jaffa was a major port, and Beirut was a small port town. Things began to change so much early in the 1900s when many Europeans began migrating into Palestine, a place for people of all religions. It was prosperous and peaceful. That is when we came to Lebanon. Opportunities seemed to be better here for us, so my family came to Beirut. My wife Ramza's family lives in the South. They have stayed there because we are Sunni Muslim, and the *Shimal*, the North, is mostly Christian. Of course, the Druze live in the Shouf Mountains east of Beirut. You know, Mr. Thomas, it was the same in Palestine from centuries ago. We had Christian villages like Bethlehem, the birthplace of Jesus, Ramallah and Nazareth. Others consisted of Jewish villages or Sunni or Shia Muslim. We each stayed with our own kind, even though we all got along with each other and traded among the villages. However, we all prefer...no, I must be honest... required our children to marry within our own religions. But we got along very well even throughout World War II. That is, until the 1947 war."

Having listened to Kassem recall his story for twenty non-stop minutes, Alexander, unable to resist as he realized more and more he was getting very close to Douma, responded by briefly telling his own story, including aspects that included Madeleine. While some things were simply no one else's business, he felt almost comfortable sharing his emotional burden to this driver whom in all likelihood he would never see again.

"I left my village as a very young man...just a boy actually, in 1920. My older brother chose to stay in the mountains, but I felt a better future awaited me in America. My mother urged me to follow my father there to find my future. And since I trusted her wisdom completely, I did just that. I have not returned to my village for more than forty years, Kassem. I don't even know who is still alive here. So, this is a very significant trip for me. While I believe I have accomplished all I could in America, I am very happy to return to Lebanon, yet, I have no idea what awaits me in Douma."

"My friend," Kassem replied, "there are many destinies in our lives, I believe. Only *Allah* knows what will come."

Just at that moment, near the top of the mountain, Alexander spotted a familiar large stone on the valley side of the road just ahead. He almost shuddered at the familiar sight. It was still elongated, flat, and about three feet tall and five feet long. "Stop the car, Kassem," he shouted. "Stop the car right here. I want to get out for a few minutes right now."

Alexander waited for the Mercedes to completely come to a stop before opening his door. "I'll need a few minutes, Kassem." He walked across the road to the stone, gazing down the valley, seeing the village of his birth far below with the houses strewn along the steep terraces. He chuckled as he fondly slapped the stone as if it was his close friend. Not much had changed in the village...

"See how the village looks like a scorpion from here, Kassem? He said, admiring his village, pointing below. "And see how almost all the rooftops are red? They are that way because legend says that it is to remind everyone of the blood that has been spilled here over the ages by our young men in protecting these mountains from the invaders. Sixteen times, Kassem. Can you believe it?"

Alexander, gesturing in various directions, told his new friend of the ancient cedars, how so many had disappeared at the hands of everyone from the Phoenicians on, ultimately defacing the mountain ranges of northern Lebanon.

"See those olive trees there on the valley floor by the river? Some of those trees are more than a thousand years old."

"Yes, Mr. Thomas, I know. My family had many ancient olive trees in Palestine."

"Up there," Alexander said, pointing up the mountain to his right, "are the orchards, or what's left of them."

"Legends say my family has lived here since before Christ. And yet, I went away like many others to seek a better life."

"And now," Alexander continued speaking with his head looking down, "I am returning to the place of my birth. My father is gone now; my mother died many years ago, and I'm not sure what I'm going to find. I'm searching for my brother and cousins."

"Mr. Thomas, I believe your heart is filled with emotions and that you might be a little afraid of what awaits you down there, but I also think that you must accept whatever you find. Sir," he beckoned softly, looking at his watch, and gestured to the car, "I think it is time to drive on to the village."

Before Alexander moved, he looked at the ground, digging his hand into his pocket and endearingly feeling the stone he had carried from this very spot so long ago when he last looked back at his beloved village. As he held the stone memento in his fingers, he looked again to the rooftops below. He recalled the very sensations he had felt that morning so long ago when he left Douma to seek his destiny in America. His eyes began to moisten from nostalgia as he remembered his mother and his childhood. He thought of his brother and how he had watched over him. He remembered his mother's gentle hands. His heart began to swell as he felt himself breathe deeply, looking, wondering what awaited him.

Then, he stood tall, squared his shoulders, wiped the light perspiration from his forehead, and turned to Kassem.

"Let's go. It is time for me to walk in Douma once again. But it is difficult for me. Do you understand?"

"Of course," Kassem replied, "it is always difficult to go back home, and for you...after all these years..." his voice trailed off.

The black four-door Mercedes slowly entered the main street of the village at the south and reached the center of the town's *souk*.

"See the stone sarcophagus there with the cedar tree at each end in the middle of the *souk*, Kassem?"

"*Na'am*," he responded.

"There..." continued Alexander, "you can read the plaque...it has the date of 350 B.C., acknowledging the arrival of the six Chalhoub brothers and their families to this place. Legend tells of my ancestors who came so long ago from the Golan in Syria to settle here. The plaque speaks of that date as the founding date of this village. Remarkable, isn't it? At the time, this was a heavily forested mountain range thick with wildlife: bear, deer, even lions, some say, and birds of all kinds."

Kassem slowly continued driving down the village road.

"We are here, Mr. Thomas," the driver intervened. "Point to your house."

"Over there, Kassem. You see the small square stone building? That is where I was born. It looks so much smaller now. My God," Alexander exclaimed with a drooping mouth, viewing the modest...no...almost barren structure about eight feet in height. "You see this, Kassem? That is where five of us lived. My God, this is too much," Alexander whispered again, feeling a strong sense of humility, of warmth, of reconnecting to his soul. "I am stunned with memories, Kassem. I can't really describe my feelings. There are so many...my youth, joy, pain, agony, love...they are all there." He reached deep into his pocket and withdrew his stone companion, fondling it in his hand. *We are here, my friend, we are home again.*

They stepped from the car, and looking at the house, Kassem asked, "Yes, Mr. Thomas, but what of the very large house next to your birthplace? What is that?"

"That must be the new home my father built when he returned to the village after the Second War. He told me that he would build a new, larger home for Milhelm and his family. That must be it. He would never sell the land. No one in my family has ever, for centuries, it seems, sold our land. Soon after he finished the house he wrote to me about it, but I haven't heard from anyone else in years. Only after the war when they needed help. Then the letters stopped."

Alexander stepped from the taxicab, asked Kassem to return in two hours, and turned to walk the ten steps up to the newer main house, stopping at the top to look at the old stone house...hovel?...to his left.

"Milhelm?" he yelled at the door as if he had left only the day before. "Milhelm?" he repeated his call.

"*Na'am?*" came the response from a woman's voice inside. He heard footsteps and then the heavy front door opened. "*Ahlen wa sahlen.*" A pretty, young woman spoke with a smile, customarily stretching out her arm as a gesture of welcome, beckoning Alexander to enter her home. He reckoned she was in her early thirties.

"*Mahrharbahr,*" spoke Alexander, smiling. "Is this still Beit Chalhoub, the Chalhoub family home?"

"Yes, yes it is. *Shooishmee?* What is your name?" she asked, looking directly at the visitor.

"I am Iskandar Thomé Chalhoub," Alexander replied, and then asked, "*Shooishmee?*"

"*Ishmee* Katrina." With a friendly, innocent smile, she responded, sensing her visitor was American.

Alexander couldn't believe his eyes. The vivacious fair-haired, light-complexioned, young woman looked so much like his mother the last time he saw her so long ago. He was totally caught off guard by his mother's name. "Katrina, you say?" he gasped.

She smiled broadly as the rays of the sun stroked her auburn hair when she stepped outside the door to speak to this man who was unfamiliar to her and surely to almost anyone in the village. Of that she was certain. *But his face would certainly fit in the village*, she thought. *He could easily be part of this family.*

Alexander was struck by the familiar aromas emanating from the kitchen in the rear of the house. There was an unmistakable smell of the blending of sautéed onions with a hint of garlic, and fresh bread baking in the oven. His thoughts raced to his youth, remembering the very same aromas he would smell as he came home from school to find his mother at the fire in their one-room home.

His sensations were almost overpowering: peace, a touch of sadness, compassion, and comfortable familiarity. Eager now to enter the house, his heart was filled with a deep sense of "coming home."

Katrina couldn't take her eyes off her visitor's face. "You could be my Uncle Iskandar, son of Ibrahim. You look so much like my father."

"Yes, that is exactly who I am," he replied with a broad smile.

"But Iskandar Thomé *Ibn* Ibrahim Chalhoub is in America. I have never met him, but I believe he is there. Why do you now come here, sir?"

"I am here because this is my home. I am with a group returning to celebrate St. Jude Hospital in America, and to visit my family." He smiled, hoping to reassure the attractive young woman who reminded him of his own daughter. "I have come to see my brother." He added softly and endearingly, "You look very much like someone I knew many years ago."

Alexander hoped there were elders inside because she was not yet convinced. His eyes looked beyond her into the sparsely furnished home with its smooth, white plaster ceiling and walls, and large Oriental rug on the colorful, polished Lebanese marble floor. The austere walls had framed family photographs placed strategically over the couch and in the adjoining open dining room.

"*Ishmee* Katrina, youngest daughter of Milhelm Thomé Chalhoub," she said proudly, but in a friendly tone.

"Katrina?" Alexander asked. "Did you say Milhelm is your father?"

"Of course. I have two brothers and a sister. Mother and I take care of *Biyee*. He is not well, you know."

"No, I do not know. I must see him immediately. What is wrong?" Without waiting for an answer, he stepped to the side of Katrina and strode into the living room, looking for the only apparent place that could lead to a bedroom. "Is he upstairs?"

"La," Katrina shook her head. "His bedroom is there," she replied, pointing with her hand. "But who are you, sir? I heard you say your name, but I don't believe it."

Losing his patience a bit, he sharply replied, "I *am* your uncle. Now take me to your father...*please.*"

Surprised by the stranger's authoritative response, Katrina quickly led Alexander to her father's bedroom.

As he stepped through the doorway, his eyes went straight to the bed on which his older, beloved brother lay, then focused on the face on the pillow.

Alexander felt a sense of shock in his body as he saw his big brother.

"Milhelm," he said hurriedly as he stepped quickly into the room to the bedside. "Milhelm," he whispered. "What is the matter, *khai-yi?* What has happened?" He saw that his brother, always a very large man, was thin and weakened, without much energy. He looked so forlorn in his plain white *dishdasheh*, his body-length, cotton robe. Alexander, eyes moistening from his emotional impact, sensed that this was what he must now wear all the time.

Alexander turned to Katrina and whispered. "What happened, Katrina? Tell me, what is wrong with my brother."

Now convinced Alexander indeed was her father's brother, she opened up to him. "My father suffered a severe stroke many years ago and hasn't been able to speak much since. It has been very difficult for him. He was so strong, so important in the village. But now..." her voice trailed off as she looked sadly into Alexander's eyes. She continued, "He will know you, I am certain, even though I didn't recognize you, uncle. Go to him. Embrace him. Let him know you are here and how you love him."

Alexander softly stepped to the bedside of his brother. "Milhelm," he whispered in his ear, "Milhelm, it is Iskandar, your little brother. Oh, my Lord," he said as he bent over and kissed his brother's cheek. As he did, he felt a teardrop on his brother's cheek, and then saw his brother's eyes were filling with tears. A slight, but growing smile of familiarity formed on Milhelm's dry lips. His right arm and hand were clearly limp across his chest. Alexander had seen the signs of stroke in Florida's VA hospitals.

Alexander pulled up a chair to the bed and reached over to hold his brother's strong left hand, thankful now that he didn't further delay seeing him.

"His hand is still large, much larger than mine, and it is warm," Alexander said to Katrina as he turned his head to look at her through his own tear-filled eyes. "And he just squeezed my hand. His grip is still very strong," he sighed in relief. Then, looking up at the ceiling, he thought, *Oh, God, I pray I am not too late to be with my brother. Thank you, God.*

"His left side is still very strong. But his right side is weak and paralyzed. He cannot speak well," Katrina told him.

"Does he have adequate medical care?"

"Some. But he could use more. He has been depressed much of the time, but perhaps with your visit, he will feel better about trying harder. Aside from his paralysis and inability to speak, he is in good health. But he is sad most of the time."

Alexander gestured as he asked Katrina to leave him alone with his brother for a few minutes. Welcoming a respite, she exited, looking over her shoulder at the two men touching each other in joyful reunion.

"Oh, Milhelm, I'm so sorry I took so long to come home." As he began speaking to his brother of his life, his children, and his love, both Alexander's and Milhelm's eyes filled with tears, grateful for this surprise visit, remembering their youth together.

"Forty years, Milhelm. Forty years. It's been so long...too long, *khai-yi.* I love you, and we must do whatever is necessary to help you get well."

Two hours later, when Kassem returned to the house at the appointed time, Alexander asked him to leave him and return later in the day.

"I wish to stay today with my brother as much as I can. It has been too long. We have so very much to share."

Throughout the remainder of the day, Alexander stayed with his brother, taking a break at times to let him rest or sleep. He accepted Katrina's offer to walk to the *souk* with her.

As Katrina took her uncle's hand, they went down the stone steps to the now paved street.

"Let me show you our church, uncle. It is old, but it is beautiful. You know how much a part of our family life it is, don't you?" Then, she added, "We can pray for your successful return and for *Biyee*."

"Oh, yes, Katrina," Alexander replied proudly. "The church has always been very important to this family. It was for me when your father and I were very young."

After entering the solidly built stone edifice with the steeply sloped, red-tiled roof, and enormous hand-carved cedar front doors, they sat in the family pew to pray together for Milhelm's recovery. As Alexander leaned back, he instantly felt his body press against the familiar hand-hewn wooden seat and backrest. The sensations reminded him of the many Sundays he sat next to his mother, with his older brother on her other side. Sweet memories of his childhood and of the devotion and love of his mother enveloped him. He subconsciously gripped his niece's hand tightly.

After silent prayers, he turned to his niece and whispered, "Faith, Katrina... faith can move mountains, your grandmother would always say. So, we will look to God for His healing power. You know, Katrina," he continued, looking around the wood and stone interior of the ancient church, "this church looked enormous to me as a boy, but it doesn't seem so large now. Ahhh...the same icons are here."

"It's a small church, and ours is a small village, but I'm sure it seemed different to you as a boy." Then, simply looking at his saddened face in wonder for a moment, she added, "I'm so grateful to be here with you, Uncle Iskandar."

Then she smiled, trying to change his melancholy mood. "Let's go to the *souk*. Perhaps you will see some familiar faces."

As they walked the village's main street to the center, Alexander noted that the short lanes sloping up or down off the street were still mostly gravel and unpaved. The steepness up the slopes was still severe, demanding superior leg strength. He recalled how, as boys, he and his brother always felt strong.

"It hasn't really changed all that much has it, uncle?"

"No, Katrina, it hasn't. It seems very much like I remember. Even after forty years. A few homes are new and larger, of course."

As they got closer to the *souk*, they exchanged greetings with more and more pedestrians strolling in the opposite direction, some of whom appeared familiar, most not.

"By the way, Katrina, how is Aunt Sara?"

"Aunt Sara? Oh, uncle, she passed away three years ago."

"Oh, I'm sorry." He felt that now familiar poignant sense of guilt. *Too late again*, he agonized.

"She and my father spoke often of you. They missed you so much over the years. I think when Aunt Sara died, she took with her many family stories... even secrets," she smiled. "She knew everything, didn't she? Everyone always deferred to her. She could have been the sheikh of the village if she were a man."

"She was the matriarch of the family, for sure. And very strong," Alexander added with a smile.

Then she turned to him and asked, "Are there any people you would especially like to visit while you are here?"

"Actually, Katrina, I'm really here to see your father and our family, and to just walk the streets of the village. I think I'll sit here in the *souk* for a few minutes until we go back to the house."

After he looked around for awhile, watching the villagers stroll in the market area, Alexander noticed he was feeling an almost overpowering swell of nostalgia with a mixture of joy and sadness, yet, embracing the warmth of being "home."

"Look up there, Katrina," he said to his niece sitting behind him. "That small grove of cedars is where your father and I played together back in the early years when we were boys. We would go up the mountain to the apple grove, then climb the cedars so we could look at the sea. And down there, in the valley, we would join in the olive harvest. Ah me," he sighed, "those were the simple days. We were very poor then. But everyone in the village was poor.

"We too are without much, uncle. And I have to say, compared to cousins in Beirut, we are very poor here in the mountains. But we survive, and we are happy. We have a saying here... 'We *wish you enough.*' Don't you see? Enough...enough food, enough sunshine to brighten your life...enough rain to provide for your needs...but not necessarily do we wish for more...'things,'" she smiled. "I like that view, and that is why I am very happy here watching over my father. My brothers and sisters are in Beirut. But I like it here in the mountains. We feel very rich here, although we have little money. The summers are cool, dry, and we have many visitors. Of course, the winters can be very cold, as you know. But it is true, my heart is here," she added after a sigh, looking across the *souk*.

"Well, Katrina, I too feel your sense of pride, of contentment here. Now, let's go back to the house and see your father."

Alexander stood, stretched his arms, and gave his niece a warm embrace. "I am very proud of you, Katrina, for your dedication to your father. And your mother? By the way, where is she?"

"Oh, *Imei* is in Tripoli for the day, visiting her sister. She will be disappointed that she didn't see you. But you will return soon, won't you? I know she will look forward to your next visit as will my father."

"I will be back, Katrina. Perhaps tomorrow, depending on what happens at our event in Beirut, but surely by Monday. So tell your mother I wish to see her. Let's assume Monday. Alright?"

"Yes, uncle. Monday for sure. Now, let's walk back to the house."

As they turned, Alexander's eyes moved across the small village *souk*, up toward the mountains, then down to the terraced vineyards...the fruit trees in the distance lining the slopes... the olive groves below... remembering. Everything reminded him of his childhood days. Some made him smile. Others made him sad. *That was my past and it's still here. Now I must look to the present and the future as I treasure my past.*

He shrugged his shoulders and responded to Katrina's call, "Come, uncle. We must go." She was still full of life, exuberant, and totally concerned for her father's welfare.

He stepped toward her, following until he caught up with her, and then together they began to briskly walk back to *"Beit Milhelm,"* Milhelm's family home.

Alexander stumbled abruptly on an uneven step and decided to sit on the bench under the family grape arbor next to the house. He patted the seat and beckoned for Katrina to sit beside him.

"He saved my life more than once, Katrina," he exclaimed fervently, "and now it is my turn to help him. Oh, Katrina, I am so sad for him...I waited too long to come." Alexander was angry with himself. "How I looked forward to sharing this time with your father. I love him so much. He watched over me all those years of my youth. He was so alive, so strong. Katrina. Your father was my hero. He literally saved my life when I was caught in a snowstorm up there," he said in a soft voice while pointing to the ridge of the mountains above them. "And now, he cannot speak to me with his voice. Damn!"

"But he is speaking to you with his eyes. You have made him very happy with your visit. Yes, he would have so much enjoyed sitting here, visiting with you. Before his stroke, he spoke about you all of my life, Uncle Iskandar. He still tries sometimes but it is too difficult for him. He told all his children how carefree and daring you were and how proud he is of you," Katrina said consolingly. "Always he has spoken of you with pride. He sometimes regretted not going with you to America. But I believe he has been very happy here in the mountains. It has been hard, to be sure. We have had to do without much, but we also have our family, our friends, the family church, and our heritage. We are people of the mountains. You understand, don't you?"

He nodded with an understanding smile.

"We all looked to you during those very hard days after the war. There was a food shortage and we had few clothes. The shipments you sent us helped us through those harsh, cold winters. We survived as a family and stayed together. I don't know if my father wrote to you then." She shrugged her shoulders. "Perhaps it isn't part of our culture. Anyway, then he got sick and very depressed and *couldn't* write." She smiled. "My father is a wonderful man...a kind man. He never succeeded in business, but what a good man."

Alexander thought how very different this was from his own prosperous way of life. Listening to Katrina's soft voice of compassion, he realized her presence had brought him to renew his appreciation of his family here in the village of his birth. "I have so much to be grateful for, Katrina," he said as he gripped her hand, looking into her eyes. "For so many years I was mostly absorbed in my work. I lost my son, Michael, during the war. Then, when Helene, my wife, went to sleep, I became very lonely. I am sorry now that I didn't come back then. But I never received any answers to my letters, so, I thought everyone was fine and doing well. But now, I can see what happened."

Katrina spoke to him, bonding with her uncle, "Perhaps I can tell you now, knowing you will understand. My father was a proud man as you are and could not write to you to tell you he needed help. He could never have done that. He didn't want to bother you all those years. And then," she took a deep breath, pausing, "when he suffered his stroke, he wasn't able to speak or write. He suffered in silence. He didn't want us to tell you. I don't know why. We didn't know what to do. And we don't know what secrets he has inside. But I am sure he is very happy you have come now. And now he may regret our not writing to let you know. Men are too proud, I think," she shrugged. "Maybe your visit will help him get better."

Alexander frowned slightly, "I should have come years ago. I think I have waited too long for too many things. I have missed very important appointments with two people I love very much. And now I must live with the knowledge of what might have been here, Katrina, and in Marseille."

"Marseille?" she asked.

"Yes," he replied, "but it's a long story. It began when I was very young, on my way to America. Perhaps one day I will tell you about it. But not now. We must only look to helping your father. And now, I need to use your telephone."

"It's in the living room, uncle. We just got our telephone only two years ago. It's been very hard to obtain one ever since the war."

"So long?"

She shrugged again, accepting.

They stood and embraced.

"Let's go into the house now."

Alexander sat for a moment thinking, calling on his nearly fifteen-year involvement and financial support at the VA hospital's therapy programs in Tampa where he had devoted himself after his son died. He had also been supporting a prominent rehabilitation clinic in Orlando. He knew more could be done for Milhelm, and although he was not sure how much his brother would improve physically, he knew having regular therapy sessions would certainly improve his attitude, and, he knew that as his spirits improved, so too would his physical condition.

"I will have a new sturdy wheelchair sent to you, Katrina," Alexander told his niece. "Whatever is available, I will have it sent to my brother as soon as I get home. Then you can take him to the *souk*. He'll like that." Alexander didn't need reminding of his brother's needs. Nor did he need any request to act. He became totally preoccupied with his brother's welfare. "We'll do what needs to be done, Katrina. I'll need your help though."

His initial call was to St. George Hospital in Beirut. He spoke in Arabic to the Medical Director. Alexander was determined to succeed in bringing help to his brother.

"I want the best physical and speech therapists you can find. Full time. Let them alternate every other day at the hospital and then here with my brother. I will be responsible for their full salary and travel costs. If you will agree, then I will pay you in advance for six months at a time." On a roll now, he added, "In addition, I'm sure you have certain needs at the hospital that we can discuss. Oh," he remembered, "and a new wheelchair. We need a wheelchair now." After reviewing the various options the hospital could offer to a paying family, a welcomed situation to be sure, they both agreed the hospital would begin treatments immediately. Relieved at what the director told him, he responded, "*Shookrun*," confidently as he completed the call, feeling helpful and assured.

"Katrina," he said as he placed the telephone in the cradle, turning to her, "I have arranged for St. George Hospital to provide whatever your father may need in medications, therapy, and for his comfort. I know you will continue to watch over him and be my liaison. We will communicate regularly and I will arrange for you to be properly paid. I want to do anything and everything I can do for my only brother. For him and for our mother and father. Do you understand?" He wrote on a notepad as he spoke. "Here is Dr. Nabeel Zein's name and phone number. He is the man I just spoke with. Stay in touch with him."

"Of course," Katrina replied, "but Uncle Iskandar, I cannot accept any payment from you. I will ask that you give it to St. Mary's, our family church, instead."

"Certainly, how 'American' of me." He smiled, understanding. "Yet I want to provide for your needs whatever they become. You are my brother's daughter, which makes you my daughter as well."

"And now, uncle, let's walk to where your mother sleeps. She's up there on the hill by the church next to your father, my grandfather, my *jiddou*."

They walked side by side up the winding path, and as they came closer to the graves, Alexander again felt his chest heave with emotion, catching his breath, remembering his mother's gentle, enduring love, and his father's love and strength. The moment they arrived at their graves, he fell to his knees.

"Thank you, Lord," he spoke softly, "thank you for bringing me safely to my home, to the place of my birth, and to my brother. And thank you for reminding me of so many blessings you have bestowed on me." He felt it. He knew where his heart was. His transformation was becoming complete. He covered his grieving face with his hands as his tears overflowed.

As he spoke, Alexander felt himself experience a sense of willingness to accept whatever might come into his life. He was wonderfully impressed by Katrina's unselfish devotion, but not surprised at her exuberant acceptance of her life, of having so much less in a material sense than he had experienced. So refreshing, and so lovely.

"Thank you too, Katrina, for teaching me simply by being who you are. But I shouldn't be surprised. Your father was, at the same time, incredibly strong physically, and yet generous and giving, with the sensitive soul of a poet, like Gibran.

Later, as Kassem held the Mercedes car door open for him, Katrina whispered, "*Allah ma'ak*, Uncle Iskandar, go with God, and know we all love you. Please come back soon. And next time bring Helena." They kissed each other's cheeks. She eagerly hugged her uncle, wrapping both her arms around him.

Alexander pulled his face back a few inches and said, looking at her face, "You have the face of your beautiful grandmother, Katrina. So lovely, so alive. You and Helena both carry her in you. *Allah ma'ak*, Katrina," Alexander whispered once again as he lingered, looking into her eyes before climbing into the waiting taxicab.

Now speaking from inside, before he closed the door, he said, "I must go to Beirut now, but I will return Monday before I leave for America. And I will come to see you and my family very soon after. You have restored my faith. *Shookrun*, dear Katrina, *shookrun*. You are my family, and you have entered my life at a very important time."

He sat back into the front seat of the taxi, heaved a sigh, and looked back to see his niece dabbing the corners of her eyes with her lace hankie as he too felt an overflow of tears and wiped them from his cheeks. She is such a joy.

The taxi surged up the mountain road as Kassem confidently pressed the accelerator pedal, calling on all 300 horsepower under the cab's shiny hood he had buffed during the afternoon.

After a few minutes as the powerful car climbed the steep incline to the ridge, Alexander called out, "Kassem, there is the stone on the right! Stop the car. I want to look from there one more time for a few minutes."

Alexander emerged from the front seat of the cab and stepped to the familiar stone once again. More at ease with himself, and having filled his thoughts with Katrina and Milhelm, recalling so much of his childhood, and feeling better about the fact that he had not been successful in his two-year search for Madeleine, he became absorbed in the view of his village, the mountains, the valleys, the olive trees, and his beloved cedars in their clusters on the mountain slopes.

Finally he spoke. "Well, Kassem, I have come full circle now, more than a full lifetime, more than forty years later, and I *have* fulfilled my destiny. I have achieved my mother's wishes and gone *beyond the cedars*...she was so wise. Even more, Kassem, I have returned to my roots. Now where will my life lead me? I must think about that."

"My friend," Kassem replied as he stood beside Alexander and put his arm around the shoulders of his new friend, "you have indeed fulfilled your mother's dying wishes. You know that she and your father sleep together in peace, and you know they wish only for your peace of mind. So, do that for yourself. Find your heart, follow it. Do as Gibran admonishes, and realize that we do not know what *Allah* has in store for us. Muslims believe, as He speaks in the Quran: 'Only God, and there is only one God, knows what awaits us even in the next minute. So dear friend, now that you have returned to your homeland after so many years, you have found your youth, your brother, and your family, and perhaps you have found *yourself,* the most important thing. You must live, truly live, knowing God has something very good in store for you." Kassem smiled and returned to his place behind the wheel. "We must be on our way to Beirut where you must begin the rest of your life."

As Katrina watched the black Mercedes leave the village and ascend the winding road up the mountain, her eyes focused on the sharp bend in the road higher up where she knew the car would stop.

That's the spot everyone enjoys a brief, but important moment to look down on the village rooftops. Then, as she saw the Mercedes pull to a stop, she smiled. *There...yes, it did stop.* She knew he couldn't see her from such a distance, but she waved her arm anyway, connecting to her father's beloved brother one last time. But he did see her and once again nostalgically remembered Madeleine standing on the pier in Marseille.

As Katrina turned and walked up the stone steps to the door before entering her home, she hesitated, looked again up the mountain road and thought for a moment. *Uncle Iskandar said he thought he was too late for two important people in his life, and he mentioned Marseille. I wonder if he meant the woman who came here during the war when I was a little girl. She was from Marseille. Yes, Madame Moreau was very beautiful. And she had a handsome son who looked just like Uncle Iskandar.*

Katrina leaned against the door, thinking...and smiled, closing her eyes.

Didn't she move to Beirut? My father would know. I wonder if that woman is the same person Uncle Iskandar spoke of? I wonder if he knows she's in Beirut even today?

CHAPTER 59

Beirut

Knowing nothing of the sort, Alexander, deep in his memories as a young boy, sat quietly thinking as Kassem drove. He couldn't take his eyes off the surrounding mountains as the taxi wound its way down the narrow, winding road to take him back to Tripoli, then the hotel in Beirut where he would dress to attend the President's gala that evening.

Alexander recalled, "It snows so much up there, another 3000 feet above the village, that we had to put a door in the roof so we could enter the building when the snow was deeper than the building was tall." He laughed, remembering. "It was so hard then. My life was terribly difficult here as a boy...we had nothing. *I mean nothing*, Kassem. My mother was a saint. I loved her so much. And my brother, Milhelm. What a man. But how he suffers now."

Kassem, concentrating intently as he carefully steered the Mercedes at a slower rate of speed this time, replied, "Yes, I am sure it was hard, Mr. Thomas, but wouldn't you agree that your difficult experiences as a child better prepared you for the years to come?"

"Oh yes," Alexander replied with a smile, "I'm certain you are correct. For sure, it has been very hard most of my life. Life during my youth somehow taught me it was not supposed to be easy later, that it would be difficult, and," he laughed, "there were times when I thought it was too difficult to continue."

"But you never gave up, did you?" Kassem smiled.

"Give up? Never!" Alexander responded firmly, shaking his head. "Giving up was never part of our way of life. We were always taught to believe we were given certain capabilities from God and that it would be an insult to squander those talents. Besides, when you are born in the mountains as rugged and as harsh as these, my friend, you cannot give up or you will suffer too much. When you are shown this as a child, then as you get older, you don't question the tests of your skill and determination. Your youth is your foundation. Here, your future is a rocky one. It is not so easy just being born in Lebanon anyway. We Lebanese use our abilities, our skills, and our tenacity just to survive. We have no riches, no valuable resources, such as oil or enormous farmlands. So we have learned to call on our minds, our values, our culture, our determination, our faith, our heritage...even in America."

Alexander felt himself becoming more and more aware of his blessings, and more accepting of his life as he experienced this time in the mountains having seen his village once more, being with his beloved brother and Katrina. In many ways, he was drawing on the psychic reserves that had waited for him for so many years. He was still experiencing an epiphany of spirit that bode well for him. And he was becoming braced in strength for what may come.

"Kassem, you were correct when you spoke to me at the stone on the curve in the road overlooking the village. Only God knows what the future holds for us. When I was having trouble in my business and things were going bad, like when the freeze killed our entire harvest and almost wiped us out, I said I will do this or that and my father used to tell me: 'If you want to make God laugh, tell him your plans.'"

Kassem laughed at the joke, turned his head to look at his passenger beside him. "Your father was a wise man, sir, and you must know that your abundance comes only from Him. Therefore, be still...and wait for Him." Then, changing the subject, he asked, "I think tonight you and your friends will be with the President at the gala. Isn't that so?"

"Yes, we are all here from America. Danny Thomas is our leader. We are here mostly because of him. He is a great, kind and wonderful man."

"This is a wonderful honor, Kassem. Most of us were just simple peasants who left our homeland when we were poor and very young. Now, we are Americans. But we always remember our Lebanese heritage with pride. As Danny often tells his friends, 'He who does not honor his heritage has no heritage.' And he is correct."

"So," Alexander continued, looking at his intently listening driver, "we come here to restore our love of our homeland and our heritage. In America we have extended our culture, our beliefs and our history." He chuckled proudly as he continued, "We came from the Phoenicians, and, now we return to be with our families and are being honored by our homeland. Some have labeled us "the New Phoenicians." Maybe that is so, and therefore one could think our work is complete, but it isn't. I personally still have one more very important task to complete. After I go to Douma to stay with my brother, I must return to France to conclude one way or another my search for someone very important to me. I pray she is still alive."

Kassem, still listening, pulled the taxi to the curb as they reached the port city of Jounieh, just north of Beirut. "I want to show you something," he said to Alexander. "I will show you a place with the most beautiful sight of Beirut and the sea. There you must be quiet for a moment, pray to God and ask for his blessing."

After a short drive up the winding mountain road, tightly lined by small homes, trees, and bushes, Kassem turned the car onto a paved overlook.

"We are here at my mosque. Speak with God here as you view this most incredible sight."

Alexander stepped from the taxi, washed his hands in the fountain, removed his shoes, walked into the mosque and knelt on the carpet to pray.

After thoughtful solitude and prayer, Alexander emerged from the mosque feeling much better and silently climbed into the taxi.

He was quiet for the rest of the drive into the city.

"Thank you, Kassem, for stopping at your mosque," Alexander said to his driver as he exited the cab at the front entrance to the Phoenicia Hotel.

"Shall I come pick you up early Monday for your visit to your brother?"

"Yes, I'll see you here at nine o'clock."

"*Inshallah*," Kassem replied as he skillfully pulled the Mercedes away from the curb into the noisy, busy street.

"Iskandar!"

He heard his name as he entered the lobby. It was Archbishop Antony Bashir.

"Hello, *Sayedna* Bashir," he replied as he wrapped his arm around his cousin's shoulder.

"Did you have a good visit in Douma? It's still beautiful, isn't it?" the Metropolitan asked. "We all had a wonderful time. But I ate too much *kibbee* and *hummus*. I'm full!" he laughed as he patted his stomach.

The lobby was active with others in small groups, chatting and gesturing, who had spent the past two days at the villages of their parents, where they were born.

"We went to Ehden and Bsharre way north. It was very cold there, I must say!" Danny was speaking to the cluster of men in the lobby. "Isn't this great?"

"Yes, Zahle is so much bigger then I remember," added George Simon, with a proud smile.

"And the Bekaa is very busy… there are vegetables, wheat, vineyards, even citrus trees. I couldn't get over the rivers and ponds," said another.

"Well, it's quite a homecoming for all of us I must say. This is amazing. Looks like the Marines cooled this place down in '58," said Emile Hajar.

"Just in time, I'd say," interjected Joe Ayoub. "They've had a bunch of trouble here. There always seems to be political turmoil in this part of the world."

"And it might get worse in the '60s some have said, especially in the South," spoke a new face with a familiar voice. "I'm glad I live in California. The Bekaa was wonderful, but California's San Joaquin Valley is where I live now, and for that I am grateful."

"Butrus, is that you?" Alexander turned his head as he heard the voice that jarred his memory. "My God, Butrus," he exclaimed, using Peter's Arabic name. "How the hell are you? I didn't know you were here. I didn't even know they allowed Californians here," he added, laughing at his own joke.

"Yeah," Anthony added, "Floridians are always surprised when Californians are invited too."

"You know, guys, that's exactly how we feel in California about Easterners, especially those from that backward state of Florida. You should come out west if you want to see how the more advanced Americans live."

They all laughed at the friendly rivalry, relishing in their common bond.

Recalling their trip to New York, Peter pulled Alexander aside. When they were sufficiently separated from the group, he embraced Alexander, kissed both his cheeks and started speaking excitedly, "Iskandar, it's been so long...forty-two years! I don't know why we never get together. My home is your home, you know."

"I know, Butrus, but the first years were so hard. I worked with my father six, sometimes seven days a week, just trying to get ahead. Times were very hard...then later the Depression...when times got a bit better after the war, I had too much to do, it seems. I don't know where the time went, *khai-yi*, but it's been too long that's for sure."

"Well, when we get back, we'll have to do something about that, *khai-yi*. Besides, I understand your wife died. There are lots of nice ladies in California if you ever find enough time to come visit. I live near Stockton, and there are some wonderful Greek families there." He paused, "Wait a minute, Iskandar, what ever happened with that beauty you fell in love with in Marseille? What was her name? Let's see..."

"Madeleine, Madeleine DuBois." Alexander reacted quickly since she seemed to be on his mind most of the time.

"Yes! Madeleine. She was a lovely young girl. Boy, Iskandar, I remember how totally in love you were, and how you suffered on the ship to New York. My God, you were miserable. But then, if I remember correctly, both of us were seasick and throwing up most of the voyage. I haven't been on a boat since." He laughed heartily.

"Me either," Alexander replied. "I don't even go on the boat fishing in the lake at my home anymore. I did agree to take out my son and daughter when they were young; they loved it. Not me. Boy, I hated that ship."

"Well," Peter asked, "what ever happened to Madeleine? You said a hundred times on the ship you were going to go back and get her. Did you?"

Alexander wasn't prepared for this exchange with Peter, the only person in the world who would know about Madeleine. He took a deep breath, and answered his friend from 1920, "No, *khai-yi*, I never went back. I wrote her many times...many times," he reiterated, "but she never responded to my letters. Now, I'm convinced I waited too long. My French investigator thinks she passed away."

"Yes, I see. That's a shame, Iskandar," Peter interjected. "I remember you wrote her on the ship almost every day. You were a lovesick puppy, Iskandar. I never saw a man so in love. No letters? How can that be?" He was surprised.

"I was eighteen, Butrus, and she was sixteen."

"Hey, is that the ring she gave you that night, Iskandar?" he asked as his voice pitch went higher while he stared at Alexander's finger.

"My God, Butrus, you remember that too?"

"Of course I do. Hell, you rubbed that ring all the time. Do you wear that ring everyday, even now?"

"Yes. Yes I do. I have never forgotten Madeleine. I was a good husband and a good father to my two children, but I must confess, I have never stopped loving her. It's not something you do...it's just something that happened to me, and I've never gotten past it. But I didn't let it impact on my marriage. Since Madeleine didn't respond to my letters, I was able to devote myself to Helene...she was such a wonderful wife to me, and mother to our son and daughter. I couldn't betray Helene. But after her death, Madeleine re-entered my mind, and I have been searching all over Europe for her for nearly two years."

"Two years?" Peter repeated startled. "My God, Iskandar, it's been more than forty years! That's a long time to stay in love with someone you haven't even seen for so long!"

"Maybe I'm being incredibly foolish. I don't know. But I do know she has been in my heart all that time, and I cannot stop wanting her with me now. I didn't ask for this, Butrus, but it's something I can't explain...even to myself."

He continued, putting his hand on his friend's shoulder, and looking directly into his eyes, affirmed, "I tell you, if she is still alive, I will find her. I will never forget her."

"And if she is married? And has a bunch of children? And grandchildren? And if she's not even alive?" Peter asked quizzically.

"Well, I haven't thought about that possibility because I can't. She was only sixteen, for heaven's sake. Married? Not possible."

They both laughed, easing the tension of their conversation.

"If she's married, then I'll shake her hand, shake his hand, and wish them a happy life."

"Liar. You couldn't do that. I sure as hell couldn't do that. You're fooling yourself. After the love of your life shows up again after forty-two years, you think you could do that? I don't think so. I think," Peter continued with a mischievous smile, "if you find her..."

"*When* I find her..." Alexander corrected him.

"Okay, *when* you find her. But I think you won't even be able to speak. Forty-two years? You'd better have me with you, my friend."

"Sure," Alexander laughed. "Sure, I'll find her and bring her to California."

They both laughed, nervously to be sure, but they laughed, remembering their closeness as youths.

"Gentlemen," Danny said as he walked up between them, putting one arm around each, "we all need to begin to get ready now. The bus that will take us to Baabda, the Presidential palace above Beirut, will be here at seven o'clock. Why don't you two join the rest of the guys in my suite for a quick drink, some conversation, and some local tidbits like *hummus, fistok,* and *jibneh*? Say in an hour?"

"Thanks, Danny. See you there."

Later, as they left the bus at the President's palace overlooking the city, the sun was just setting into the Mediterranean.

"Beautiful sunset, isn't it?" more than one asked a friend standing nearby looking at the sea.

"Yes. My God, that too reminds me of Madeleine, Butrus. The most wonderful evening of my life was that day I loved Madeleine on a grassy spot on the cliffs overlooking the Mediterranean Sea in Marseille. I always felt if I were to die after that, I had lived the most wonderful full life."

"Everything reminds you of Madeleine, Iskandar," Peter laughed. "Maybe some things more than others, I suppose, but you haven't stopped saying her name since I met you."

"I suppose you are right. Maybe I need to find a way to just hand it over to God."

"You think?" Peter laughed. "Now you're making some sense. Look for her, sure, but don't let it take over your life, Iskandar." Then stepping to the entry, he beckoned. "Let's go inside and have a wonderful time with the President."

The visiting delegation walked as a group from the buses to the broad, polished, Lebanese marble staircase, climbed the dozen steps to the landing at the door, and one by one entered the anteroom at the foot of an arched stairway that led to the reception area. They gathered together and were led up four more marble stairs. They almost gasped as they entered the enormous ballroom with ceilings almost forty feet high, ornate décor, multiple huge sparkling French Renaissance chandeliers, and, at the far end, an elevated stage. To either side were many tables with cream-colored damask cloths set for eight each. A large number of people were already in the room enjoying beverages and hors d'oeuvres served by the abundant number of strolling white-gloved, formally attired servers, men and women, dressed in black trousers or skirts and white shirts.

One of them approached the group asking graciously, "Champagne? Wine? Orange juice? Tea?"

The servers, sensitive to the various religious constraints of the mixed populace, offered the variety of beverages customary in the more westernized Arabic countries of the Middle East, among them, Lebanon, Jordan, Iraq, and Syria. Juices were offered for those of the Islam faith.

Danny spoke to the group that had not yet dispersed. "I understand there are individuals here who live in Lebanon, mostly in Beirut, who also are receiving awards for their philanthropy from the President this evening. I think it best we not cluster together, but rather, mingle around the room with the local guests. Let's get to know them and introduce St. Jude to this crowd."

At his cue, Alexander and Peter began a slow stroll across the gleaming marble floor, admiring the grand ballroom.

"Extraordinary, Iskandar, isn't it?" Butrus asked, still deferring to Iskandar as he had on the ship when Alexander was eighteen and he was fifteen. Peter waved his arm in a sweeping motion, indicating the spacious room, accoutrements and décor that were deserving of their attention. They stopped briefly to listen to the soft background music played by the orchestra on the stage at the far end of the ballroom.

"The music is really nice too, don't you think?"

"Yes," Alexander replied. "You know, Butrus," he continued after taking a sip from his champagne glass, "when we lived in Lebanon, we were so poor, so apart from the political world here, I doubt we could ever have dreamed of entering this building even as employees. Now, we are here being honored by the President. Extraordinary! This whole experience is extraordinary." He lowered his head and whispered softly, "I'm sorry now that I didn't talk my daughter into coming with me."

"Yes," Peter acknowledged, nodding, "But we didn't expect this. I know I certainly didn't. I thought we'd have dinner and receive a decorative box containing a certificate maybe. Not this. Look at this room...the marble floors, the impressive Corinthian columns, the glistening chandeliers. It's magnificent. I must say, the President sure knows how to throw a party! We all came from the most humble origins, Iskandar, and in America, our people today stay away from politics, even in our smallest towns. So this really was never part of our consciousness. Maybe it will take another generation."

"You think? Let's walk across the room," Alexander suggested. "We have a few minutes."

They strode together across the great room toward a cluster of men and women standing in a small group with the smiling, hospitable President. The women were in expensive, elegant evening gowns, most direct from Paris, hair coiffed to perfection...and the jewelry...so opulent, so exquisite, and so tasteful. These were the crème de la crème of Beiruti society for sure, Alexander thought.

His eyes suddenly focused on a tall, dark-haired elegant woman in the distance who stood very straight, arms gracefully at her side. She looked like an international fashion model. Contrasting with her tanned skin, her ivory sequined gown shimmered in the glow of the myriad of lights emanating from the crystal chandeliers. She was strikingly beautiful. The close-fitting strapless dress accentuated her slender figure. Many of the other women standing nearby were also dark-haired, some fair-haired, with olive or fair complexions, but not as tall or slender as this particular woman. Her elegance was pronounced by her subtle smile and her regal stature. As he looked from a distance of a hundred feet across the large room, his eyes focused on her face, her almond-shaped eyes with sensually lowered eyelids, her thin, arched eyebrows, the straight aquiline nose...Alexander's eyes were frozen to the woman's face. He was captivated. He couldn't move his eyes. She was the most beautiful creature he had ever seen. She seemed strangely familiar.

Who is she? Everyone in the cluster seems to know her, especially the President. And who is the young man standing beside her? While certainly she is a mature woman, dressed as though her gown was designed for her, the man beside her appears to be much younger than she. Yet her body language belies her fondness for him.

"My God, Butrus, look at that woman. She is lovely, so exceptional. I feel like I've seen her before."

"She's pretty, yes, Iskandar."

"Does she remind you of anyone? Who could she be?"

"I don't know, but I'll try to find out," he answered as he stepped away.

Alexander knew he couldn't stand in the middle of the room by himself. He would be too obvious. He looked around the room to obfuscate his stare; he didn't want to appear rude. He stepped to the side, toward a small cluster of men to blend in with them.

His eyes quickly returned to the woman. He couldn't help himself. After a few moments, he took two tentative steps toward her. She was still conversing with the young man. He watched as she placed her hand on his arm and laughed. Their faces were near each other's. Both were smiling at each other affectionately. *Her companion? Some mature women are attracted to younger men. Her son?* he wondered.

Alexander's emotions began a roller-coaster ride. He was drawn to her, wanting to be near her, to speak with her. But who was *the man? Go toward her...no, stop...no, get closer. Something is pulling me to her. Why?*

An aide standing beside and slightly behind the President leaned toward him and discreetly whispered near his ear. "Sir, the American delegation has arrived. You asked me to inform you."

The President smiled silently, and nodded. Then, gesturing to another aide who quickly came to him and asked, "Sir?"

"Joseph, tell my wife the Americans are here. We will allow them thirty minutes to socialize before I need her beside me for my welcome. Kindly inform her now."

"Yes, sir." The aide bowed, turned sharply on his heel and strode across the room to the President's wife who was at the moment standing, visiting with her longtime friends, Mr. and Mrs. Kabani.

Tilting her ear to the aide, she listened to the message, smiled graciously, turned to her husband and nodded in acknowledgement. Then, returning her attention to the Kabanis, she alerted them. "My husband expects to speak in half an hour after the Americans have had time to visit. I will go to him shortly."

Alexander again tentatively took a few more steps toward the President's group as if he might join them. At least he hoped that's what the others in the room would perceive.

I'm sixty years old. What's happening here.. Who is she? What am I doing? he thought nervously as he sipped from his glass.

A waiter, noticing his empty glass, stepped up to him. "Champagne, sir?"

Alexander nodded and exchanged his empty flute for a freshly filled glass from the proffered silver tray which he in turn nervously gulped down. "*Shookrun,*" he said as he handed back the glass.

Then he discreetly asked the waiter, "Who is the handsome woman speaking with the President?"

"She is a prominent, well-respected lady here in Lebanon. She supports children's' hospitals, clinics, and young artists. She is quite well known and much admired. Her name is Madame Moreau."

"Moreau? Moreau did you say?"

His mind began to race. *My God, could it be? The detective in Paris told me Madeleine had married a man named Philippe Moreau. Could she be Madeleine? Is it possible? Is it Madeleine? Could it be that she is here in Beirut? Then she isn't dead. Oh, my God...no...maybe a Lebanese woman who simply looks like her. That must be it.*

He felt his pulse quicken. His lips felt dry as his memories flashed by in his mind...that first night in Marseille.

His eyes magnetically returned to the beautiful woman. He saw her turn to the President, listen to him, smile and nod, then turn to the young man next to her.

Alexander, now emboldened, decided he had to find Peter who was across the room. To do so, he had to step even closer to the woman. Not wanting to be seen by her, he avoided her eyes, stayed behind the guests gathered in groups between them, and swiftly walked away in search of Peter.

The room was growing more crowded with several hundred attendees in formal attire who stood or strolled while conversing, laughing, sharing stories, some louder than others, some gesticulating, waving an arm, most smiling, all adding to the cacophony so loud that one could barely hear the soft classical music in the background. For Alexander, the air was getting thicker, making it hard for him to breathe.

"Butrus," he said as he finally found his friend.

Before Alexander could speak, Peter turned to him and smiled, whispering, "Iskandar, I found out who she is. Her name is Madame Moreau. She is French, not Lebanese. But she has lived in Lebanon since before the war, more than twenty years now. But she's only lived in Beirut since after the war. No one knows where she was in the country before that. I was just asking this man who she was and he offered all this information. She seems to travel in the finest circles of Beiruti society, and is here tonight because she too is being honored by the President for her outstanding support of under-privileged, handicapped Lebanese children. Can you imagine? She is quite the philanthropist and has raised millions of dollars to build children's health clinics, hospitals and schools. She is beloved here, they say."

Alexander nodded his head excitedly. "I have to meet her, Butrus. I must find out who she is. She could be Madeleine."

"Do you think? Go, Iskandar, and good luck," he said as Alexander turned toward the area across the room where the woman stood. The great ballroom, with its high ceilings and ornate décor, was now almost filled with people. Some older couples were already seated at partially occupied tables, and mostly Lebanese nationals and government officials were standing in groups, laughing and speaking in Arabic or French, sipping from long-stemmed crystal flutes. The volume of voices was substantial. It was growing louder, reflecting the exuberance of the gathering of honorees and their families and friends. But as he watched the woman near the President, he realized he was not hearing the din of voices as before. Suddenly, the room was becoming silent to him as he focused only on her, noticing the exquisite way she tilted her head, smiled, and gestured with her hand. Her movements seemed somehow wonderfully familiar to him.

He also knew that very soon an announcement would be made urging all the guests to take their places and then it would become very difficult if not impossible for him to get near her. He realized he would have to do something soon. He had only a moment to make his move. If the woman indeed was Madeleine, he had to know immediately. His hands began to moisten, reflecting his increasing pulse rate and anticipation. He felt his heart pounding in his chest.

Then, mustering his courage, he finally began to walk toward her, determined, yet very nervous. He anxiously stopped once again and stood very still while gazing at her. His pulse grew faster as his breath became shallower. He pulled his handkerchief from his breast coat pocket and wiped his damp brow. *Is it possible? Could it truly be her? Am I going to make a fool out of myself?...Who cares!...I must get a bit closer.*

He looked around and realized he was nearly by himself in the middle of the room. People involved in their own conversations were walking quickly past him across the room to their assigned tables. His nervousness was certainly noticeable to himself if not to others.

After an agonizing moment he took a few more steps and watched her turn as she lifted her head, laughing with the President. Her somehow familiar laughter stopped him again as his gaze froze on her. He was becoming more convinced now it must be Madeleine. *But is that her?* His feet felt stuck to the floor, unable to move further.

Madame Moreau's hair was swept up in a French twist, held with an elegant silver comb, revealing her entire beautiful profile. Her neck was long and slender as he remembered. Her shoulders and arms were graceful as she gestured with her hands while speaking. It was so long ago.

My God! It is Madeleine, he finally realized as he dared to step even closer, emotions exploding within him. He watched as she delicately brought her champagne glass to her full red lips and gracefully sipped the clear amber bubbly liquid.

His eyes couldn't leave her. At that moment, she laughed aloud and smiled at the President, apparently her close friend, as she lightly touched his arm.

There was no sign that she was with anyone else except the younger man. *He is handsome, but he is much younger than she. Who is he anyhow?* he thought as she smiled at her companion and affectionately tucked her arm through his. Alexander was now perplexed and felt a sinking sensation as he wondered if indeed the man was her escort. *Oh God,* he prayed, *let it not be after all these years. Please...*

He stood still as though his knees were locked in place, his eyes never leaving her. All the years since he met her in Marseille seemed to flip through his mind...all those years of unanswered letters...his two years of an empty, frustrating, fruitless search. *And here she is...in Beirut! How can this be?*

Time seemed to stand still. It was as though his legs couldn't move. The world stopped for him as he gazed on her and the younger man.

Not knowing quite what else to do, he took just three steps, tentatively walking slowly toward her, and was startled to realize he was now only twenty feet from her. Embarrassed, he stopped abruptly.

Suddenly, he felt she had sensed his approach. She tilted her head slightly in his general direction, but not directly at him.

Then it happened.

Her eyes turned directly to Alexander's. She still had the same smile on her lips she had a moment before as she paused to study the tall, dark, handsome man in the expensive silk tuxedo coming toward her. Perplexed, she thought, *Who is this man facing me?*

Then her expression changed. *Is it he? ...Iskandar? Oh, my God!* Her smile widened slowly as she felt this vaguely familiar man's eyes focus totally on her. One hand went to her mouth for a brief moment.

Drawing a deep breath, she stiffened with sudden recognition. *Oh, my God! It is Iskandar!* She felt an electrical surge throughout her body and thought she could actually hear her heart pounding in her breast. Her knees grew weak and her body trembled as she recalled the first time they met...the feel of his arms around her.

The loud sounds of voices in the room morphed into absolute silence for both of them.

Alexander felt their silent connection as his arms became limp. Now his legs seemed to disconnect from his body. Aware of the emotional sensations rising within him, he thought, *She sees me now...Oh, my God, she's even more beautiful than when I last saw her.*

It was a magical moment when their eyes met and remained fixed on each other's as they stood motionless in a room filled with the sounds of music and conversations, but totally silent to them.

Waiting for her signal before continuing toward her, Alexander glanced at the younger man, then back to her. She nodded slightly to Alexander, beckoning him to come to her. Her breathing quickened. He seemed to be holding his breath as he stepped cautiously to her. Their faces became very close. Electricity filled the moment. Each became overwhelmed with the pent-up emotions they had harbored deep in their hearts for more than forty-two years. *Forty-two years!* At the same instant, they recalled their moment of embracing and loving on the grassy place on the cliffs of Marseille and giving their eternal love to each other

Her eyes nervously left his and went to his left hand. *There! There is the ring I gave him. There is my father's ring. That ring! My God! He still wears it. He never stopped loving me. Oh, my God! My dream...my life...my destiny. He is here with me!*

She was sixteen again, innocent, in love for the first time all over again. Madeleine brushed a tear from her cheek and smiled, still looking at

Iskandar, her true love had returned. He was just a step away from her now, close enough to speak.

"It is you, isn't it, Iskandar? It is you," she cried in a whisper, then lifted her arms wide, inviting him to her.

Now he was eighteen again...at *Place de Lenche* that evening they first met and fell in love.

Alexander quickly responded as he too opened his arms wide to embrace her. She gazed deeply into those sensuous, liquid brown eyes she remembered so well, eyes that were now brimming with tears of joy.

They embraced gently at first, then brought the other even closer. Tenderly, they held each other in love. They were together at last.

Their moment was filled with their singular sense of ecstasy. This was their *Precious Present.*

Time froze as their emotions embraced them tightly together, like a warm cocoon, as they wrapped their arms tightly around each other.

She felt his body press against her; he felt her warmth all over his body. Years of love enveloped both of them.

"Oh, Iskandar, *je t'aime,*" she whispered passionately in his ear. He could feel the warmth of her breath as she brushed her lips on his ear. "I knew you would find me. I have yearned for you for so long."

He whispered, "Madeleine, you make me deliriously happy. Happier than I have ever been in my life. I love you so much."

Finally, as they reluctantly and gently released their embrace, but keeping their faces near, he asked, gesturing to her companion, "And, Madeleine, who is this handsome young man?"

Smiling softly, she looked directly into his eyes and whispered, "Iskandar, meet your son, François."